Readers LOVE *The Perfect House*!

'A gripping story that I couldn't put down'

'Wow. All the wows . . . I couldn't believe my eyes when I was reading this book . . . everyone must read it'

'A stunning thrill ride of a novel! Left me speechless and thinking about it long after I'd finished it. A must read!'

'A thrilling story that keeps you reading until you reach the shocking ending'

'There's a sense of unease that grows as the plot progresses that is magically done and like nothing I've read before! A fantastic thriller with intriguing characters, I read it in one sitting. A must read!'

'Kept me guessing and I read it in 2 days flat!'

R.P. BOLTON lives in Manchester with her partner, son and three lively rescue dogs. When she's not reading, writing or walking the dogs, she'll be at the gym, a concert or indulging in her passion for nature. *The Perfect House* is her debut thriller.

Visit R.P. Bolton online at rpbolton.com or on Twitter @RachintheFax.

The Perfect House

R.P. BOLTON

ONE PLACE. MANY STORIES

HQ
An imprint of HarperCollins*Publishers* Ltd
1 London Bridge Street
London SE1 9GF

www.harpercollins.co.uk

HarperCollins*Publishers*
1st Floor, Watermarque Building, Ringsend Road
Dublin 4, Ireland

This paperback edition 2021

1
First published in Great Britain by
HQ, an imprint of HarperCollins*Publishers* Ltd 2021

ISBN: 978-0-00-850378-9

For Tim and Christian

Mary, Mary,
Quite contrary

Prologue

A strip of light wakes her. The banister creaks. She knows what this means: he is back. Holding the tiny bundle close to her chest, she pulls the blanket over her head. Perhaps this time the cocoon of wool will fool him into believing the room is empty.

It never does.

The bolts are drawn and there is breathing, laboured from the climb. Smells of alcohol and damp earth.

Peering through the weave in the blanket, she sees him silhouetted in the doorway. His disgust crawls across her, but she won't be ashamed. She *won't*.

'Be a good girl, Mary,' her father says.

1. Now

It was fate.

Or luck. Something like that anyway because after eight hours of soul-siphoning tedium in the offices of Craftmags Ltd, Ellie Wight wasn't thinking about estate agents or house hunting or property auctions. Truthfully, she wasn't thinking about anything except getting home and taking her bra off. But as soon as she stepped outside, the Manchester heavens opened.

Rummaging through her bag for her umbrella, she ducked into the doorway of a nearby office block. A second later, some guy with skin as grey as his suit skulked in beside her, cupping his hands around a lighter. He glanced down at her belly and, with an I-don't-give-a-shit shrug, sparked up. The billowing smoke followed her into the rain and almost to the next doorway, the entrance to Raja Property Services.

'And that's when I saw it,' she told her mum over FaceTime when she finally got home. 'Right there in the window. The perfect house.'

Carol leaned forward to top up her glass and Ellie suddenly yearned for the Spanish sunset lighting up the screen. For a large, chilled Pinot Grigio of her own. And for her mum to not live a plane ride away.

'That certainly sounds like fate to me,' Carol said. 'What's it like?'

'Perfect. Three bedrooms, garden. Look.'

Pushing her glasses to the tip of her nose, her mum peered at the printout Ellie held to the phone. 'It's too fuzzy – you'll have to send me a link. When did you say the auction was?'

'Next Monday.'

Laying the A4 sheet on the bed, Ellie tried to keep her voice this side of no-big-deal. Even so, her mum's eyebrows shot off the screen.

'Can you afford it?'

'Just about. I've got Dad's money plus the deposit from the flat and we've saved loads living with Howard.'

Right on cue, the grotesque sound of Tom's dad revving his throat filtered through the floorboards. Ellie breathed out slowly.

'The baby needs a proper home.'

'I know, love,' Carol said. 'But an auction? You won't know what you're getting till it's too late.'

'I've booked a viewing for tomorrow and downloaded the pack with all the legal stuff in.'

Her mum frowned. 'How are you going to cope with a new baby and a house?'

'You know Tom loves a challenge. We'll manage.'

'If it weren't for this bloody thing' – Carol tapped the metal frame encasing her leg from toe to knee – 'I'd come with you.'

'When are the pins coming out?'

'Depends on when they can operate again. Hopefully before your due date.' She smiled and lifted the wine glass. 'Uppermoss Park is near that house. Me and Dad used to take you when you were little. Do you remember feeding the ducks?'

Ellie had her mouth open to say *Yes, I do* when Roger, her mum's partner, interrupted from the depths of the villa.

'Carol? I'm dishing up.'

'I'm on the phone, Rog. Won't be a mo.'

She returned to the screen. 'Before I let you go, I've ordered flowers for Anita and David for next Tuesday. You haven't forgotten, have you?'

The anniversary. Her heart thudded.

'Because they love hearing from you,' Carol added. 'And it'll be ten years this time, remember.'

3

Did she seriously think Ellie could *forget*?

'Ten years,' Carol repeated quietly. 'Poor Mia. Poor family. I don't know how they've kept—'

'I'm bringing it out now,' Roger shouted.

'Lovely,' her mum called before adding in an undertone, 'His first paella, bless him. Can I ring you later?'

'Sure.' Ellie plucked at the duvet cover. 'I'm not going anywhere.'

Yet.

They said goodbye: her mum to eat seafood in the Majorcan warmth and Ellie to sit like an overgrown teenager in Tom's childhood bedroom.

The bed protested as she straightened her aching legs. God, she missed their old apartment. Living in a converted mill in the Northern Quarter could be noisy and cramped, but at least when the front door closed, it was just the two of them.

Although they hadn't officially been trying for a baby, they hadn't exactly *not* been either and with two about to become three, suddenly the flat was all wrong. So it made sense when Tom suggested moving in with his dad to save money. Of course she should be grateful to Howard. She *was* grateful. But right now, her gratitude had thinned to the point of transparency.

Downstairs, Howard coughed again. Ellie stared at the ceiling and breathing-techniqued the hell out of her irritation.

No way could they bring the baby up here.

An ache gripped her skull. And why did her mum have to mention the anniversary?

Don't think about it.

She shifted a little straighter and the movement rustled the printout. The only photo was a small image of the front of the house, but she had read the blurb so many times she had no trouble conjuring up the interior.

'*For Sale by Auction. An incredible opportunity to buy a family home in the sought-after location of Uppermoss near Stockfield. One*

4

reception, separate kitchen/diner, three bedrooms, storage attic and extensive gardens to front and rear.'

It had to be fate that had led her to the Holy Grail of first-time buyers: 'Affordable' in a 'sought-after' location. Every 'affordable' three-bed currently on Rightmove was in an area she was too scared to drive through, let alone live in.

But the cherry on the icing of the cake was that the house backed on to Mosswood. A pocket of protected woodland that had survived decades of developers nibbling away at the edges. Something about trees had tapped into her recent desire to build a life away from taxi ranks and takeaways. Food cravings, well, they were a given. But nature cravings? Completely out of the blue. Green. Whatever. One minute, she was urban to the bone; the next, she'd gone off city life as completely as coffee.

She stroked gentle circles on the mound of her belly.

'This is for you, baby girl,' she whispered. 'Me and Daddy are going to give you the best life. Parents who love you, a beautiful home, space, fresh air, a garden to explore. We'll—'

A fusillade of coughs rattled through the floorboards and Ellie bunched the pillow around both ears.

Bollocks to affordable.

She didn't *want* that house, she *needed* it.

She was still awake when Tom crept up the stairs, exceeding his overtime yet again.

'How was work?' she murmured, squinting in the glare of the bedside lamp.

'Not stopped all day.'

'Did you see my text about the house?' She shuffled towards him in small, effortful movements, unable to stop a grunt escaping her lips. Taking pity, Tom kissed her on the forehead.

'Yeah, I didn't get chance to check the link though.' The last syllable disappeared in a yawn.

'Never mind. We've got a viewing at nine tomorrow.'

Tom groaned. 'I'm on earlies, love.'

'But we have to. This is Uppermoss village, Tom. Size, location, price … it's too good to be true.' She wrapped her feet around his, pulling him close. 'We can't let it slip through our fingers.'

'We can't let my job slip through our fingers.'

'Go in a bit later. Please? You can't hang about on a property like this.'

He sighed. 'I guess they owe me for staying late tonight.'

With her lips pressed against his arm, the words were muffled. 'Thank you. I promise you're going to love it.'

'*You* might not love it.' He leaned across to turn off the light. 'I mean it, Els, don't get your hopes up. You said it yourself: at that price, it's too good to be true.'

He kissed her, dropped on the pillow and within seconds, his breathing slowed and deepened. But Ellie's mind refused to switch off. She watched blue lights sweep over the boxes stacked against the walls. Trinity squirmed in her belly while the estate agent's blurb looped in her mind.

Affordable. Semi-rural. Family home.

Tom snored gently and Ellie hooked her little finger around his. Six Moss Lane was going to be theirs.

She could feel it.

2. Now

According to the satnav, Moss Lane was a forty-minute drive taking them past Stockfield, the town where Ellie spent her childhood. Away from the bypass, the traffic thinned to an occasional car flickering past hedgerows and flat green fields dotted with sheep and cows. It was one of those days when the weather can't decide between summer or autumn and through the Mini's windscreen, the sky arced a cool watercolour blue.

'Beautiful, isn't it?' Tom said.

She murmured in agreement. If they lived here, away from the pollution of the city, she could breathe. The baby could breathe. Speaking of which … She straightened to relieve the pressure of tiny feet on her lungs.

'You OK?' Tom laid his hand on her thigh.

She screwed her face up. 'Backache. Heartburn. The usual.'

At the last antenatal clinic, the nurse had frowned at the number on the scale before flicking her eyes critically over Ellie's body.

'We recommend a one- or two-kilo gain a month at most. But I think you've gone slightly over.' Pause. 'Again.'

Well, no shit, Nurse Sherlock. Seriously, did the woman think she didn't own a mirror, or toes she hadn't seen for weeks? What Sister Obvious failed to recommend, however, were strategies for controlling uncontrollable hunger. Hunger that dispatched Tom to the twenty-four-hour garage at all hours. Even picturing that family-sized Dairy Milk set her stomach rumbling a rebellious duet with the satnav's calm directions.

In half a mile, turn right.

Tom glanced up from his phone. 'That's not bad, you know. Should be a pretty straightforward run to work for both of us.'

Ellie clicked the indicator and drove down a sheltered lane lined with high hedges until the sign came into view:

Private Road. Entry for Residents and Their Guests Only.

Stones spat out from under the tyres and she skirted a pothole. As the car bumped along, she lusted over the detached Edwardian villas lining both sides of the peaceful cul-de-sac. Beautiful, ornate, in-my-dreams-but-not-on-my-wages houses. Number 1, 2, 3, 4, 5 …

Your destination, 6 Moss Lane, is on the left.

Her heart soared. The photo hadn't lied.

'Oh God, it is perfect,' she breathed.

Peering through a huddle of dark conifers, she saw the well-proportioned house from the brochure: three good-sized windows and a small porch in an off-white façade, like a kid's drawing of the perfect family home. Set back from the road, number six sat modestly alongside the Gatsby-esque elegance of its neighbours. But it was miles better than any other property they'd considered, and she had been scouring the internet for months.

'Can't knock the location,' Tom said, opening the passenger door.

Scents of earth and pine filled her senses. Cool, pure air soothed the pulsing in her head and she breathed easily for the first time all day. Even the baby seemed to sense a change, shifting her position to relieve the pressure on Ellie's ribs.

From the greened fence to the knee-high weeds lining the driveway, nature had staked her claim on the land. The ancient trees of Mosswood were visible above the roofline and also off to one side, cocooning the house in soothing green. Not a chicken shop or taxi rank in sight. In fact, no other cars were parked and it was almost nine …

'Where's the estate agent?' Tom said, reading her mind.

Moss clung to the gatepost, and she picked at the spongy fronds and looked back down the silent street.

'We're a bit early. I can give him a call.'

Tom's phone shrilled.

'Work. Sorry, I need to …' His voice carried as he walked up the road. 'Hey, Tanya, what's up?'

Digging a crumb of soil from her thumbnail, Ellie took a step forward. They had an appointment, so it wouldn't be trespassing. Not technically.

A gust of wind shook the leaves into whispers, whipping a lock of hair across her eyes, and she fished for a bobble in her cardigan pocket. When she looked up again, a woman had emerged from the passage at the side of the house.

Ellie held her hand out. 'Hello, Ellie Wight and Tom Hartley. We've got an appointment to view.'

If the woman heard, she made no sign. Instead, she continued staring at a point in the distance. Her grey-black hair was scraped into a tight updo and the shapeless black dress and scuffed shoes didn't exactly say 'meeting a client'. When she drew level, she ignored Ellie's outstretched hand and, with an expression like she'd just sat on a hedgehog, sailed on past.

'Excuse *me*?' Ellie said, taken aback.

But the stranger didn't bat an eyelid, and continued heading towards Tom, who was talking animatedly into his phone at the end of the street. Despite the strengthening breeze, the woman's helmet hairstyle remained rigidly in place.

Potential buyer cold-shouldering the competition?

The owner, pissed off at being forced to sell?

Rude.

Still, maybe it would be better to wait for the estate agent. Leaning against the fence, Ellie rotated one puffy ankle then the other, scrolling though emails she couldn't be bothered to open yesterday. Deadlines, queries, someone's leaving do. A passive-aggressive rant Joan the Moan, her line manager, had cc'd her in on. With a sigh, she tipped her face to the watery sunshine, feeling the soft air caress her skin. Truly, maternity leave could not start soon enough.

'It's all kicking off at work,' Tom said, putting his mobile in his pocket as he walked towards her. 'And we're short of bodies again.'

Ellie smiled sympathetically, knowing Tom's frustration at the budget cuts that regularly shrank his team at the police station.

They both turned their heads at the sound of an approaching car. A Mercedes pulled up and a man with slicked-back hair and a very groomed beard got out.

'Ellie and Tom?'

The black overcoat flapped in the breeze, revealing a turquoise lining.

'Shan Raja. So sorry you've had to wait. Honestly, the centre of town is in gridlock. I swear the cones were breeding before my very eyes.'

'No worries,' Tom said, shaking his hand.

'Shall we?' Shan gestured towards the house.

A tapestry of weeds covered the driveway, leading them to the porch adorned with saggy grey cobwebs. There was an untidy pile of free newspapers and junk mail in one corner and a lopsided number 6 screwed to the frame, the flaky black paint revealing rust underneath.

Ellie hesitated. 'Is anyone still living here? Just that a woman came out a few minutes ago.'

'I didn't see anyone,' Tom said, sounding surprised.

'She walked right past you!'

Shan tapped his phone against his lips. 'The vendor lives in Canada. But the next-door neighbour's been keeping an eye on the place so it must've been her. Anyway, let's …'

Neighbour? Hmmm. Would she really want to live next door to that thousand-yard stare?

Shan turned the key and the hinges gave an OTT haunted-house creak. Trapped air rushed out to greet them.

The hall, papered in the same textured stuff as their old uni flat, triggered a memory: Mia in her biker jacket, digging her thumbnail in the little bumps until it was peppered with crescent moon scars.

Stop thinking about Mia.

Shan misread her hesitation. 'A bit of TLC, that's all it needs. Here. Great size lounge.'

Tom murmured appreciatively. Ellie breathed in eau de run-down charity shop and saw a faint sepia patch blooming across the ceiling. Seventies carpet. Stone and copper fireplace.

Meanwhile, Shan scanned the room with an appraising eye. 'Honestly, I should be bidding myself. What an incredible investment opportunity.'

Ellie stared at the sad, ghostly outlines where pictures had once hung. *Too good to be true.* Tom's warning rang in her mind and the exhilaration she'd felt outside crumbled. 'I don't want an investment opportunity,' she said. 'I want a home.'

Her emotions lurked so close to the surface nowadays that they could manifest without warning. Mortified by the crack in her voice, she rummaged up her sleeve for a tissue.

'Love!' Tom exclaimed.

Shan smiled kindly. 'I sell a lot of auction properties – trust me, this one is in an excellent state of repair. Everything that needs doing is purely cosmetic. Lick of paint, carpet fitter and bingo, the perfect family home.' He patted the fire surround. 'Maybe an hour with a sledgehammer.'

She blew her nose and gave a shaky laugh. 'Oh, I don't know. A room needs a focal point.'

Tom squeezed her shoulder.

'Well, if retro's your thing,' Shan continued, 'wait till you see the kitchen.'

Kitchen: universal heart of the home, and the marbled Formica units and off-white tiles reminded her of her nan's. But the resemblance ended there. Instead of mingled aromas of Stardrops and Victoria sponge, the air smelled of drains. Two bin liners spilled their contents in the corner.

The heart of this particular home had ceased to beat some time ago.

Shan tutted and tied the tops of the bags into bunny ears.

'Sorry, someone was supposed to clear this.'

She lowered her gaze to the lino. Sensing her mood, Tom slung his arm around her and gently guided her to the window.

'Check out the garden. That view!'

Nature had run wild in the back too, creating a dense tangle of weeds and waist-high grass to match the front garden. But shrubs flanked the lawn and slap bang in the middle was – what would you call that wooden thing? A pergola? An arbour? – which proved this overgrown jungle had once been tended and loved. Beyond it, the pale birches, dense evergreens and swaying canopies blurred where the garden ended and Mosswood began. Above the treeline, paint-stroke birds circled in the blue sky.

'Wow,' she whispered.

'Marvellous, isn't it?' Shan said, behind them. 'I don't show many three-beds with an en-suite woodland.'

Tom brought Ellie's hand to his lips and kissed the knuckles. 'Think of the potential. We could have people round for barbecues. Even get a pizza oven. Sit under the trees in the summer. Get Trinity a treehouse. Grow our own veg, maybe. It's perfect.'

His enthusiasm reignited her own. A dated interior was hardly a deal breaker. For the price of a skip and a few tins of paint, the baby could have a perfect outdoorsy childhood. Her mind leapt ahead, visualising her daughter in the fresh air climbing those trees, making dens, playing football on the lawn.

As though reading her thoughts, Trinity kicked. Hard.

'What do you think?' Tom murmured in her ear.

'It's beautiful,' she replied from the side of her mouth. She took a series of pictures with her phone. 'Mum will go nuts for this place.'

'Wait till you see the views from the bedroom,' Shan said, ushering them towards the stairs.

Under the nursing home décor, the master had great bones. High ceiling, square proportions.

'Views to die for,' Shan said, gesturing at the picture window that ran almost the full length of one wall.

Tom nudged Ellie and, grasping her hand, squeezed lightly.

'Anyway.' Shan headed back on the landing. 'You'll be pleased to hear the bathroom is completely functional. Any works are cosmetic only.'

'Cosmetic only', Ellie now realised, was estate agent speak for 'knackered'. Worn fittings, cracked tiles, faded lino. The world's most corpulent spider crawled leisurely across the pink bath. But the disappointment of earlier failed to materialise. She flushed the loo – fine. Ran the taps – fine. Nothing else mattered. Only the potential mattered.

Dimly aware of Tom and Shan discussing renovations and building regulations behind her, Ellie's imagination sketched the room. She visualised a new white suite, metro tiles, walk-in shower with a glass screen. Chrome freestanding tap arching over the bath. Herself like a smiley mum in an advert, expertly wrapping their new-born daughter in a fluffy towel.

'Bedroom three,' Shan continued. 'Same fabulous views.'

Sunlight cast a golden glow over the tired boxroom.

'Cosmetic only, right?' she said with a grin.

'Exactly. Take your time or gut the whole place in one go. Either way, someone is getting a real bargain at the auction.' He looked at his watch. 'Right, I have to be elsewhere, I'm afraid.'

He ushered them back down the stairs, carpeted in Seventies swirls, and out into the porch.

'Email if you have any queries.' The front door juddered closed. 'Otherwise, best of luck.'

They all shook hands and he strode towards his car, black coat flapping like the wings of the crows flying over the roof.

Tom fiddled with the zip on his parka. Too busy for a haircut recently, his fringe flopped over his eyes and when he pushed it back, almost twelve years peeled away to reveal the boy she first saw in the student union, nodding to an Oasis classic with his best mate, Danny.

Danny, Mia's boyfriend.

Do not think about that. She touched her bump instinctively. *Not now.*

'So it needs updating,' Tom said, head down. 'But nothing major. We'll see anyway when we've gone through the property pack with the solicitor.' He finally pulled the stuck zip free. 'What do you reckon?'

Her reply tumbled out quickly, 'I think we're never going to find anywhere else this perfect and I'm not bothered about the work or how long it takes. I just want us here when the baby comes, not squashed in one room with a million boxes. And I'm not being ungrateful to your dad. He's been amazing. But the smoking with the baby ...'

'I know.' The rough cotton of Tom's parka brushed her cheek as he pulled her close into a toothpaste-and-soap-scented hug.

Suddenly exhausted, Ellie tugged at the neck of her T-shirt and tried to catch her breath.

'Can you drive? I'm knackered.'

'Course,' he said, taking the keys. 'So, the verdict is it's definitely a project, but currently liveable. The commute to the station or Craftmags isn't bad. Dad would help out with the work.' Pursing his lips, he studied the house. 'I can really picture us living here, you know.'

He started the engine, and Ellie peered through the conifers as she fitted the seatbelt under her bump. At some point in its past, this house had known love. Someone had chosen those carpets and that wallpaper; put that pergola up and tended the rose beds. Maybe like Nan in the months before she went into the care home, the owner had got too frail to keep on top of the maintenance.

Under the layers of dirt and neglect, 6 Moss Lane was clearly begging for someone to come along and restore its beating heart.

Someone like Ellie.

Back at Howard's, they waded into a fog of cigarette smoke.

'For God's sake, Dad,' Tom snapped, wafting his hand.

'Didn't expect you home yet.' Howard sucked on the filter, eyes screwed tight with effort. 'Sorry, I'll put this out. How was it?'

'Perfect,' Ellie replied, with a cough.

At Tom's glare, his dad gave an apologetic shrug and beat a retreat to the kitchen, closing the door behind him.

'Come upstairs,' Tom said, holding out his hand. 'You look wiped out.'

Even with his guiding arm around her, climbing the stairs left her gasping. The excitement of Moss Lane had been overtaken by the need to lie on her bed with the blind down.

Concern spread across Tom's features.

'I don't think I should go into work,' he said. The bed creaked as he helped her to lower herself onto the mattress.

Almost dizzy with the relief of being off her feet, she dropped against the pillow. What she wanted was Tom to hold her until the stabbing pain in her temples subsided. Instead, she mustered up a smile. 'Go. I just need a nap, and if you stay, I won't sleep. Please?' After reassuring him yes, she meant it and yes, she'd ring if she needed anything, he left with a promise to return 'as soon as the new DC is up to speed'.

Downstairs, Howard rattled around in the kitchen, arguing with the radio. Ellie pulled the pillow around her ears.

This was Howard's house. He had a good heart, fixing things at the flat and letting them stay rent-free. With any luck, they'd be in their own house soon.

Be grateful. Be grateful. Be grateful. For a few seconds, 6 Moss Lane lingered behind her closed lids. Not the version from today, with peeling paint and a neglected garden, but a spruced-up version, six months, a year down the line with fresh paint and cared-for flowerbeds.

She rolled over and propped herself awkwardly on one elbow. Scrolling through her phone, she selected the most 'cosmetic only' images of the house's immense potential – no damp patches or scattered dead flies – and WhatsApp'd them to her mum with the message:

You were right: it was fate. We've found our perfect house xx

3. Now

'Try not to get your hopes up, love,' Tom warned gently, dropping the butter knife in the sink. 'Any house in Uppermoss is bound to fly at auction.'

Ellie picked up a slice of toast. 'Nope. It's ours. I know it.' And she did. Even last night when they'd sat together on the bed surrounded by boxes in their cramped room and inputted the scary figures into the calculator for the hundredth time that week, she knew it. Of course, Tom, frowning as he scribbled numbers on a pad, focused on the practicalities. The mortgage had been approved and thanks to their savings and her inheritance from Dad, the deposit was sorted. It was doable … but only if they stuck to the plan: £310,000 and not a penny more.

And this morning, although he'd sworn only a national emergency could force him to work, Ellie had taken the precaution of setting his mobile to *Do not Disturb* while he was in the shower. She had also emailed Joan the Moan to pull a Monday sickie and asked Jess to cover. No guilt there. Why trek into Craftmags when she could work from the comfort of her own dressing gown later?

To minimise the worsening heartburn, she chewed her breakfast slowly and carefully while checking her messages. One from Jess. No text, just a string of crossed-finger emojis and hearts.

One from Mum. *Let me know how you get on at the auction x.* Followed quickly by a second: *Please call David and Anita. Anniversary tomorrow. Don't forget. x*

The sudden pain in Ellie's chest had nothing to do with heartburn. She'd lived every day of the last ten years in the shadow of Mia's death. She wished she *could* forget.

A spiky weight shifted inside her skull when she bent to tie her laces. Bloody hell, not *another* migraine. While luckier women bloomed in late pregnancy, Ellie wilted under the burden of endless niggles and there was *still* another five weeks to go. *I need my body back*, she ordered the baby. *Hurry up.*

In the car, the DJ's smug lad banter got on her already taut nerves.

'Can we have the radio off?'

'It's for the traffic news,' Tom said apologetically. He adjusted the rear-view mirror and pulled away from the kerb. 'I'll turn it down.'

Through the window, houses gave way to tatty shops, and while her eyes registered graffitied shutters and tired signage, her mind strolled around the garden at Moss Lane. They'd been back twice since the first viewing. Not inside, but to sneak up to the windows and wander the street to 'get a feel for the area'. Howard had brought binoculars to check the roof tiles and the gutters and pronounced them 'sound as a pound'. They had all been scratched and stung negotiating the tangled mess of garden. Ellie had half-expected the moody neighbour to give them an earful about trespassing, but they didn't see a soul and had left still feeling completely bewitched by the house.

Rain hit the windscreen like a handful of stones and Tom switched the wipers on.

'Remember we said three ten tops. Even then we'll be skint.' He coughed a disbelieving laugh. 'It's crazy. I mean, it took me nearly a month to choose these trainers and now I'm sinking everything into a house I didn't know existed till last week.'

'I get it. Massive mortgage stress. Debt. No new trainers ever again.' She adjusted the seatbelt under her bump. 'You're not getting cold feet, are you?'

'No, I love it. I'm just saying we need to act with our—' He tapped his temple. 'Not our hearts. Stop me if I look like I'm getting carried—'

He paused mid-sentence and tilted his head towards the radio.

'Sorry, love.' The indicator clicked. 'Motorway's shut. We'll have to come off here.'

Lulled by the swish of the wipers, the tap of the rain on the roof, she relaxed into the seat. The individual shops disappeared, replaced by a tired retail park and then a series of industrial buildings. A pedestrian stepped off the kerb, head down, and Tom slowed.

'Here we go,' he said.

A pair of magpies chattered on a sign that read 'Stockfield Auction Rooms'. Two for joy, as her mum would say. Tom pulled into a space and put the handbrake on. 'What I mean is, I know we've got our hearts set on it, but if it's not meant to be ...'

'Head not heart,' she said. 'Promise.'

Her first auction, and the swirl of adrenalin temporarily masked her physical discomfort. The décor was twenty-first-century uninspired: nylon carpet, fluorescent lighting, ceiling tiles. Crammed with mismatched chairs but strangely not with people. Apart from half a dozen other audience members and a man in round glasses, the room was empty.

'Where is everyone?' she whispered.

Tom replied from behind the auction card, 'Maybe the motorway crash? Listen, there's something I need to tell you. Something the estate agent said.'

'Sssh,' she hissed. 'They're starting.'

The man in glasses had stood up and she realised he was on a platform. He peeled a sheet of paper off the desk.

'Good morning, ladies and gentlemen. Lot number one is a detached family home on the outskirts of Uppermoss village. Covenants restricting any redevelopment are detailed in the property pack. Let's start the bidding at 220,000.'

Tom leaned forward and tapped the card on his knee. At two fifty, he did nothing. Two eighty.

The auctioneer clicked his mouse, announcing, 'The internet is out at two ninety.'

As the bidding continued, the urge to prod Tom grew until finally – finally! – he put his hand up.

'Three hundred thousand with the gentleman at the front,' the auctioneer said.

Ellie twisted her fingers in her lap. This was the moment the other bidder would bow out. The moment the man would slam his little hammer down.

But he didn't.

'Three ten.'

Tom slumped. Ellie sensed his grip loosening on the card.

You belong there, her heart said. *You deserve it. One more.*

The auctioneer peered over his glasses. 'Five then?'

Her pulse throbbed erratically. She looked at Tom. He looked back.

'Oh, what the hell,' he murmured and waved the card.

'Three fifteen with the gentleman at the front,' the auctioneer said. 'Sir?'

The rival bidder nodded.

'Against you at the front.'

Tom waved the card. 'Three twenty … three twenty-five … three thirty.'

After what felt like minutes, the rival bidder shook his head and the auctioneer picked up his pen.

'Sold for £330,000 to number 143.'

Tom sat back in the chair and exhaled long and hard, as though someone had let all the air out of him. An overwhelming urge to giggle gripped Ellie. They did it! They won!

'Oh my God,' Tom whispered, helping her out of the seat. 'What have I done?'

A youngish man in a jumper with 'Stockfield Auction House' embroidered on the chest sat in the office, smiling as they approached. Tom's lips returned a shell-shocked smile.

'Won't be a moment,' the clerk said. 'I'll just get the paperwork.'

Grey metal filing cabinets lined the office walls. They both sat on uncomfortable plastic chairs, shooting secret pleased-dazed looks at each other.

'We got it!' Ellie mouthed and Tom leaned across to give her a loud smacking kiss.

While Tom and the clerk sorted transferring the deposit, Ellie side-eyed the vendor's details on the desk: 'Ms Catherine Wilson' and a street address in Toronto. Shan had mentioned the owner lived in Canada. No wonder the house felt so forlorn.

The man brought documents over, still warm from the copier. A couple of signatures, a final handshake and 6 Moss Lane was as good as theirs.

'I'll be in touch with the completion date soon. Congratulations and …' The clerk hesitated for a few seconds before he added, 'Best of luck.'

Tom groaned and dropped his face into his hands. 'I can't believe I did that. What was I thinking?'

Ellie, who was mentally cartwheeling across the car park, peeled his fingers away and covered them in little kisses. 'You were thinking we couldn't lose our perfect house for the sake of a few thousand, same as me.'

In the car, his panic ballooned as the reality sank in. 'Head not heart, I said. I told myself I wasn't going to get carried away. Where are we going to find an extra twenty grand?'

'I'll sell my car.'

'Won't cover it. We'll have to increase the mortgage or use our savings.' He pulled his phone out and tapped. He frowned at the screen and when he spoke, it was tinged with incredulity. 'How can I have seven voicemails?'

'Sorry. I put it on silent.' She manoeuvred the seat back and stretched her tired legs into the footwell. 'I was worried you'd miss the auction if the station called.'

Easy-going was Tom's default setting, but as he listened in grave silence to the messages, the dial had definitely turned to 'rattled'. Ellie closed her eyes. The adrenalin of the auction had trickled away and from her toenails to her ponytail, every inch of her ached. She leaned against the headrest and tugged the bobble from her hair, massaging her scalp with her fingertips. No matter what happened, the house was theirs. That was all that mattered.

Only the occasional phrase of Tom's monologue filtered through as they drove back to his dad's. 'Work stuff … Monthly repayments … Contingency budget … Nursery fees … Ask Dad for a loan.' And it wasn't until he said her name that she realised they had parked outside Howard's.

'I'm sorry about your phone,' she said weakly, opening the gate.

'Don't worry about that.' He grabbed her hand, rubbing his thumb over hers. 'Are you sure you're all right? I can ask if I can have the rest of the day off.' The air shimmered at the edges like a heat haze.

'It's just a bit of a headache,' she lied. 'You go. I've already dropped you in it enough at work for one day.'

He held her face with his palms and scrutinised her carefully. 'OK,' he said. 'I'll sort this one thing and be straight back, then we can celebrate. I'm sorry I panicked about the money. Everything's going to be fine.' He kissed her. 'In fact, everything's going to be perfect.'

Somehow, she arranged her features into a convincing smile. When the rumble of the car's engine had merged into the traffic, Ellie dragged herself upstairs and collapsed onto the bed. Colours exploded behind her eyelids in a migraine supernova and the pain scouring the inside of her skull scrubbed thoughts of Tom, the baby, 6 Moss Lane, everything away until nothing existed apart from clean, shining pain.

She closed her eyes and everything turned black.

4. Now

Someone was moaning. *She* was moaning.

A knuckle tapped the door. 'Are you all right, love?'

The 'No' was a groan, but it was enough. Floorboards creaked. Smoke drifted in.

'Wait there,' Howard said.

Like she had a choice.

After that came a chaos of blue lights and sirens. Pain skewered her temples. A woman with a Geordie accent held her hair while she vomited.

'It's all right, pet,' she said. 'We'll soon have you sorted out.'

Minutes, maybe hours later, she bumped down a ramp and was wheeled along corridors smelling of school dinners and Dettol. Lights flashed and dimmed. When the trolley stopped, a faceless man tried to get her to wee in a bottle. A curtain rattled on plastic rings, caught in a flurry of hushed movement.

'Where's Tom?' she whispered. The Geordie accent promised he was on his way.

A needle of light pierced the darkness. Ellie's pupils contracted. Behind the glare, she saw the woman in black from Moss Lane. But then she clicked off the torch, turned to speak to a masked man and the resemblance disappeared.

A band tightened, beeped, tightened again on Ellie's upper arm. Fragments of conversation broke through. Protein. PCR test. Blood pressure. Theatre. Another stranger warned her to expect a 'sharp scratch'. Sleep sucked her down a black hole and she fell gratefully in.

5. Now

She woke to the sound of sniffing.

Slowly, a dim cubicle swam into focus. On the left, a plastic jug and a cardboard bowl. Under her, a rock-hard mattress. Level with the pillow sat Tom with his hair stuck up at odd angles. He was blowing his nose on a piece of toilet roll.

In the twelve years they had been together, she had only seen him cry twice. The first was the night Mia died. The second, in the visitors' lounge at Willow Lodge.

Had they sent her back there?

Tom poured water into a scratched plastic beaker and held it to her lips, one hand curled under to catch the drips.

'Here.'

Water streamed down her chin as she gulped.

'Sip it.' He moved the cup out of reach. 'You'll make yourself sick.'

'What's happened?'

Tom blinked bloodshot eyes. 'Don't you remember anything?'

Pain. Geordie accent. Sirens. Willow Lodge? No. That was years ago. Ambulance?

Now that rang a bell.

'Sweetheart, I am so, so sorry.'

At the misery in Tom's voice, the bell became a shrieking klaxon.

Panic thrust her forward, but a sharp sting halted the movement. What was that? A plastic thing stuck to the back of her hand. A thin tube that led to a drip. She stared, struggling to recognise this pink swollen hand as her own. It looked like an inflated rubber glove.

She felt strange. She felt numb. She felt … empty.

'What's going on?'

He brought her hand to his lips.

'You've had an emergency C-section.'

Her mind scrabbled for a foothold.

'Your blood pressure went sky high and Dad rang the ambulance,' He drew in a deep, shuddering breath. 'It's all my fault. I am so, so sorry. If I hadn't gone on about the money and my phone. If stayed with you after the auction, you wouldn't have got so stressed and …'

His voice slid over her ears. Was this even real? The baby wasn't due for five weeks. It was as though she had wandered on to the set of a soap opera and any minute now, the director would yell 'Cut' and she would still be pregnant.

She wasn't pregnant.

'Where's the baby?'

Tom tried to smile. 'She's in neonatal intensive care.'

Shivers convulsed her. Her teeth chattered cartoon-style, but there was nothing remotely funny about any of this. Tom draped the blanket around her and lowered his face to hers. His eyelashes sparkled.

'The baby's small, and she needs some help to breathe. But she's going to be fine. And she's beautiful, just like her mum. See.'

He took out his phone. Click. A pinkish blur appeared, swamped by a nappy and wearing a red knit cap. Spread-eagled in an incubator, tubes and wires snaking to machines.

Trinity. Their daughter, so small and red and new. She reached to stroke the image. He brought the phone closer. Even the simple act of scissoring her fingers drained her energy. She zoomed in on the baby, her face, her miniature fingers and toes. Her ankle, circled with a tiny plastic ring.

'I know the breathing stuff looks scary, but it's just a precaution,' Tom added. 'The doctor said she should be taken off it later today.'

'I want to see her.'

He kissed her knuckles. 'I'm sorry, love. They said you've got to stay here under observation for forty-eight hours.'

Forty-eight hours? She shuffled up the bed, or at least, her brain sent the order but her legs refused to obey. Instead, something cut into the soft skin of her belly like wire. She retched and Tom rushed to pour more water, but she waved the jug aside.

'I'm not waiting for two days.'

Tom half stood and lightly pressed her shoulders. 'Stay still or you'll rip your stitches. You've got to let yourself recover. Listen, I know it's hard, but she's in the best care.'

'Let me look at her again.'

He tilted the screen showing the close-up of the baby's hospital tag. Ellie stared.

Baby Wight, it read. *September 12th.*

Realisation crashed around her. 'What day is it?'

'Tuesday. Just gone eight in the morning. You've been here since last night.'

September 12th.

The anniversary.

She dropped back on the pillow and closed her eyes. You could spend your days believing you had escaped the past. Every time today turned into yesterday, the secret guilt sank a little further from the surface until one day, you woke up and your first thought wasn't 'Mia's dead'.

'Ellie?' Tom whispered. 'I promised your mum I'd ring when you woke up. I won't be long.'

After a few seconds, his lips bumped her ear. Too much coffee had soured his breath. The curtain rattled on its track and his footsteps retreated.

September 12th. Her daughter's premature birth and her best friend's premature death. Present and past, forever entwined.

It's my fault, Tom had said. But it wasn't. It was hers.

Rain drummed on a flat roof. A distant machine beeped and

every few minutes, an ambulance sped under the window. A faulty light flickered and her mind, which should have been filled with the baby, swarmed with images of Mia.

Karma hadn't forgotten her at all.

6. Now

The time passed in a chaos of tests, injections, blood pressure spikes but the physical pain was eclipsed by the pain of not seeing the baby. What if they looked into each other's eyes and felt nothing?

Unable to sleep, Ellie listened to the pulse of the night shift. Swishing mops, murmured conversations and the soft beat of the cleaners' shoes transported her to the months after Mia died. With comfy beds and their own stuff – books, posters, teddies – Willow Lodge was meant to have a laid-back home-from-home vibe, not a hospital feel. And it could have worked, except at home, your mum didn't swipe you in and out or confiscate your nail scissors. Oh, and there was nothing laid-back about Willow Lodge.

Lying in the narrow hospital bed she remembered a resident, Alina, whose baby had been taken into emergency foster care. On her first day at Willow Lodge, she smashed her forehead so hard against the visitors' lounge wall that her blood stamped poppies on the plaster. Although Ellie never knew what happened to Alina, or her baby, she understood the girl's anguish. The pain of separation.

When Ellie was finally wheeled in to her daughter, a rolling wave of love swept away her fears. A fierce love that started in her gut and roared through every cell in her body. She looked in her daughter's eyes and felt *everything*.

Determined to make up for lost time, she followed the midwife's instructions as though they were carved on tablets of stone. Expressed milk. Cupped those doll-sized feet. Stroked the peach-soft limbs. Lay skin-on-skin. Kissed each one of her tiny, perfect fingers and toes. Ellie held her and sang to her and did everything she could to make up for the fact she had so royally screwed up Trinity's arrival on the planet.

But every inch of her hurt. And she was so tired. Whenever she cajoled the baby to latch on, the tiny fists would flail: *You're doing it wrong!* By the time they mastered feeding (Ellie lying on her side, holding the baby like a rugby ball and almost not wincing) she'd overshot the miracle of motherhood and landed squarely on knackered where she remained, permanently dazed, for the next five weeks.

Days and nights merged in a jumble of blood pressure complications, feeds, nappy changes, check-ups, and a surgical site infection that extended their stay until Ellie thought they would never be discharged. Visitors came with flowers and helium balloons. And Tom, worn out from juggling work with moving, brought the completion paperwork and photos so she could plan how to put their stamp on 6 Moss Lane.

At last both of them were well enough to leave. Ellie dressed Trinity in a ladybird vest Jess had brought in and covered her with the white cellular blanket, exactly as she had been shown.

'Home tomorrow, baby,' she whispered. 'Daddy's been working hard to get everything ready for you.'

When Trinity sank into the twilight calm of the hospital, Ellie tried to follow. But the other patients' nocturnal coughs and moans kept jerking her back to wakefulness. She weaved in and out of uneasy dreams, until a new sound caught her attention: the carefully subdued swish of the curtain. She hugged the covers.

Go away. Need sleep.

The cot wheels gave a tiny metallic squeak.

Ellie's eyes flew open.

A woman stood in the cubicle. No nurse's uniform. The greying crown of a head and black-clad bumps of spine leaned over the cot.

'Hey!' Ellie said, struggling to extricate herself from the paralysing sheets.

The stranger lifted a finger to her lips. Dirt lined the creases and a grimy crescent marked the nail. Glasses. Iron-streaked dark hair.

'I know you,' Ellie said, louder. 'I saw you on Moss Lane. What are you doing?'

In reply, the woman reached her filthy hands into the cot. The track rattled as the curtain whipped open and she vanished into the darkness of the ward before the baby's blanket even hit the floor. A silver 'It's a girl!' balloon bobbed in her wake.

Ellie thrashed her legs. 'Come back!'

The covers pinned her to the mattress. She twisted and kicked, but they held her tight. Grunting with effort, she tore at the taut fabric. She couldn't do it. She couldn't save her baby.

'Stop her! Help!'

Ignoring the ripping sensation across her stomach, she yanked the call bell, but a nurse was already striding towards the cubicle.

Finally, the covers came free. She swung her legs over the side. 'She's stolen my baby! Quick, catch her.'

The nurse jogged the last few feet and caught Ellie's elbow.

'Nobody's taken your baby. Look, she's right there.'

Ellie followed the nurse's gaze to the cot and did a double take. Trinity lay in her ladybird vest, delicate fists curled, her face tranquil in deep sleep.

Some of the other patients began calling out, asking what was going on. *What's the fuss?* A new-born launched a thin wail and it didn't take long for others to join the chorus.

Panic made Ellie's voice shrill. 'I saw her. She tried to snatch my baby. I know where she lives.'

Around them, the murmurs intensified. *Taken a baby? Where? Who?*

An eerie glow emanated from one of the bays as a phone screen illuminated. The nurse addressed the small side ward, pleasantly but firmly.

'Everything's fine, ladies. Someone's had a bad dream, that's all.' Frowning at splotches of dirt, the nurse stooped to pick Trinity's blanket off the faded tiles. 'Let's get you a clean one.'

'She must have walked right past you,' Ellie insisted, clenching fistfuls of hospital sheet. 'Why didn't you stop her?'

The nurse shook out a fresh blanket and expertly tucked Trinity in.

'Anyone coming through that door walks past me,' the nurse said crisply. 'And I haven't seen another soul all night.'

'Then you can't have been looking. I saw her.'

A cloud crossed the nurse's face. 'I can review the CCTV and note your concerns on your file if you like.'

Skin slick with sweat and weakened by ebbing adrenalin, Ellie flopped back onto the pillow. Stupid. The security was watertight. A member of staff buzzed everyone in and out and checked their ID. Only that morning, she'd seen an irate dad refused entry.

'It seemed so real,' she said quietly.

The nurse's irritated expression softened. 'You had an SSI and you've been put on blood pressure medication, right?'

'Yeah. I had pre-eclampsia and it hasn't gone back to normal yet.'

'Well, vivid dreams can be a side effect. Have you had any other symptoms? Low mood, anxiety, confusion?'

Ellie shook her head. 'Just tiredness.'

'Well, I'm sure every new mum has nightmares about something happening to the baby, especially if there have been complications. Try and get some sleep now. You'll feel better in the morning.'

The white clogs shushed across the tiles to the midwives' station. In the cot, Trinity slumbered on, her blanket rising and falling with each fluttering breath.

With the covers up to her chin and her heart beating erratically, Ellie tried to relax her muscles in turn the way they'd been taught at Willow Lodge. Soften the cheek muscles, loosen the jaw. But her forehead stayed tense. Something was … off. What was it?

The answer appeared as she drifted into sleep: even if she had dreamed the woman in black, that didn't explain the mud on the blanket.

Or how it had ended up on the floor.

7. Now

'I should really be carrying you over the threshold,' Tom said, opening the passenger door. 'But we can save that for another day.'

He hooked his arm under hers and she leaned gratefully into him as she climbed out, wincing at the pull on her incision which was still tender from the wound infection. Outside, the cool Moss Lane air washed the lingering traces of hospital dinners and antiseptic from her nostrils.

'It's so good to finally have the pair of you home,' Tom continued, easing the baby from the car seat with meticulous care.

'Hear that, Trinity?' Ellie said, her eyes taking in the whole of number six. 'We're home.'

Although the exterior hadn't changed much since she'd last seen it, the porch had been swept clean. Welcoming light spilled from the hallway as Tom unlocked the front door and, with one hand on the small of Ellie's back and the other cradling the baby against his chest, ushered them inside.

'Do you want to look round?' he said, dropping his keys into the wicker basket on the windowsill. 'Or have a cuppa first?'

Patches of drying plaster in the hall and the dark stains under Tom's eyes testified to long hours of graft since they'd completed on the house only a couple of weeks earlier. The hall smelled of deep cleaning and, in the kitchen the old-fashioned tiles and cupboards gleamed. No wonder he'd looked so exhausted every time he came to the hospital.

'Tea, please,' she said. He lowered Trinity into the baby bouncer. Nestled in the elephant-printed fabric, she seemed impossibly tiny and, removed from the safety of the hospital, entirely vulnerable.

Vulnerable. Jesus. The thought weakened Ellie's knees and she sat heavily.

Tom boiled the kettle, chatting on about the work he and Howard had planned for the house. Meanwhile, Ellie took a deep breath, rested her forearms on the table she'd inherited when Mum moved to Spain.

Back when she was a kid, this kitchen table had been a place to eat, talk, play and occasionally argue with Mum and Dad. In the Northern Quarter flat, the familiar wood became a dumping ground for junk mail and Tesco bags. But now future meals and board games and homework beckoned, right here under her elbows. The table represented family.

Tom put the steaming mug on a coaster. 'Should be champagne, really.'

The tears came without warning and she blinked them away. 'You realise I'm crying because I'm so happy?'

'I do make an incredible cuppa,' he replied, deadpan, and held his own mug in the air. 'Cheers. To us.'

'To us,' she echoed over the clink. 'I can't believe how much you've done already.'

'Most of it was Dad. We would've done more, but there were a few ...' he twisted his mouth to one side '... unexpected jobs that cropped up and needed sorting first.'

'But *this*. It's like new.'

'Original Seventies joinery. Built to last. Unlike the ...' he pointed at the lino, greyed out by years of foot traffic. 'We could get some cheap laminate for the time being if you like.'

Despite selling her car and parental handouts, their joint account, never exactly healthy, had slipped into a terminal decline.

'Let's wait and do it properly when we can afford it.'

Above Mosswood, the setting sun pinkened the sky. Crows cawed and flapped their ragged wings on their way to roost.

'Have you got used to the view yet?'

'I'll never get used to that view,' he replied, placing a hand on either side of the sink. 'I keep having to pinch myself.'

'Even though we'll be living off beans on toast for the next ten years?'

'Luckily, I love beans on toast,' he said. He drained his tea and picked up the baby. 'Anyway, me and Dad didn't want to do too much decorating without your say-so, but we have done one thing. Do you think you can manage the stairs?'

The paint on the banister had worn away in patches, revealing the wood underneath. It creaked when she grabbed it. Less than a year ago, she could run 5k without breaking a sweat and now she was panting over a few stairs?

Pregnancy had given her new respect for her body. And fed up as she was of elastic-waist jeans and tent tops, she had no issues with the nine months on, nine months off rule. But energy, strength and effortless stair-climbing? Those she missed. Wiping her palms surreptitiously on her thighs, she reached Tom standing in the doorway of the front bedroom. He shielded the baby's eyes.

'Surprise!'

And it was. From the palm-print curtains to the jungle animal lightshade, somehow he had delved inside her mind and plucked out the dream nursery.

'Oh, Tom, it's perfect,' she said.

'I've set the Moses basket up in our room,' he continued, 'but I thought it'd be nice to have all her things together, even while she's in with us.'

'I love it.'

Ellie stroked the giant panda Jess had sent; peeked into the basket on the changing table that Tom had filled with reusable wipes. Opening each drawer released a fresh lavender scent from orderly rows of vests, tights and onesies. Her toes dug into the soft pile of new carpet and she ran her fingers along the shelves built in the chimney-breast alcoves. Shelves that would soon be filled with books and toys.

Trinity flung out her arms and gurgled.

'She loves it too!' Ellie said in wonder.

Tom sniffed tentatively. 'Or maybe …'

He laid her on the changing mat and undid the poppers of her onesie. The air no longer smelled of lavender.

'Jesus Christ,' Tom muttered, frowning at the contents of the nappy. 'Is it supposed to be that colour?'

Ellie handed him the wipes. Above the changing table hung framed family photos, and she smiled sadly at grandparents Trinity would never meet keeping watch over her.

'I knew you wouldn't want pink and fluffy,' he continued, balling up the dirty nappy and dropping it in the bucket. 'Your mum told me to check out your Pinterest board for ideas. Which reminds me.' He pointed at a box under the window. 'She sent us this.'

Ellie took the baby while he lowered the blackout blind and plugged the light in. One click and a soft glow filled the room. Another and it revolved, dappling the walls in a soft kaleidoscope of light. 'And there's more. It's a night-light, disco light and also …' soft piano music played '… singer of lullabies. Good, eh?'

The ache of missing her mum sharpened to acute misery. She kissed Trinity's soft scalp and the baby wriggled and flexed her fingers.

'Lion,' Tom said and pointed to the squares on the wallpaper border. 'Giraffe. Elephant.'

The baby's face crumpled, as did her dad's, his dismay so palpable Ellie couldn't help but laugh.

'Don't worry, she's just hungry,' she said, already unfastening her bra.

'Give me a shout if you need anything,' he said. 'I'll unpack your stuff.'

The nursing chair she'd bagged on eBay stood in the corner by the window. She settled into it as 'Twinkle Twinkle' segued into 'Oranges and Lemons', triggering a memory of running under her primary schoolmates' arms in the playground. *Here comes the candle to light you to bed.*

She cupped the baby's silken skull, fragile as glass, in one hand. The greedy mouth clamped on and tears tingled the back of Ellie's nose. Honestly, whoever decreed this the most natural thing in the world had to have nipples of granite.

After a few minutes, she switched sides and the pain eased. The sucking slowed in a dribble of milky bubbles and when she patted Trinity's back, she was rewarded with a thunderous burp. But Ellie's grin turned to a frown over the baby's shoulder.

'Tom!' she called.

Pulling dirty clothes from the hospital holdall, he emerged from their bedroom.

'That mark on the floor,' she said. 'Is there a leak?'

With Trinity wedged against her chest, she nodded in the direction of a large stain on the carpet. It was roughly rectangular and longer than the cot.

While he held the wooden cot rail and knelt, knees clicking, to press his palm down, Ellie mentally ran through the layout of the house. Lounge, front bedroom, overlooking the road.

'Remember that damp patch downstairs when we viewed?'

He sniffed his fingertips. Shrugged. 'It's definitely not wet.'

'Can you see the mark though?'

He examined his palm and stood back with a shake of his head.

'No, and there can't be anything. The boards are new; the carpet was only fitted yesterday. Why don't I ...?'

He clicked the main light on. Shadows shifted and rearranged in the sudden glare.

'Better?'

She cocked her head and scrutinised the floor. No dirty marks, just dim lighting on the springy pile of a new carpet.

'Better,' she agreed, relieved.

Trinity wriggled and yawned, revealing an expanse of pink gum and milk-streaked tongue.

Tom brushed fluff from his jeans. 'What do you want to do now? Eat?'

'Honestly, I would love a bath.'

Tom lifted something from the shelf.

'OK, I'll do dinner, you have a bath and we can test the baby monitor out. The guys at the station had a whip-round for it.'

One tap and the object in his hand illuminated with a colour view of the entire room. Two parent heads, changing table, cot. Another tap, and the baby's head filled the screen.

Ellie looked from TV-Trinity to actual Trinity and back again.

'That is such a clear picture. Where's the camera?'

'It'll be clearer once we've got Wi-Fi.' He nodded at a white box by the chimney breast and circled his fingertip. A green bead of light appeared and a lens swivelled like an eyeball.

'The sound is just as clear. You can hear and talk to her from anywhere in the house.'

'Fancy.'

'I know. If NASA did baby monitors, right?'

Ellie shook her head and said regretfully, 'But we can't leave her on her own, even with that. Sorry. You'll have to take her down with you.'

'Good point,' Tom said, scooping the baby up and speaking into her face. 'Are you going to listen to the footy with Dad? Are you?'

Time had stopped circa 1985 in the bathroom. With a heartfelt 'Ugh!' she inched back the pink shower curtain. Speckled with black mould, it was one of those old flimsy things that would smother you given half a chance. She'd order a new one tonight. The water trickled out of the taps, but at least it was hot.

Tom hadn't got far with their bedroom. Their bed stood on bare floorboards with the stand for the Moses basket at the foot. Work clothes hung on a clothes rail and the rest were still packed in suitcases. She selected fresh pyjamas and returned to have another look at the nursery. *talkSPORT* played through the baby monitor and she smiled, listening to Tom explain to Trinity why the pundit didn't have a clue.

While the bathwater trickled laconically, she rearranged the wipes and double-checked the nappy supply. Pastel light swirled over the walls and a male vocalist sang 'Hush Little Baby'. She opened the top drawer and grabbed a handful of Trinity's dainty vests, smoothed out non-existent creases and folded as the chop of vegetables downstairs gave way to the sizzle of oil. Shame she couldn't sleep in here yet, but the guidelines said six months with parents and—

'Major Tom calling mother ship. Can you hear me, mother ship?'

The disembodied voice sounded as if he were standing right beside her. She clutched her chest.

'Loud and clear, Major Tom. God, I nearly had a heart attack.'

'Sorry, I meant to tell you, you can download the monitor app to your phone. Give us a wave.'

The green-lit eyeball swivelled and she stuck her tongue out at it. 'What about privacy? I could've been up to anything.'

Adopting a TV voice, he intoned, 'Day 1 in the Hartley-Wight household and does Ellie have something to hide?'

Stuffing a pair of woolly tights in the drawer, she replied, 'You don't know the half of it, mate.'

'I solemnly swear I will never spy on you,' Tom said. 'Now, are you getting in the bath?'

When she turned to switch the light off, she paused, one hand on the doorframe. The stain under the cot had returned and, if anything, had grown wider and longer. She blinked, hard. Looked again.

No, not a stain. Fluffy pile on a new carpet. Tomorrow, she would find where Tom had hidden the hoover and deal with it.

The bathroom was filled with steam and the bath half-full. She undid her jeans and gingerly shucked them off. Lowering herself

39

into the bath took some effort, but she sank gratefully under the bubbles, feeling her limbs relax. *Home.*

When she emerged, she pushed the wet hair from her eyes and groped for the towel to wipe her face. How lovely of Tom and Howard to finish the nursery. And exactly how she would have done it herself. Thoughtful, too, not to get too stuck into the rest of the house so she could be involved. Maybe money was too tight to get everything done straightaway, but stripping the layers of wallpaper? Well, that was one job she could do. Then what? Easy fixes first: white paint job, sand the boards, rugs from IKEA, blinds, a light fitting from the twenty-first century. Eyes closed, she grinned and slid under the water, picturing the 'Before' and 'After' images she'd post of herself, the fireplace and a mighty sledgehammer.

As the gentle splashes of the bathwater quietened, she became aware of music. The night-light in the nursery played the first notes of … what was it called? 'Mary, Mary, Quite Contrary', that was it. Even as she thought it, a less harmonious sound drowned out the music: the baby was crying. Ellie's breasts immediately tingled. She raised her eyes to the ceiling in disbelief. How greedy could a kid be? She must have had five pints already.

The volume increased and she felt a flicker of irritation. Why had Tom brought her back up to the nursery?

'Coming,' she said through the wall. She dried herself quickly and dragged on her pyjamas.

Out on the landing, the crying escalated beyond Trinity's usual cat-like sounds. Hairs prickled on the back of Ellie's neck. What the hell? This was nothing like Trinity's mewling demands. This was loud. Urgent. This was a cry of pain.

8. Now

She pushed the nursery door. Nothing happened. She pushed again, this time braced against the wood and rattling the handle. The door still refused to budge.

'Tom!' she shouted in rising panic towards the stairs. 'Get up here.'

How could this be happening? Surely she'd left it open. She yanked the handle. Or tried to. The mechanism clicked and shifted. The baby's wailing pierced the unyielding wood.

Ellie shoved again, ignoring the warning stab in her still-healing belly. Nothing. She may as well have been trying to smash through the wall.

'Tom!'

She could hear him blithely singing along to a radio jingle. How could he ignore the cries filling the house?

Fighting to control her hysteria, she placed her mouth against the cold wood.

'It's all right, baby. Mummy's coming.'

She threw her full weight at the door again, sending shock waves from her shoulder to her fingertips. It flew open and she stumbled inside, panting, just as the crying stopped dead.

Ellie stared. The cot was empty. The room was silent under a constellation of projected stars.

Then the final notes of 'Mary, Mary' broke the suspended hush. Pain radiated down her arm and the incision across her belly burned.

'Tom!' she shouted, and this time he heard.

He stood at the bottom of the stairs, holding a steaming pan. 'What's up, love?'

'Where's the baby?' she said.

He put his finger to his lips and pointed back into the kitchen. 'Don't wake her up.'

In the Moses basket, Trinity lay like the poster child for peaceful slumber. Her face read 'Do not disturb'. Her chest rose and fell in regular rhythm. Her forehead wasn't hot, wasn't cold. Ellie put her cheek to the baby's mouth and felt the reassuring tickle of even breaths.

Tom returned to the sink and drained noodles through the colander.

'Was she crying?' Ellie said.

'More grizzling than crying, but then she just nodded off. How was your bath?' He tipped the steaming noodles into mismatched bowls.

Ellie chewed the inside of her cheek. 'It sounded like she was in the nursery, crying. Really crying.'

'You must have heard her through the baby monitor. Maybe we should adjust the volume.'

'Maybe,' she said, keeping one hand resting lightly on the basket.

'Are you ready to eat?'

He eased the cap off a beer bottle and took a long swallow.

'Yeah, it smells great,' she said, but her appetite evaporated as he put the dishes on the table and sat down.

'Make the most of it,' Tom said, curling noodles around his fork. Drops of pale green sauce spattered on the table. 'We're back on the beans tomorrow.'

She prodded a sliver of broccoli. 'So, I tried to get in, but the nursery door wouldn't open.'

'It'll be catching on the new carpet. I'll get Dad to plane the bottom.'

'But it was so scary. She could have been ill, *really* ill, and I couldn't get in. It was completely stuck.'

'Well, she wasn't actually in there,' he pointed out. 'But I'll do the hinges with some WD-40 as well. Speaking of doors, the woman at number five dropped our house keys round the other day. She's been keeping an eye on the place, apparently.'

Ah. Miserable woman in black.

'Hair tied up in one of those …?' She mimed a Princess Anne updo. 'Unbelievably rude? She's the one I saw when we came here with the agent. Remember?'

Tom's forehead crinkled. 'Not this one. She's got short hair, blonde-ish, friendly. Like the TV cake woman.'

'Mary Berry?'

He pointed the bottle at her in affirmation. 'She said to knock if there's anything we need. She also said she was a health visitor at the village surgery till she retired. I liked her.' He took a swig of beer. 'Anyway, keys are in the basket. Saves us changing the locks till we replace the doors.'

With the first few noodley mouthfuls, her appetite perked up. After six weeks of lukewarm hospital slop, it tasted good.

'Are you happy with the nursery?' he said.

'Love it!' She took a sip of elderflower, letting the bubbles dance across her tongue.

'Good, good,' he said, absently.

A drop of water splashed on the pots and pans piled in the sink. Tom stabbed at a cube of chicken then cleared his throat.

'Els, I've got something to tell you. It's about work. You know we have major staffing issues?'

She had lived with a police officer long enough to suspect where this was heading. Her heart began to sink.

'*Had* staffing issues,' she corrected. 'You've got a new DC now.'

'Yes, Tanya. But things have blown up on the job and she doesn't have the experience, so the boss rang me …' He tailed off with a shrug. 'Sorry.'

Suspicions confirmed, Ellie's heart plummeted to the worn lino. 'I get it. They've cancelled your leave.'

'Not cancelled.' His chin rasped as he rubbed his two-day

stubble. 'Postponed. They've given me so much time off already, I don't think I can say no. Plus Tanya really needs the support.'

'*We* need the support. Me and your daughter.'

He spread his arms in a *what's a man to do?* gesture. 'I know, love, but I'll be here most of the time and what we're on to now is massive. And we are this close' – he held his thumb and finger until they almost touched – 'to taking some truly evil bastards out of circulation in the next few weeks. People fight to be posted to this unit.'

'Well, let one of them do it, then. You promised you'd have the first week at home.'

'The job's at a crucial stage right now. There's a raid coming up. You know I can't tell you details, but if all goes to plan, it'll make the news.' He put his warm hand over hers and clasped her knuckles. 'And apart from that, I've used all my paid leave.'

She withdrew her hand. 'Oh, so this is about money.'

The crease between Tom's eyebrows deepened. 'Come on. You know it's not.'

She interlocked her fingers and looked away. The entire length of the worktop was littered with vegetable scraps and cutlery resting in sticky puddles. Where Tom cooked, chaos followed. With an exaggerated sigh, Ellie collected their empty bowls and stacked them by the sink.

She heard chair legs scrape and felt his arms around her. He rested his chin on the top of her head and for a moment the kitchen light haloed their reflections, merging their washed-out faces with the darkness outside.

'Look, if you really want me to stay home, I'll call the boss and explain.'

She was about to say, *yes, you do that*, but she caught herself. They needed the money, simple as.

She broke away. 'No, don't. It'll be fine.'

'OK. Well, if you're sure, I'll stick this in the fridge,' he said, poking at the leftovers in the pan with a spatula. 'There's enough for your lunch and I'll take the rest to microwave at work.'

The penny dropped.

'You're going in *tomorrow*?'

'I told you the other day. I'm on court duty for a job from last year.' Water gushed in the sink and bubbles frothed like meringue, spilling over onto the worktop.

She wrenched the tap off. This wasn't the homecoming she'd imagined. 'We haven't been home for twenty-four hours yet.'

'Why don't I ask Dad to come over if you're worried about being on your own?'

'I don't want Howard,' she said, blinking back tears. 'I want *you*.'

'Love,' he said, reaching towards her, but she stiffened, her arms at her sides.

'Don't. Just don't.'

Bathing Trinity took forever. When they'd been supervised by the nurses, the whole process had seemed so easy, fun even. But at home, instead of singing and games, there were debates over how warm was 'warm'; the best way to fill the small plastic tub and the safest hold for a squirming, slippery creature hellbent on sliding under the water. Even the towelling technique merited discussion.

By the time Trinity slipped into clean, milky oblivion at the side of the bed, backache and tiredness had set Ellie's bones in concrete. Too exhausted to shower away the day's grime, she collapsed into bed hardly noticing when Tom climbed in beside her.

But it seemed as though she had barely shut her eyes before Trinity's plaintive cries prised them open again. The only light in the bedroom was the red glow from the bedside clock: 11.37. Tom, unperturbed, snored faintly and turned onto his side.

Stumbling out of bed, Ellie grabbed her dressing gown, lifted Trinity from the Moses basket, carried her to the nursing chair and the pattern for the first night was set. Cry, feed, sleep, repeat.

By 4.37, the line between reality and dreams had blurred. There didn't seem much point returning to their bedroom, so she put Trinity in the cot and curled up in the nursery chair alongside with her dressing gown draped over her like a quilt.

She woke to gentle singing.

Mary, Mary, quite contrary,
How does your garden grow?

Long dark hair tumbled over the shoulders of the figure next to the window. Her fingernails were painted black. Ellie blearily watched her dig her thumb over and over into textured wallpaper that wasn't there.

Just a dream. Just a dream. A dream.

With silver bells and cockle shells.

Her eyelids grew heavy.

And pretty maids all in a row.

9. Then

'Welcome to Henderson Hall!' the laminated sign read. 'Flat and room numbers displayed below. Collect keys from desk. Please read the rules.'

Eighteen-year-old Ellie Wight shrank against the wall, overwhelmed by the herd of laughing, shouting, chatting strangers. A girl with long dark hair styled into a quiff fiercely hugged an equally tall woman, knocking her sunglasses from the top of her head. Next to her, a white dog batted its tail against the legs of a handsome man.

'Calm down, Smudge,' the man said, patting the dog's head.

An image of her own mum getting home to darkness and silence flashed through Ellie's mind. She forced the picture away and mustered a nervous smile.

'Room six, please.'

'Name?'

'Eleanor Wight.'

The woman rifled through a plastic crate and selected an envelope. 'Here you are. Keys and rules. Shared kitchen and lounge for eight. You've got your own shower and loo. Big key is the external door.' She jerked her thumb at the entrance. 'And the little one is your room. Enjoy.'

After they'd carted the last box from the car to the tiny bedroom, her mum hugged her tight.

'I'd better go now to beat the traffic,' she said. 'Take care, love.' She sniffed a couple of times and her wedding ring dug painfully into Ellie's scalp. For someone so strong, she felt unbearably fragile.

'I promised myself I wouldn't get upset.' She pulled away, wiping tears from the side of her nose. 'But Dad would have been so proud of you.'

'I love you, Mum.'

'I love you too.' With one final squeeze, she was gone.

Ellie perched on the unfamiliar bed, surrounded by boxes, and slid the keys on the key ring her mum had given her for her eighteenth. They clinked against the initial E and the silver heart that contained a photo of her dad. She stroked it absent-mindedly with her thumb and tried not to freak out.

A minute or so later, there was a knock, followed by a cheerful 'Hello?'

Ellie quickly wiped her eyes and opened the door.

The voice belonged to the girl with the glamorous parents. Tall and lean, she wore a leather biker jacket over a jumper shot through with glittery threads; skinny jeans tucked into clumpy-soled boots. She held her hand out to shake. Her fingernails were varnished black, her skin streaked with paint or pen.

'Hi, neighbour,' she said with a smile Ellie couldn't help but return. 'I'm Mia.'

10. Now

'Morning.' The man in the porch presented a laminated ID. 'Connection services.'

Ellie stared at the card until the man's arm drooped along with his smile. Conscious of the crusty cardigan, bedhead tangles and general disgustingness caused by three nights of bad dreams and round-the-clock feeds, Ellie felt herself go red.

The man nodded at the top sheet on his clipboard. 'Six Moss Lane, is it? I'm here to connect your phone and broadband?'

Right. Of course. She remembered now. After assuming baby brain was a myth to patronise new mothers, discovering the truth had been a shock. Tom had reminded her last night and before he left for work. It had been on the calendar since they'd come home from the hospital. And yet the arrival of a man in a boiler suit on her doorstep still took her by surprise.

She didn't want a strange man here. She didn't want anyone here.

But she did want superfast broadband.

'Sorry. Yes. Come in.' She smiled, remembering a second too late that she hadn't brushed her teeth. Oh no. Did he actually wince? 'I've just had a baby,' she added, apologetically.

She offered him a cup of tea, realising too late it was the last of the milk. And, apparently, Tom had unpacked the kitchen stuff blindfolded meaning she had to ferret through every drawer to find a clean teaspoon. Also, he'd rushed off leaving his cereal bowl pebble-dashed with rock-hard granola. And at some point he must have traipsed mud across the lino *and just left it*.

Black coffee and the whine of the engineer's drill battered

further at her tired mood. With every mopping and scrubbing movement, a sour yoghurt smell wafted from her because she couldn't get in the sodding shower until the sodding man left. From her head to her feet, everything ached. Even her gums. Her sodding eyelashes.

And of all mornings, Trinity had picked this one to flex her tantrum muscles. Ellie followed the care instructions suggested by Google, but singing, feeding, walking, rocking, nothing eased the relentless whimpering.

'Sorry, I didn't catch that?'

The engineer stood in the kitchen doorway. Ellie paused, mid-way through drying a plate and rocking the bouncer with her foot.

'Sorry?' she said.

The engineer gestured at the door. 'When you came in just now, I didn't hear what you asked me.'

'I didn't come in. I haven't moved out of here,' she said, half-smiling, half-frowning.

There was an infinitesimal pause.

'Oh.' His face was a question mark. 'You didn't come into the lounge and speak to me just now?'

'Definitely not.'

'Blimey. I could've sworn …' He laughed and shook his head. 'Oh well. Must be going daft in my old age. Anyway, I'm all done now.'

She watched him peel a sticker from a sheet and smooth it on the router saying something about codes and giving it a whirl in half an hour. Or was it an hour? All she could think about was standing under hot water with a bar of soap.

His van bumped away over the potholes, silence settled on the house and she breathed a long sigh of relief. Broadband: good. Not having to act normal: even better.

She added his empty mug to Tom's breakfast dishes dripping on the draining board then settled Trinity in the Moses basket on the landing and finally stood under a cascade of warm water and scrubbed and rinsed until she felt almost human again.

'There we go,' she said, wrapping her hair in a towel. 'All better.'

Trinity stared up with awe and reached her hands out, clutching at the air.

'Gorgeous girl,' Ellie said, blowing a gentle raspberry on the back of her neck. 'Thank you for not crying.'

The letterbox rattled and the baby gave a surprised gurgle.

Holding Trinity to her chest, Ellie gingerly bent her knees to retrieve the scattered letters from the hall floor. The wound had flared up after barging the nursery door on their first night home and while she took the itching as a sign of healing, the little jabs of pain were less welcome. She set aside a clothing catalogue stamped with 'M. Brennan' and a couple of letters for Tom that looked suspiciously like bills. And examined the last, a handwritten envelope addressed to them both.

'Another card for your collection?' she asked Trinity, extracting what her mum would describe as a 'tasteful' Beatrix Potter card. She opened it. Read.

Dear Ellie and Tom,

We hope you are settling into your new home. We were delighted when Carol told us your wonderful news. Congratulations to both of you on the safe arrival of Trinity. Such an exciting time!

We often think of you and please do remember that you are always welcome to visit.

With fondest love,

Anita and David Goldsworthy

Anita's writing matched her completely: elegant and effortless. Ellie pictured her bent over the farmhouse table, considering each word carefully. Strolling to the post box, with a dog trotting by her side. Not Smudge, the friendly old soul Ellie had become fond of when she'd stayed with Mia's family, but a descendant.

She gulped down a sob, and she knew if she closed her eyes, Mia would be there. Not the funny, beautiful, talented daughter Anita and David loved, but the other one. The broken one, lying on the tarmac on a rainy night. Time might have a habit of blunting memories, but that image only sharpened over the years.

Trinity's eyes rounded with curiosity. Drool dripped down her chin and Ellie wiped it gently with the sleeve of her cardigan.

'Don't worry, baby,' she whispered. 'Mama's fine.'

But she wasn't. The sly voice in her mind had returned, as insistent as ever.

You don't deserve to be happy.

She hadn't had a panic attack since Willow Lodge, but the signs were unmistakable. Acting on autopilot, she cupped her free hand and exhaled, pushing against the tightness in her lungs. She sat heavily on the sofa, only a second before her legs gave way. *Anchor your breath. In. Out.*

The distant shrill of her mobile pierced the haze. 'One, two, three, four.' She counted the rings aloud, like a mantra until the blurring at the edges of her vision receded.

She covered her face and groaned. Through splayed fingers she saw the card on the coffee table. She wanted to bury it at the bottom of the bin.

Trinity grizzled. Had she been squashing her? Anita must have nuzzled into Mia's infant neck like this. Did she make the same feverish plea to the universe? *Keep her safe and I swear I'll do anything you ask of me.*

Ellie leaned against the sofa's upholstered back and screwed her eyes shut. How much courage would it take to congratulate a new life after your own had been ripped apart?

Anita had signed the card, 'With fondest love.'

What would the poor woman write if she knew the truth?

11. Now

A subdued thud startled her from the edge of sleep. One of the sofa cushions had slipped to the floor and reaching to retrieve it, she heard a muffled cry. *The baby!*

Trinity was wedged between Ellie's thigh and the arm of the sofa. Oh God! Was her skin dusky? Lips. Too pale? Bluish? Ellie ran her fingers frantically over the baby's face.

Then her daughter gurgled, bending then straightening her legs with a forceful kick.

With one hand supporting the delicate neck and the other under the pudge of Trinity's bottom, Ellie slumped against the armrest, winded by shock.

How could she be so careless? During her pregnancy, she had pored over parenting books, magazines, and websites, confident that if there was a GCSE in 'Theory of Motherhood', she'd get a Grade 9. And yet every article she'd read warned about the dangers of napping with a new-born.

Babies tumbled to the floor.

Babies rolled into gaps.

Babies fell asleep and never woke up.

Trinity wriggled and whimpered, her nose softly bumping against Ellie's shoulder.

'Are you hungry, sweetheart?' She lifted her T-shirt and the baby wobbled as Ellie's eyes went glassy.

Simple enough things, really – food, comfort, physical safety – and she couldn't even meet her daughter's most fundamental needs. What use was theory if you failed the practical?

The phone rang again when she was wiping traces of milk from Trinity's chin.

'Hi,' Tom said over the noise of traffic. 'I rang before but you didn't pick up. How are things?'

Last night's curry hung in the air and wet laundry lingered in the machine. The floor was filthy, the nappy bucket overflowing. She needed to brush her hair. And, judging by the taste in her mouth, her teeth.

And she had almost killed their daughter.

She put on her brightest voice. 'All great, thanks.'

'How's the broadband?'

'Speedy,' she said, making a note to test it when he got off the phone.

A female voice called his name and he put his hand over the mouthpiece, muffling their conversation.

'Sorry, Els. Promise I'll be home soon as I can.'

After the call ended, she opened Favourites and pressed her mum's name. Paused. Clicked the phone off. Outside, birds darted in a cloudless sky and the trees, some already leafless, some with curled brown leaves stubbornly clinging on, swayed in the breeze.

'I think you and I need to blow the cobwebs away, baby girl,' she said. 'Fancy a walk?'

12. Now

With a little help from a YouTube tutorial, Ellie fitted the baby sling snugly against her chest. She double-checked the straps and hip positioning. Safe and secure. Trinity wiggled her legs experimentally, intrigued by this new experience.

Keys? Wicker basket in the hall. Her fingers found two scratched and worn mortise ones and a Yale, rusting at the edges. They hung on her key ring between the silver E and the photo of her dad. Since she left home, it had only ever held rented keys, but these actually belonged to her. She clasped the bunch tightly. *Her* keys. *Her* house.

But as she stepped into the autumn sunshine, her confidence faded and a sliver of panic lodged in her chest. After weeks cooped up inside, the sky suddenly seemed too wide; the birds too loud. The breeze through the trees was a sinister whisper.

For a fleeting moment, she imagined unfastening the sling and barricading the two of them indoors. But then where would that lead? Keeping her daughter locked up forever, like a princess in a fairy tale?

She set her shoulders back. If she wanted Trinity to grow up fearless rather than fearful then she needed to lead by example.

'Let's be explorers,' she said firmly.

Although Howard and Tom had cleared a path through the garden, the forlorn atmosphere lingered. Wet grass and brambles wound around her ankles and left streaks on her jeans. She stopped at the rose bed where the greened wood of the pergola had splintered into lethal, jagged spikes. An old plastic chair lay on its side next to a planter filled with blackened dead things.

Total eyesore.

Shielding the baby's head with her hand, Ellie stepped hesitantly across the uneven stepping stones that created a makeshift path through the weed-filled rose beds. Slimy clods of vegetation coated their concrete surface and the whole shoddy thing was a death trap, never mind a mess.

Her dad had loved gardening. He would have known when to sow lawn seed and what to grow where. She pictured him teaching Trinity the names of the trees and flowers, just like he'd done when she was small. Peppering her daughter's head with kisses, she let the wave of sadness break over her and recede.

Then she lifted Trinity's legs clear of the nettles, carving a path through whorls of tall grass until she reached the fence that separated them from Mosswood.

'Hold on tight,' she sing-songed and carefully clambered over.

From the house, Mosswood was a uniform mass, but over the fence the trees revealed their unique personalities. Patterned bark, different-shaped leaves, multi-coloured moss. The sun shone through the canopy, dappling patches of late flowers and grass with light. Tiny birds chirped as they flitted from branch to branch. Nature, clean air, peace: this was what the move to Moss Lane meant.

Mum and baby walking in the woods on a crisp October day. What could be nicer? Twigs crunched underfoot as she headed to the sandy path, ducking under the low branches that blocked their way.

'Follow the yellow brick road,' she chanted, clicking on the Maps app. 'We're that blob and the other blob is home. Easy. We won't need to drop breadcrumbs and we definitely won't meet any big bad wolves.'

But it didn't take long for the weight of the sling to grow more noticeable and only slightly longer before her back began to ache. The baby's solid warmth made sweat pool between her breasts.

'Mummy is so unfit,' she said, wafting away a cloud of tiny black flies. 'Shall we head back home?'

As she finished the sentence, they arrived at the edge of a fairy-tale clearing complete with wildflowers and a sparkling pond. Pine trees circled a patch of sunlit grass and in the exact centre, a dead tree held court, its bleached bone-smooth limbs lending it a skeletal beauty.

Trinity hadn't uttered a peep since they left the house, but when Ellie stepped off the path her bottom lip began to tremble. Up close, the dead tree looked more sinister than sculptural and when she touched one of the thick branches, she was surprised by the cold that greeted her fingertips. Even the birds stayed on the margins, silent. Trinity wriggled, letting out a cry that echoed through the clearing.

'Sssh, sweetheart,' Ellie said. 'Look at the pretty pond.'

On closer inspection, she saw that clusters of flies hung above the still water. Sunlight sparkled on stagnant depths and the reeds, green and healthy from a distance, were streaked with black rot. The pretty pond was actually pretty rank.

Some foetid smell – sewage or gone-off chicken – caught in her throat and suddenly, Ellie was certain they weren't alone in the clearing. A shadow flitted across her peripheral vision and she snapped her head round to see a crow flap by on lazy wings. Goose bumps plucked her arms. She couldn't see anyone or hear anything other than the whine of the wind in the trees, but something felt wrong. Peculiar. Nothing she could pin down, only an ancient do-not-linger that tingled her nerves, telling her to leave this place.

Now.

She wasn't up to jogging, especially with a squirming, squealing baby strapped to her chest, but she moved briskly, crossing her arms to protect Trinity. The dark-green canopy of leaves stirred into ominous rushing, like a fast-flowing river carrying her away from home. Brambles and twigs grabbed at her clothes. Every snap, every rustle was a threat. Dread pushed her deeper into the woods. She blundered through a dense thicket of rhododendrons, only stopping when she tripped over an exposed tree root. With a painful crack, her knee hit the trunk and she shot her hand out to right herself against the rough bark. Black spots danced in front of her eyes, but the jolt had dislodged her phone from her back pocket, lighting up the screen.

'OK, baby girl?' she said, grunting as she stooped to retrieve it. Trinity howled in reply.

Thank you, Google Maps. The creepy clearing they had just left was called Moss Pond and, miraculously, they were heading in the right direction for home. Limping slightly now, she hurried along the route on the screen until she caught the first glimpse of the neighbour's red-tiled roof followed by their own.

With every step, the baby had gained a pound and by the time she reached the fence, she had to grab her sore leg and physically lift it on to the bottom rung.

She retraced their steps through bent grass to the house, digging her keys out of her pocket as she stepped carefully under the splintered pergola. Once inside, she leaned against the closed door for a few seconds and caught her breath.

Home.

The kitchen was exactly as she'd left it: breakfast dishes draining on the rack. Laundry piled on the table. Floor in need of a mop. Wet washing in the machine.

Safe.

She took the baby from the sling and sat down. As Trinity fed, Ellie's heartbeat slowly returned to normal. She blew out of the corner of her mouth to unstick a strand of hair glued by a trickle of sweat and briefly considered asking Tom to come home but then thought better of it. What could she say?

In the reassuring ordinariness of the kitchen, the spooked half-jog seemed a ridiculous over-reaction. After all, she hadn't actually heard or seen anyone. And even if she had, why wouldn't someone be in the clearing? Dog walkers, joggers and nature lovers flocked to Mosswood. In fact, it would be weirder *not* to bump into someone. Trinity flicked her little hands open and Ellie swapped her to the other side.

'Your mum is such an idiot,' she announced. 'Scared of her own shadow.'

The kitchen was a mess. Muddy tracks across the lino mirrored a black smear on the back door and either she'd brought the rotting pond home in her nostrils or the house stank.

A plump fly buzzed over the nappy bucket and, not for the first time since leaving hospital, Ellie questioned her commitment to reusables. Another example of real-life experience kicking theory's butt. She grimaced and opened the window, ushering the blue-bottle out. The house needed a clean. She needed a distraction.

'Come on. Be productive,' she ordered herself, dragging a knotted assortment of wet clothes and nappies from the machine and sniffing. They'd have to do. Where had Tom hidden the pegs? She opened the cupboard under the sink, felt a twinge in the base of her back as she straightened and as she did, caught sight of a stranger's face overlapping her reflection.

13. Now

The face in the window broke into a warm smile and moved to one side. Unlike hers, it wore make-up and was framed by neatly brushed hair. Smart-casual in a fuchsia bodywarmer over a Breton striped T-shirt, the owner of the face was younger than Mary Berry, but Tom had the comparison nailed. Through the glass, their new neighbour mouthed, 'May I …?'

Ellie smiled and opened the back door. The woman held a newspaper-wrapped bouquet, water dripping from protruding green stalks.

'Hello, I'm Diane from number five. Welcome to Moss Lane.'

'Hi. Of course. Come in.' Ellie stepped back.

Their new neighbour folded a corner of damp newspaper over the stems. Her nails were painted a subtle pink. 'I could pop back later if this isn't a good time?'

'No, it's fine. Honestly.' Ellie smoothed her hair down. 'Sorry, I'm just having one of those days.'

'I was a health visitor for nearly forty years, so I can tell you "those days" are universal.' She beamed down at the baby, eyeing her with curiosity. 'And this beautiful young lady must be …'

'Trinity.'

'What a lovely name. Now, these are the last of the roses from my garden. I can't remember them ever blooming this late.'

Ellie took the bundle and buried her nose in the sweet petals. 'They're gorgeous. Thank you.'

'You're welcome. I just wanted to introduce myself and to see how you're settling in.'

'Getting there, slowly.' Ellie gestured at the boxes and balls of crumpled newspaper, clothes spewing from the washing machine. 'Would you like a cup of tea?'

'No thanks. It's a flying visit. I wanted to mention the play-group my grandson, Freddie, goes to. My daughter-in-law is a volunteer there. Asha – she's very friendly. Australian. It's from ten every Tuesday and Friday at St Michael's on the high street.'

Trinity sighed and bubbles formed on her wet lower lip.

'That's really kind of you, thanks.'

Diane stroked the baby's cheek. 'It is such a pleasure to see a family in this house. We're such a lot of old fuddy-duddies on the Lane now all the children have grown up and moved away. I'm sure Mary would have been thrilled.'

'Mary?'

'The lady who lived here before.'

Ellie frowned, recalling the documents on the auction office desk. 'Wasn't she called Catherine?'

It was Diane's turn to frown. 'No, Catherine's Canadian. They were cousins, I think. She inherited the house last year when Mary passed away.'

Ellie digested this new information. 'I'm sorry to hear that. Were you and Mary close?'

'No.' Diane paused a beat before adding, sadly, 'I wish we had been. Maybe things would have turned out differently for poor Mary.'

Ellie waited for her to elaborate, but the older woman just fiddled with the zip on her gilet.

'Different how?' Ellie prompted.

There was a pause during which first confusion then shock crossed Diane's face. Her hand went to her mouth.

'Oh my goodness. I am so sorry. I assumed you knew.'

'Knew what?'

'Dear me. I only meant that I wish I could have …' Dismay clouded the older woman's features. She cleared her throat. 'Mary passed away in the house. Nothing sinister – she had a weak heart.' She tailed off and edged towards the door. 'I'm afraid I've put my foot in it.'

The poor neighbour looked horrified.

'No, it's fine,' Ellie heard herself say.

But her mind reeled even as she tried to put Diane at ease. Someone died *here*?

Diane gave a weak smile. 'Please believe me when I say you are exactly what Moss Lane needs. Life and laughter. Children. And if there's anything I can do, you know where I am. And again, I apologise.'

'Honestly, there's no need,' Ellie said, mustering a smile of her own. 'I'm not superstitious.'

A draught fluttered the baby photos stuck to the fridge and Diane left with a final promise she would speak to her daughter-in-law about the playgroup. Even before her footsteps had retreated up the path, Ellie had her phone out.

'Tom Hartley is unavailable …'

She sucked in a deep breath. Held it. Ended the call without speaking.

This wasn't information you could just casually drop into a voicemail. *Hi, can you get some milk on your way home. Oh and by the way, a woman died in our house.*

Holding the phone to her lips, she processed Diane's revelation while her emotions shuttled through a range of reactions. Did she feel scared? Angry? Grossed out?

Shocked, definitely. But even as she registered that, her mind took her back to the viewing and the forlorn atmosphere of a home that had lost its beating heart. She had sensed, even then, a sadness.

And after all, this wasn't the first time she'd lived where someone had died.

When the oncologist told them Dad's lung cancer was no longer treatable, Mum drove him straight home. Spending his last weeks with them had felt natural. The best possible solution to the worst possible situation.

She unwrapped Diane's roses and stuffed the wet newspaper in the bin. She couldn't deny it was a shock. But plenty of people slipped away with no warning at home. And, given the choice, who wouldn't die in familiar surroundings rather than a hospital or a hospice?

Every vase was already filled with flowers from family and friends, so she filled a pint glass at the tap and, without looking at Anita's card, placed it in the centre of the mantelpiece. Had the previous owner died in here, watching TV? Or peacefully in her bed surrounded by family, like Dad?

A blast of wind moaned down the chimney, sending little puffs of soot onto the floorboards. She zipped up her hoodie. If this house had stood empty for a year, that explained why it was so bloody freezing. She found the dustpan and brush on top of Tom's sports gear in the under-stairs cupboard and swept up what hadn't fallen between the cracks in the floorboards.

Back in the kitchen, Trinity had nodded off. Ellie tiptoed across the floor and carefully picked up the laundry basket. Balancing the peg bag on top of the wet washing, she went outside.

The clothesline stretched between a tree and a rusty metal post. She slid a damp cloth the full length, cleaning off umpteen years of black and green gunk. A couple of greyed-out clothes pins, the old-fashioned dolly kind her nan used, spun with the vibration and Ellie considered them carefully. How many times had the old owner used those pegs to hang her own sheets and towels?

With clean whites flapping on the line, she set the empty basket on the kitchen table next to her phone. A notification from Tom had arrived while she was outside. She read it and bit her lip, snorting softly down her nose.

Typical.

Trinity twisted, clenching her fists like a miniature boxer. Ellie leaned over the basket saying, 'Daddy's going to be late because he's helping the new lady at work.'

Trinity grumbled a response.

'You're absolutely right. Daddy should tell her to get lost and come home.'

No, that wasn't fair. Especially as he had nodded off revising for his sergeant's exams last night. The textbook lay splayed face down on the bedroom floor. She picked it up and wedged it against the nursery door.

Shafts of autumn sunshine lit the room and a few late insects batted against the window. The baby settled on the nursing pillow and within seconds, began to suck rhythmically and more importantly, near painlessly. Progress at last.

Diane was right. This house needed a family; Ellie had sensed that from the first time she saw it. And if someone died here, so what? Sad for the woman, obviously, but people had been dying in houses for thousands of years. Half of Manchester was built over defunct mass graveyards, for God's sake. No point getting all Stephen King about it.

Still.

Despite her pragmatism she suppressed an involuntary shudder. Against her will, her brain picked over the conversation with Diane, filling in the gaps with speculative whens and wheres and hows.

Stop it.

She shoved the macabre thoughts aside firmly.

The baby unfastened herself with an audible pop. On the changing mat, the tiny eyelashes fluttered and limbs softened while Ellie stripped, wiped, and changed. By the time the Velcro on the nappy rasped into place, Trinity's muted whimpering signalled she was on the cusp of sleep.

With the baby snoozing in the Moses basket at her side, Ellie dusted the laptop screen with her sleeve then entered the wireless code the engineer had stuck to the router. Success. The screensaver was a happy blast from the past. A reminder of the Australian leg of their trip of a lifetime that seemed way more than a lifetime ago. They'd stayed on a campsite near Uluru infested with ghostly flying crickets the size of sparrows and a plague of flies whose sole purpose was to sip the moisture from your eyeballs.

In the photo, twenty-two-year-old Tom and Ellie radiated love. Fingers entwined, they bathed in the dying rays of a sun that cast bruise-coloured shadows on ancient rock and even after all this time, she recalled the deep spirituality that had flooded her veins. How standing in the presence of something so inexplicable, so sublime, so beyond the limits of human understanding had consumed her with total awe.

But sitting on the sofa eight years later, that total awe was directed at her younger self. She looked seriously amazing. Why had she ever wasted a minute on being self-conscious?

Reconnecting with the world of social media meant fielding a never-ending stream of other people's sun-soaked holidays and heavily filtered nights out. Her world, too, not that long ago. But while their glamorous lives carried on unchanged, hers had entered a new dimension, one filled with dirty nappies and nipple balm. She uploaded some cute pictures of Trinity ('sorry for the baby spam!!!') and cringed at some shockers on Tom's page. Her own head, blotchy and bloated, loomed over their daughter's perfect peach of a skull. At least the comments were kind.

Her stomach growled. She ate a jam sandwich over the kitchen sink, watching the washing ripple in the breeze, obscuring the view of the garden beyond.

Was it previous owner Mary who had built the pergola and tended the rose beds around it? She must have picked out the pink bathroom suite, the bobbly wallpaper, and the crazy copper fireplace. The newsprint smudges around the front door, which at some point Ellie would have to clean, were made by her fingers. Or had there ever been a Mr Mary? Kids? If she left the house to her cousin, maybe not.

A gentle gasp came from the Moses basket. Trinity opened and closed her chubby fists, then settled again with a sigh. Calm and safe.

Torn between not wanting to know and the pull of morbid curiosity, she found herself eyeing the laptop. If she knew the truth, then she could move past it, right?

Decision made, she brushed crumbs from her top into the sink and made a mug of decaf.

'Right, Mary,' she said to the laptop. 'Who were you?'

Maybe she'd get lucky and discover Mary had a Yeti-sized social media footprint, although that was unlikely, given the absence of broadband. But the first hurdle was her surname. Ask Diane? No, too weird. Think laterally.

The vendor was Catherine Wilson. Mary Wilson, then.

'Mary Wilson' brought up millions of hits. She scrolled through the first few, but it was hopeless. She sat back, defeated, and stared out of the window. A shirt flapped on the line, startling a couple of crows into cawing flight.

Ah. The clothing catalogue. She fished in the bin for the package she'd dumped earlier. And suddenly there it was – M. Brennan printed on the address label. She was immediately back on the laptop. How about Moss Lane + Mary + Brennan?

Jackpot. Several links to newspaper articles appeared. She clicked on the top, from the *Stockfield Express*: 'Woman's Body found in Uppermoss'.

Although she'd been half-expecting it, the picture loading under the headline jolted her. Six Moss Lane, their new home, with blue-and-white tape stretched between the gateposts. White-boiler-suited figures loaded boxes into a police van parked on her drive.

Police tape? Boiler suits?

Nothing sinister, Diane had said.

Police were called to a house in the Mosswood area of Uppermoss today where the body of a woman, believed to be the homeowner and in her late fifties, was removed. Forensic officers remain at the scene. However, a police spokesman has confirmed the death is not being treated as suspicious. It is believed the body may have lain undiscovered for up to two weeks before a postal worker reported seeing a large number of flies.

Ellie blinked. Lifted the laptop off the table and held it closer. She'd misread that, right?
But the black typescript stared back, unchanged.

The body may have lain undiscovered for up to two weeks.

14. Now

'And the estate agent never mentioned it?' Carol said.

'Nothing. Or the auction house.'

Ellie hugged the hoodie tight around her. Above Mosswood, the first stars blinked coldly in the autumn twilight. It got dark so early here, away from the light pollution of the city streets.

'There must be a law,' Carol said.

Wedging the phone between her chin and shoulder, she walked to the light switch. Cold lino penetrated through the woollen socks.

'I googled it. There's no obligation to tell house buyers if it's a natural death.'

'When did it happen?'

'Last summer.'

'Well, I don't think you should dwell on it, love. Most houses have had someone die in them.'

Ellie clicked the loudspeaker icon and put the laundry basket onto the table. She tipped the line-dried clothes out. Daddy bear, mummy bear, little baby bear.

'I know that, and it's not the dying bit that bothers me, particularly, it's the two weeks aspect. Two weeks, Mum, and no one missed her. It's awful.'

'What does Tom think?'

'He doesn't know yet.'

'I'm sure he's seen worse at work,' Carol said. 'At least the poor woman is in a better place now.'

Ellie suppressed a sigh. As a kid, she loved stories of ghoulies and ghosties and things that went bump in the night. Even now, give her a vampire box set on Netflix and she's in her element. But while she knew they were just that – stories – her mum's beliefs leaned towards a spiritual pick and mix of major religions and New Age sage-burning shit.

A muttered 'oof' followed by a clunk came out of the phone and Ellie seized the chance to redirect the conversation away from Mary Brennan.

'Any news on the leg?'

By the time Carol updated her on the pain ('awful') the inconvenience ('a nightmare') and the prognosis ('pins out soon'), any further spiritual chat had been deftly circumvented.

'And as soon as I'm cleared by the consultant, I'll book the first flight over.'

'That's brilliant.' Ellie's voice thickened. 'I can't wait to see you.'

'Oh, love. You don't know how much I want to be there with you and little Trinity.'

The events of the day – Anita's card; falling asleep with the baby; the walk in the woods; the shock of Mary Brennan – surged inside her. Everything would be so much easier with her mum here.

A tear rolled down the side of her nose and she sniffed noisily. 'Sorry, I don't know what's got into me. I keep crying over nothing.'

'Being a first-time parent isn't "nothing". I didn't have anything like the difficulties you had and I was still a wreck for months after you were born. Everyone is. And anyone who tells you different is either very rich or lying. And you were such an easy baby. You slept right through the night from the word go, always smiling.'

When Ellie replied, she spoke to her reflection in the kitchen window. The gloom outside sapped her complexion while her voice sped up, spilling the pent-up emotions of the day.

'I worry when she cries that I've done something wrong. Or that I won't even realise something's wrong. And I can't even go for a walk without messing up. And Tom never said his paid leave ran out so he'd have to work because the money stupid things like paint and curtains cost is ridiculous. And on top of all that, there was a body in the house for two weeks. In *summer*. Everything feels so weird.' She caught her breath and blinked hard before adding more steadily, 'I'm just so up and down. One minute I'm fine, the next I'm crying.'

There was a pause before Carol spoke. 'Have you mentioned it to your health visitor?'

Despite the deliberately upbeat tone, Ellie could read her mum's mind like a book. And not a tricky one, either. An early reader with small words and big font.

'I'm not depressed, Mum.'

'But it can't do any harm to speak to someone, can it?'

This was textbook Mum behaviour. Ellie rolled her eyes to the ceiling. 'Being emotional and being depressed aren't necessarily the same thing, Mum. Look, I'll have to ring you back. Trinity's waking up.'

It wasn't entirely a lie. Trinity had uttered a low grumble, often the prelude to a full-on wail.

'Well, take care, love,' Carol said, reluctantly. 'I'm going to physio in a bit but you call me anytime – you know that.'

Ellie ended the call. A sudden draught, as though a window had opened somewhere, made her shiver. She bent sideways to touch the radiator. Freezing. The orange light on the boiler shone, but without any accompanying whirring or clanking to suggest action. She flipped the control panel open and examined the ancient workings. Pressed a few buttons. Nothing.

How she had missed the dirty mark on the cupboard earlier, she didn't know. But there it was, a long smear of mud across the painted surface. She picked up a cloth and ran the hot tap. Icy water gushed out. Great. She scrubbed the stain and rinsed the cloth as best she could.

The kitchen went from cool to cold. She tucked Trinity's

blanket in and switched the kettle on, only remembering as she touched the fridge door that there was no milk. No tea then.

'I give up,' she told the ceiling.

Tom's phone went straight to voicemail. As instructed, she left her message after the beep.

'Hiya, love. I thought you said you wouldn't be late. The boiler's stopped working. Oh, and can you get some milk?'

With a black coffee warming her hands, she checked the hall radiator. Freezing. Lounge?

A cloying odour hit her from the doorway. Stagnant like the pond in the clearing, it caught in the back of her throat and stopped her in her tracks. Where was it coming from? Please don't let a bird have fallen down the chimney. She scanned the room.

The flowers.

The pint pot was exactly as she'd left it in the centre of the mantelpiece. But inside, every one of Diane's roses had withered on the stem, their old-fashioned scent transformed into sickly-sweet decay. She tilted the glass. It was half-full, not of fresh water, but a greenish liquid that clung to the now slimy stems. How could that happen in a couple of hours? Perhaps she had bleached it and forgotten to rinse it. Or the room was too cold. Diane said they were the last ones. Maybe they were already dying or she'd cut the stalks too much.

With a prickle of unease, she scooped up brown petals, crisp and curled at the edges, from the mantelpiece. Bone-dry, they crackled to the touch and a couple drifted to the hearth like drops of dried blood.

Ellie was emptying the petals into the bin as headlights illuminated the hall. Tom, home at last, pulling the door closed with a slam.

'I have had such a bad day,' he announced, kicking off his shoes.

An eddy of autumn leaves had rustled into the hall with him. Ellie quickly swept them into the dustpan.

'I've been ringing you all afternoon.'

'Sorry, I had to turn my phone off in court.' He nudged his shoes so they roughly lined up with the skirting. 'Then I had to drive Tanya to the station and then I went to Tesco.'

He held out a shopping bag. She peered in.

'Milk,' she said, slightly mollified. 'You read my mind.'

He kissed the back of her neck with a loud smack. 'It is so good to be home. Is the baby asleep or can I …?'

'Course. I've just put her down,' she said, her irritation fading with each of his exhausted footsteps. 'How did court go?'

He unknotted his tie. 'Oh, the usual. Their side picks holes in a witness and months of investigation unravel on a technicality.'

Trinity lay curled like a squidgy comma. Tom leaned over to stroke her forehead. When he straightened, he started to unbutton his shirt.

'Right, I need a quick shower.'

'I left you a voicemail. There's no hot water or heating.'

He blew his cheeks out and exhaled a blast of air. 'Awesome. Replacing the boiler, just what we don't need.'

But he hadn't even touched the controls before there was a click and the thing came to life, followed a second later by a gurgle from the kitchen radiator. A few drops of water escaped from an exposed pipe and he dabbed at them with a tea towel.

'I swear it wasn't working,' Ellie said. She put her hand on the radiator, feeling the beginnings of warmth.

'What can I say?' He waggled his fingers. 'Magic touch.'

She sighed in mock irritation. 'Have you eaten?'

'Not had time. And I can't be arsed to cook. Can you be arsed to cook?'

'I can stick a pizza in.'

While Tom showered, Ellie scraped the frost off a pepperoni box and turned the oven on. The issue of Mary Brennan still loomed large in her mind. How could she break the news? After a rough day at work, the last thing anyone would want was more gloom at home. But as her mum pointed out, years

72

as a police officer meant Tom was used to dealing with the dark side. Then again, this was the first time the dark side had followed him home.

Bad news was easier to digest with food. Best to wait until he had a mouthful of pizza before dropping the 'and the worst part is no one found her for two weeks' bomb.

Ten minutes later, he reappeared in joggers and a faded Sonic Youth T-shirt. Although his clothes were fresh, his face was anything but. Bruised shadows ringed his eyes and new wrinkles fanned from their corners.

'You OK?' she said, concerned.

He rubbed his cheeks and sighed. 'I'm just pissed off about court today.'

'What exactly happened?' She peered in the oven. Another couple of minutes should do it.

He dragged a chair out and propped his elbows on the table. 'OK. So, we have the guy nailed. We know he did it. He knows he did it. The young woman he did it to certainly knows. As do her parents. But because he refuses to admit to the sick fuckery he's committed, she has to endure a cross-examination by some condescending twat who—' He broke off. 'You know what? Never mind. Sorry I couldn't get to the phone. How was your day? Apart from broadband. And temperamental boilers.'

Now or never.

'Well, something did happen.'

'Go on.'

'The neighbour came round, Diane, the one who looks like Mary Berry. And we got chatting about the woman who lived here before – who was called Mary too. Except not Berry.'

She pulled the oven gloves off the cooker rail and slipped them on as she spoke.

'And neighbour Diane told me that this Mary died in the house. Our house. And so I googled it and … brace yourself.'

'OK.'

'Not only did she die here, in this house, but they didn't find her body for two weeks.'

Tom chewed the skin around his thumb and didn't reply.

'Two. Weeks. And only then because the postman saw the flies.'

'Is that pizza burning?' he said, sniffing in the direction of the oven. 'Because I can smell burning.'

She yanked the oven open. A wisp of smoke curled out. Bollocks.

'Never mind.' He sprang up and went to the cutlery drawer. 'It's only caught the crust. We can scrape it off.'

He took the pizza wheel and carved it into pieces, picking off the charred bits. Ellie went up behind him and gently squeezed his shoulders.

'I'm really sorry to break such a horrible thing to you like this. Especially when you've had a rough day.'

He slowly chewed a slice of pizza and steadily met her gaze.

Ellie stepped back. Her hand shot to cover her mouth.

'Oh my God. You already knew?'

He shrugged and swallowed.

'How?' she said.

'The estate agent told me a couple of days before the auction when I rang to query something in the property pack.'

Cosmetic Only Shan was in on it too? It got worse.

Her mouth dropped open. 'He should have told me. *You* should have told me.'

'I was going to. Remember? Right before the bidding.'

She flashbacked to the auction house. Tom tapping the card against his thigh.

'Listen, there's something I need to tell you. Something the estate agent said.'

He continued, 'You kept saying it was our dream house and I didn't want to put you off. Then I was going to tell you afterwards, but everything happened with your blood pressure and the baby and I couldn't stress you out more. I've been waiting for the right moment. Do you think it's a big deal?'

'Don't you?' Her voice came out high-pitched.

'Honestly? No.' He thumbed crumbs away from his lips. 'Obviously, I feel sorry for the woman, but she died over a year ago so I don't see how it affects us. I mean, if you'd known the history before the auction, you'd still have bid, right?'

'Maybe.' She paused, considering. Would she? Probably. 'But how could you keep something that big a secret? One, it's creepy as hell and two, it's unhygienic. After two weeks in summer, the poor woman must have been a bag of liqu—'

Oh.

She pictured the sepia stain she'd noticed at the viewing. The stain directly below where Trinity's cot now stood.

'Tom, tell me she didn't die in the nursery.'

He didn't need to answer; his expression said it all.

Oh God.

She could hardly get the words out. 'The water damage on the lounge ceiling. Was it?'

'No, no, no …' he said quickly. 'There are rules about cleaning up. Empty houses get damp patches and that was definitely water. Do you honestly think I'd let us move into a biohazard?'

Repelled by the idea of physical contact with the house, she lifted her feet off the lino and curled them round the rung of the chair.

'Why didn't you tell me when we came home from hospital?'

He picked up a slice of pizza and bit down, severing the strings of mozzarella with his teeth as he said, 'Because it was too late and anyway, I knew you'd over-react.'

The unfairness infuriated her. 'You call *this* over-reacting? Our daughter is going to have that room. How do you think *she's* going to react?'

'Ellie,' he said, putting the pizza back on the plate. 'I'm sorry I didn't tell you, but seriously, me and Dad stripped everything out. Replaced the carpet, the underlay, floorboards, ceiling. New window. Redecorated. The lot. There is nothing original left.'

He reverently lifted their sleeping daughter from the basket, holding her against his shoulder.

'Do you honestly think I would put her in danger?'

His face was tinged grey with exhaustion. Tiny red lines threaded through the whites of his eyes.

'No. Of course I don't.'

'No,' he said. 'Let me tell you something. In court today, I watched the victim's dad sob his heart out while the arrogant prick who attacked his daughter sat there smirking. And all I could think was if anyone laid a finger on Trinity, I would rip their balls off. So, if you ask me whether I think it's a big deal that the previous owner died here, I'll say no.' He kissed the baby's velvet skull. 'Because it's the living we need to protect our daughter from, not the dead.'

15. Now

'He was only trying to protect you,' Carol said, over the sound of heavy traffic. 'Not that way, Roger, left. Left!'

Ellie stood at the bedroom window, listening to Tom singing bath-time songs to Trinity. As the evening sky edged towards night, Mosswood formed a restless darker patch, ruffled by the strengthening breeze. After the perma-lit Manchester streets, the darkness out here took some getting used to.

'He should have told me. We tell each other everything,' she said.

'No one tells their partner everything, love. Everyone has secrets.'

'We don't,' Ellie said, drawing the second-hand curtains that didn't quite meet in the middle.

'Well, I'm sure after everything you've been through, Tom didn't want you to … ROGER!'

A horn blared and Roger bellowed a string of swear words.

'Oh, for heaven's sake,' Carol muttered. 'Look, I'd better go before he kills us both. I agree he should have told you, but don't be too hard on him, love. The past is the past. It's the future that matters.'

During the evening, the wind intensified to a gale that rattled the windows but the house felt sturdy, secure. Like it had weathered far worse storms than this.

She draped her legs across Tom on the sofa. While she was in hospital, he had developed an obsession with property shows and was currently heavily invested in the renovation of a crumbling chateau.

The presenter's hard hat wobbled as he nodded earnestly at the camera. With his hi-vis and rolled-up sleeves, he had the aura of someone to be taken seriously.

'A home is more than bricks and mortar. It has a backstory. And this place has been bruised and battered, almost beaten by decades of neglect. This noble lady can't be resurrected with a mere' – he wafted his hand at the bare wall – 'coat of paint. She needs to be nurtured and nourished, loved, in order to grow into the warm family home she deserves to be. And with sheer guts and graft, I think these two may just manage to bring her back to life.'

'Guts and graft,' Tom scoffed over the theme music. 'Not to mention a film crew, a team of builders, a massive budget ...'

Ellie smiled, but the presenter had a point. Maybe neglected houses did need an emotional as well as physical overhaul before they could become homes. Like this one.

Despite the bare floorboards and boxes stacked against the walls, the furniture from the flat seemed more at ease in the lounge now. The floor lamp contributed to the homely feel and the warm pool of light even subdued the monstrous fireplace.

The credits ended and Tom took the last swallow of beer, tipping the bottle right back. Ellie slid in closer, tucking her head under his chin, feeling her hair rasp on his stubble.

'Sorry for giving you a hard time about the Mary thing,' she said.

'Mary?' He hooked a strand of hair behind her ear. 'No, I'm sorry. You're right – I should have said something sooner. Is it really stressing you out?'

Carol's words echoed in Ellie's consciousness: *everyone has secrets.*

'I think ...' she said slowly, 'that it was a shock because it's so recent. And it might take a while to completely get my head around it. But the same could have happened ten, twenty years ago in the flat or at your dad's or in any house and we'd never know. So I guess—'

Tom interrupted with a yawn. 'Sorry, tough day at the office.'

'No more secrets?' Ellie said.

'No more secrets,' he repeated, squeezing her leg just above the knee. 'Right, I need my bed. You know I was half-asleep when I got to work this morning and I put the wrong date on all the paperwork. If it hadn't been for Tanya double-checking the file, the whole job could have been screwed. She totally saved my bacon.'

'Tanya's the new DC?'

'Yes, she's an absolute diamond.' He stretched again then clapped his hands on his thighs. 'I'm going to lock up. Do you want to go to bed and I'll sort Trinity?'

'No, she'll need a feed. I'll take her up now.'

As Tom stood, the motion caused his T-shirt to ride up. In the not-that-long-ago, a quick flash of that ripped stomach would have kindled a flare of lust, but now the taut smooth skin just kindled envy. And while she wasn't knocking equality with the childcare, an equal share in the child*bearing* would be even better. Nothing major. A few pounds here, a reciprocal stretch mark there.

She settled the baby on the nursing pillow and braced herself. Maybe even a sympathetic cracked nipple or two.

By the time she put a sated Trinity down, Tom was under the covers, one arm flung above his head and his mouth slightly open. Outside, the gale continued to rage, but whatever magic he had wrought on the boiler had worked: the bedroom was toasty. Ellie quietly squeezed alongside him and winced as the mattress dipped, but he turned over without waking.

Cosily safe, she snuggled deeper under the covers. Peace settled on the house. It was like the earnest TV presenter said: the story of a house was constantly being rewritten by the people within its walls. And while Mary Brennan's death marked a sad time for 6 Moss Lane, her chapter was closed now. And Ellie, Tom and Trinity would be writing the rest.

16. Now

It seemed only minutes later that a noise jerked her from a dream-filled slumber. The wind had toppled something, rolling it around the concrete with a booming underwater sound.

Tom snorted and turned on his side, hugging the duvet. The digits on the alarm clock switched from 2.36 to 2.37. Outside, the booming object rolled again. What the hell was that?

Fingers of cold moonlight crept around the curtains and insinuated themselves in the gaps. And it was cold. So cold that her breath puffed out in a cloud.

She shuffled to the foot of the bed to avoid disturbing Tom. But he slept the comatose sleep of the overworked. Slow rhythmic exhalations culminated in a throaty click.

She inched the curtains open. Although clouds scudded across the sky, the bright moon still frosted the tops of the trees.

A bone-white flash caught her eye. The dead climbers whipped like broken ropes, revealing a glimpse of a pale face. Something, no, someone, was down there in the rose bed. Her heart skipped a few anxious beats and she pinched the doughy flesh of her inner arm. Sucked down a squeal. Not a dream, then.

'Tom,' Ellie whispered urgently.

He didn't stir.

She grabbed his foot. He startled upright, legs kicking wildly, fists flailing.

'What the hell!'

'Ssssh. Listen. Can you hear it?'

'Hear what?'

'Someone outside.'

'Who?'

'I don't know. Come and look.'

Tom tugged at the covers. 'Els, go back to sleep. You'll wake the baby. It's just your meds giving you nightmares again.'

She pulled the duvet away. 'I wasn't asleep. Come and look. Please, Tom.'

With a groan, he slid out of bed and joined her at the window. The moon ducked behind the racing clouds and the garden writhed with shadows.

'Where?'

'In the rose bed. There!'

'There's no one there,' he muttered, rubbing the gooseflesh on his upper arms. 'It's the wind blowing stuff around.'

She clutched his arm so hard her nails dug in. 'Can't you see them? There's someone there.'

'Sssh. The baby,' he hissed as he dragged on yesterday's joggers. 'All right. I'll go down.'

Almost twitching from her heightened nerves, she followed him. At the back door, Tom stuffed his feet into trainers and switched the torch on his phone. When the door opened a crack, the wind stormed in, tossing a pile of bills and invoices on the floor.

Chill air battered her skin as she stood in the doorway watching Tom pause to right the fallen bin on his way to the rose bed. He turned to the house and shouted, but the storm buried the words. Ellie picked the fluttering bits of paper from the floor.

When Tom reappeared, he passed her a white plastic bag. Ellie stared dumbly.

'This was flapping in the rose bushes,' he said. 'A bag, not a person.'

He locked and bolted the door with one hand, sucking the fleshy base of his thumb. Blood welled in long scratches up his arm. He tore off a piece of kitchen roll and pressed down.

'Are you OK?' she said.

'Fine,' he replied, sounding anything but. 'If there's nothing else, I'm off back to bed.'

She smoothed the bag out on the kitchen table. Standard-issue white plastic with an unreadable black font on one side, slashed by thorns and daubed with streaks of Tom's blood.

The bedroom door closed followed by the creak of floor-boards as Tom sank back into bed. Ellie double-checked the bolts. Definitely locked. She flipped the bin lid releasing the sweet decay of dead rose, and quickly stuffed the plastic bag on top.

Her finger was poised on the light switch when she heard a voice.

Let me in.

No, no, no, no, no. Of course there was no voice. Only the wind and her tired imagination playing tricks on her. She scurried upstairs without looking back.

Trinity slumbered on, but she'd kicked the blanket down again. Two long streaks of mud marred the snowy sheets, like tracks on either side of the baby. Mud, too, on the blanket, clumped as though it had been clasped in a muddy fist. Ellie touched the woven basket handle and rubbed her fingertips together. Sniffed the cold, damp smell of earth.

For God's sake. Could Tom not have washed his hands before he checked on the baby?

With a feather-light touch, she rolled the baby over, trying to strip the mattress without disturbing her but Trinity had other plans involving indignant yelps. Soothing her required yet another feed and by the time she'd changed the sheets and settled the baby, Ellie tiptoed back to bed on feet of ice.

Her head swam with fatigue as she slid under the duvet and rolled towards Tom.

'Sorry,' he said, shifting to the edge of the bed. 'I've haven't slept a wink and I've got to be up in two hours for a meeting.'

Outside, the wind moaned. Ellie squashed the pillow tightly

over ears that rang with Tom's observation from earlier. 'It's not the dead we need to protect our daughter from.'

Her last conscious thought before exhaustion dragged her under was he had it all wrong.

If the ten years since Mia's death had taught her anything, it was that the dead could do just as much damage as the living.

17. Then

'Come on, you'll enjoy it,' Mia said, head tilted as she applied mascara. Her reflection grinned at Ellie in the mirror. 'One drink and I promise if you hate it, we'll leave. Deal?'

Fairy lights, a giant Audrey Hepburn poster and a vase of red roses transformed Mia's Henderson Hall bedroom from student cell to quirky cool.

Ellie shrugged. 'I don't know. I won't know anyone.'

'You'll know me,' she said, pumping the wand into the tube. 'And Danny said he'd be there with some of his mates.'

'Dan Dan the flower man?' Ellie said, pointing at the roses. 'Hasn't he got a girlfriend at home?'

Mia licked lipstick off her tooth and poured vodka into two mugs.

'*Ex*-girlfriend,' she corrected. 'He finished it. Come on, there'll be people from your course, I bet. It'll be a good night.'

And it was.

Bodies thronged the Union bar and Ellie had to politely push her way through crowds of students talking and cackling over the thumping music. They'd only been at uni for one term and already Mia had a hug and a word for every second person.

'Budge up,' Mia shouted. A good-looking ginger-haired lad obligingly shuffled up the upholstered bench and they squeezed through the gap. Ellie smiled shyly and sat down. The tabletop was sticky and covered in torn shreds of beer mat.

'Ellie, Danny,' Mia said.

He lifted his pint glass in a salute. 'Hiya.'

'Hi.' She smiled in return and clutched her pint glass in both hands, trying not to trail her sleeves in the pools of spilled beer. So, this was potential new man Danny.

Nice, she mouthed when he wasn't looking and Mia screwed her face up in a joyous beam.

Friday night at the Union was the biggest event of the week. Mia was right about seeing people she knew: a trio of girls from Henderson Hall waved fivers impatiently at the barman; a lad from her course leaned over the pool table.

'Do you fancy another?' Danny said, gesturing at Ellie's almost-full glass.

Lager swirled in her stomach, mingling with the unwise vodka shots she'd downed with Mia earlier. Vodka in a mug. Mugshots. She stifled a giggle.

'No, I'm good thanks.'

Danny jogged the table as he stood, sending the collection of glasses into a chorus of clinks.

'I may be some time,' he said, launching himself into the crowd.

As soon as he was out of earshot, Mia widened her eyes. 'Well? What do you reckon?'

Ellie watched Danny fight his way towards the bar. 'Yeah, he seems really nice.'

'He is,' Mia said, twisting a thick strand of hair around her finger.

'You like him then?'

'This much.' Mia stretched her arms back to touch the velvet booth.

'What about his ex-girlfriend?'

'Oh, she'll get over it,' Mia said, dismissively.

'I still feel sorry for her, though.'

Mia shrugged. 'Me too, but at least he's honest, telling her he's met someone else. Better than stringing her along.'

Ellie took a long sip of lager. 'I don't mind heading off if you want to be on your own. I've got an essay to finish.'

'On a Friday night? No chance.'

'I'm off to the loo anyway,' Ellie said, pulling her bag crossways over her chest. 'Wish me luck.'

Why did the men never have to queue? Ellie shifted her weight from one foot to the other. Everyone huddled together, laughing, or singing, only separating when a cleaner pushed past, carrying a mop and bucket. Perfume mingled with a hundred other scents: chewing gum, smoke, hard-working deodorant.

Inside, the lights were bright and fluorescent strips over the mirrors greyed out an anxious Ellie. A girl squeezed herself in at the sink with a 'Sorry'.

'No problem,' Ellie said, but the girl was too engrossed in fluffing her hair to hear. The hand-dryer added to the cacophony and set her head spinning.

In a parallel universe where her dad hadn't died in her GCSE year, a different version of Ellie thrived on this raucous atmosphere. That other Ellie had celebrated birthdays and exam results with wild nights in pubs and clubs, not at home with her mum and an empty seat at the kitchen table. The real Ellie had spent the last few years hiding behind a wall of grief until her school friends stopped trying. She couldn't blame them.

She practised a friendly smile in the mirror. The girl next to her smiled back.

Things were different now, weren't they?

Wiping her nearly dry hands down her jeans, she excuse me'd her way back to Mia. Oasis played over the speakers and a gang of red-cheeked lads yelled along, arms around each other's shoulders.

She spotted Danny's red hair from halfway across the room, next to Mia and another guy who had just sat down and was shrugging off a green parka. He pushed his floppy fringe out of his eyes, nodding in time to the beat.

'Ellie!' Mia shouted, waving her over.

Zigzagging through the mass of bodies, she caught eyes with the new guy. He smiled and Ellie half-smiled back, dipping her head, so her hair hid her face.

'This is Danny's flatmate,' Mia said, her eyes glassy. 'Name's Tom. He's lovely. I'm just going outside for a ...' She stuck a Marlboro Light in the corner of her mouth, tip first, frowned and took it back out. 'Come on, Danny boy. Let's get some fresh air.'

Danny put both palms on the tabletop to steady himself. 'See you in a minute.'

Mia picked shreds of tobacco from her lip. 'I'll leave you two lovelies to get to know each other.'

Ellie's cheeks flamed and she hugged her bag to her chest. Did Mia have to be so obvious?

But Tom didn't seem fazed. He shuffled up the bench and Ellie squeezed in next to him.

'So, you're friends with Mia,' he said. 'Are you on the same course?'

'No, we're next to each other in halls. I'm doing Marketing. Are you doing Art as well?'

'No, I went to school with Danny. I'm doing Psychology,' he said. 'Don't worry, I'm not going to analyse everything you say.'

She smiled. Her fingers fussed with the bag buckle while she mentally begged Mia to hurry up. Throughout sixth form, these kind of interactions invariably ended up with Ellie tying herself in mental and verbal knots that made her cringe for days.

Meanwhile, Tom chatted about his course; described his new part-time job in a restaurant and she chipped in with genuine-sounding responses until, after a few minutes, they *were* genuine. From the corner of her eye, she studied him: nice hair, kind eyes and a smile that made her want to smile back.

And when Mia and Danny finally returned, smelling of mint-laced smoke and with their arms wrapped around each other, Ellie didn't care when Tom shuffled along until his leg was centimetres from hers.

By the time the barman shouted, 'That's your lot,' the only weird thing she'd discovered about Tom was that he didn't make her feel weird at all.

'Can you see the others?' Tom said, reaching for his phone.

Ellie blinked in the sudden harsh light. She hadn't even realised they'd gone. 'There's Danny. Where's—?'

'There she is,' Tom said.

Mia appeared by the bar. Her hair was mussed up and her mascara had run, turning her dark eyes into black holes. Red lipstick smudged into the corners of her mouth. Danny took her hand and caught sight of Tom.

'Buddy,' he shouted gesturing. 'Come here.'

Tom briefly caught the tips of Ellie's fingers in his as they walked across the pub. Something fluttered in her belly and she bit her lip to hide an emerging grin.

'We're going back to ours,' Danny said.

Mia, who was buttoning her coat wrong, looked up. 'Only if that's OK with you, Ellie.'

'Er, yeah. Course,' she said with a shrug.

'I can walk you home if you like?' Tom said, raising his voice on the last syllable.

'Are you sure you don't mind?'

'Why would he mind?' Mia kissed the side of Ellie's head.

Ellie laughed. 'You are going to feel so rough tomorrow.'

'I'll be fine.' Mia tucked her long black hair into the collar of her coat. Sudden panic crossed her face. 'Damn, I hadn't thought. What time are you going out in the morning?'

'I don't know yet. Why?'

'I don't think I've got my keys.'

She patted her pockets then rummaged hastily through her bag. 'Nope, definitely no keys.'

'Again? You are hopeless.' Fishing in her pocket, Ellie's fingers located the silver E. 'I've got mine. Give me a shout when you're outside. I'll let you in.'

18. Now

The wind had disappeared by morning. As had Tom.

Picking up where the storm left off, Trinity wailed at a volume that belied the size of her lungs.

'Mummy's coming,' Ellie said.

Trinity clamped on with terrier-like ferocity, bringing tears to Ellie's eyes. Usually, feeding soothed the baby, but not today. Coaxing those wriggling limbs into fresh clothes was like wrestling a bad-tempered octopus. Sweat trickled between Ellie's shoulder blades as she fastened the final popper but sneaking off for a shower seemed as unlikely as getting a decent night's sleep.

In the kitchen, the noisy protest showed no signs of abating. Yesterday, the bouncer was a safe space. Today, it was a torture chamber. A painful knot twisted in Ellie's guts. Was the baby ill?

The thermometer gave a normal reading. Ellie ran her finger along the hard pink gums; no bony bumps to indicate emerging teeth. And still, while the kettle boiled and she made some toast, the baby raged on.

'I've fed you, changed your nappy and rocked you till my arms ache. I've got nothing left. Let's see what Netmums has to offer.' Ellie took out her phone, hesitated. Sniffed. What was that—?

Smoke snaked up from the toaster.

'Oh for God's sake.'

She pinched at the blackened slices of bread with her fingertips and lifted them carefully out of the slots. Grey wisps curled off their charred sides. Surely they'd only been in a few seconds?

Trinity arched her back and cranked the howling up a notch.

'Please shhh,' Ellie said, flipping the bin open. 'One minute.'

The burnt toast landed on top of the dead roses and the torn plastic bag she'd stuffed in there yesterday which, in the morning light, looked nothing like a woman's face.

She tipped cornflakes (stale because Tom had neglected to close the box) into a bowl. Chewing spoonful after spoonful without tasting, she scrolled through pages of Google advice on her phone and rocked the bouncer with her foot.

When Trinity's howls finally faded to weary bleats, the phone pinged a calendar reminder – Playgroup, 11 a.m.

'We're going out today, baby girl. That'll be fun, won't it?' Ellie whispered as she gingerly lifted her foot. 'But first …'

Quietly, she dragged a heavy white tangle from the washing machine and hung the peg bag from the crook of her arm. After last night's storm, stray twigs and broken branches littered the garden. She shook off the fat raindrops that trembled on the washing line, wishing she could shake last night's events off so easily. The pale face among the roses; the voice that had seemed so real.

Back in the kitchen, there was a missed FaceTime from Mum. The phone rang out two or three times before she answered and clicked the speaker icon.

'Hi, darling,' Carol said cheerily. 'Look, they took the cage off. I can walk again.'

She waved the phone down her body to the grey plastic boot on her left leg.

'Fantastic. How does it feel?'

'Achy and I can't stand on it without crutches, but it's just so good to be up and about. Weeks of bedrest is more than I can bear.'

Ellie wet a cloth and wiped mud off the back door. Honestly, Tom could be such a slob. Fair enough, she sent him out in the middle of the night, but he could have washed his mucky hands. She chucked the cloth in the sink. Through the window, last night's bassinet sheets hung clean and motionless alongside Tom's work shirts, Trinity's vests, and assorted muslin cloths.

'Weeks of bedrest sounds good to me,' Ellie said. 'Why don't you come over here for it?'

'Oh, love,' Carol sighed. 'I wish I could, but I need to be near the hospital and you'd end up looking after me as well as the baby. How is my little girl?'

Ellie propped the phone against the fruit bowl, angling it towards Trinity.

'This is the first time she's stopped crying for hours. I've tried rocking her, feeding her, winding her … everything.'

'Probably a touch of colic,' Carol replied. 'It won't last long. Have you tried lying her across your legs and rubbing her back?'

Pale lines of light criss-crossed the kitchen, but there was no warmth in them. Boiler on the blink again? Ellie touched the radiator then snatched her hand away. Nothing wrong with the heating. Maybe Howard could check for draughts when—

'Are you still there?'

'Yes. Sorry. Go on.'

She shivered and put the back of her hand against Trinity's forehead. Warm as toast.

'I said the weather looks good there. What are your plans for the day?'

She picked a hoodie from the clean washing pile and threw it over her head, muffling the reply.

'There's a mum and baby group at the church hall in the village. But I don't know if I'm up to it today.'

'Sounds like a great idea. You won't remember, but I used to go to one with you when you were tiny in the same room you went for Brownies. You got to play and I got to have a bit of a break.'

Ellie leaned over the sink. Weird how after the chaos of last night's storm, the garden stood as still as a painting, apart from a single magpie swooping between two trees.

Mum carried on, 'It was the only time I ever got to drink an entire cup of tea while it was still hot. And to speak to adults. Of

91

course, your dad was at work and I was desperate for a conversation. We all were.'

A dewy glitter sparkled on the lawn and Ellie shivered. How could sunshine make a room colder?

'I don't know. I mean, I'm not sure I'm up to a twenty-minute walk yet and we sold my car, remember?'

Carol put her serious voice on. 'Staying in the house all day is going to drive you mad. I'm sure Tom'll take you.'

A spider had spun a web of crystal lace in the corner of the window. Ellie traced the intricate outline with her finger. 'Except he's at work. As always.'

There was a very short pause.

Then Carol said, 'Ellie. If Tom's at work, who is that standing behind you?'

19. Now

Ellie whirled around.

Empty chairs. Table. Clothes and assorted junk. Fridge freezer. Dizzy with panic, she scanned the ceiling and the walls, glanced between the locked back door and the hall.

No one.

She fumbled with the straps on the bouncer and clutched Trinity tight, her forearm flat against the baby's spine, her palm cradling the delicate skull.

'Not funny, Mum. Not funny at all,' she shouted in the direction of the phone.

The reply was tinny and distant. 'Please pick the phone up.'

With her back to the wall, Ellie shuffled around the perimeter of the kitchen until she reached the table, barely registering the hot radiator against the back of her thighs.

Carol's voice continued, 'Just let me put my glasses on. It's very bright, isn't it? And it's hard to see properly on a little screen.'

Ellie felt the sting of tears. 'Why did even you say that? That's so mean.'

'I didn't mean to scare you,' Carol said, distraught. She hesitated, then laughed. 'Oh. I'm such an idiot!'

'What?'

'It's just a shadow. Look, can you see it?'

Ellie turned to see a figure appear and dissolve: a shirt on the line, magnified by some optical illusion, topped by the rounded canopy of a distant tree.

Jesus.

The sun rose above the trees, flooding the kitchen with

light. Instead of shivering, sweat prickled across her upper lip and exhaustion and relief turned her legs to rubber. She closed her eyes and drew in a deep, controlled breath. 'As if I'm not freaked out enough already, Mum. You nearly gave me a heart attack.'

'Oh, love, I'm so sorry. I wasn't thinking about the poor woman who died. I just want to put my arms round you, both of you.'

'I know.' Ellie shifted her bum along the radiator.

'Listen,' Carol said. 'Do you remember the floorboards upstairs at the old house? How they used to groan when the heating came on?'

'Yeah, Dad said it was the wood expanding with the heat.'

'That's right. But you always pulled the covers over your head, thinking someone was coming up the stairs. You were so jumpy when you were little. And the extractor fan in the bathroom that used to click round and round when it was windy.'

She nodded, remembering. 'I thought a witch was tapping on the window.'

'Exactly,' Carol said. 'Even here, Roger bought the villa off-plan but when the wind funnels down the chimney, it's like someone moaning. Scared me to death the first time I heard it.' There was a brief pause. 'What I'm saying is houses have their own funny ways and on top of finding out about the previous owner, what's-her-name?'

'Mary Brennan.'

'Poor old Mary Brennan. What you've been through in the last few weeks is enough to send anyone round the twist. Love, go to the playgroup. It'll do you the world of good to get out. Have a chat with the other mums and you'll soon realise everyone's in the same boat.'

Linear shadows of slender-trunked trees fell like bars across the kitchen wall. She said goodbye to her mum as the magpie swooped on to the apple tree, staring with one shark-blank eye while confrontationally flicking its tail. Cocky bastard.

Ellie slapped her palm against the glass. 'Shit on my clean washing and you die.'

Round the twist.

Maybe Mum had a point. She needed to get out of the house.

Her mental health craved normality right now. A quick Google Maps search confirmed the route to the church hall would be straightforward. Fresh air, exercise, other humans. And the truth was, apart from the meeting-new-people nerves fluttering in her belly, she didn't have a reason not to go.

She unfolded a cute pair of dungarees for Trinity. Red, embroidered with little monkeys, they fit snugly around her chubby ankles. Stripy socks and a vest added to the cuteness overload.

'You look so gorgeous,' Ellie said, tickling the baby's tummy. 'Yes, you do.'

Choosing for herself proved more of a challenge. Considering the narrow criteria of a) will fasten and b) not pyjamas, this should have been simple. Instead, she was stuck with the maternity jeans with the fraying high waist. Again.

She brushed bronzer on the apples of her cheeks to liven the zombie mum skin and tied her hair up in its usual lazy ponytail, noting how desperately her roots needed doing.

With Trinity in the pram in the hall, mittened fingers flexing and clenching to an inaudible beat, they were ready to set off. Ellie fastened her coat buttons. Purse. Check. Phone. Check. Keys.

Keys?

They had been in the back door. One hundred per cent. She remembered hearing the *chink* when she took the washing out. Except they weren't there. She scanned the lino in case they'd fallen out. No. And they weren't on the sill or under Trinity's pram. Or on the kitchen worktop, in the empty fruit bowl, on the coffee table, in the bathroom, her coat pocket or on her bed.

Maybe she hadn't seen them today after all. She tapped her phone with her fingernail.

Had Tom moved them before he left for work?

'Hiya love,' he said over the office soundtrack of ringing phones and babble of conversation. 'I tried to ring before, but it was engaged.'

'Yeah, I was talking to my mum. Look, have you seen my keys?'

'In the wicker basket?'

She peered down the back of the bedside table. 'I've checked. I thought I'd left them in the door, but they're not there and I'm about to go to the playgroup. Remember? I told you last night.'

'Listen,' he said. 'About last night. I'm sorry I was such an arse about being woken up. I know you're having these bad dreams and it was so noisy with the storm.'

'It's OK,' she said, only half-listening. She pulled back the curtain to view the corner of the windowsill. 'I actually think the sleep deprivation is sending me a bit doolally and—'

There was a clinking sound from downstairs. She hurried down to the hall. Stopped. Stared.

The silver letter E swayed in the lock.

20. Now

She stepped back hastily and knocked against the pram, shocking the baby into a yelp.

'Ssssh, it's OK.'

The yelp upgraded to a high-octane wail of confusion and Ellie had to fight the urge to join in.

'Ellie?' came Tom's worried voice. 'What's happening?'

'Nothing. I tripped over the pram. I'll call you later.'

She didn't hear his goodbye as she slowly curled her fingers around the key ring. The prongs of the E bit into her skin. She thought she'd checked the front door, but she couldn't have done. Her eyes felt full of grit and she rubbed the corners. Too forgetful, too tired.

'Oh, dear what can the matter be?' she sang under her breath. 'Mummy is losing her mind.'

With the house locked and the keys securely zipped in her pocket, she pushed the pram up the driveway, ignoring the magpie's chattering commentary.

Clouds had drifted over the sun and the low grey sky stretched on forever, broken here and there by black circling birds. Although the road to the village seemed flat in a car, on foot the slight incline was steep enough to leave her breathless.

She set her jaw and pushed past trees that grew further apart and houses that crept closer and closer until they touched the pavement and turned into shops.

Uppermoss clung to its identity as a village, but over the years, the bustling high street had evolved into something closer to a small town. Workers on a break hurried by. The road widened and cars bunched up to let an ambulance pass. A black dog sniffed the buggy's wheels while his owner talked loudly into the phone.

'You don't deserve her. Not after what you did.'

Ellie halted in the middle of the pavement. Cold dread stole her breath. The dog walker eyed her with undisguised curiosity, stepped into the gutter and tugged at the lead until the dog reluctantly trotted off.

A random comment from a random stranger. That's all. Her knuckles gleamed on the buggy handle. She tucked her chin to her chest and ignored the rising buzz in her ears.

Get a grip.

The pavement swarmed with laughing, shouting, staring faces. So many faces. And so much noise. After the peace of Moss Lane, it felt like the volume had been turned up on everything: sound, colour, movement raced around her like a film on fast forward. Conscious of a damp prickling under her arms, she willed herself to the pedestrian crossing. Her raised finger shook.

Push the button. Wait. Cross.

She breathed a sigh of relief as she reached the sturdy modern building. Wooden half barrels bloomed with flowers under banners that advertised a tea dance, a choir, an artisan market. A no-nonsense space next to the fancy Victorian twiddles of the church, inviting her to sit in peace with a cup of tea. Pre-baby, Ellie would not have given a church hall a second glance, but right now, with sweat on her forehead and the weight of lost keys on her mind, the relief was like getting into bed after a hard day.

The metallic jab in her front pocket reassured that, yes, the keys were still safe, as she opened the door into a beige-carpeted vestibule that smelled of furniture polish and custard creams. Conversations punctuated by the occasional wail emanated from behind a wooden door. A woman emerged carrying a toddler. Ellie attempted to push the buggy through.

'Oh sorry.' The woman smiled. 'You have to leave that in the pram park under the stairs. First time?'

'Yeah.'

'Everyone's super friendly. When you go in, ask for Asha – she runs the group.' She shifted the toddler to the other hip. 'The loos are just down the corridor on the left if you need them.'

The woman's friendliness brought tears to her eyes, and she murmured her thanks.

The baby changing room gleamed. A box next to the spotless mat, printed with rows of happy ducks, contained lotion and a free supply of wipes. Thoughtful. She quickly rubbed one over her face and under her arms.

'You're OK,' she reassured her reflection. 'You got this.'

A noticeboard headed *What's on in Uppermoss*? hung from a nail. Someone clearly made an effort to keep it cheerful and updated. Was this Diane's daughter-in-law's handiwork? She scanned through the yoga classes, allotments and nearly new sales and her eye was caught by a poster. *Join I love Uppermoss on Facebook. A friendly group to discuss issues concerning our beautiful village.*

With a couple of clicks, she'd sent a join request. The village community. Playgroups. Mothers and babies. This was her new tribe.

But one glance around the hall snuffed out any hope of finding fellow zombie mums. With their uniform of striped tops over skinny jeans, these women had a collective aura of success in all areas. Expert motherhood just another tick on life's to-do list.

She ought to have put on some lipstick and blow-dried her hair, or at least tamed the frizz that sprang from her temples. But she'd been too tired and, frankly, hadn't expected to find herself gate-crashing a Boden photoshoot.

A huge soft area, dotted with play gyms and various well-behaved and beautifully turned-out children, dominated the centre of the room. Chairs lined the walls and by the stage, a trestle table held glasses and vintage cups and saucers alongside an Italian coffee maker. There was a fruit basket. Home-made cupcakes and biscuits adorned a three-tier cake stand. Porcelain, not plastic.

'We are going to have fun,' she ordered Trinity, laying her under a baby gym. 'Yes, we are.'

Ellie's hand wavered for a nanosecond over an apple, then helped itself to a biscuit. She poured a coffee and took the closest available chair. In the adjacent seat, a woman glanced from her phone long enough to bestow a dismissive half-smile, then returned to scrolling through the virtual lives of more interesting people.

Go for it. Join the tribe.

She leaned into the woman's sightline and gestured to the mat Trinity lay on. Lights flashed and bells rang on the play bar above her mesmerised eyes.

'Fruit machines for babies. And in a church hall!'

The joke fell flat.

The woman's manicured finger hovered over the screen for a second longer before she dropped her phone in a leather bag.

'Hi, I'm Norah.' She reached under the chair for her coffee cup. 'First time?'

After the initial introduction, it didn't take long to establish that Norah's greatest love was talking about herself. About as long as it took Ellie to regret choosing that particular chair, in fact.

'Just the one? Lucky you,' Norah said, taking a long sip. 'Whenever I used to meet people who said, "I'm a full-time mum," I'd think, all you do all day is watch CBeebies and go to things like this.' She waved vaguely around the room. 'And then I had the twins, and the hard work started. Then Harry came along. And just when I thought I knew what I was doing, he does something totally unprecedented and I'm back to square one. If I were at work, I'd call it upskilling, I guess. Harry is upskilling me.'

She laughed then took a dainty bite of an amaretti biscuit. While her mouth was otherwise occupied, Ellie shoehorned in a sentence.

'It's certainly been a steep learning curve with Trinity.'

Norah laughed, daintily dabbing at the crumbs. 'Trust me, one is a piece of cake. Don't even think about complaining till you've got three. And you know what's weird? All the time I was working, I hated it. Office politics, sicknote colleagues who took a fortnight off if they sneezed. But at least I could go out for a drink to unwind. Now I'm always at home and I've been breast-feeding so long, I've forgotten the taste of gin.'

'What did you do before?'

'Journalist.' She dunked the remaining biscuit. '*Stockfield Express*, but I'm moving into freelance feature writing now.'

Norah tucked her caramel-highlighted hair behind one ear, and Ellie made a mental note to ask about a local hairdresser.

'I was – I am – a copywriter for a craft magazine. But we've just bought a house to do up, so maybe I won't go back for a while.'

'Have you bought in the village?'

'No, just outside. Moss Lane. Do you know it?'

Her eyebrows twitched. 'I certainly do. We walk the dogs in Mosswood most weekends. Very nice. Which one are you?'

'Number six.'

She frowned.

'Boxy-looking one set back from the road?' Ellie offered.

Whichever part of Norah's brain dealt with gossip lit up like a fruit machine.

'Number six. Well, that's interesting. I heard it had gone up for auction.' She leaned forward, balancing the mug on her knee. 'How are you finding it?'

Ellie settled back in the chair, pulling her top down where it had ridden up over her belly.

'Well, we've only just moved in and it needs quite a bit of work, as you can imagine, because it was empty for so long. But the garden is amazing and obviously the views are lovely, so …'

Like Joan the Moan, Norah was the kind of listener who peppered conversations with absent-minded *uh-huh*s and *oh* *really?*s to kill time before she got to the important stuff. *Her* stuff. When Ellie paused to inhale, Norah pounced.

'It was sad, the whole situation. Very sad. I'm assuming you know?'

'About the owner's death? Yes, we do.'

'And the rest? Did you know—' The pointy tip of her tongue darted out to moisten her lips. 'The full history before you bought the house? Everything about the Brennan family? Does it impact on the way you feel now you're living there or do you prefer not to think about it? Do you have any regrets?'

Norah fired questions quicker than Ellie could hear, let alone answer. She took a bite of her hobnob in lieu of a response.

Perhaps realising she was being too intrusive, Norah flashed a sorry-not-sorry smile. 'Hey, once a journalist …'

She stayed quiet for a beat, brushing a few invisible crumbs from her cashmere jumper. 'Some good came out of the situation, you know. My paper started a campaign after Mary died. Combatting loneliness. Old people, the vulnerable, the invisible. My boss said it was a …' Norah mimed air quotes '… Community Awareness Initiative, but honestly, I think he read that story and saw his future. Divorced three times. Not on speaking terms with his kids. Staring down the barrel of old age. I mean, Mary wasn't old but dying in that horrible way after such a tragic life. Losing her mother so young and then her father committing suicide. And then all the scandal at the council, of course.'

'Mummy! Mummy!' A twin hurled itself at Norah's knees.

Dregs of coffee from the mug threatened to spill.

'Shi-sugar!' she exclaimed, tilting it back just in time. 'Silly Mummy.'

Another took firm hold of Norah's sleeve. 'Mummy! India called me a poo poo!'

Norah swung the little girl up into her arms.

Ellie was still knitting together the last strands of the conversation. 'What do you mean by a scandal?'

But Norah's focus had shifted entirely away.

'Don't kick Mummy. You little … *poo poo*.' She threw Ellie an apologetic smile, revealing slightly pointed canines, like a vampire's. 'Lovely meeting you. See you next week?'

'Sure,' Ellie replied to Norah's retreating back.

She watched the clusters of other mums chatting while their children played for a minute or two. But the coffee swirled uncomfortably in her guts at the thought of gate-crashing one of those tight cliques, especially after the bizarre interrogation from Norah.

'Time to go, honey,' she said, picking up Trinity who immediately wailed. 'Sssh.'

She was elbowing the door open when she spotted a woman in gym gear and holding yellow rubber gloves slaloming through the play area.

'Ellie?' The Aussie accent was unmistakable. 'Sorry I missed you. I'm Asha, Diane's daughter-in-law.'

'Hi.'

'I was about to come over, but some little monkey stuffed a whole loo roll down the toilet and now I need to …' She flapped the gloves. 'You know how it is.'

Trinity gurgled and Asha leaned in close. 'Hello, gorgeous. What's your name?'

'This is Trinity.'

'I'd introduce you to Freddie, but he's …' she turned '… toddled off somewhere. Are you going already?'

Ellie's sinuses ached. Oh God. Was she actually about to cry? 'Er, yes.'

'Everything all right?' Asha said, kindly. 'Did you get to meet some people?'

'I talked to Norah.'

'Okaaay,' Asha drew the final syllable out. 'Well, come back next week and I promise I won't let Norah monopolise you. She can be quite …'

'Full on?'

Asha laughed. 'That's a nice way to put it. Look, I was thinking, I'm up at Diane's a lot. Maybe I could drop in for a coffee if you're not too busy?'

'That would be lovely.'

'Great.' Asha tugged the rubber gloves on. 'I'd better get back to the chaos. Nice to meet you.'

'You too,' Ellie said, meaning it.

Using her back to open the exit into the vestibule, she didn't see Norah standing by the buggy park until it was too late. She was applying glossy beige lipstick with the help of a gold compact. No screaming kids in sight. And *bloody hell*, she was standing right by the pram, so Ellie couldn't even pretend she hadn't seen her.

'Oh, are you going already?' Norah said.

'Yes, things to do,' Ellie replied, dragging out the pram. 'You know how it is.'

The net on the base caught on a Bugaboo and she bent over to shake it free.

'I do indeed. Try having three,' Norah said with a dismissive wave. 'Nightmare. Oh …' She extracted an immaculate leather purse, drew out a business card. 'That's my number. Anytime you want to talk, about the house or, you know, anything.'

Ellie put her coat on, ready for the long walk home. Her caesarean scar itched under the jeans' elastic waistband and the keys dug through the thin pocket lining. More sweat ran freely down her spine, sticking her top to her back, and to make matters worse, one soaked nursing pad had folded over and slipped down, forming a sticky rosette on the front. She buttoned her coat and prayed the stain wouldn't show through the fabric.

She hunched over the pram and, head down, wheeled past the graveyard, the playground and out on to the high street.

How could Norah say that caring for one baby was 'nothing'? And the way her face lit up like a lottery winner when delivering bad news reminded her of Joan the Moan delivering redundancy notices.

It was more than Norah deserved, but at least Ellie waited until she was on the edge of the village before she flashed her own sorry-not-sorry smile, crumpled the card and dropped it into the gaping mouth of her bag.

21. Now

Ellie folded the buggy and locked the front door, placing the keys carefully in the basket.

'Keys,' she murmured into the baby's head. 'Definitely in the basket, right?'

At their old flat, the thin walls and plentiful neighbours had provided a 24/7 human soundtrack. And living on the main road at Howard's, with the screech and rumble of non-stop traffic, had her craving peace and quiet. She'd certainly got that on Moss Lane. Apart from the faint whisper of Trinity's breath in the cot, a deep hush settled on the house and she almost jumped off the nursing chair when her phone dinged a message from Jess.

When are you coming into the office? Everyone's dying to meet Trinity.

Let me know when good for you, Ellie tapped back. *No car so will have to organise a lift.*

Any lunchtime good for me but will have to check with Joan.

Ellie responded with a GIF of a fire-breathing dragon and an unexpected yearning for the daily gossip, laughs, the mutual hatred of management. Even getting up at freezing o'clock to drag her weary arse through the Mancunian rush hour had acquired a nostalgic glow.

Silence rang in her ears, pushing against her temples. She switched the night-light on. The faint notes of the lullaby were just enough to take the edge off and the room welcomed her. It was cosy. Relaxing. And yet, her traitorous mind would not stop picking at Norah's conversation – interrogation – at playgroup.

Do you have any regrets?

Did she? Her subconscious flashed up a slideshow of unwelcome images. Mary Brennan in bed, clutching her chest. Mary Brennan praying for help that never came. Mary Brennan's body lying undiscovered day after day. Looking round this tranquil space, it was hard to imagine it as the setting for such a sad event.

A flicker by the cot caught her attention. A moving black dot that buzzed above the singing from the night-light.

'Ugh.'

A fat bluebottle alighted on the carved cot rail and rubbed its cellophane wings together.

'Gross.'

She opened the window and flapped until it buzzed out. Then she wiped the sleeping baby's face and hands just in case, shut the window and sprayed and rubbed the fly-walked furniture. Then sank back into the nursing chair.

Trinity slept on. The night-light played on. Ellie drummed her fingers on the wooden chair arm. Could she ring Jess for a chat? No. Wouldn't be fair to bring the wrath of Joan upon her. Not Mum either while she was still feeling wobbly and liable to burst into tears. Better to send some all-is-well photos instead. Very quietly, she snapped a few shots of Trinity and pinged them off with the message: *Sleeping beauty! xx*

What had Norah meant about a scandal? Before she could persuade herself poking around Google was a bad idea, she typed 'Stockfield Express Moss Lane' into the search bar. The picture of her house with police tape across the drive appeared. Buried right at the foot of the article was a link:

Join this paper's Campaign against Loneliness by N. Aryan.

N for Norah? Ellie curled her legs up on the chair and began to read.

The House on Moss Lane

Secluded, exclusive and affluent ... Moss Lane in the pretty village of Uppermoss is not the kind of place you would associate with human tragedy. But recent police activity has sent shock waves through the neighbourhood. And perhaps it has forced the local community to face some uncomfortable home truths: is this once close-knit village falling apart?

No one can tell us much about Mary Brennan, the woman whose body was recovered from number six Moss Lane. Close neighbours seem reluctant to talk, perhaps uncomfortable at the damning coroner's report that confirmed that Mary lay undiscovered on the floor of her bedroom for up to two weeks during the hottest days of the year.

The sad truth is, we know little for certain about the circumstances of Mary's death. The cause of death was given as 'inconclusive' due to the deterioration of the body. The report also stated that she was diagnosed with high blood pressure and put on a course of medication by her GP in 2011. But she never collected the drugs. Did she have a heart attack? A stroke? How long did she lie dying in bed waiting for help that never came?

We will never know.

What we do know is that Mary Brennan died a victim. A victim of a society that no longer cares for its vulnerable and lonely members. A victim of neighbours who turned a blind eye to the invisible woman at number six. In life, Mary's tragedies were ignored and in death she lay forgotten.

She is the hidden face of misery, a recluse who no one cared for and no one missed and her death poses many unanswered questions. She may have had no family or friends, but she had neighbours. Neighbours who had lived next door to Mary Brennan for over forty years. Why didn't they notice something was wrong at 6 Moss Lane? Why were they so unwilling to help?

Had the postman not glanced up to the first-floor bedroom to see a swarm of flies at the window, who knows how much longer Mary would have lain undiscovered?

The question we must all ask ourselves now is: how many other Mary Brennans live in our town and villages? How many other men and women live alone among neighbours who turn a blind eye to their suffering?

That's why we at the Stockfield Express have decided to launch our campaign against isolation. Over the coming weeks, we'll be focusing on local organisations that work within the community to combat loneliness and promote togetherness. Perhaps Mary Brennan's legacy will be to teach us all to be better neighbours.

Ellie clicked her phone off and rubbed her leg, digging both thumbs into the muscle. When she curled her toes into the carpet to stand, pins and needles shot through her calf and she winced.

You had to hand it to Norah, it took talent to be a bitch about the neighbours while writing a plea for community kindness. One of those women with #bekind in her bio and venom at her fingertips. Still, Mary's story seemed more sad than tragic. Unless by 'tragic' Norah meant the neighbours' ignorance.

She reached into the cot and gently stroked Trinity's cheek. There was a stack of laundry to sort in her own room, but it didn't seem fair to wake the baby. Surely she'd be OK for a few minutes?

The nursery door hadn't stuck since the first night but better safe than sorry, she propped it open with one of Tom's giant trainers and tiptoed across the landing. She tipped the clothes onto the duvet, bent to retrieve a stray bra that had slithered to the floor and found the TV control half under the bed. The picture wasn't great up here, and the old TV had an annoying purple stripe across the top of the screen, but she needed something to lure her brain away from Mary Brennan.

With a yawn, she clicked the volume down to not-wake-the-baby level. Flick, local news. Flick, cookery programme. Flick, property show and back to the chateau.

Today the presenter wore a hi-vis vest over his suit and was patting an interior wall. 'This old lady has been through so much.' He smiled wryly. 'But hessian wallpaper? Heinous.'

Ellie shook out a star-print onesie. The mums at playgroup probably ironed theirs. Should she …?

On screen, the camera panned up and over a faint water stain in one corner of the ceiling. The chateau owner's eyes were glazed with unshed tears as she wailed, 'And on top of everything, we've got a damp patch in the lounge.'

Ellie rolled her eyes. Call that a damp patch?

The boiler rumbled and the radiators made a ticking sound and as the room grew warmer, her eyelids grew heavy. She folded the baby's soft cotton vests and stacked clean nappies in a monotonous rhythm until her brain and limbs felt anaesthetised. Setting the basket to one side, she kicked her slippers in the air and lifted her legs on the bed. Two minutes, then she would get the baby.

On the TV, Mrs Chateau sobbed. 'Every day in this house is a nightmare and I just can't wake up.'

Ellie laid her cheek against the pillow and, succumbing to the weight of her tiredness, let the presenter's calm voice drift into her subconscious:

'If these old walls could talk, imagine the stories they could tell.'

22. Now

The low murmur of voices dragged her back to consciousness. How long had she been asleep?

She clicked the remote control. Nothing. The batteries were dead. Swinging her feet to the floor, she rolled her stiff shoulders. Through sleep-smeared eyes she saw the tumbledown chateau had been replaced by a modest family home in equal need of updating. The camera tracked through a hall covered in textured wallpaper. Stair treads creaked under the weight of ascending feet. Hairy fingers curled to grip the banister. Flesh puffed around a gold signet ring. Heavy, laboured breathing accompanied the visuals.

The painted banister and landing light resembled theirs. As did the carpet, patterned like mould in a petri dish. When the camera reached the top of the stairs, it zoomed in on a door identical in every way to the nursery, except for the handle with a key sticking out of the lock. And the thick black bolts, top and bottom.

She stared, alert now, as the hairy fingers turned the key and drew the bolts. Through the crack in the door, the camera filmed a sliver of yellow-papered chimney breast illuminated by the bare ceiling bulb and a single bed. Huddled under a woollen blanket, someone was crying.

Then a phone started ringing.

Not *a* phone, *her* phone.

Her eyes opened and she felt the pillowcase under her cheek. On the TV, five women sat around a table, laughing raucously at a joke she'd missed.

Groggy with sleep and confusion, she rubbed the corners of her eyes and scrabbled for her mobile.

'Hello?'

'Is everything OK?'

'I …' Ellie struggled to marshal her thoughts. She swung her feet to the floor, rolled her stiff shoulders. 'I must have fallen asleep.'

'Look at her! She hasn't got a clue,' the dark-haired presenter said in a broad Yorkshire accent and the studio audience roared with laughter.

'You need to check on Trinity. Now. Please.' There was controlled panic in Tom's voice.

That's when she realised Trinity was crying. Yelling, in fact. How had she not woken up?

She put Tom on loudspeaker and hurried to lift the squirming baby, cheeks puce with outrage, from the cot.

'She's not hurt, is she?' Tom said.

Trinity's legs battered the changing table. Ellie wrinkled her nose at the reek of dirty nappy.

'I don't think so. No. She just needs changing.'

One of the Velcro tabs had come undone and greeny-black sludge caked the baby's thighs and back. With a grimace, Ellie pulled it free and tugged the vest up to Trinity's armpits. A glob caught in the press studs and smeared across the baby's pudgy belly.

'Sorry,' Ellie murmured, reaching for the wipes while addressing the phone. 'How did you even know she was crying?'

'The app,' Tom replied. 'Look at the camera.'

Steadying the baby with one splayed hand, she glanced up. Sure enough, the green pinhead of light shone steadily. Her panic changed to annoyance.

'Were you spying on me?'

'Not you, the baby. But the point is I'm in *Manchester* and I could hear her, love. She's been screaming for at least ten minutes. I don't understand how you could be in our room and sleep through that.'

Even to her ears, Ellie's reply sounded defensive. 'I was up nearly all night.'

'I know,' he said, more gently. 'I'm not having a go. I was just worried.'

Squirming against the touch of the wipe on her mottled skin, the baby's foot hooked the nappy, spraying the contents over the mat before it landed, wrong side down, on the new carpet.

'Balls,' Ellie muttered. She glared at the camera. 'Switch it off, Tom, it's creepy.'

'I'm coming home,' he said.

Standing on tiptoe, Ellie draped a muslin cloth over the camera's prying eye.

'Ellie, don't be—'

She cut the call.

'Backseat bloody fathers,' she said loudly in the direction of the camera. The green light winked out with a click and, seconds later, her phone beeped with an apology from Tom.

Not spying. Home soon. Sorry. X

The theme tune to a game show blared from the TV. Loud presenter, louder contestants.

A warm bath failed to dissolve Trinity's tantrum. Ellie patted her dry and gently rubbed cream in the reddened creases at the tops of her thighs.

'I'm sorry. Mummy was just really tired,' she said. 'I promise I won't fall asleep again.'

Beyond placating now, Trinity's mouth persisted with a long wail of misery, only stopping a minute before Tom pulled into the driveway. When he walked through the door, Trinity squealed.

And when he held out the bag from the takeaway, Ellie almost did the same.

'I thought we'd both be too knackered to cook,' he explained. 'So I picked up a curry. Got you a garlic naan too.'

The evening passed pleasantly enough, with Tom extra solici-tous and tactfully avoiding mentioning the baby monitor. Instead, between mouthfuls of rogan josh, he talked about the progress the team were making.

'The new intelligence has meant we're closing in on the bastards, finally. One last push next week and we'll have them. Then I promise, no more overtime and no more weekend shifts.'

After he'd washed up, they slumped in front of the TV. Tom placed a cushion behind his head and put his arm around Ellie, pulling her close.

'How was playgroup?' He slurped the foam off a glass of beer, flicking his tongue to catch the drips.

'Good,' she said. 'I met next door's daughter-in-law, Asha. And I got talking to a journalist who covered the story about Mary Brennan dying in the house. How strange is that? She told me the paper used it to start a campaign about looking out for vulnerable people. Apparently, her boss …'

But she had lost her audience. Tom sat upright, fingers flying over his phone screen in response to a message alert.

'Sorry,' he said, taking his beer and getting up. 'Tanya's emailed me about tomorrow and I need to answer it if I'm not going to be …'

His voice trailed off as he left the room. Ellie rested her head briefly against the back of the sofa then lifted the laundry basket onto the coffee table and began to pair up socks.

Much later, while Trinity drifted off in her arms following the 3 a.m. feed, Ellie tiptoed out of the nursery and back to their room. And stopped. Bathroom, bedrooms, airing cupboard … she looked at each door in turn. Their worn and tarnished handles had to be the originals. Not the nursery, though. That was the origin of the weird dream, then. Subconsciously, she must have noticed its shiny brass handle was the odd one out.

Light glinted on the still-visible outline of the previous handle. And there were indentations on the door, top and bottom. Gouges in the wood with barely visible screw holes. Bolts? Possibly. But why would you put bolts on the outside of a door?

She rubbed her thumb over the thick layers of paint that almost obscured the shallow dents.

Almost.

23. Then

'I don't know,' Ellie said, unlocking the kitchen door. 'My mum likes me home in the holidays.'

Wrinkling her nose, Mia squashed last night's curry cartons into the already overflowing bin bag. 'It's only for a few days. You'll still have ages with your mum. Anyway, isn't she off on a romantic Easter break with Roy?'

'Roger, and yes, but only to Palma for a week. And I thought Danny would be staying at yours.'

A look of resignation passed over her friend's face. 'He's having one of his too-much-commitment freak-outs again. I'm sick of it. You're so lucky with Tom, you know. He's so reliable. Predictable. Loyal.'

'You make him sound like a Labrador.'

Mia put the bin bag outside and leaned against the wall, flicking her lighter on and off. 'I mean, he doesn't let ex-girlfriend guilt get in the way. He's straightforward, whereas Danny … One minute we're hunky dory, the next he's got the Josie angst again. But if he wants to get back with her, that's fine by me. Plenty more *poissons dans la mer*.' Click. The little orange flame danced. 'Ignore me. Please come and stay. I'm going to be bored out of my tiny mind.'

'I don't want to put your mum and dad out.'

'They'll be thrilled to see you. Anyway, they'll be working at the clinic most days so I'll be on my own.'

Mia's parents had made the long journey north from Surrey twice since the start of the year. The first time, they'd taken Mia and Danny out, but the last they'd invited Ellie for a pub lunch

116

and although shyness had tied her tongue at first, their warmth soon melted her nerves.

She scrubbed at a clump of rice stubbornly clinging to the plate.

Mum and Roger wouldn't want her hanging around for four weeks, would they?

'Go on, then,' she said. 'I'd love to.'

A farmhouse kitchen, all quarry tiles and ancient pets milling around, was the beating heart of Mia's family home. Bunches of dried herbs hung from the rafters and scented the air with sage and lavender. A battered Aga dominated the space, heating the water that clanged through the pipes. It was like stepping into the pages of a Famous Five book.

Every wall told the photographic history of the four Goldsworthy siblings from cute to gawky to gorgeous. Anita and David were the most welcoming of people, although Ellie felt slightly awed by the combination of Anita's whip-quick brain and David's Hollywood looks.

The view from Mia's bedroom contained fields, trees and about a thousand miles of blue sky. Hardback books lined the windowsill and more were precariously stacked on the bedside table. A faded patchwork quilt covered the bed, clashing with the daisy-print curtains. The whole effect was girly and slightly old-fashioned. In other words, completely unlike the Mia Ellie knew. In fact, the only classic Mia-like touch was the string of fairy lights wrapped around the wooden beams. Nothing contrived or planned, but in the context of this family, this ideal home, it was perfect.

On the first night, David offered to drive them into the village to go to the pub.

Mia rumpled her dad's hair. 'No, it's fine – we can walk, Dad.'

The tender gesture sent a shock wave of loss and envy through Ellie and she had to turn away so they wouldn't see.

Only a few tables were taken at The Hare and Hound, but

the landlady broke into smiles when Mia walked up to the bar and the sound of their friendly chatter followed Ellie to a nook at the back of the pub. Horse brasses lined a fireplace piled with logs, but unlit on this mild evening. She adjusted the worn red cushions and when an enormous dog with curly grey fur ambled over to sniff her leg, Ellie scratched behind his ears.

'Hello, boy,' Mia said, putting two pint glasses down, the old-fashioned sort, with panelled glass and thick handles. The dog wagged his tail before wandering over to another table.

Mia took a swig of beer. 'Danny's asked if I want to share a house with him when we move out of halls.'

So this was why Mia had invited her to stay. Ellie's heart sank. She'd kind of taken it for granted that they'd find somewhere together, a flat or maybe a house and now Mia was about to shatter those plans.

'What do you think?' Mia said, twirling a beer mat between her fingers.

'I think ...' Ellie said, hiding her disappointment as well as she could, 'that if that's what you want, it's a great idea.'

Mia tapped the mat on the table. 'Yeah, I told him I'd think about it, but I already know I'm going to say no. I mean, we've only been together for nine months and we're not exactly rock solid while he's feeling guilty about his ex. I was surprised he suggested it, actually.'

'They had been together since Year 7,' Ellie said mildly.

'I know and I do feel bad,' she said, pulling the corners of her mouth down. 'But it was Danny's decision to end it with her, not mine. Have you and Tom talked about getting somewhere?'

'No.' She picked up her pint. 'Same as you, it would feel a bit rushed.'

The truth was it hadn't even entered her head. While Mia and Danny's relationship had been characterised by intense ups and downs from the start, Tom and Ellie were on a much slower burn.

'Really? If Danny were anything like Tom I'd definitely be

considering it,' Mia said. 'But if you don't have any plans in that direction, shall we look for somewhere together?'

'Yeah,' Ellie said, happiness radiating through her. 'That sounds great.'

On their way back to Mia's, the hedges rustled with nocturnal creatures and when an owl hooted, Ellie jumped and clutched Mia, sending them both into breathless bursts of laughter that echoed in the still night air. Giggling and with her arm linked through Mia's, she felt herself emerge a little more from the sadness that had plagued her for so long.

'I'm free,' she said. She flung her arms in the air and twirled, slightly unsteadily, down the pitted lane. 'I'm a butterfly.'

'You're a tit,' Mia replied affectionately, sending them both into renewed drunken hysteria as they approached the sleeping farmhouse.

When they reached the gate, Mia patted her pockets. 'Balls. I've lost my keys. We'll have to go back and find them.'

She ran in the direction of the road, peering into the darkness. Ellie caught up and grabbed her arm, whispering, 'They could be anywhere, maybe you dropped them in the pub. Let's look tomorrow.'

Mia grimaced, glancing up at the dark windows. 'I don't want to wake Mum and Dad up.'

Ellie shrugged. What else could they do? She tried the door handle but it didn't budge.

There was a scratching sound against the wood, followed by a whine.

'Easy, Smudge,' Mia murmured to the dog. 'It's only us.'

She hitched her skirt up and turned to face Ellie.

'Right, I'm going to climb up to my room, then I'll come down and let you in, OK?'

'What? No way.'

'Nah. I used to do it all the time when I was younger.'

'After two pints and three Jack Daniel's?'

Mia grinned broadly. 'Often after substantially more than that and still without a scratch.'

Ellie followed her around to the side of the house and a heavy black drainpipe. Through the French doors, she could see the dog's nose pressed against the glass and she put her palm against it.

Twinkling lights glowed through a part-open window.

'Up the drainpipe, onto the conservatory roof and through my window. See you in a minute.'

Before Ellie could protest any further, Mia swung her foot onto the bracket holding the pipe to the wall and put her hand onto the low roof. The pipe creaked in protest.

'Get down!' she hissed. 'Mia, don't be stupid.'

Without replying, Mia heaved herself up to standing and carefully balanced on the ridge. The buckles on her boots glinted as she hugged the ivy-covered wall, shuffling slowly towards the windowsill.

'For God's sake, be careful.'

Ellie watched, half in terror, half in admiration as Mia grabbed the stone windowsill and reached through the crack to pull the window fully open. With a thud and a mumbled 'oof', she dragged herself over the sill and disappeared inside. A second later, a figure appeared, silhouetted in the window.

'Go to the back door,' Mia said hoarsely, tugging the hem of her skirt down to straighten it.

When they had crept silently up the stairs, past the sleeping parents and into Mia's room, the pair of them collapsed into giggles while the dog ran round, licking their faces and bashing them with his tail. And the hysteria only increased after Mia stood stock-still, staring at her bedside table with a stunned, 'What the hell?'

Ellie followed her gaze, putting her hand over her mouth as realisation dawned through the alcohol haze.

'You are joking.'

The keys dangled from her black-painted fingertips. 'I didn't take them.'

'Sssh,' Ellie giggled, putting a finger to her lips.

Of course, the burden of losing her dad and the gradual loss of her friends could never disappear completely, but at that moment, lying in Mia's bedroom in the grip of a major giggling fit, the familiar weight felt lighter than it ever had.

'I don't want to go all health and safety,' Ellie gasped when she could speak again, 'but climbing up the wall like that is so dangerous. You could actually kill yourself.'

Mia peeled a strand of long, dark hair from where tears had glued it to her cheek and stood by the window, looking down at the flat porch roof.

'Relax. I've done it a million times and I'm still here, aren't I?'

24. Now

'Have you seen the car keys?' Tom popped his head round the bathroom door.

'On the kitchen table.' Ellie cast a critical eye over lank hair, skin lifeless as cold porridge. Her spirits sagged. 'I just need five minutes,' she said and opened the cabinet.

The shelves contained a guilt-inducing arsenal of products for the new mum in search of her old self – oils, creams, vitamins – none of which made much difference to the exhausted face in the mirror. She tapped the bronzer brush against the side of the pot and swirled the bristles over her forehead and cheeks. Applied tinted lip balm.

After weeks of little to no sleep, she had to cut herself some slack. Things would improve once Trinity started sleeping through the night.

When he returned, she noticed Tom was equally leached of life, his eyebags the colour of builder's tea.

'Where's the changing bag?' he said.

'In the hall.'

The rapid thud of feet was followed by a shout, 'No, it's not.'

Scraping her hair into a functional ponytail, she went into the nursery. The changing bag was by the cot.

'Sorry. Could've sworn I'd brought it down.'

It took him three attempts to manoeuvre the buggy into the car and squash the changing bag on top.

'We need to be back by twelve to let Dad in.'

'Uppermoss Park is only twenty minutes,' she said. 'We'll be back in plenty of time.'

He slammed the boot. 'Sounds good. Can you lock up?'

Did Mary Brennan have a trick for locking this door? Ellie coaxed the worn shaft of the mortise to engage with the mechanism and an image appeared of cold fingers turning this same key for the final time, unaware she would never leave the house again. Alive, anyway.

It locked with a solid click.

Trinity snoozed for most of the journey, cutely cosy in the tiger-striped hat and mittens Danny and Josie sent, allowing Ellie to watch the landscape blur into a green and brown banner. Watery morning sun warmed her face through the glass and childhood memories paraded through her mind like jerky home videos. Her dad running alongside her bike on the paths. Throwing stale bread crusts for the ducks, her shrieking at the greedy geese. The excitement of queuing for a 99 after paddling in the stream.

'Here we go,' Tom said, pulling into the car park.

Parkrun had just finished and the last stragglers, their hi-vis vests spattered with mud, panted along the concrete path. An unfeasibly fit woman pushing a three-wheeled buggy brought up the rear.

'We could do this,' Tom said. 'Would you like that, Trinity?'

Ellie zipped the snuggle blanket around the baby's legs.

'Yeah, you could go fast with Daddy or slow with Mummy.'

'You'll be back to your PB in no time.'

Ellie hooked her arm through his. 'I really hope so.'

The air was cold but crisp and the blood pumping round her body released a burst of energy. Mum had been right – she had been cooped up for too long. Being outdoors was working wonders on her mood – and Tom's. He chatted away to Trinity, pointing out the trees and the bushes. By the lake, an off-lead dog ran up and sniffed the pram, wagging its tail.

'Trinity. That's a doggy,' Tom said. 'There are some ducks.'

Ellie was transported back to her own childhood and her dad's hand warm and strong in hers, beard tickling her cheek as he knelt to name the ducks. Despite the exhaustion claiming her body, walking among these happy memories smoothed some of the jagged edges of the last few weeks and she felt her anxiety melt a little in the weak sun.

'Technically, that's a mallard,' she said to Trinity, 'and a Canada goose. And that show-off over there is a Mandarin.'

Tom pulled an approving face. 'Impressive duck knowledge, Wight. Any other hidden talents you'd like to share?'

She waggled her eyebrows and he grinned.

They crossed over the stone bridge where she'd played pooh sticks with her dad, rounded the corner and stopped in front of Uppermoss Hall. The textbook Tudor mansion had tiny leaded windows, cockeyed chimneys, and a huge, studded door in front of which stood a man in a Henry VIII costume handing out leaflets for a guided tour. A very un-Tudor length of tinsel hung around his neck like a shiny feather boa.

Tom whistled. 'This place certainly puts our house maintenance woes in perspective.'

He leaned across the pram to kiss her, but the mosquito-buzz of his work phone interrupted.

'Sorry, I've got to take this,' he said. 'You keep going. I'll catch up.'

Tom's voice drifted over. 'Hiya, Tanya. What's up?'

Ellie chewed the inside of her cheek. Was he not allowed one weekend off?

Trinity sneezed wetly, flinging her whole body into it, and flashed a wide-eyed look of surprise.

'Oh, sweetheart,' Ellie said and reached into her pocket. 'Let Mummy wipe your nose.' The tab of the tissue packet stuck to the lining and when she tugged, her keys dropped to the ground.

Before she could bend down to retrieve them, Henry VIII materialised by her side and picked them up with a flourish. 'Allow me.'

Close up, she could see elastic hooked round his ears to anchor the ginger beard in place. She smelled Lynx and felt the brush of his suede gauntlet against her palm.

'Thank you.'

He smoothed his gloves down his doublet. 'Would madam like to discover the macabre secrets of Uppermoss Hall in our Christmas Ghost Experience tour?'

'Not today, thanks,' she said and pressed a tissue against Trinity's cherry-red nose. She took the proffered leaflet and, with a smile, stuck it in her back pocket.

'What's that?' Tom said, still holding his phone.

'Just a leaflet about the ghost tour. What did Tanya want?'

'Nothing important.'

It was on the tip of her tongue to say *why did you take it then*? But Trinity interrupted with another ferocious sneeze.

'Do you think she's OK?' Tom sounded concerned. He touched her forehead. 'She doesn't feel hot. Maybe being outside is tickling her nose.'

A kid, clutching an ice-cream cone like his life depended on it, narrowly avoided crashing into the buggy. His parents followed holding bacon butties, ketchup oozing through the paper serviettes.

'Shall we try the café?' Tom said.

Ellie frowned. 'It's a bit expensive here. Why don't we wait till we get home?'

'Aw come on.' He set off with the pram. 'Let's go crazy. A piece of cake isn't going to break the bank.'

Under the awning and sheltered from the breeze, Tom removed Trinity's hat, smoothing down the static wisps of hair. Ellie basked in the weak sun, spooning foam from the top of her cappuccino, and carving bits off a piece of carrot cake.

'You know, Danny and Josie gave us that hat and gloves set, and I haven't sent them a thank-you card yet. I haven't sent any.'

'People understand,' Tom said. 'Especially if they've got kids of their own. They must understand it gets a bit full-on in the first few weeks. Months. Anyway, don't worry, I said thanks to Danny the other night when he rang.'

'How are they all?'

'Fine. We mainly talked about you and Trinity and the house.' Tom dabbed at the baby's nose. 'Dan was saying they went down to Anita and David's on the anniversary. Put some flowers on Mia's grave.'

Ellie carefully squashed cream cheese icing onto the back of her fork. They were having a nice time. Why did he have to mention Mia?

'They went for lunch,' Tom continued, oblivious. 'Mia's brothers were there too, with their kids. Danny said it ended up being quite a party.'

'We should definitely invite Danny and Josie to stay, once the house is in better shape. What is the next project, anyway?'

She half stood and brushed crumbs from her jeans. Maybe he realised she was changing the subject, maybe he didn't. Either way, Tom took the bait, describing his plan to get the garden sorted for spring while she nodded, chipped in with suggestions, and pushed away images of nephews and nieces who would only ever know their Auntie Mia through photos and stories.

Five minutes later, they had paid the bill, tucked Trinity in the buggy and set off. They walked past Henry VIII leaning against a tree, smoking a roll-up and checking his phone. A billboard above his cushiony hat depicted a blissful bride and groom. *Ask about our beautiful weddings!* it read.

Some chance. She and Tom talked about getting married now and then, but there always seemed to be something else to save up for. And now, at the rate the house gobbled their savings, they'd be walking up the aisle on Zimmer frames.

They reached the playground and Tom stopped and knelt next to Trinity. 'Doesn't that look like fun? When you're a bit older you'll be able to play on the swings and the slide like those big boys and girls.'

It had changed a lot since her childhood visits. Rubberised flooring replaced the lethal concrete and the rusty swings were long gone. A pirate ship complete with slides, climbing wall and tunnels attracted hordes of kids screaming with laughter.

'We'd better go home for Dad.' Tom's knees cracked as he straightened. 'I wish my mum could have met Trinity.'

Ellie followed his line of sight to an older lady helping a toddler in rainbow wellies splash through a puddle. The older woman mirrored the toddler's delight and Ellie felt an intense wave of longing for her own mum.

'She'd have loved being a grandma,' Tom continued.

Ellie curled her lips in a sad smile. 'Yeah. My dad would have loved bringing Trinity here. Teaching her about the trees and the wildlife.'

'That's the kind of life I want for our daughter,' Tom said, gazing up at the leafy canopy. 'Roaming about in nature, not hemmed in by concrete, worried about pollution and traffic. Once the house is sorted and the pressure is off at work, we'll appreciate what a good move this was for us.'

A squirrel skittered across the path and into the bushes.

'I already appreciate it,' Ellie said. 'And I'm really sorry I've been such a pain these last few weeks.'

'Don't be daft.' Tom braced his thigh against the pram and reached for her. He smelled of autumn and his arms were solid and warm.

'I should be doing more around the house, but I'm knackered,' she said into his chest. 'And then I feel bad for moaning because you're working flat out and even more knackered. I feel like I'm lazy and useless.'

He hugged her even tighter. 'You are definitely neither of those things. You're a brilliant mum and we're lucky to have you.'

She hugged him fiercely in return. Why was she even worried? He loved her, she loved him. They both loved Trinity. Nothing else mattered.

He planted a kiss on her forehead. 'Come on. Let's go home.'

Home.

Obviously, it was her imagination playing tricks, but as soon as the word left Tom's lips, she felt the keys burn, cold and metallic, through her jacket pocket, her jumper, her T-shirt to her skin.

25. Now

Howard's van was already parked on the driveway when they arrived home. The rear doors were open and a set of stepladders rested against the porch.

'Dad beat us to it then,' Tom said over the crunch of gravel. 'He must be round the back. Why don't you open up and I'll tell him we're home?'

She unclicked her seatbelt and took her jacket off the back seat while he lifted Trinity out.

Ellie rummaged in her zippered pockets. Phone, purse, tissues. She sat back.

'I can't find my …' She lifted her hips and patted her jeans pockets. 'The house keys. I can't find them.'

'Have you checked under the seat?'

But her groping hand found nothing there except the ice scraper and an old Yorkie wrapper. They hadn't slipped under the footwell mat, either, or in the gap between the seatbelt and the door.

'It's OK,' Tom said, jangling the bunch at the open window. 'I've got mine.'

But he didn't need them. As soon as he touched the handle, the front door swung open.

'I thought you locked it?' he said and she heard a tinge of irritation.

The memory of turning the key in the lock lay so close to the surface she didn't even need to search for it. Hand, fob, thinking of Mary, lock.

'I did. Your dad must have opened up.'

'We haven't given him a key yet,' Tom pointed out on his way inside.

Howard emerged from the passageway at the side of the house. He was wearing a faded lumberjack shirt over paint-spattered cords and heavy-duty work boots.

'Did you have a good walk?' he said, pulling his gloves off.

'Was the front door unlocked when you got here?' Ellie said.

'I didn't think to try, to be honest.'

'Hi, Dad,' Tom said from the porch. He had the basket from the hall in his hand. 'Look, Els.'

He held her keys up by the silver E.

She stared. 'Where did you find them?'

'In here.' He shook the wicker basket, rattling the jumbled contents.

She felt her forehead crease. 'But that's impossible. I locked the door and put the keys in my jacket pocket before we went to the park.'

'Never mind. At least we've found them now,' he said. 'Anyway, Dad, I was thinking I can get stuck into the garden while the weather's good and you could look at the heating. What do you reckon?'

Before Howard could respond, Ellie stepped forward. 'I'm being serious, Tom. I definitely locked up and I definitely took those keys to the park.'

Trinity gave a melancholy wail and writhed in Tom's arms.

'All right, love,' he murmured into the baby's head. 'Look, I'll change her if you bring the stuff in.'

Her body acting on autopilot, she carried the changing bag into the kitchen while her mind looped back to dropping the key ring in the park. The touch of the man's suede glove. The cold burn of metal in her pocket.

Yale for the top lock, years of grime embedded in the grooves. Lost in confusion, she shrugged off her coat and hung it on the back of the chair. Slim brass mortise, worn smooth by Mary Brennan's fingers. The memory was sharp.

'I said' – Howard cleared his throat – 'I saw one of your neighbours just now. She came into the garden.'

She hadn't even been aware he was speaking. She smiled and adopted a fake-bright tone. 'Sorry, Howard. I was miles away. Yeah, that'll be Diane from next door. She's really nice, isn't she?'

He made an embarrassed sound, a kind of cough-laugh. 'I don't know about that. I said hello, but she completely ignored me. I think she took one look at the overalls and decided I wasn't worth talking to.'

'Really? What did she look like?'

'Dark hair, glasses.' He shrugged. 'Miserable. Anyway, Tom told me the electrics are playing up.'

'Yeah, and the boiler,' she said absently. 'I think that woman is another one of the neighbours. Sorry.'

Howard chuckled. 'I'm not bothered, love. But you can do me a quick sandwich if you want to make up for it.'

'Of course,' she said, gathering herself. 'Ham OK?'

A whiff of sour milk emanated from the fridge. She took out the ham, a shrivelled end of cucumber and a jar of mayo and quickly assembled Howard's sandwich.

On the other side of the window, Tom waded through the brambles. He had a spade in one hand and a roll of black bags in the other.

She turned to pass Howard his lunch and something fell out of her back pocket: the wadded-up leaflet about ghost tours.

'Cheers, love. I'll have this while I'm bleeding the radiators,' Howard said, taking the plate. 'It'll probably just be air in the pipes, if the system's been shut down for a while.'

As she smoothed the creased paper flat, her memory returned to the clatter of the key ring hitting the tarmac. The suede glove. The cold burn of metal.

But the keys were in the basket. She saw Tom get them.

She realised Howard was probably waiting for her to say something.

'Thanks for all your help. There's no way we could have done so much on our own.'

'Don't be daft,' Howard said in a gruffly pleased tone. He selected a metal thing from the toolbox. 'No point paying cowboys a fortune to do a bad job. Right, I'll start upstairs.'

Within a few minutes, alarming gurgles raced through the pipes and Ellie, tapping crumbs off the breadboard, half-smiled at Trinity's open-mouthed astonishment.

Observing the unique human emerging from generic babyness fascinated Ellie. One day, she saw Dad in the line of Trinity's jaw. The next, Tom's hairline emerged from the fuzzy scalp and that little fold at the top of her left ear mirrored his and Howard's. Dad lived on in the rounded curve of the chin and Mum in the perfect bow of the lips. And a shift in light could turn the murky navy of her eyes to deep brown, like Tom's.

Brown eyes like King Henry's. The rash of pimples; the elastic hooked around his ears, the cigarette smoke on his breath when he handed the keys over. How could she have imagined such detail?

Outside, Tom karate kicked the wooden structure in the middle of the rose bed and Ellie imagined rather than heard the splintering crack of rotten planks. It lurched and tilted but, anchored by the thick bushes entwined around the bars, didn't collapse. Instead it hung lopsided while Tom wiped his forehead, stepping back to decide his next move.

A reel of events unfurled in her head. She saw herself lock the door when they left. Put the keys in her pocket. Get in the car. Everything was so vivid. So real. Only two possible explanations presented themselves: either her sleep-deprived memory had short-circuited and imagined the whole scenario.

Or Tom had taken them out of her pocket and hidden them in the basket.

Metal flashed as he sawed through the thick, thorny stems.

Even from the kitchen, she could see the line of sweat soaking through the back of his grey T-shirt. Poor Tom. Whether he was at home or at the station, he never stopped working.

And in the unlikely event it was a stupid joke, he would have confessed as soon as he saw she was upset. She must have got it wrong. She gave her head a little shake. No, there was no way he would have taken the keys without telling her.

Because why would he want her to think she was losing her mind?

26. Now

'Cup of tea?'

The question cut through deep layers of sleep. Thick-headed and with a nasty taste in her mouth, Ellie swam to consciousness. In the days since the incident at the park, she'd had the same surreal dream about vanishing keys and lost babies and dead roses almost every night. She rubbed her gummy eyes.

'What time is it?'

'Just gone eight.'

'Jesus, Tom.' She kicked the duvet off. 'Why didn't you get me up?'

'Because you were dead to the world,' he whispered, nodding at the Moses basket. 'And because Trinity is still sleeping off the expressed milk I gave her at six o'clock.'

A quick glance confirmed Trinity was indeed fast asleep. The blood pressure meds were in the bedside drawer and she chased them down with a swig of tea. The health visitor had suggested taking them in the morning, but so far it hadn't made any difference to the dreams.

'Shouldn't you be at work?'

'We're taking the baby for her injections, remember.'

'Oh God.' She shuffled up the headboard.

'Relax. We don't need to set off till ten.' His patchy stubble tickled her cheek as he leaned in for a kiss. 'How are you feeling now?'

She mentally scanned her body, top to toe. 'OK, I think. Tired.'

'Look, we need to talk about last night,' he said. The mattress sank as he sat down. His tone was serious.

She looked at Tom, *really* looked. Hollow-eyed and unshaven, T-shirt on inside out.

'What do you mean?'

There was a tiny pause while an expression she couldn't immediately identify clouded his face. Then he gave a weak smile and squeezed her hand. 'You were sleepwalking.'

Sleepwalking? She hadn't done that for years. Something flickered at the back of her mind. Searching for something. The cold ache from kneeling on a hard floor. But it slipped away before she could examine it. She brought her knees to her chest and hugged them.

'What happened?'

'You were well out of it,' Tom said, shuffling over to put his arms around her. 'I heard banging and it woke me up. You'd opened the kitchen cupboards, chucked stuff out. I got there when you were trying to unlock the back door. You kept saying "the baby's gone".'

He got up and crossed to the window. Dust motes sparkled in the sudden light as he opened the curtains on a crisp blue sky. He leaned his forehead against the window.

'In the end, I had to get Trinity to show you so you'd come back to bed.'

'*The baby's gone.*' She saw the woman in black bending over the cot. But that had been in the hospital. And a dream.

'Sleepwalking is an anxiety thing, right?' he said, turning around. His concerned tone matched his expression. 'Because it's totally understandable, after everything that's happened.'

'It must be,' Ellie said slowly. 'I had the same dream when I was in the hospital, about someone taking the baby. I can't believe I went through the cupboards, though. That's so weird.'

He wiped a patch of condensation from the window. 'How are you feeling now?'

'I'm fine,' she said, checking the wobble in her voice. 'I can't remember anything. And I'm sorry for keeping you awake.'

135

'Don't worry. Listen, why don't you try and get a bit more sleep now? I'll be out in the garden if you need me.'

The stairs creaked as Tom descended. Ellie dropped back on the pillow. Only once she heard the back door open and close did she let the wave of panic engulf her. What the hell? She hadn't sleepwalked since Willow Lodge.

And since the thing with the keys, nothing else weird had interrupted the gentle rhythms of daily life. Ellie had reassessed the situation and accepted she'd made a mistake. Her pockets constantly leaked random junk – tissues, Polos, loose change – whatever Henry had passed her, it hadn't been keys. She'd left them at home in the basket.

She'd made a mistake, that was all.

Like Tom had said.

A mewling sound came from the Moses basket. The sheets rustled as the baby woke.

Ellie swung her legs out of bed. Her dressing gown lay in a heap at the end of the bed and as she dragged it on, she caught sight of Tom in the garden, standing by the remains of the pergola. The spade was buried in the muddy ground and he leaned on the handle. But he wasn't digging. He had his mobile phone clamped to his ear and even from this distance, she noted his hunched shoulders. He glanced up at the house and she stepped quickly back from the window.

Trinity stirred again, crying more loudly this time.

'You certainly get your appetite from me, young lady,' Ellie said, picking her up.

Relax. Relax. Relax. Don't think about sleepwalking. Just relax.

Exhaling slowly, Ellie focused on her body and how it occupied the chair, held the feeding cushion on her lap. *Drop the shoulders, loosen the grip on the cushion.* It worked. Her limbs softened, and she closed her eyes.

After a few minutes, when the greedy sucking had diminished and Trinity entered the intermittent tugging phase that signalled she had almost finished, Ellie heard the hinges creak and Tom's careful footsteps.

'It's OK,' she murmured. 'Not sleeping.'

A cool breeze drifted in from an open window somewhere in the house, carrying the scents of autumn.

She could sense him watching.

'You promised not to spy on me,' she said drowsily. He didn't respond and she ordered her eyes to open, but the lids refused to obey.

Her chin drooped to her chest and a vision materialised of Trinity kicking her legs in the brilliant sunshine. Under her, the lawn was a green velvet carpet and the whispering trees of Mosswood framed the scene. On the edge of sleep now, she murmured, 'Have you finished in the garden?'

But in place of an answer, a distant yell catapulted her to wakefulness. Trinity let out a confused cry and Ellie started, almost flinging her off the cushion.

Downstairs, work boots scuffled on the kitchen lino. The house reverberated with the door slamming.

'Bastard thorns!' Tom shouted. 'They've cut me to ribbons again.'

The sun ducked behind a cloud and the nursery darkened. Silent tiger, lion, elephant eyes from the motionless mobile watched Ellie clutch the baby and stumble on to the landing. How—?

Tom stood in the kitchen doorway, streaks of blood mingling with mud on his T-shirt. He tilted his head at the top of the stairs.

'Look at that!'

He lifted a wad of paper towel from his forearm and brandished deep parallel scratches, like claw marks.

Ellie stared down. Her mouth opened and closed but couldn't formulate a reply.

'Have we got any antiseptic cream?' Tom said, dabbing at the cut. He looked up. 'Ellie?'

137

She shook her head slightly, trying to rearrange the chaos in her head.

'In the drawer,' she said faintly, edging down the stairs and then placing Trinity in the bouncer. 'Did you just come up to the nursery?'

'No,' he answered distractedly, already rattling around in the kitchen. 'Which drawer?'

The bouncer rocked as Trinity kicked her little legs in fury. Plasters, ointment … nothing was where it should be. It was as though a whirlwind had passed through the house, upending drawers and scattering the contents. She found the first-aid box in the cupboard under the sink, just as Tom turned the tap on and water deflected off last night's unwashed plates. He jumped back, but too late to prevent the water splashing onto the muddy floor.

'Here, clean it off with that.' She passed him a baby wipe. 'What happened?'

With the cap off, the tube released the reassuring smell that took her back to Dad treating her childhood bumps and scrapes. She dabbed the cream first on her fingertips then his arm.

'I tripped and landed right in the rose bushes.' He screwed his face up and opened his fist to reveal a matrix of thin lines studded with scarlet beads. 'Those thorns are like razor wire. They really had it in for me.'

'I think you need to do this,' she said, propping his elbow on the table so his wrist was at shoulder height. She added, casually, 'Are you sure you didn't come upstairs?'

'Not me, I was too busy being mauled by feral vegetation.' He gave her a sharp glance. 'Why?'

She peeled the backing off a wound dressing. Despite the pounding in her ears, she kept her voice light. 'No reason. Just thought I heard you, that's all.'

'OK well, we need to set off for the clinic in about an hour, but until then …' He pulled his gardening gloves back on. 'Man versus plant. Round two.'

Watching Tom make his way through the weeds, she rinsed the cloth under the tap and the faint pink of diluted blood swirled down the plughole. When he reached the debris of the rose beds, he turned and flexed his biceps like a body builder. She gave a double thumbs-up and from the bouncer came the sound of Trinity smacking her lips.

'That's right,' Ellie said, unbuckling the straps on the bouncer seat. 'Silly Daddy. Come on, let's get you ready for your injections.'

She noticed the mud as soon as she walked back into the hall. And the handprints on the banister. She dabbed it and fresh dirt smudged under her finger, still wet. How had she not noticed when she came down? And there, too, on the carpet, almost invisible in the green swirls, were glistening patches left by muddy feet.

It didn't make sense.

Why would he lie about coming upstairs?

27. Now

Uppermoss Medical Centre appeared to have outgrown its car park some years earlier. After two expletive-filled circuits, Tom pulled back out onto the main road and began systematically trawling the side streets.

'Permit holders only,' he muttered. 'Double yellow lines.'

Ellie glanced at her watch. 'Why don't you drop us outside and come in when you've parked up?'

'Don't worry. We'll make it.'

But the only free space was streets away and although Tom had the added weight of Trinity, it was Ellie who panted as she tapped her date of birth and initials on the touchscreen in the overheated foyer. God, she was so unfit.

Shan the estate agent would have marketed the waiting room as 'vintage'. Fifty shades of beige, from the fraying fabric seats to the cream walls covered in faded public health posters.

Caring for your new-born. Staying mentally healthy. Fighting fatigue.

Tom jiggled Trinity on his knee.

'Will the nurse ask how you are as well?'

Ellie gave him a sidelong glance. 'Why do you ask?'

'Oh you know.' He adjusted the strap on Trinity's dungarees. 'I wondered if it might be worth mentioning the sleepwalking and stuff.'

Her heartbeat picked up. 'What do you mean "stuff"?'

'You know, tiredness, losing the keys and emptying the cupboards, cleaning, that kind of thing. Look' – he nodded at the board – 'our turn.'

The nurse who popped her head round the door wore a navy tunic, a harassed expression and a straight-to-the point attitude.

'One parent only. Waiting room, please,' she said, waving Tom back down the corridor. She ushered Ellie. 'Weight and three lots of vaccinations …'

Five minutes later, Trinity had been weighed, measured, swabbed and injected. Questions had been asked and answers given regarding sleep patterns and feeding. Comments made about introducing solids and the importance of tummy time because 'No one wants a flat-headed baby, do they?'

Ellie rocked Trinity against her shoulder while furtively inspecting her skull bones. What was the woman trying to say?

The nurse finished plotting new graph points in Trinity's record book and put her pen in her breast pocket.

'She'll be unsettled for a few hours. If she gets worse, please give us a call. The good news is she's gaining weight nicely and everything seems fine.' She edged towards the door as she spoke. 'Anything you're concerned about? How is your health?'

Ellie hesitated, then said, 'I'm tired and I keep getting confused. But that's probably because my sleep is so disrupted.'

The nurse's hand hovered on the handle. 'I can get you in with a GP if you like. There may be a wait though – we're very busy today.'

'No, no,' Ellie said quickly. 'It's nothing.'

Holding Trinity awkwardly, she slipped the little red book in her bag and exchanged a look of worn-out solidarity with the next mum waiting in the corridor.

As long as those graphs kept heading in the right direction, her fears eased a little. Trinity was healthy. Trinity was fine.

At least she would be once she stopped screaming.

Plastering on a bland smile, she scanned the waiting room. Eyes peered over newspapers or lifted from screens, but Tom's bloodshot baby browns weren't among them. She pushed the foyer door open with her elbow and saw him, pacing as he chatted into his phone.

He jerked his head as the automatic doors slid open.

'What's their team saying about that?'

Biting his lower lip, he nodded to whatever the other person said. When they'd finished, he closed his eyes briefly and said, 'Shit, shit, shit. OK, I'll be in within the hour. Bye.'

He raked his fingers through his hair, then set his shoulders back and found a smile. 'Poor baby, did that hurt?'

'She was very brave,' Ellie said, passing the still-squalling baby over. A second later, his phone beeped. He read the message quickly over Trinity's head, as they walked to the car.

'Tanya?' Ellie said tightly.

He nodded and lowered Trinity into the car seat. She drummed her feet furiously against the upholstered edge.

'Yeah, there's been a complication. Look, will you be OK if I just pop into work after I've dropped you home? I wouldn't ask except it's an emergency and Tanya can't do it on her own.'

I can't do it on my own.

With effort, she swallowed the reproach and dropped her bag into the footwell. Unwanted angry tears stung her eyes and she dipped her head so he wouldn't see.

'Lucky Tanya. She sees more of you than we do,' she said, lightly.

But he wasn't even listening.

28. Then

She heard them before she saw them. Their laughter escaped under Mia's door and into the communal hallway of block B Henderson Hall where Ellie stood, fumbling for her keys. That foghorn of mirth belonged to Mia, proprietor of Manchester's most raucous laugh. But whose was the low, masculine murmur? Danny was still in the library when she left half an hour ago.

An unchained bike leaned against the electricity meter cupboard. Tom's bike. When she left his flat this morning, he told her he was working straight after lectures finished. He didn't know she would be home early. And she wouldn't have been, except two lads sharing a bottomless bag of Doritos plonked themselves next to her in the library.

She paused on the small landing and listened to the wordless cadences of animated conversation. Two people getting along well. *Very* well.

She took a deep breath and knocked.

'Come in,' Mia called out. 'It's not locked.'

On the bed, one leg curled under her, Mia sat holding a mug. Tom sprawled on the floor inches from her.

How cosy.

He jumped up and wrapped her in a bear hug. And if he noticed her stiffen, he didn't act fazed.

'We thought you weren't back till later,' Mia said. 'I said Tommo could wait till you got back.'

Tommo?!

'Well, the library was heaving,' Ellie replied as she extricated herself from Tom's embrace. 'And I've got a bit of a headache.'

Mia unfurled herself. 'I've got some paracetamol somewhere.'

'No, I'm good, thanks. You coming, Tom?'

Mia stretched and a yawn creased her perfect features. 'See you guys later.'

Behind her own closed door, Ellie leaned against the wall to kick her shoes off.

'I thought you were going to the gym?'

'I am,' Tom said, gesturing down his body. Which, admittedly, was clothed in shorts and a neon yellow vest. 'But ...'

He held her mobile phone out.

Of course!

As soon as she saw it, Ellie remembered. She'd been brushing her teeth in Tom and Danny's tiny bathroom when her phone beeped. Danny knocked to ask how long she'd be and in the rush, she must've left it on the side.

'Thanks.' She picked it up. 'I thought I'd left it in here.'

After the initial surge of relief came guilt accompanied by irritation. Not with Tom, or Mia. Herself. Talk about paranoid. Tom wouldn't cheat. It wasn't in his nature. And as for Mia. OK, she did have that 'all's fair in love and war' attitude with Danny's ex, but ... she shook her head. No way.

Tom fastened his cycle helmet. 'See you later, yeah?'

Ellie hesitated, twisting her fingers together. He smiled expectantly.

The words burst out from nowhere. 'I love you.'

Tom broke into a broad grin. 'I love you too.'

29. Now

Ellie hadn't sleepwalked since she was discharged from Willow Lodge, almost ten years earlier. The key to her recovery, the centre director had explained in her soft Scottish accent, was to learn to exist in the present. That was the ethos at Willow Lodge, and from mindful colouring after breakfast to thoughtful yoga before bed, an activity was allocated to every minute.

Real life with a baby didn't leave much time for mindfulness, but mindlessness? That she had by the bucketload. Two minutes scrubbing the brown stains left by Tom's casually dropped teabag. A further ten chipping limescale off the bath taps. A good hour rearranging the jumble inside the kitchen cupboards. Hoovering. Mopping. Mind-numbing, yes, but right then, a numb mind was her aim. Plus by the end of it, she could cross a few items off the to-do list on the fridge door.

Stifling a yawn, she wiped Trinity's sticky face and hands. If her lack of crying was anything to go by, the pain of the injections had eased off.

'Tummy time,' Ellie said, unrolling the playmat.

Trinity lay on her belly looking comically startled at the sight of her reflection in a mirrored panel.

'Zebra. Lion. Tiger.' Ellie pointed at the squares then at herself. 'Mummy.' Swooped in to tickle the baby's tummy. 'Trinity.'

A dimpled fist thumped a square, a bell tinkled and the baby gazed in astonishment, searching for the source.

Trinity changed day by day, hour by hour. It was fascinating to watch her infant intellect working like a database with each sense inputting infinite pieces of information from the world around her. This time last week, she couldn't lift her head and today, here she was goggling at the messy collection of boxes by the fireplace.

'Clever girl,' Ellie exclaimed. 'Are you telling Mummy to get on with the unpacking?'

Thanks to Roger whisking her mum off to Spain, she didn't have a family home to store her childhood possessions and this pile constituted the archive of Eleanor Wight.

She rocked back on her heels. When you viewed it as the history of her life so far, there wasn't much.

The first box contained memories of a happy childhood. Photos of Dad in a paper hat, lifting a glass to the camera. Christmas the year she got her first bike. Ellie squinting in the sun from high on her dad's broad shoulders. Memories of his terrible jokes and surprisingly slick dance moves. Everything swept away by the tsunami of a cancer diagnosis.

Looking back on it now, Ellie understood that losing her dad had changed her on a molecular level. Overnight every cell of her blistered with the knowledge that the flip side of love was loss. And while the sharp corners of grief had rounded with time, Trinity's arrival had carved a new route to the pain. The pain of knowing that her daughter would never meet the grandad who would have idolised her.

With a stab of sadness, she carefully replaced the lid and set it to one side. She sipped cooling tea and stared at the next box. Innocuous enough, this tatty shoebox with 'uni stuff' scrawled over an orange Sale sticker. No need to look. Straight in the loft.

But when she picked it up, the lid slipped off and a grubby tangle of wristbands slithered out. Under them was a collection of cards, all hand-drawn. The top one read 'Happy 20th Ellie' above blue anime eyes and a sweep of brown hair.

Her stomach clenched and she turned the pile over. Underneath lurked curling photos printed on the old machines at Boots. Some were in paper wallets and others loose, studded with scraps of dried Blu Tack. Their power surged through her fingertips, but she wouldn't turn them over. Not now.

Last was an illustrated girl on card, like a fashion drawing of Audrey Hepburn. Smoke twisted from her sketched cigarette, the grey ribbon writhing into a single word: *Mia*. Its Ellie counterpart was long gone, but these had been their doorplates for the year or so they'd lived in the flat.

Right at the bottom of the box was a picture frame. Ellie laid her palm flat on the card backing and chewed her lip. She didn't need to turn it over to see it.

The two girls in the photo wore vest tops and artificial daisies in their hair. Mia had round pink sunglasses on and Ellie was squinting happily at the camera. The grubby tail of Mia's wristband hung over her collarbone as she hugged her friend. Her other hand toasted the camera with a pint of lager in a plastic pot. The lager had been warm, Ellie remembered, and bits of grass floated in the amber liquid. She could taste it in the back of her throat now.

Their tent was pitched too far from the stage and too close to the toilets, but by the second night, she barely noticed the smell. Looking back, she had never felt as free as she had that weekend. Dancing and drinking and laughing in the sunshine. The Mia in the photo smiled like a girl with a long, happy future stretching ahead of her.

A bird cried outside the window, bringing Ellie back to bare floorboards and half-unpacked boxes spewing bubble wrap. Existing in the present might well be the key to recovery. But how could you focus on the present when the past was all around you?

She put the lid on the shoebox. Somehow, half an hour had passed and if anything, the room was more untidy. As she rapidly divided the rest into bin, store or sort piles, she heard the bird again. Louder. Closer.

Bird?

She cocked her head. Trinity lay dozing on the mat, a string

147

of drool hanging from her rosebud lips. The TV was off. Radio same. Phone too.

Not a bird. A baby. The whimpering escalated, unmistakably human.

She looked up at the ceiling and little hairs bristled on the nape of her neck. The house waited. Ellie tiptoed towards the hall.

Somewhere upstairs, a baby coughed out angry staccato cries.

Ellie's heart pumped the blood so fast it pounded in her ears, almost muffling the sound of the stranger baby. The baby that couldn't possibly be crying because there couldn't possibly *be* a baby upstairs.

With her eyes locked on the landing, she moved towards cries that now blared like emergency sirens. She grabbed the handle, half-expecting the door to stick.

Instead it swept smoothly over the carpet and into the empty nursery.

The cries hung like an auditory after-image in the air, then vanished, replaced by the mocking caw of a bird.

Had she imagined the baby crying? She peered at the cot, the nursing chair, the changing table with the photo of her dad above.

Of course she'd imagined it. The silence pressed in around her, squeezing her until she could hardly breathe.

Trinity dozed on, unperturbed in the lounge. Very quietly, Ellie picked up her phone. More than anything now, she needed to hear her mum's voice.

She was about to hang up when Carol finally answered.

'Sorry, love. My phone was right at the bottom of my bag. We're out for lunch.'

Background chatter and the clink of cutlery came down the phone. Normal sounds.

'That's OK,' Ellie lied. 'I only rang to say hi.'

She never could fool her mum.

'What's wrong?' her mum said sharply. 'Is it the baby?'

Ellie went to speak then stopped. How could she explain

what had just happened? Instead, she said, 'No, she's fine. We're all fine.'

'Hang on. I'll just go somewhere quiet. Let me get my crutches.' There was a clattering and then the background noise cut abruptly. 'There's something wrong. I can hear it in your voice.'

'Nothing's wrong.' Ellie blinked rapidly. 'Just fancied a chat. Being on my own in the house feels a bit ... weird.'

Her mum spoke with reassuring briskness. 'Well, that's understandable. Like I said before, new houses have their quirks. You've been through a lot and ...' she paused '... don't bite my head off, but I still think a visit to the doctor's might be a good idea if you're anxious.'

'I didn't say I was anxious.' Ellie stroked Trinity's pudgy arm. 'Anyway, if I say I've got anxiety then they'll think I can't cope.'

'Rubbish,' Carol scoffed. 'They'll see a fantastic mum having the same doubts and fears that all parents have, but who is also having to deal with the after-effects of some health issues and a new environment.' Her tone took on an edge. 'Unless there's something you're not telling me?'

The shiny copper fireplace warped Ellie's reflection like a fairground mirror.

I emptied the kitchen cupboards and I can't remember doing it, she could say. *I dreamed I saw my house on the TV. I thought I heard a baby crying upstairs.* But even Carol, who believed in auras and angels, would baulk at that.

'No,' she said, deliberately upbeat. 'New-house jitters, that's all. Anyway, I saw the nurse this morning when I took Trinity for her injections.'

'That's good,' Carol replied, still with a hint of doubt. 'And have you spoken to Tom?'

She nudged a box straight with her toe. 'He's stressed enough with work.'

'But that's what partners are for. Especially when you're parents. You need to lean on each other, trust each other.'

149

'I guess so.'

'You know so,' her mum said firmly. 'And on that note, I'd better go before Roger thinks I've run off with the waiter. I've got physio later but call me if you need to.'

When they'd said their goodbyes, Ellie listened intently to the sounds of the house. But no matter how she focused her ears, the stranger baby's crying had stopped.

Still, she upped the volume on the TV. Vacuous laughter blared. The camera followed the shiny blonde presenter from the fake kitchen back to the couch. 'Next up, it's our favourite granny in the garden.'

A smiling woman in wellies appeared next to a stunning flowerbed.

The presenter nodded approvingly. 'Look at those perfect roses, will you? Now there's a woman who knows how to look after her babies.'

30. Now

Buzz.

Ellie frowned. What was that? She turned the TV off. There it was again. *Buzz.* Like the rusty death throes of a bluebottle.

'Hello!' a voice called from outside.

Someone stood in the porch, distorted by the dimpled glass, and flipped the letterbox.

'Hi. Hope I'm not disturbing you. It's me, Asha. Diane's daughter-in-law from the playgroup?'

Ellie opened the door. 'Hi, how are you?'

A V-necked tank top and turquoise leggings matched the thin weatherproof jacket tied around Asha's shoulders. Her glowing complexion owed nothing to make-up and tendrils of wavy hair escaping from a topknot followed the curve of her face. Asha was so intensely perfect, she probably sweated Jo Malone.

Ellie tugged self-consciously at her stained T-shirt and wished she had brushed her hair.

Asha grinned. 'I'm good, thanks. I've brought this from Diane.' She offered a tin printed with cheery cupcakes. 'Lemon drizzle. But I can leave it and come back another day if you're busy.'

'No, come in. But you'll have to excuse the mess.'

'You should see my place.' Asha laughed, a genuine throaty sound. 'Like a nuclear bomb's gone off.'

She followed Ellie into the kitchen. 'We viewed this house, you know, when it came on the market. Adam was very keen.'

There was an expandable folder on the chair stuffed with bills and receipts, which Ellie quickly moved to the worktop.

'Have a seat,' she said. 'You weren't at the auction, were you?'

Asha shook her head. 'Don't get me wrong, I think it's a great place, but I don't have the imagination or the energy for a doer-upper.'

'It is a lot of work, but it's largely cosmetic. Sort of,' Ellie said with a rueful smile. 'Do you want tea or coffee?'

'Coffee, please. Black. And how are you finding life on Moss Lane?'

'Quiet. Nice to have more space.' Ellie plated slices of cake and put them on the table. 'We were living with Tom's dad for six months and before that we had a flat in the Northern Quarter.'

'I'm not surprised it seems quiet here.'

Ellie put two mugs on coasters and poured milk into hers.

'We wanted the peace, you know once we had the baby. And I grew up near here. I've always loved the area.'

'Thanks.' Asha wrapped her hands around the mug. 'Is your family close by then?'

Through mouthfuls of lemon drizzle, Ellie explained about her mum moving to Spain and then Asha countered with how much she missed her own family in Sydney and Mumbai. That led on to trading stories about how they met their respective partners. Ellie 'met Tom at uni', Asha 'met Adam backpacking'.

'And you never went home?'

Asha shook her head. 'Got a job in accountancy, had Freddie and stayed. I like it here. Friendly people, green spaces. Miss the beach, though.'

'I bet you do,' Ellie said.

'Mainly miss having my mum around. I love Diane to bits, but it's not the same, is it? And how are you getting on here?' Asha said, gazing around the kitchen.

'Slowly,' Ellie said, straightening the coaster under her mug. 'We're doing as much as we can ourselves. Or rather, Tom and his dad are.'

'As if having a new baby isn't enough work. I'm impressed.'

'Really?' Ellie crossed her arms over her chest. 'There was so much we weren't prepared for with the house. Not just the DIY stuff, either.'

Asha pulled a sympathetic face. 'Diane felt terrible letting it slip about Mary. I couldn't believe no one told you before you moved in.'

'She shouldn't feel bad. Tom already knew; he just decided not to tell me because he didn't want me to freak out.' She flicked her eyes up at Asha. 'Is that the real reason why you didn't put an offer in? Because you knew what had happened here?'

'Crikey, no,' Asha said with a laugh. 'Honestly, I'm far too lazy to pick up a paintbrush, never mind start from scratch. Someone dying here wouldn't have put me off. Does it bother you?'

'I can't deny it creeped me out, especially because of the body not being found straightaway. Still does if I'm honest. But I'm getting more used to the idea and it's made me think …' Pause. 'It's made me think we have more of a responsibility to turn the house into a happy family home. Put the heart back in it to honour Mary.' She tutted. 'God, that sounds so pretentious.'

'Not at all. You want to exorcise the sad vibes, I get it,' Asha said, licking crumbs from her fingers. 'And I know Diane's glad you're here. She says you'll be a breath of fresh air after everything that's happened. New beginnings and all that.'

'I hope so,' Ellie said, draining her tea. 'Did you ever meet Mary?'

'I saw her now and then when I was round at Diane's. Sitting at the bottom of the garden where that rose—'

She waved towards the pile of splintered wood and dead rose bushes. A three-legged plastic garden chair sat on top, like the Guy on a bonfire.

'Oh, the pergola thing has gone. Wow, huge improvement. I never understood why anyone would interrupt that view. Anyway, one time I was jogging on the path in the woods and I said hi, tried to introduce myself, but …' She passed her hand back and forth in front of her eyes. 'Nada. Not that she could have said anything, of course.'

'How come?'

'She didn't talk. Couldn't.'

'Couldn't?'

'A medical condition, that's what Diane told me but I don't know what the actual diagnosis was. Just that Mary used to speak and then after her dad died, she stopped. Some kind of PTSD, I guess.' Asha rubbed her fingertips together, scattering crumbs onto the plate. 'Which is understandable considering she was the one who found his body.'

Another death? Here? Giddy with déjà vu, Ellie stiffened. Her horror must have been obvious because Asha instantly let out a regretful yelp.

'Oh God. He didn't die in *here*,' she said hastily. 'Not in this house. He took his own life out by Moss Pond. It's a local beauty spot, kind of over there.'

Her ponytail swished as she turned to jab her finger to the left of the window.

'Oh,' Ellie said slowly. 'I think I went there on a walk with Trinity the other day.'

Asha grimaced. 'What I should have said was he left a note for Mary and she went out and found him. I'm really sorry, I didn't mean to give you a heart attack.'

'It's OK,' Ellie replied, although her heart was threatening exactly that. 'I think there have been so many now that I'm kind of getting used to the revelations. Has Diane mentioned anything else?'

'You know, the whole topic is a real sore spot,' Asha said. 'People were horrible to her when Mary died. Like she was too stuck up to help or she must have been involved in some way with what happened when she was a kid. But I can tell you, if Diane had known what was going on, there's no way she would have turned a blind eye.'

Oh God. Was there more?

'Turned a blind eye to what?'

'Mary's dad. He was a bully. A serious tyrant.' Pressing the lid on the cake tin, she shrugged. 'Diane knows more than me, obviously – she's lived here forty-odd years. But from what I gather, Mary got pregnant in high school and that was, you know, a big taboo for her big-shot council leader dad and he basically had the child forcibly adopted. Of course, Diane didn't know this until afterwards.'

Ellie turned her mug round and round as Asha spoke. It seemed sad secrets permeated every brick of this house. Everyone she spoke to presented different versions of Mary. They fitted into one another like Russian dolls: the lonely recluse. The voiceless woman. The motherless child. The childless mother.

'And people really had a go at Diane for that when Mary died?' she asked.

'None of the papers named her, thank God, but Uppermoss has its fair share of self-professed witch finders.' Asha whistled slowly. 'Trial by social media. Community Facebook groups, comments page of the *Stockfield Express*. And Norah, the reporter you talked to at playgroup, stirred the pot big time with all that *where were the neighbours?* stuff.' Asha stretched her arms above her head. 'And on that note, I'd better pick Freddie up. Are you coming to playgroup tomorrow?'

'Definitely.'

'Great. We can talk about happier topics then.' She put her jacket on at the front door. 'For what it's worth, I don't think it's pretentious what you said about putting the heart back into this house.' She looked around the hallway. 'Nowhere deserves it more than this place.'

31. Now

Despite the heavy clouds that had gathered outside and the heavy topics they'd discussed, Ellie's mood had lifted. Asha was down-to-earth, easy company and only lived down the road. Definite friend potential.

The wind moaned around the side of the house and down the chimney, scattering soot onto the hearth as Ellie sank onto the sofa and, with a wary eye on Trinity in the Moses basket, plumped a cushion for her back. Next on the list for today: online shop. She peeled the last banana and picked up her phone.

But while she located the Tesco app, her mind went back to Asha's comments about Mary. It felt strange to know so much about someone's death and yet so little about their life. Rude, even.

While Mary Brennan lingered in the pink bathroom, the fake wood candelabras and the petri-dish-effect carpets, she was part of their home. She was part of their *life*.

Ellie clicked on Google. Hesitated. Folding the banana skin carefully on the coffee table, she stared at the screen. Did she really need to know any more? Once those worms started slithering out of the can, you couldn't stuff them back in if you didn't like where they went.

But if strangers were going to keep springing revelations on her, it would be better to discover every skeleton herself, right? Be prepared. Lessen the shocks.

Her finger made the decision by entering Mary Brennan + father + scandal in the search box. Hundreds of results instantly appeared as outside, the rain that had been threatening all morning began to fall.

'In Plain Sight: lessons to be learned from the Stockfield scandal.'

Ellie skimmed through search results littered with the 'leafy suburb of Uppermoss', 'affluent area', 'behind closed doors' – phrases beloved by the media until a by-line caught her eye. An in-depth exclusive by Norah Aryan. 'Scandal in Suburbia: dead councillor William Brennan named in historic bullying and abuse inquiry.'

She tapped the screen and, settling deeper into the sofa, began to read.

Who was disgraced former councillor William Brennan?

William Brennan was a well-known local figure. Born in 1933 to a teacher father and housewife mother, he attended the local grammar school and, after the war, secured a post with the local council's planning department where he met his future wife, Elizabeth 'Betsy' Walker. They bought a plot of land and built number six Moss Lane on it. Sadly, Betsy died less than two years after giving birth to their only child, Mary. Becoming a widowed father to a small child did not hinder Brennan's progression through the ranks and, by 1971, he was deputy leader of Stockfield Council.

However, dark secrets lurked under this respectable façade. Allegations of widespread corruption had begun to surface as early as the mid-Seventies. Rumours of a culture of bullying and abuse circulated around the chambers of Stockfield Town Hall. Most worrying of all, were the allegations of sexual misconduct made by junior members of staff against members of Brennan's inner circle. Time and time again, they fell on deaf ears or were quickly quashed by Brennan, a man who seemed, at the time, untouchable. These were different times, times when influential men everywhere had the power to brush the misdemeanours of their friends under the carpet.

Perhaps this situation would have continued indefinitely but for the brave actions of a whistle-blower who described Brennan as a cruel bully and a tyrant. Although no charges were brought at the time, the spotlight turned on members of the council and an internal investigation began. Accusations levelled against the council leader, William Brennan, included bribery, violent attacks on staff, embezzlement and, most sickening of all, turning a blind eye to abuse in council-run children's homes. However, the investigation folded with no further action. So why, only weeks later, did William Brennan take his own life at Moss Pond, a beauty spot a short distance from the Brennan family home? Did guilt finally get the better of him?

His daughter, Mary Brennan, only eighteen years old at the time, continued living in the house on Moss Lane until her own recent death. She consistently refused to co-operate with both the initial and the most recent inquiry.

In the light of other reopened historic cases, Greater Manchester Police has been re-examining the evidence submitted at the time and a recent appeal led to many other witnesses coming forward. Numerous council employees and former children's home residents have also given evidence against the few surviving members of the council. For the majority of the others, William Brennan included, justice will be served posthumously.

Rain lashed against the window and the late-afternoon gloom wrapped around the house. Ellie switched the light on. There was a sharp plink, like the flick of a fingernail on glass, as one of the candelabra bulbs burned out. She glanced at the ceiling, blinking in the sudden brightness that blazed like her anger.

A traumatised woman who literally did not have a voice

'refused to co-operate with the inquiry'. How could Norah, a woman with daughters of her own, write such self-righteous victim-shaming bullshit?

Six decades earlier, Mary's mother must have stood in this spot and kissed the velvety skin stretched across her daughter's unfused skull bones. She must have murmured the same promises to love and protect her, not for a moment imagining the tragedy of her own death. And Mary finding herself scared and pregnant under the roof of a tyrannical father. Had she cradled her own child here years later before he or she was taken away?

Ellie's heart ached for the two women.

She held Trinity close and impossibly long eyelashes tickled her. So vulnerable, so tiny, so dependent. She lowered her face to the baby's. But those round navy-blue eyes swivelled upwards, to the smooth white plaster and the nursery above.

A room with bolts on the outside in a house owned by 'a cruel bully and a tyrant'.

Poor Mary. Tears leaked from between Ellie's closed lids and ran down her cheeks.

'I will always keep you safe from harm,' she whispered, burying her nose in the sweet, fresh hay scent of Trinity's scalp. 'You know that? No one will ever touch a single hair on your head. I will protect you and—'

The lights flickered.

There was a bang.

Ellie screamed.

32. Now

Darkness. Absolute darkness. And a smell, like fireworks or just-pulled Christmas crackers.

Gunshots? No, of course not.

Light switch. Flick. Flick. Nothing. The red standby light plinked off on the TV. Ellie scrabbled for her phone and found the torch icon. Fragments of glass sparkled on the coffee table. She tipped her head back: the candelabra held six brass bulb holders. Each one no longer containing a bulb.

'Shit!'

Using her fingertips, she delicately examined the exposed areas of Trinity – scalp, face, hands – and blew gently across her face, trying to dislodge any dust. No sign of glass, thank God, but she needed to get her in the bath to be sure.

It was even darker in the hall. No reassuring lights winked from the boiler or the appliances in the kitchen and Tom's phone rang out until his voicemail kicked in.

This is Tom Hartley. Please leave a message.

'Are you nearly home? The bulbs exploded in the lounge and I don't know where the fuse box is.'

Her own phone beeped – only one per cent battery remaining. She hung up, switched the torch off.

No power, no heating. No phone. A shudder engulfed her.

The only light was a beacon glow from Diane's conservatory. She whispered, teeth chattering against Trinity. 'Come on, baby girl. We're going next door.'

She trailed her fingers along the hallway's cold wall. And

stopped. Tom had stripped the embossed wallpaper and repainted. So why did her imagination feel ridges and swirls?

The darkness eddied around her. A cold panic trickled down her spine and she groped frantically at the front door handle.

Where were the keys?

Her blind fingertips probed the wicker basket, assessing and discarding objects.

No keys.

Even the faint glimmer of streetlamps had been snuffed out and darkness wrapped around her so tightly she couldn't tell if her eyes were open or shut. Silence swelled and her mind convulsed with the terror that someone – or something – was about to materialise.

Like the air above a candle, the darkness shimmered. She slid to the floor and drew her knees up as close as the baby's body would allow and, like a child herself now, she huddled small and motionless, knowing if her foot sneaked out of the blanket, a monster would grab it.

Blood pulsed in her ears and she knew she wasn't alone.

She held her breath. The house held its breath.

Upstairs a voice began to sing very quietly.

'Mary, Mary, quite contrary,
How does your garden grow?
With silver bells and cockle shells …'

Ellie moaned, pressing her hand over her eyes until colours exploded against the lids.

'And pretty maids all in a row.'

33. Now

'I think I got all of it,' Tom said, pressing the pedal to open the bin. The broken glass tinkled off the dustpan. 'But we haven't got any spare bulbs. I'll get some tomorrow.'

The radiator threw out a force field of heat, but the bone-deep chill remained. Ellie clasped the hot mug so tightly her fingers burned.

'Trust me. Someone was upstairs,' she said for the third time. 'I heard singing.'

Tom closed the bin lid with a soft thud and set the dustpan on top.

Carefully, he pulled out a chair and sat by her side, his knee touching hers as he rubbed the circulation back into her still frozen hands, one at a time.

'You're completely safe now. I've checked and there is no one in the house apart from us.'

The boiler hummed. The innocuous sounds of a house getting on with the business of being a normal family home. Not a place where things exploded and invisible women sang in the dark.

She gnawed the skin around her thumb, teasing a tiny strip with her teeth. The irony was the fuse box had been inches away, to the left of the front door. If instead of freaking out, she'd reached a hand across, she would have felt the little brass knob of the meter cupboard.

Which is exactly what Tom had done when he'd finally managed to push the door open. Terror had slowed time to a crawl although in reality, only a few minutes had passed before

Tom found her cowering in the dark. With a flip of the tripped switches, the hallway flooded with light.

'It's OK, love,' he had said, gently helping her to straighten her stiff, cold legs. He took the baby and with a sniff, said, 'Someone needs their nappy changing.'

His reassuring smile jarred with the deep frown line between his eyes.

The aftermath of terror turned her hands to claws and it was only when he winced she remembered the deep scratches on his arm.

'Please don't take her to the nursery.'

'She needs a bath and a clean nappy. Clean clothes. All those things are upstairs,' he said. 'Why don't you come with me and we'll do it together?'

With Trinity cradled in one arm, he started up the stairs. After a second's hesitation, Ellie followed.

But there really was nothing to be scared of. Everything in the nursery – the baskets, the mat, the sad-eyed teddies – sat neatly under the pastel glow of the night-light. Benevolent jungle animals gazed down from the wallpaper. Hanging on the back of the nursing chair was the fleece hoodie she'd been wearing earlier. Cosy, warm, and scented with fabric conditioner.

In fact, the only note of discord came from the baby bawling on the changing mat. The nappy sagged almost to her knees and when Tom unfastened the Velcro, foul sludge oozed out.

'Why don't you have a lie-down for half an hour?' Tom suggested, reaching for a wipe. 'Go,' he said, kindly when she didn't move. 'I've got this.'

When Trinity was clean and safely tucked up in their room, Tom led Ellie back into the nursery and to the night-light.

'Can you see the timer?' he whispered, tapping the controls at the side.

She nodded. If that's what the clock icon next to the on/off switch symbolised, then yes.

'Well, when the bulbs blew, they tripped all the fuses downstairs, but the sockets stayed on up here. It must have triggered the night-light to start playing.'

His lips grazed her forehead. 'What I don't get is why you didn't go round to Diane's. I'm sure she wouldn't have minded.'

'I told you. We were locked in and I couldn't find the keys.'

'But they were in the basket.'

When she replayed her fingers frantically sifting through pens, coins, sunglasses, earbuds, a plastic sack for a charity collection, all the flotsam of ordinary life, the keys hadn't been there.

Had they?

'I'm not surprised you missed them, though,' Tom continued. 'It was pitch-black.'

'What made the bulbs blow?' Ellie said.

Tom shrugged. 'I don't think the wiring is dangerous, but maybe it's more knackered than we originally thought.'

'Knackered but not dangerous,' she said. 'Is that me or the electrics?'

There was a short pause.

'Me. You. The house. Everything,' he answered. 'Look, Els, it might be a good idea to go to the doctor's tomorrow to change your blood pressure meds to one without so many side effects. I know they said it'd settle down when you got used to them, but it doesn't seem to be happening.'

Ellie was about to say, 'No thanks' or 'Don't start, I get enough of that from Mum'. But then she had a fleeting vision of herself, wild-eyed, numb with cold. Ranting about keys and mysterious singing.

Change the medication? That simple?

'Yeah,' she said. 'I think that's a good idea.'

In the lounge, the floor lamp cast a warm glow over their baby sleeping peacefully in the basket. Ellie squashed a cushion against the arm of the sofa and sank onto it. On screen, the chateau couple stared horror-struck at the scaffolded exterior wall. The camera zoomed in on a cordon of orange tape and panned across fallen clumps of render, like plaster scabs picked off to reveal old brick. Standing next to a *Danger: Falling Debris* sign, the presenter made a show of jamming his hard hat down.

'Buying this grand wreck was a huge leap of faith for this young couple and I admire their passion for seeing the potential beyond the crumbling façade. But still.' He let out a regretful sigh.

'Every day presents new problems, new setbacks. I hope I'm wrong, but I can't help thinking that these two young people have no idea of the horrors still lurking within these neglected walls.'

Hours later, hours after they'd gone to bed, something woke Ellie.

A woman's voice, whispering so close to her ear the soft breath caressed her skin.

'Pretty maids all in a row.'

Ellie's eyes sprang open and she scrabbled back against the headboard. Except the headboard had gone. She flung her arm out but her groping hand couldn't find Tom's reassuring bulk. Instead of the warm cocoon of duvet, cold air wrapped around her.

A moan escaped her throat and she frantically scanned the shapes emerging from the gloom. Where were the chest of drawers, wardrobe, the Moses basket?

She flailed wildly, desperate to find a landmark to orient herself. Reaching, grabbing, kicking. Invisible objects scuffed across the floor. Her left elbow connected with something solid and darts of pain fired to her fingertips. She grasped her arm with the other hand, hugging it to her hip.

Then there was the sound of footsteps. A door creaked and Tom's voice came out of the darkness.

'What's going on?'

The light switch clicked and she blinked in the sudden glare. His silhouette filled the doorway. It took a few seconds more for the familiar shapes of the kitchen to register.

She was sitting on the floor facing the table with her spine pressed against the drawers. There was the boiler. The fridge. The pile of bills.

'Are you all right?' Tom said.

She bit her lip, hard, trying to quell the rising panic. How had she got down here?

'Come back to bed,' he said, shutting the cupboard doors. 'We can sort all this in the morning.'

'All this', she realised, was the contents of the kitchen cupboards. Packets and tins, old Tupperware, place mats and assorted jumble littered the floor. When she didn't move, Tom squatted down on his haunches.

'Come on, love. It's freezing down here.'

'Where is she?' she gasped, digging her fingers into Tom's arm.

'She's fine. She's upstairs asleep in our room.'

'Not Trinity. The woman.'

Tom rubbed his eyes and stifled a yawn. 'It's just a dream, love. Let's go back to bed, eh?' She held on to his arm and he helped her up the stairs, murmuring all the while: 'That's it … come on … everything's fine.'

Trinity slept on in the basket, her lips pursed in an 'o'. Ellie laid her hand very softly on her daughter's chest and felt the reassuring patter of her heartbeat against her palm.

The toilet flushed, water ran and then Tom's quiet footsteps came back into their room. He held a glass of water and rummaged in his bedside drawer as he spoke.

'Els, we can't go on like this,' he said. He popped two paracetamol from the foil packet and swigged them down. 'We're both going to be ill at this rate.'

'I'm sorry,' she said in a small voice.

He folded her into a hug. 'Doctor's tomorrow. Let's get it sorted. I know that must have been terrifying for you.'

His hand slid over to cradle her face and she felt his thumb rub rhythmically against her cheek.

'Let's talk about it in the morning,' he said finally, getting under the covers.

Less than a minute later, Trinity started to cry.

Tom moulded the pillow around his ears but Trinity's lament swelled to don't-ignore-me pitch and he started to get up.

'I'll take her in the nursery,' Ellie said, already grappling her arms into her dressing gown.

She faltered at the end of the bed. *Nothing to be frightened of. No one there,* she told herself.

As Trinity sucked, every part of Ellie strained to believe Tom's explanations. The timer started the singing. She'd missed the keys in her panic. As hard as it was to admit, she must have started sleepwalking again. She knew it made sense.

But an insistent voice clamoured against all the rationality, because she had heard the night-light's rendition of 'Mary, Mary' a hundred times before.

And every time, the vocalist had been male.

34. Then

'Come on, you know it makes sense.' Mia placed both hands on Ellie's windowsill at Henderson Hall and gazed out at the grey Manchester sky. 'Attic of a Victorian house overlooking the park. Kind of. One minute from a tram stop and' – Mia did jazz hands – 'only a couple of streets from the boys.'

'It does sound good,' Ellie said cautiously.

'Good?' her friend echoed in mock incredulity. 'It sounds abso-bloody-lutely perfect.'

Ellie unzipped her rucksack. 'But I told you: I've got a lecture at eleven.'

Mia glanced over her shoulder. She was wearing denim dungarees and holding an apple. Her eyes were ringed with black liner and she'd wrapped her hair in a Fifties headscarf, like a glamorous Rosie the Riveter.

She bit into the apple. 'Can't you get the notes from someone? I only got us in because she's showing the flat underneath at nine thirty.'

'Can't you ring her back and see if we can go later?'

Exams were coming up and while Mia and Danny's portfolio work had them up all hours of the night, Ellie's course required her to hit the books, same as Tom, and it hadn't left much time for flat hunting.

'It's the perfect flat in the perfect location. And I've already told the landlady we'll be there. We can't let it slip through our fingers. Come on. *Please?*'

The thing about Mia was her enthusiasm always hooked you

in. Even now, with revision lectures and reams of tiny, scribbled notes calling, Ellie found herself replying, 'Give me ten minutes.'

A little under half an hour later, they alighted at Victoria Park, walked across the main road and up a side street lined with trees where once grand Victorian homes had been swallowed by the expansion of the universities and divided into flats.

'This one,' Mia said, coming to a halt outside number twelve.

There was no denying the house had seen better days. A few of the railings were missing and the garden wall surrounded a courtyard filled not with flowers, but tarmac, patches of bare soil and numbered wheelie bins. Ivy cloaked the façade and the stained glass in the front door had a crack running its entire length.

'Do we buzz or what?' Mia said, her finger hovering over the entry bells.

Ellie was about to answer when the door swung open and a woman in leggings and a Mickey Mouse sweatshirt poked her head out. 'Help you?'

'Yeah, I'm Mia. We spoke on the phone about the top-floor flat.'

The woman got a packet of cigarettes out and moved past them onto the steps. She jerked her thumb inside.

'Flat six up the stairs. It's open.'

She clicked a lighter. 'I'll be down here.'

'Thank you!' Mia sang out, taking the stairs two at a time.

Ellie followed at a slower pace. Not that she was expecting much, but the wobbly banister, grey with the fingerprints of long-gone tenants grossed her out as did the huge cobwebs slung like dusty hammocks in the ceiling corners. But the wide communal hallway had a mosaic floor under the carpet of pizza flyers. And she had to admit, the proximity to Tom was a major selling point.

'Servants' quarters,' Mia said, her voice reverberating down the tiled stairwell. 'It's fab.'

Despite being sequestered at the top of the house, light flooded in through a pair of balcony doors. Admittedly, the textured wallpaper could do with a coat of paint, but at least there were no visible stains on the carpets and the cooker and fridge seemed reasonably new. Both bedrooms had double beds and wardrobes and the cramped bathroom lacked a bath, but the shower looked decent enough.

'Check out that view,' Mia said, turning the key on the double door that led to the minuscule balcony.

'I'm not sure you should go out there,' Ellie warned, peering at the narrow iron base. 'It looks dodgy.'

'Nah. Solid as a rock,' Mia replied.

She grabbed the top rail and the entire structure rocked. Tiny pieces of masonry rained down, exploding into dust when they struck the tarmacked front yard.

'Shi-i-t,' she said stepping back inside, eyes almost popping out of their sockets. She laughed breathlessly and laid her hand on her chest.

Ellie shot her friend an *I told you so* glare.

Unperturbed, Mia twanged the washing line strung between the furthest railings. 'At least it's somewhere to hang your knickers.'

'I don't know,' Ellie said. 'I don't think it's safe.'

Mia pulled the door to and locked it. 'Then we don't use the balcony,' she said. 'But come on. Location, price, size … everything else is spot on, right?'

'Compared with some of the dumps on offer, I guess it's not too bad.'

Mia perked up. 'Really? Shall we tell her we'll take it then?'

Ellie looked at the view. She could almost see Tom and Danny's flat behind the trees. Positivity surged through her.

'Yes,' she said firmly. 'Let's take it.'

35. Now

Ellie had lain awake until the cold grey dawn broke, feeling energy, hope, patience … every positive emotion trickle from her. And now, staring at herself in the health centre's loo mirror while Trinity howled, she added self-esteem to that list. She washed her hands then folded a paper towel to a point and wiggled at the foundation coagulating in her pores.

In the beige waiting room, Tom jiggled Trinity on his lap, her wet cheeks crimson with sustained crying. The other patients flipped through ancient magazines or checked their phones and pretended to ignore the noise.

He leaned across. 'How do I get her to stop?'

'Do I look like a professional baby whisperer?' Ellie hissed back.

Tom raised his eyebrows. 'All right.'

'Well, don't you think if I knew, I'd already be doing it?'

Two seats away, a man coughed a dry bark of irritation and shook the pages of his newspaper.

'I'm going to take her outside, see if that helps,' Tom said. 'If I'm not back when you go in, make sure you tell the doctor everything this time.'

'What do you mean?'

'The nightmares and the sleepwalking.' Using the pad of his index finger, he smoothed a crease out of Trinity's red corduroy pinafore. 'Maybe mention Willow Lodge. The PTSD. Mia.'

'This has nothing to do with her,' she hissed and turned away to signal the conversation was closed.

A buzzer sounded. The bad-tempered man tucked his newspaper under his arm and strode under the Exit sign. Holding

Trinity against his chest, Tom followed and Ellie half-imagined a collective sigh of relief from the other patients as peace descended. She let her gaze wander over the beige Wall of Woe.

Temper troubles?

Can't sleep?

Overthinking the past?

Yeah. All of the above.

Forget the pain of losing a parent. Forget falling in love or buying a home or starting a family. Whenever anything major happened, Tom always managed to circle it back to Mia. He was obsessed.

Eleanor Wight Dr Monk Room 4 flashed on the screen. Ellie picked up her bag.

Not obsessed, cursed. That was the word.

Dr Monk was young with a sleek chin-length bob and make-up-free skin glowing with health. Vitality radiated from her, as though she could backflip over the desk at any moment.

'Good morning. Please take a seat.' The doctor crossed her legs at the knees, smoothing the wrinkles from her skirt. 'How can I help?'

Ellie breathed slowly. 'I've got a two-month-old baby, and my partner thinks I'm not coping as well as I could.'

'And do you think you're not coping?'

'Hmmm,' she replied. 'Sometimes.'

The doctor scrutinised the computer screen, reading notes Ellie couldn't see.

'You had pre-eclampsia and your baby was born early, right?'

'She's fine now, though. Doing really well.'

Tapping on the keyboard, Dr Monk continued, 'That's good. But it's still a huge trauma. So, is there anything specific that you're struggling with?'

Ellie hesitated, the desire to unburden herself muddied by remembering Willow Lodge and Alina. The baby taken into foster care. As nice as this woman seemed, with one phone call she could have Trinity spirited away quicker than you could say 'unhinged mother'.

'Well, I am quite moody,' she began slowly. 'And when I do manage to get some sleep, I have bad dreams. And I'm so forgetful.'

Dr Monk nodded encouragingly. 'In what way?'

'Losing my keys. Going into a room and forgetting why. And sometimes I feel so useless.'

The pressure of tears built behind her nose.

'Why useless?'

'Like I'm letting her down when she cries. I can't work out what she wants me to do.'

'Do you feel tired?'

'Constantly.'

Dr Monk's smile was conspiratorial. 'Tired doesn't begin to cover it, right?'

'Not even close.' The truth erupted in a sudden honest rush. 'I don't get it. I used to work all day, go to the gym after, then the pub and I'd be fine. Now some days I hang the washing out and I need a lie-down. And I can't complain because my partner works such long hours.' She looked up at the ceiling, willing the tears not to fall. 'I've never done less and I've never felt more exhausted.'

Dr Monk's neat fingernails clicked on the keys. 'You said you were moody. Can I ask if you have experienced any thoughts about harming yourself or the baby?'

Careful.

'God, no.' She exhaled sharply. 'Never. If anything, I'm the total opposite. Ridiculously overprotective.'

The doctor sat back and twiddled her pen. 'What about feelings of depression?'

Shaking her head, she replied, 'Nothing like that. I'm just … knackered.'

Dr Monk placed the pen on the desk. 'You've had major surgery, hormonal changes, lack of sleep plus a new baby to deal with. These things make huge demands on you physically and mentally. I've met countless mums in here and I can assure you I have yet to meet one who doesn't share some of those concerns. The forgetfulness and mood swings are your body's way of saying take it easy.'

She moved the mouse and ran her finger down the PC screen. 'Now I can prescribe you something to help you to sleep better, but it would interfere with breastfeeding.'

For a moment, Ellie let the temptation of deep, unbroken sleep linger in her mind. Then she shook her head sadly. 'I can't.'

'Then I think you need to take off as much of the workload as you can. Is there anyone who could help?'

'My mum should be here, but she broke her leg. She'll be coming as soon as she can.'

'Well, my advice is to forget about perfect. Stick to the bare minimum to keep yourselves fed and clothed and rest whenever you can. I'll just check your blood pressure while you're here. How are you finding the tablets?'

The cuff tightened.

'I actually think they're part of the problem. They give me nightmares.'

The doctor smiled and the pressure released.

'Still a touch on the high side, so I wouldn't be happy with you coming off them altogether, but we can try one with fewer side effects. In the meantime, try to eat healthily, get plenty of rest. See how you get on over a week or so and then ring for a follow-up appointment.'

She wasn't losing her mind! A weight lifted with each step towards the waiting room. No one was going to take Trinity away from her. All she had to do was change the medication, go home, forget about perfect and practise being a normal mum.

But the other members of her little unit weren't in the waiting room. Or the foyer. The toilet lock read Vacant, so they weren't having a pit-stop in the baby changing room either.

The exit doors slid open as she approached and she spotted Tom with his back to her, jogging a mercifully quiet Trinity while deep in conversation on the phone.

'Tom,' she called, walking towards them. 'Tom!'

He turned his head and she heard him say, 'Gotta go, Tan. Speak to you later.'

He popped the earphones out. 'Sorry about that. How did you get on?'

Ellie stroked the baby's cheek. 'Really well. She said it's normal, especially after a difficult birth.'

He opened the back door and secured the baby in the car seat.

'Good, good,' he murmured, then breathed in, ready to say something else. Then didn't.

Driving home, the crowds and shops soon dissolved into the blur of passing countryside. Forget about perfect. Now there was a mantra Ellie could live by. No matter what social media claimed, real women didn't inhabit a bubble of yoga, white jeans and gleaming marble worktops. Popping that bubble felt good. The weight in her chest lightened a little more as she curled the green prescription slip between her fingers. Not a revival of mental health issues. Side effects. A fact confirmed first by a midwife and now by a doctor.

Tom rubbed the back of his neck.

'So did you mention your time at Willow Lodge? Or the PTSD?'

Her buoyant mood deflated like an old balloon. 'Not this again.'

From the back of the car came a grunt. A familiar smell filled the car.

Ahead, a man stood next to a truck, the dashboard rammed with hi-vis vests, newspapers and takeaway cartons. As their car approached, the man turned his lollipop from green to red.

STOP.

'Great,' Tom said with a sigh and pressed the brake.

Ellie reached behind to give the baby's hand a gentle squeeze, the tiny fingers wonderfully squidgy under her fingertips.

'This little piggy went to market; this little piggy stayed at home.'

Tom drummed his fingers on the steering wheel a couple of times.

'You literally never mention Mia or the PTSD and whenever me or your mum do, you shut down.'

Here we go again. 'Because it's not relevant. There's no point dragging up the past.'

Trinity's fretful cries increased. A magazine article she read had explained how the pitch was calibrated to get on your nerves. An evolutionary move, apparently, so babies couldn't be ignored.

'It's not actually in the past though, is it? Not really,' he said. 'I'm worried it's starting up again. I'm worried about *you*.'

'Mia has nothing to do with what's happening now.' Ellie folded her arms to underline the point.

The workman nonchalantly flipped the sign to GO in a way calibrated to get on Tom's nerves.

It worked.

'Wanker.'

36. Now

'Can you get two plates out?' Tom said. He was grating cheese onto the chopping board. Four slices of toast browned under the grill.

They had driven the rest of the way home in tense silence only broken by the endless pinging of Tom's work phone. Panic always made Ellie snappy and not much panicked her more than discussing Mia. Especially with Tom.

Without replying, Ellie opened the cupboard by the fridge. Random tins, shoe polish, organic weedkiller ... no plates.

'They're in the one over the microwave,' he added. 'With the mugs. Sorry, I didn't have time to put everything back straight.' He took the toast out and liberally sprinkled cheese on the top. 'We can have a proper sort-out at the weekend.'

She put the plates down. Tom rattled the grill pan, dropping shreds of cheddar all over the bottom of the oven.

'Listen,' he said. 'We really do need to talk. And before you do that thing where you change the subject, please will you hear me out.'

He dug the butter-smeared knife *straight into the jar of chutney.* Ellie clenched her fists.

'So, about last night,' he said. 'I'm worried that your PTSD could be flaring up. Which is totally understandable, given what you've been through with the pre-eclampsia.'

She picked a shred of cheese from the plate. 'I'm fine.'

'But you weren't fine when I found you in the dark in the hall,' he said. 'Or when you're sleepwalking. Or hearing mystery women. All the stuff about keys and lost babies. Look, I've done some research and there is such a thing as postnatal PTSD and it's much more prevalent in women who have experienced traumatic births or who have a history of mental health issues. All your symptoms fit. But things have moved on since you were at Willow Lodge. There's absolutely no stigma around mental illness and no need for you to keep suffering like this when professional help is available. You can be well again; you just need to accept there is a problem and ask for help. They are the first steps to recovery.'

Toast forgotten, she pushed her chair and the legs scraped across the floor. 'Well, thanks for the TED talk, Dr Google, but I'm good.'

His brow puckered. 'Don't be like that, Els. I'm trying to avoid things going back to how they were.'

The unspoken 'after Mia died' expanded to fill the silence that followed.

A surge of adrenalin ripped through her tiredness and she wanted to pick Trinity up and run away. Throw the front door open and just leave him, leave the house, leave all of it behind.

Instead, she rooted in her back pocket.

'According to the doctor, it's actually all about side effects.' She slapped the prescription slip onto his palm. 'See? Not crazy. Don't need therapy, just different medication. Pick these up for me and I'll be sorted.'

He read then folded the paper, slowly scoring the crease with his thumbnail. When he spoke, he sounded concerned.

'No one is calling you crazy, and no one's judging you for having a history of mental illness, love. I don't know why you've got such a bee in your bonnet about it. I just wish you'd ...' He pinched the bridge of his nose. 'OK. Mia's death had a massive impact on both of us and I don't want us going through that again. Especially not now when we've got Trinity to consider. I'm doing the best I can for all of us. Anyway, I'll go to the chemist now.' As he stood, he pushed his plate across the table. 'Here, I'm not hungry. You can have mine.'

She stayed in the kitchen long after Tom's tyres had spun in the gravel and he'd driven away. The slump following the argument left her shaky, craving carbohydrates. She polished off the cheese on toast then crammed a chocolate digestive in her mouth. Still holding the packet, she slumped on the sofa.

Forget about perfect, Dr Monk had said.

Well, that was one piece of advice she could certainly follow. She demolished another biscuit, then another, and stretched full-length on the sofa, curling one hand under her head. Her reflection, rippling and distorted by the copper canopy, drew her eye to the mantelpiece and Anita and David's card.

A traitorous part of her almost wanted Tom to make the connection between the sleepwalking, the anniversary and Trinity's birth. Once he'd joined the dots, the true picture would emerge and at last, Ellie could purge herself of the toxic guilt she'd carried inside for ten years. But then what? Her mind spun 180 degrees. The relief would be short-lived, lasting until Tom slipped seamlessly from boyfriend to detective mode. Quizzing and questioning. Probing. Judging.

Exactly as he was doing now, in fact.

Her stomach cramped with dread. Had he already made the connection?

37. Now

Of all the bullshit wisdom people loved to share, 'sleep when the baby does' had to be the most bullshitty. Ellie shuffled up the nursing chair, wincing as her neck cricked painfully. She'd barely opened her eyes before the phone pinged twice in rapid succession.

The first message was from Jess. *Are you OK for lunch this week? X*

And the second from Tom.

Been to the chemist for your blood pressure tablets. But now at work. Sorry. Emergency x

She waited for the threat of tears to pass before she dialled him, but it went straight to voicemail.

Muffled whimpers came from the cot. The hump of blanket undulated and the whimpering turned to a whine that scraped down Ellie's eardrums like sharp fingernails. Hard to believe that such a gorgeous child was capable of such an ugly sound.

'Mummy's here,' she said.

Get up! she ordered her legs. *Things to do.* But her traitorous body refused to co-operate. It was so warm, so seductive, so easy to sink deeper into the cushioned seat. Babies were tiny dictators, torturing with their endless, shrieking demands. Perhaps if Ellie closed her eyes and stayed completely silent, Trinity would let her snatch another half-hour. Perhaps if she—

Her phone buzzed against the changing table mat. Tom.

'What's going on?' he said, his tone worried but controlling it. 'I'm on the baby app now and ...'

The loud hiss of a coffee machine drowned the rest of the

sentence. As it faded, other sounds filtered in: music, conversation, laughter.

'Where are you?' Her voice came out a croak.

'Costa,' he said.

'Costa?' she echoed, suddenly alert. 'You said you were going to work.'

Chair legs scraped across a hard floor. Crockery clinked. A woman laughed, very loud, very close.

'I am at work. We're just picking up something to eat.'

'We?'

'Me and Tanya,' he replied, impatient now. 'Els, look at the baby, please?'

When had the baby started screaming? She got up clumsily from the chair. Her legs were stiff, as though she hadn't moved for a while. The baby kicked, face turned to the wall. Where were the nappies? The wipes?

Robotically, she changed Trinity's nappy. A hundred excuses for sleeping through the baby's screams sprang to her tongue, vanishing before she could choose the right ones. Meanwhile, Tom sat in Costa. With Tanya. Watching her.

She draped a onesie over the camera's spying eye. Tom's voice came out of the phone, sounding echoey and weird. She couldn't talk to him now. Wincing, she rubbed her knuckles into the small of her back. Falling asleep in that chair was a bad idea.

The dark stain had returned, oozing from under the cot and, despite the warmth, Ellie shivered. She hesitantly dabbed the carpet with her toe then felt her sock. Dry. A shadow, then, not a stain. From the corner of her eye, the green light glowed faintly through the fabric of the onesie and she withdrew her foot, scooped the baby up and slunk out of its spying range.

The pinhead light continued to glow. So, she was still being watched.

Was Tanya self-consciously sipping her latte while Tom

frowned at his phone screen? Or were they thigh-to-thigh on a squishy sofa, shaking their heads at her lacklustre parenting?

Watching her.

Criticising.

Conspiring.

38. Now

Ellie screwed the lid on the nail polish and puffed sharply on her fingertips. Dove grey to match the new ASOS top hanging on the front of her wardrobe. Trinity lay gurgling on their bed, flexing her tiny fingers towards the plush giraffe Tom danced above her.

'Give me a ring when you're finished and I'll drop you back home,' he said. 'I've already told Tanya I'll be nipping in and out today.'

Tanya.

She took a slow breath and carefully scraped a hair's breadth of polish from a cuticle.

Within an hour of his I'm-in-Costa-with-Tanya call yesterday, he'd returned with her new blood pressure pills, two bags of groceries and an apology for sounding like a TED talk. Ellie, too exhausted to argue, let him feed the baby while she crawled back to bed. But sleep refused to come. Instead, she stared at the repeating swirls on the Artex ceiling and reasoned with her brain's Department of Paranoia.

Tom's one of the good guys. He would never do anything to hurt me.

Oh come on, Paranoia had sneered. *You know that's not true.*

'We'd better get going soon,' Tom said, swooping Mr Giraffe to tickle Trinity's nose.

'Give me ten minutes.'

Tom took the baby downstairs while Ellie pulled on black opaque tights, wiggling the waistband over her belly. Buttoned a black A-line skirt and slouched into the grey top. She tied her hair back and tugged a few strands loose at the front.

From the bathroom, she could hear him chattering away to the baby. Speedily and efficiently, she applied make-up to the face reflected in the mirror. Her real face was hidden behind a zombie filter, all thready eyes and lifeless skin, and while she couldn't conjure up eight hours of sleep, she did have the miracle of make-up. Foundation, concealer, a big swipe of blusher, two coats of mascara that did little to minimise her puffy bags. Not miraculous, but better. Human, at least.

She pinned a smile in place and went downstairs.

Half an hour later, they pulled level with a queue of blank-faced commuters. Tom jumped out and opened the boot before Ellie had even taken off her seatbelt.

At the rumble of an approaching bus, the queue shuffled forward.

'Are you sure you don't want me to park up and wait?' he said, clicking the car seat onto the buggy. 'Or walk you to the office?'

'We'll be fine.' She kissed him. 'Don't worry.'

He sped away just as the bus pulled into the bay, leaving Ellie and Trinity on the pavement. Diesel fumes clouded around them. Normal women in office clothes talked, shouted, laughed. There were signs of Christmas everywhere: a stall selling hot chestnuts. A busker singing 'Fairytale of New York'. Cheerful Santas hung in shop windows and shoppers clutching multiple bags streamed by. She leaned against the Perspex bus shelter. Breathed. Adjusted Trinity's fleecy hat, tucked her blanket in. Breathed again.

For almost five years, her daily commute had taken her along this street. Now as she wheeled the pram past bars and stores that used to swallow her monthly pay, it was like strolling down a street on the moon. But the street hadn't changed – she had.

Keep going. Nearly there.

Craftmags occupied the whole of the second floor of Regal House. She paused at the ramp next to the steps. Behind that soot-streaked façade, her replacement sat counting the hours till she could slip away.

The double doors slid open. Same magazine titles fanned on the coffee table, same plastic ferns no one ever bothered to dust, same drab pictures on the same drab walls.

If the walls of Regal House could talk, they would bore you to death.

Different receptionist, though, currently delicately picking at a spot with her long, pointed fingernail.

'Ellie Wight, here to see Jess Peel at Craftmags.'

The girl handed her a visitor pass and pointed at the lift. 'Fourth floor.'

Trinity goggled at the lift's mirrored interior.

'Going up,' Ellie said.

Jess was waiting outside Craftmags' office. She rushed towards them, arms held wide.

'Hello, you,' she said, hugging Ellie. 'Wow, you look fantastic. And Trinity!' She hitched her skirt up slightly to kneel by the buggy. 'I can't get over how much she's grown since I saw her in the hospital.'

On the other side of the glass wall, colleagues vigorously tapped keyboards and chatted on phones. The first to see her was Liz from accounts, and Ellie returned her enthusiastic wave with a smile.

Olly, Layla and Sarah from design gathered to coo over the pram, followed by Penny from HR. Boring work and toxic building aside, Craftmags wasn't a bad place to work. With one notable exception.

'Hello, Joan.'

The line manager offered an insincere smile. 'Well, this is a surprise. And this is …?'

'Trinity.'

'How cute,' Joan said in a tone that implied the exact opposite. 'And can I just say I think it's great you're not rushing to lose the baby weight. So refreshing.'

Before Ellie could reply, Fehmida from IT asked about the renovation project and that led to everyone chipping in with their own nightmare builder stories. Joan's smile stretched thinner and thinner, until she said loudly, 'I hate to spoil the fun, but ...'

Jess pulled her coat from the back of her chair and wound a long, striped scarf around her neck.

'I'm going out for lunch now with Ellie. See you later.'

Joan's smile set like rigor mortis. 'Don't be late back. Deadlines don't meet themselves.'

The pair of them waited until they were in the lift before collapsing in fits of giggles.

'I hate to spoil the fun,' Jess said, mimicking Joan's tight-lipped delivery. 'Bollocks. She *exists* to spoil the fun. She is like the Funspoiler General.'

'Not rushing to lose the baby weight,' Ellie said, inspecting her side view in the lift's mirrored interior. She smoothed her palms down over her belly.

'Take no notice of the cheeky cow,' Jess said. 'Do you fancy Nexus?'

Nexus meant birthday lunches, Christmas drinks, post-work rants about management. The perfect venue for networking, flirting, bragging, moaning and eyeballing the competition.

As Ellie manoeuvred the buggy through the doors, she realised Nexus *also* meant narrow aisles, no space to park a buggy, and, wow, had it always been this *loud*?

In short, there wasn't exactly a 'No children allowed' sign hanging over the counter. But they didn't really need one.

'What can I get you?' Jess shouted over the music.

'Sandwich?' Ellie said lifting Trinity onto her lap. 'And a latte, please.'

While Jess joined the queue at the counter, a group of suits and beards snagged the last table next to them. Really there was only seating for two, but they shoehorned a couple of extra chairs around the small table. One of them sat next to Ellie, spreading his knees so wide he nudged the buggy.

'So, I told Marcus he could fuck right off. And then keep fucking off and then fuck off some more,' he said.

This was clearly the punchline to some long-winded anecdote and the other three burst into raucous laughter. Trinity squealed and the man who told Marcus to fuck the fuck off turned around.

Angry heat flooded Ellie's face. She unhooked Mr Giraffe from the buggy and frantically waggled him.

'So, tell me,' Jess said, putting the tray on the table. 'How's it all going?'

On cue, a sustained grumble escaped from the baby.

Jess held a finger out to grab. 'Oh no, what's wrong, beautiful?'

The mirrored wall reflected Manspread's friend, beard groomed like a show pony, glancing over as Trinity rooted noisily at Ellie's chest.

Flipping between embarrassment and anger, she tried, one-handed, to shuffle the changing bag out of the base of the buggy. Manspread's lolling leg didn't move.

'Excuse me,' Jess said loudly. 'Could you let my friend get her bag?'

A few heads craned their way and he twisted completely, turning his back on Ellie.

Jess flung her knees apart in exaggerated imitation, adding gruffly, 'Me man. Me massive balls. Me need *all* room.'

Ellie laughed, but the effort of holding a squirming Trinity in place while unfastening her bra was making her sweat.

'Thanks,' she said, pulling a large muslin square from the bag. 'I haven't tried this in public before.'

'Did your mum used to hold the towel up on the beach so you could get your cossie on?' Jess said, holding the top corners of the shawl like a shield. She deftly tucked the hem under Ellie's exposed bra strap. 'Anyway, how are things with balancing the house and the baby and everything?'

Trinity began to feed and Ellie awkwardly picked up her own sandwich. 'It's been a pretty steep learning curve.'

'I can imagine. Must be lovely though, having this little angel at home.'

'It is. And also tiring and scary. And everyone has an opinion on what you're doing. I took her to a mum and baby group and all the other mums were so together. And this' – she pointed at her wet eyes and blew her nose on a serviette – 'is another drawback.'

Jess smiled sympathetically. 'I can't speak from experience, but I'm sure even the mums at your baby group feel the same sometimes. Maybe they've just learned to hide it. Trinity's OK health wise now, isn't she?'

Ellie patted the table. 'Touch wood.'

'Well, then. If she's fine, it's proof you're doing a fantastic job.'

'Thanks.' Ellie winced as Trinity shifted position. 'She is perfect but I'm a sleepless hormonal wreck.'

She took a packet of wipes from the bag and leaned Trinity against her shoulder, dabbing at spat up milk.

Jess said, 'Here, do you want me to hold her so you can have your coffee before it goes cold?'

Ellie passed first the shawl then the baby over gratefully. 'How come the temp didn't stay?'

'Joan said she was rude.'

'*Joan the Moan* called someone rude?'

'Yeah, irony overload,' Jess said and launched into an anecdote about the temp's 'lengthy' toilet breaks. Ellie's body relaxed into the sofa, craving the everyday office gossip she had been so desperate to escape from.

After five blessedly normal minutes, the muslin slid from Jess's lap to the floor. A passing waitress stooped to retrieve it. Her long dark ponytail swished and Ellie glimpsed high cheekbones, a straight nose, and huge, thick-lashed eyes.

Jess spoke, but the words didn't penetrate. Ellie froze. Time rolled back ten years.

Mia.

The thought had barely formed before the waitress straightened, her face distinctly her own. When she spoke, her lips made different shapes from Mia's. She held the shawl out, her forehead creased.

'Are you all right?' she said in accented English. 'Can I help you?'

Ellie's hand trembled. 'No, thanks. Sorry.'

'Well, let me know if you need anything.'

Taking out her cleaning cloth, the waitress slalomed through the tightly packed tables. Ellie pushed the plate with her half-eaten sandwich to one side and folded the muslin.

'Are you OK?' Jess said. 'You've gone really pale.'

The men at the adjacent table broke into leery chuckles. Ellie looked up, caught sight of her reflection.

And her throat went dry.

The mirrored wall showed the patrons of the crowded café. Framed in a tableau, Manspread and friends' reflections eyed the waitress's neat behind as she cleared a table. Jess's shiny hair bent over Trinity. Her own face stared, open-mouthed.

And one seat along, a figure in black lifted a dirt-streaked finger to her lips.

Crockery rattled and a cup fell, spilling dregs of coffee as Ellie's thighs rammed the table edge.

'Ellie!' Jess cried, the baby almost slipping from her arms. 'What's wrong?'

For a fleeting second, she thought she might be dying. Over the rushing in her own ears, she heard the coffee machine, murmured conversations and ragged breaths. *Her* ragged breaths. The mirror reflected a hushed crowd of shocked faces, but the seat next to Jess was empty.

'What's wrong?'

Shaking off her friend's kind hand, Ellie stuffed the baby's things into the buggy. 'Give me the baby. Now. Can you bring the pram?'

With her daughter clamped to her chest, she barged sideways through tightly packed tables, past the waitress who clearly wasn't Mia still holding a tray piled with empty mugs and plates.

Outside, the pavement rose up. The sky pressed down. Pedestrians swarmed, crushing her. Cold sweat prickled her upper lip.

Get away. Get away. Get away.

The pram appeared through the door, followed by Jess, pinched and frowning as she tapped her phone to life.

'I'll just tell Joan I'll be late back. Give me a—'

Ellie leaned against the window of a takeaway. 'I'm fine, honestly. I'll walk up to meet Tom at the police station.'

Rich smells of meat and fat wafted from inside the tinsel-decked kebab shop and she swallowed rising nausea.

Look normal. Smile. Lower baby into pram. Fasten straps. Breathe. Walk.

'Tell me what happened in there,' Jess said, keeping pace through the crowd. 'Are you feeling ill? You hardly touched your lunch.'

'I thought I saw someone, that's all.'

Ellie moved aside to let a double buggy pass. A pair of red-faced siblings screamed in unison and the other mum, brown smudges under her eyes, gave her a grateful smile.

'Who?' Jess said.

A young woman with headphones and cropped hair swerved around them, her heels clacking a sharp rebuke on the pavement. Not that long ago, Ellie had been that girl, irritated by dead-eyed pram pushers.

'A neighbour. But I made a mistake.'

'OK, good.' Her friend's eyebrows knitted together. 'That aside, what the hell has this neighbour done to you to make you react like that?'

The concrete and glass façade of Regal House loomed a few yards ahead.

She plucked the first random excuse that presented itself. 'Something and nothing. A stupid row about the garden. Anyway, it wasn't her, so it doesn't matter.' Her cheeks already flamed with panic, so it wasn't hard to fake embarrassment. 'I'm so sorry. Look, you'd better go before Joan has a meltdown.'

Jess narrowed her eyes for a few seconds, as if weighing up what to do. Decision made, she stepped forward to hug Ellie. 'I'm only a phone call away. Anytime for anything.'

At the top of the steps, she turned and held her fingers to her mouth and ear like a phone, mouthing 'Ring me.' Ellie nodded and smiled in return, tears prickling as her friend vanished inside.

She set her shoulders. She hadn't seen Mia. She hadn't seen the woman. Too much noise and too many people had confused her, that was all. The walk would do her good. Clear her head.

But weaving the buggy around bollards and bins and idiots who refused to move only raised her stress levels. By the time she reached the police station, her head, her arms and her bladder ached.

She scanned the car park, but Tom's car – their car now – wasn't among the ranks of parked vehicles flanking the entrance.

Please don't have gone out.

She bent down to straighten her tights where they'd gathered at her ankles and when she looked up again, a woman tapped quickly down the concrete steps. Sharp in a silky blouse and tailored skirt, with a neat cap of hair and red lipstick, she was an American cop show detective. A world away from the crumpled colleagues she'd met at the Christmas do who wore Next trouser suits and cried after too many pints.

Ellie dabbed at her sweat-smudged mascara and smoothed down her hair. She was about to head for the entrance, when a man jogged out, waving a folder.

Tom.

Ellie retreated behind a parked transit van. Too far away to

191

hear the details, she watched the woman shake her head in a rueful *Can't believe I forgot that* gesture and Tom laugh in return.

Radiating from this easy exchange was a shared sense of belonging; the camaraderie that went with working difficult cases and unsociable hours. Even from this distance, Tom looked transformed.

He looked *happy*.

39. Now

Could that *goddess* be new Detective Constable 'she's a diamond' Tanya?

From the hiding place behind the van, she watched the other woman get into a sporty red car and drive towards the exit barrier. As it neared, Ellie quickly flipped her hood up and fussed with the pram blanket. Only when the car had disappeared into the distance did she risk a glance at the station. Doors closed. No sign of Tom.

Inside the station, the desk clerk tapped his pencil against a crossword. A half-eaten sandwich rested in a cardboard box next to him and despite the Perspex screen that separated them, the smell of chutney churned her stomach. Half a dozen people sat in the waiting room, staring at their phones.

There were no signs of Christmas in here.

'Can I help you?' He sounded as bored as he looked.

She leaned close to the intercom and spoke in a low voice.

'Hello, I'm here to see DC Hartley.'

'Can I ask what it's about?'

'I'm his girlfriend.'

He gestured to the row of moulded plastic chairs, the kind that don't invite you to hang around, picked the phone receiver up and took up his pencil.

In the absence of a baby changing room and with an 'Out of Order' sign on the disabled loo, she tried to fit the pram through the door marked 'Visitor WC'. But no matter how much she jiggled it, the pram was too wide and she ended up awkwardly reversing out.

'Back in a minute,' she whispered to Trinity and parked her outside by the door.

In the cubicle, she had just enough time to turn the lock and sit down before her bladder exploded. A moan of relief escaped her and she leaned forward, bracing her elbows on her knees. Level with her eyes, a poster advertising a helpline listed forms of emotional abuse: economic control, rejection, criticism, gaslighting. A blurred woman sat with her head in her hands under the caption: 'He made me think I was losing my mind.'

There was a quiet knock and Tom's barely audible voice. 'Ellie, are you in there?'

'Won't be a minute,' she said, getting up quickly and flushing the loo.

She washed her hands quickly and shook them inside the dryer. Some anonymous visitor had written 'You don't belong' in black pen on the tiles.

'You shouldn't have left her,' Tom said under his breath when she came out, drying her hands on her skirt. 'We get all sorts in here.'

'I was absolutely desperate.'

He lifted Trinity out of the buggy. 'Next time, ask the desk to mind her.'

Behind the screen, the clerk impassively peeled his banana.

'Roy,' Tom said into the grill, 'if anyone asks, I'll be back in an hour. OK?'

He walked a few feet away, held his mobile to his ear. 'Tanya? I've just got to pop out. What time are you back?'

Pause. Laugh.

'Yeah. Quick as I can. Bye.'

He slung his jacket on the back seat. Buckled the baby in. Folded the pram. Got in the car. He said something about Jess. Something about the baby.

Tom and Tanya.

'Ellie?' He leaned across the steering wheel, forehead almost touching the windscreen to see past her. He squeezed her knee.

'I said you should have rung me. You look knackered.'

'Cheers.'

'I didn't mean it like that.' A light flashed on the dashboard and he put both hands back on the wheel. 'I'd better fill up.'

He'd replaced the cap and was striding across the forecourt to the kiosk when his phone rang. Not his work phone, but his personal phone.

Still facing the windscreen, she stretched her arm behind her and fumbled for his jacket pocket. The ringing stopped as she slipped it out, not once taking her eyes off Tom. The glass doors slid open to let him in and he joined the blessedly long queue at the till. A beep alerted her to a message.

Tanya missed call.

Ellie's mouth went dry.

The phone burned in her hand. Should she? Terrified of what she might find, more terrified of not knowing, she shuffled lower in the seat. Her finger hovered over the PIN screen.

A woman came out of the petrol station. Tom moved up the queue.

She pressed the call log button and the names of friends, family, colleagues, tradespeople appeared. Ellie. Simon. Danny. Dave Carpets. Tony Gas Fitter. Dad. Carol. Tanya. Tanya. Tanya …

Tom stood at the counter now. Ellie went to switch the phone off, but her shaking finger caught the browser button, opening the last search.

Postnatal mental illness, types of

Jumbled words and phrases leapt from the screen: *psychosis, depression, PTSD.* Swiping through the open tabs revealed more: *Auditory and visual disturbances. Paranoia and confusion. Irrational behaviour. Sleepwalking. Memory loss. Previous history of mental health, traumatic birth. Mothers can reject or even harm their babies.*

Everything inside her head rearranged itself.

Tom had googled *this*?

A flash of movement caught her eye. She clicked the phone off and stuffed it back in his jacket just as he appeared at the door.

'I got you a treat,' he said, dropping a Bounty into her lap. 'Your favourite.'

Mothers can reject or even harm their babies.

Fury rose up in her throat, choking her with a taste of bile. Then just as quickly, it drained away, taking the last of her strength with it. Everything, even her bones, dissolved into the upholstered seat. What was the point?

'You haven't said how you got on with Jess,' Tom said, oblivious.

Mothers can reject or even harm their babies.

With considerable effort, her mouth shaped a response. 'Do you mind if we don't talk? I've got such a headache.'

They sat without speaking. She pressed her forehead against the cool window. Drizzle fell on one dreary field after another while the handle of her bag scored deep lines in her palms.

Her phone dinged with a message from Jess.

I'm worried about you. Call me? xx

Irrational behaviour. Paranoia. Did Jess think that too? Did everyone?

When they arrived home, Tom took the pram out of the boot and carried the sleeping baby up to bed while Ellie remained in the hall, hardly aware of where she was.

'I'll take the afternoon off,' Tom said, startling her. 'I can stay here with you two. Maybe you could get some sleep?'

The stair carpet had disguised his creeping footsteps and now he stood on the bottom step, watching her with … concern? Curiosity? The angle of the light carved strange shadows on his face and for a moment, he looked like a stranger.

Mothers can reject or even harm their babies.

'Go to work.' She forced a light smile. 'Honestly, a couple of paracetamol and a little sleep while Trinity's napping and I'll be fine. Go.'

'Tell you what, I'll pick up some work and bring it home.' He scratched under his shirt collar. 'Be right back, OK?'

He leaned in to kiss her.

Mothers can reject or even harm their babies.

At the last second, she stepped away from him and he ended up kissing thin air.

40. Then

Ellie blinked, hardly daring to look again in case she'd imagined it. But there it was: the red 78%, boldly circled three times.

A bubble of happiness swelled inside her. Yes! Students flowed around her as she walked – no, *floated* – clutching the essay in both hands. Evenings out with Tom or Mia she'd turned down. Hours spent at the library. Late nights, early mornings. All worth it now, because of this.

Slipping the heavy rucksack off, she sat on a low wall by the bike shelter and took her phone out.

'Guess what, Mum?' she said before Carol could get a word in. 'I got seventy-eight per cent. That's a distinction.'

Carol's tone radiated pride. 'That's wonderful news, love. You really deserve it, you've worked so hard. I'm just on my way to see your dad, actually. He'll be chuffed to bits when I tell him.'

Every week without fail, while she wiped down the headstone and replaced the flowers, her mum conducted in-depth one-sided conversations with Dad. And maybe it was weird, having chats with the dead, but for half an hour every Sunday at least *something* filled the Dad-shaped void.

'I'd better go,' Ellie said, shouldering the rucksack. 'I'm meeting Mia and Tom in the refectory.'

Dad. The bubble of happiness popped and she dropped back on the stone seat, ambushed by loss. That's how grief operated. One minute, you were chatting on the phone, happy with your essay grade and life. The next, misery slammed into you. Winded you with the awful truth that no matter how much you need them, no one's love comes with a lifetime guarantee.

The rucksack's thick nylon straps had rubbed against her bare skin. She wiggled her hand underneath, trying to ease the pressure, then took it off. That's when she saw them.

Hemmed in on all sides by the lunchtime crowd, Tom and Mia sat so close they were almost touching. Ellie froze, breath suspended in her lungs as she watched. He spoke and she laughed, punctuating each burst by slapping her hands on the Formica table. Head down, her ponytail swung and her body shook with mirth. They looked so at ease. So right.

Ellie's heart gave an extra little beat.

From this distance, if you didn't know better, you'd think they were a couple.

41. Now

True to his word, she had barely enough time to feed and change Trinity and try to create order from the chaos of the kitchen cupboards before Tom returned with his work laptop, a boot full of supermarket bags and an over-the-top solicitous attitude that immediately set anxiety humming through her veins.

'Why don't you have a bath?' he said. 'I'll sort the baby.'

And now, as warm water lapped over her arms, legs, back, every part of her felt chewed up, spat out, lifeless. Except for her memory, which feverishly replayed Tom and Tanya's meeting over and over, like a GIF.

She runs out. He catches up with her. They both laugh. Tom looks happy.

Contradictory thoughts shuttled back and forth.

He's being too nice.

He's always nice.

He's cheating.

He would never cheat.

The water closed in and she swished from side to side, fanning her hair. When she surfaced, wet strands clung to her cheeks. She hooked them behind her ears, lowered her head to the edge of the bath and stared at a jagged line in the ceiling plaster directly above her.

A vision zipped in unannounced: Mary Brennan lying here, looking up at that crack growing year after year. Did she give birth alone on this chequered lino? Lock herself in here to cry when they took her baby away?

Ellie hooked her fingernail under the edge of the plug and

teased it out. Why did Mary never replace the broken chain? She lifted a towel from the hook Mary must have used. Did Mary slip on the lino; steady herself on the edge of the basin like this? Did she have a bath on the day she died? Feel dizzy and stagger out, only to collapse on her bed?

There was a soft knock. 'Everything OK?' Tom said.

Her 'Fine, thanks. I've just got out' sounded pretty convincing.

'I'll make a start on tea. Give me a shout if you need anything.'

Tom had left a pile of dirty clothes in a heap in the corner. When Ellie bent down to pick them up, she felt a sharp twinge in her back. Bloody Tom. Why couldn't he put things away? She fastened her dressing gown and gingerly crossed the landing to the nursery.

She dropped the onesie and tights in the laundry bin. The camera's pinprick light told her the parent unit was still on downstairs. No problem. If he were watching now, he would see a capable woman plumping cushions and straightening a row of teddies. A capable mother humming the melody to a lullaby while she carefully smoothed the cot sheets and straightened the blanket.

'I'm worried about her.'

Tom's murmur came out of the speaker. It was on the tip of her tongue to say, 'Oh God, what's happened?' when, with a jolt, she realised he didn't mean the baby. He wasn't talking *to* Ellie at all, he was talking *about* her.

In the pause that followed, she retreated slowly and unobtrusively out of the camera's range. She hardly noticed the frame digging in her spine as she squeezed into the gap behind the door, listening intently.

'Sleepwalking and nightmares. Confusion,' Tom continued in response to a question Ellie couldn't hear. 'Constantly cleaning.'

The cheek! She couldn't hold in the quiet tut. If he didn't leave dirty clothes and muddy footprints everywhere, she wouldn't *be* 'constantly cleaning'.

Tom's 'uh-huhs' and 'yeahs' were punctuated by longer pauses while whoever was on the other end of the phone chipped in their comments. Something went *tink*. Plates. Glasses. A cupboard door closed. 'Look, she'll be down in a minute, I'd better go.' Pause and a sigh. 'Yeah, me too. I hate the thought of leaving her when she's like this.'

Sounds of cooking resumed. Rattling pans, running water. Meanwhile, Ellie gripped the doorframe, barely registering the sharp poke of the hinges.

Leaving?

42. Now

Tom had chopped a few cherry tomatoes, arranged slices of cucumber and shaken pre-washed lettuce onto two plates.

'Help yourself,' he said, placing a steaming bowl of pasta on the table next to two serving spoons.

'This looks nice,' she said with only the tiniest wobble marring the sentence.

He didn't seem to notice.

Night swallowed the view of the garden. Even the aromas of warm tomato mingled with basil and mozzarella couldn't make her dry mouth water.

Then Tom laid his fork very precisely on the plate.

'Ellie, I need to talk to you about something,' he said. 'It's important.'

Despite his confident tone, he seemed ill at ease. He steepled his fingers together and put them to his lips. She nodded, put her own cutlery down and slid her shaking hands under her bottom.

So, after over a decade and everything they'd been through together, this was how it ended. At the kitchen table, in their first family home. Ellie closed her eyes. Waited for the axe to fall.

Tom drew in a deep breath. 'I got a message from Jess today.'

She opened her eyes.

'My Jess? Craftmags Jess?'

'She sent me a DM on Facebook. She said you got spooked in the café then ran out. Something about a neighbour and the garden which I didn't really get. She's really worried about you. So am I. And Carol.'

'You've spoken to Mum about me?'

'I rang her while you were in the bath.' He reached across to grab her hand. 'I'm sorry, but I had to talk to someone. I don't know how to help you.'

'While I was in the bath tonight?' she said slowly, drawing her hand back.

He nodded.

A wave of relief made her dizzy. She bent down and fiddled with her sock so he wouldn't see the sudden rush of tears.

But the emotion was short-lived. Rage at his hypocrisy lit her words with fury.

'So worried you take on all the overtime at work?'

'I am sorry about that. It's just so busy,' he said, sounding genuine. 'A few more days, I promise, this will be over and I'll take all my leave then. Look, about what Jess said—'

She cut him off. 'So busy that you went to Costa with Tanya?'

His brow crinkled, nonplussed. 'What's that got to do with anything? I'm talking about you and me and Trinity, love. This is important. What Jess said—'

'As important as sitting in Costa with Tanya when you should have been at work?'

He regarded her and she could almost hear his brain trying to select the right response. She watched him take a deep breath. Let it out slowly as he took a beer from the fridge.

'Trust me, at home, queuing for a butty … wherever I am, I am *always* at work. I have horrors up here' – he stuck out a finger and circled his temple – 'that I will never be able to unsee.'

His phone buzzed in his back pocket. Foam bubbled down the sides of the bottle as he set it down with a clunk and swiped to decline the call. Not before Ellie had seen *Tanya* on the screen.

'We can't go on pretending everything's fine,' he said, mopping up the spilled beer. 'Jess said you ran out of the café without even easting your lunch.'

By 'we' he clearly meant 'you'. As in *you're* paranoid. *You're* delusional. *You* might reject or even harm our baby. Images flashed. Alina, the baby-less mother. The blood-smeared wall at Willow Lodge as vivid as if it had happened that evening.

'Are you saying I'm not fit to look after her?'

'Of course not.' The tip of his traitorous tongue darted left to right, licking foam from his lips. 'You're an amazing mum – anyone can see that.'

'I guess you'd be happy if social services took her off us. Considering you never wanted her in the first place.'

Bullseye.

He flinched. 'That's not fair. Just because she was a surprise doesn't mean I didn't want her.'

Back in the Northern Quarter, with the glare of car headlights and neon shop signs, there was no such thing as true night. But here on Moss Lane, the dark square of window framed their separate anguish in a twisted parody of a family photo.

His phone pierced the silence. He hesitated, checked the caller ID, then walked out.

Which was a good thing because right at that moment, she hated him.

43. Then

Headlines boasted that Manchester was hotter than the Sahara Desert, but Mia and Ellie's flat was, in fact, hotter than the sun. Even with every window open, the air hung motionless, thick as steam and smelling of hot tarmac and diesel fumes. Mia fanned herself with a copy of *Cosmopolitan*, dirty bare feet dangling off the arm of the leather sofa. She was watching the Wimbledon Women's Final and every time the camera panned the crowd, she leaned eagerly forward, searching for her parents.

'There,' she said, pointing excitedly at a pair of oversized sunglasses and a straw hat.

Ellie pulled a half-empty packet of fish fingers from the freezer, letting the cold air fan against her skin.

'Do you want these for tea? They'll be out of date by September.'

'Bin them. We should treat ourselves on our last night. What time are you meeting Tom?'

'Around nine, when he's finished work.'

Mia shifted on the warm leather. 'OK, if we eat before then I'll stay with Danny. Tom stays here and we all meet up at the train station in the morning.'

'Sounds like a plan,' Ellie said brightly. Half-empty jars of jam and curry paste clinked as she walked to the door, picking her keys up on the way.

In the heart of London, the *thwack thwock* across the net was accompanied by a rising murmur from the crowd. Mia, glued to the screen, wordlessly stuck her thumbs up.

Walking into the hall was like entering a different climate. The tiled walls cooled the air and as she descended, her sticky flip-flops slapped on stone stairs. Someone had propped the front door open with a pile of out-of-date *Yellow Pages* and the slight draught stirred the dusty cobwebs.

Tomorrow morning she and Mia would lug their cases and bags down these steps and not come back until the autumn.

But she didn't mind leaving the flat for the summer. She didn't mind leaving Manchester. She didn't mind going home. She didn't even mind spending the holidays serving all-day breakfasts in Debenhams.

What she minded was that when Mia left for Surrey tomorrow, Tom would be going with her.

The plan stemmed from a conversation they'd had at the Union in May when Tom had been bemoaning his lack of a work placement.

'I have sent my CV literally everywhere,' he said. 'And the one offer I had has fallen through.'

'Why didn't you say something before?' Mia said, putting her pint down to reach for her phone. 'You must know my mum's a psychologist, right?'

And that was why from this Monday, Tom would spend three weeks booking clients, straightening magazines, watering plants, and observing the practical application of psychological theory at The Goldsworthy Partnership.

Which would have been perfect.

Except.

For those three weeks, Anita and David had invited him to stay at their beautiful farmhouse. With them. And Mia.

A lot could happen in three weeks.

Flies buzzed around the wheelie bins and the hot vomit stink made her cough. She wiped her hands down her shorts, batted away a bluebottle intent on exploring her ear. Gross.

God, it was so hot. Even the tarmac was melting.

Back in the flat, Mia hadn't moved from the sofa. Her legs were a deep glossy brown from weeks of lying in the park and, without meaning to, Ellie's traitorous imagination pictured them wrapped around Tom. A night at the pub. Too many drinks. Would they tell her?

A low rumble of anticipation rippled through the Wimbledon crowd. The ball flew faster and faster.

Back and forth. Back and forth.

The breathless air thickened. Sweat ran to the backs of Ellie's knees.

'The tension is incredible,' the commentator murmured.

'You OK?' Mia said without taking her eyes off the screen.

'I'm fine,' Ellie said, turning away.

Her boyfriend and her best friend. She could trust them, right?

Thwock thwack went the ball and the TV voice followed to her bedroom.

'At this point, it's anyone's game.'

44. Now

Maybe the baby sensed the earlier tension or maybe she was plain cranky. Whatever the reason, Trinity cried with clockwork regularity. At 12.37, 1.37, 2.37 Ellie stumbled from bed as the fractious syllables rose to mingle with Tom's snores and the creaks and groans of the house.

In the end, it was pointless going back to bed. She put Trinity down in the cot and curled up, exhausted, on the nursing chair. But when sleep finally arrived, it was fragmented and disrupted by dreams.

Mosswood was a painted backdrop to the motionless garden, and kneeling by the broken trellis and branches Tom had piled for burning, was a figure.

The sweet decay of dead roses cloyed the air. And yet Ellie didn't feel scared. 'Who are you?' she said, her breath clouding against the cold glass.

The figure stood. With her head dipped, two long black hanks of hair hid her face.

'What do you want?' Ellie said.

The dream woman lifted her arms and extended her palms in the pearlescent moonlight. Blackened patches of dirt clung to the skin and nails.

The next thing Ellie knew, she was in the kitchen with Tom beside her, stroking her shoulder.

'Wake up,' he said in soothing tones. 'You're sleepwalking again.'

Sweat dried on her chest. She pulled her dressing gown tight against the sudden chill.

Night slunk in through the open back door. The lino was glacial under her feet. The kind of cold that filtered through your pores to turn your bones to ice.

'Why'd you open the door?' she said.

'I didn't. You did.' He turned the key and screeched the bolts across. 'It was open when I came downstairs. Let's go to bed. We can talk about it in the morning.'

Light spilled from the bathroom and she heard Tom yawning uncontrollably as he peed. Ellie got back into bed. And did a double take.

Her bare feet were filthy.

Drying mud caked the soles and the faded red polish on her big toenail had a crusting of black. She rubbed her heel, brought fingertips sticky with mud to her nose, inhaling the ghosts of old leaves, wet earth. At the sound of the toilet flush, she quickly hid her legs under the duvet.

'Try to get some sleep, love,' Tom said, joining her. He switched off the bedside light and almost immediately fell asleep.

Meanwhile, the house groaned then stilled as Ellie watched shadows move around the walls as she searched her memory. Curling up on the nursing chair, yes. But after that? Nothing. No going downstairs. No unlocking the back door. No walking through the garden.

The dream began to fade, but the fear remained.

45. Then

From the day she returned to Manchester in September, the dynamic had changed. Thanks to their part-time jobs and Tom's summer placement, the two of them only managed to snatch a few days together here and there over the summer. And this was the final year, so the pressure of portfolios and exams loomed on the horizon. But on top of that, things felt, well, different in a way Ellie couldn't put her finger on. Tom continued to be – what had Mia called him? Predictable. Steady. Reliable. While Mia and Danny, were, as ever, the volatile opposite.

They'd only been back one day before Mia stormed home from the boys' flat and shut herself in her room. But these spikes and dips characterised their entire relationship. So while this dip wasn't good, it was hardly unprecedented. And yet … from the moment Ellie walked through the flat door, something simmered.

It wasn't her imagination.

Something had changed.

46. Now

'Morning,' Tom said, setting a cup of tea on the bedside table.

She wriggled upright. 'Aren't you going to be late for work?'

'I've taken the day off,' he said and patted her leg. 'I thought we could have a mooch round the shops. That retail park off the bypass has got an IKEA and a B&Q. We could have a look at wallpaper, get some bits and bobs. Maybe go for some lunch?'

As he pulled his socks on, the shifting weight tugged the duvet higher up the mattress. Ellie drew her feet up in renewed shock at the dried mud streaking the bottom sheet. She snuggled deeper under the duvet, trapping it between her feet and kicking it flat to hide the sheet.

'I didn't think you were off till the weekend,' she said.

He shook his jeans legs straight where they'd ridden up.

'I thought we should spend a bit of time together. Tanya said she'd cover me.'

Tanya. A clawed fist squeezed Ellie's stomach.

She tipped her chin upwards, faux casual. 'Yeah, sounds great.'

'What time is the playgroup thing this morning?'

Balls. She'd totally forgotten.

'At ten.'

He leaned down and kissed her lips. And although he set his voice to 'nonchalant', his eyes remained on 'concerned'.

'I can give you a lift to the village. Even come in if you like.'

'I'm perfectly capable of walking to the village on my own, thanks,' she snapped.

Tom looked worn out. 'I know, love. I'm just trying to help.'

Silence stretched. She swallowed her pills and swished tea

around the mug, conscious of the tightness of dried mud between her toes. *Go*, she willed him. *Go, and let me shower.*

'Right,' he said eventually, picking his hairbrush up off the chest of drawers. 'I thought I'd get the supermarket shop out of the way now, save you doing an online one. I can take Trinity with me. She'll enjoy it; they've got those trolleys with the baby seats in that make it like a pram. It'll give you a break. Why don't you have a lazy morning, get some more sleep?'

Oh God.

It was that too-broad smile that gave him away.

He hadn't taken time off because he wanted to spend time with them. Or because he wanted to go shopping or to let her get some sleep. He certainly hadn't done it because he was worried about her.

He'd done it because he was afraid of what she might do.

Ellie dropped on the pillow and pressed the heels of her hands against her eyelids until Tom and Trinity left.

She had never felt so tired.

Flying to Sydney on the first leg of their trip of a lifetime, she'd expected it when, after twenty-four hours cramped in economy, they instantly crashed out in the hostel and despite the other backpackers, the heat and the clunk-clunking fan, she fell into the deepest sleep of her life.

Motherhood was like permanent jet lag. Worse even, because every day, you landed in a new country with zero knowledge of the language or local customs. The maps were wrong, the guide books skimmed the surface and there was no sipping margaritas round the pool when you woke up.

Focus on the present, that's what the therapist at Willow Lodge said. Make your mind your friend, not your enemy.

The shower offered more of a trickle than a cascade. Watching the dirt from her feet swirl down the drain, she tried not to think about last night's sleepwalking. Tried.

She picked a small wet leaf from the plughole then scraped

her damp hair into a low bun. The mirrored cabinet revealed bags under her eyes roomy enough for a fortnight in the sun.

God, what she wouldn't give for two weeks in the sun. A week. A day.

Failing that, caffeine would have to do. But there were splotches of mud across the kitchen floor. Some undefined smudges and smears, but others clearly made by feet.

Untying and retying her trainers took more energy than she had available, so treading the backs down with each step, she went outside. Howard and Tom had trampled a makeshift path between the house and the rose beds and Ellie yawned her way down it now. Steam from the coffee mug rose into the air blurred by the remnants of early morning fog.

One of the stepping stones tipped slightly with her weight. She put a foot on either side and rocked gently, as if wiggling a loose tooth. Scattered clods of soil and foot-sized holes confirmed what she already knew: she *had* sleepwalked out here last night. Her heart sank. The dream must have been her brain's way of trying to make sense of it.

Except none of it made sense.

Even at Willow Lodge, the sleepwalking had been just that – walking. She'd just nodded off in one place and woken up in another. Not unlocked doors and emptied cupboards.

A crow flapped low and close, startling her so the mug almost slipped from her grasp. Her pulse skittered.

'I'm fine. Everything is fine,' she announced to the garden. 'Perfectly, perfectly fine.'

But it wasn't. A low hum, like the air around a pylon, plucked at the hairs on her arms, and her scalp felt strange, prickling with static as though she'd rubbed against a balloon. Phrases swarmed up from the darkest corners of her mind. PTSD. Postpartum psychosis. Depression.

Mothers can reject or even harm their babies.

47. Now

The pram wheel caught on a stone and jolted forward.

'Sorry, sweetheart.'

The baby's lips made a popping sound and her eyelashes fluttered, but she didn't wake.

'You're going to have fun at playgroup today, playing with the other boys and girls,' Ellie continued. 'And Daddy will still be at home when we get back, won't he?'

Unless Tanya clicked her fingers, obviously.

When Tom returned with the baby from the supermarket, the beds had been stripped, the washing machine churned and not a trace of mud remained on the lino. In fact, the only task Ellie still had left was erasing the unease that crackled like static through her. A storm waiting to break.

She had half-expected him to insist on accompanying her to the village. But she was alone, pushing the pram down the road that was still so cold the ground glittered. Sparkling droplets strung like fairy lights on bare branches and the smoke from unseen wood burners hung in the air.

A woman in dazzling white jeans herded three small children towards the doors just as Ellie entered the church grounds. *Whoa.* She ducked behind a banner advertising the Christmas fete, but not quick enough to avoid Norah catching sight of her.

'Hi,' Norah said loudly. 'Great, I was hoping we'd catch up.'

'Nice to see you again. Had a good week?' Ellie said, then mentally kicked herself as the other woman launched into the next instalment of 'why my life is so much harder than yours'.

'Three kids under three,' she concluded. 'Don't do it.'

'I know,' Ellie said, folding the pram. 'One's nothing, right?'

The sarcasm slid straight over Norah's Teflon-coated narcissism. She flashed her vampire's grin and said, 'Let's grab a coffee. You can tell me all about life on Moss Lane.'

Norah's children ran onto the play area as soon as they were through the door. Sensible creatures. Their mother put her handbag on a seat and coat on the adjacent one.

White jeans and a white jumper with three kids? Ellie picked at something crusty on her T-shirt and performed emergency CPR on her self-esteem. Remember what Dr Monk said: *forget about perfect.*

'I'll save you a chair while you sort out … remind me.'

'Trinity,' she offered, unzipping the pram-suit and peeling off the mittens and hat.

'Interesting,' Norah said. 'Any special significance?'

Ellie shrugged. 'I guess there are three of us now. But we just liked it.'

Norah's attention shifted to the trestle table in the corner. 'Do you take milk?'

'Yes please. No sugar.'

Friendly, but in her experience, people like Norah were only interested in people like her if there was something in it for them.

There was only one free play gym, and as she made a beeline for it, a scurrying toddler wearing a skeleton costume collided with her legs.

'Freddie, watch out!' Asha waved from behind a tea urn. 'Sorry, Ellie.'

'No problem,' she called back with an answering wave.

'Here you go.' Norah reappeared with a mug and a paper bag. 'Coffee and cake.'

While a host of off-duty Kate Middletons milled around the hall, they made small talk – plans for Christmas, the recent windy weather – until Norah shuffled a little straighter and a getting-down-to-business briskness settled on her.

'So, how are you getting on with the house? You're next door to Asha's mother-in-law, I believe.'

Ellie had taken the cupcake from the paper bag and was licking frosting off her fingers. 'That's right.'

The corners of Norah's lips twitched. 'And how do you find her?'

'Really nice,' Ellie said, cautiously.

'Freddie's at the same nursery as the twins and our paths cross occasionally.' She peered over the wide rim of the cup and said faux-casually, 'Did Diane mention Mary Brennan?'

Ah. Here it was. Norah's hidden agenda.

'Not really.'

'What about her father, Bill Brennan?'

'No. Why?'

'I got very invested in Mary's story when I covered it for the *Stockfield Express*.' She uncrossed her legs. 'And I couldn't get over the fact a nurse lived next door to that house for over forty years and never suspected a thing. I mean, if I had a vulnerable neighbour, I'd forever be checking on them.'

Ellie almost snorted coffee down her nose. *Sure you would.*

'But that's by the by, what I'm interested in happened way back when Mary was a teenager. Has Diane ever mentioned the adoption to you?'

Why did some people get off on delivering bad news? Her expression echoed that of Joan the Moan announcing redundancies. Sympathetic head tilt. Hushed compassionate tone. Oscar-winning fakery.

Ellie's smile was equally fake. 'Sorry, what is it you're asking?'

'Well, I think Mary's story has got legs for a wider audience, a national or a magazine. Human interest. Scandal in suburbia. The Stockfield Council inquiry connection. Schoolgirl mum has her baby removed. And of course, the tragedy of her death.

'I've been doing a lot of research. Archives, council minutes, that kind of thing. And according to the Land Registry, when Diane moved to Moss Lane, Mary was seventeen years old. That's also the year she left school, not to be seen again until her dad's death. How can a teenager drop off the radar? A pregnant one at that.' She held her hands up, palms out. 'I'm not implying any involvement, of course not. But Diane was a *nurse*. Who better to arrange a secret birth and adoption for a powerful neighbour?'

Norah sat upright. 'Oh hi. How are you?'

Ellie looked up. Asha stood directly in front of them.

Awkward.

Norah unhooked her coat from the back of the chair. 'You know, I promised I'd speak to Emily and I've just spotted her over there.' She took out her phone. 'Actually, Ellie, I don't think I've got your number.' She flashed an expectant smile.

'Oh sure,' Ellie said, and reeled it off before she could stop herself.

Norah typed the digits. 'Got it. That's great. Speak soon, yeah?'

Ellie nodded mutely, inwardly cursing herself for meekly handing her number over.

If looks actually could kill, Asha's would have felled Norah on the spot.

'I didn't say anything about Diane,' Ellie said quickly. 'She said she's writing another article about Mary Brennan, looking into the baby she gave up for adoption and her dad.'

'Norah digging the dirt? Well, that's on brand,' Asha replied. 'Obviously, it's your call, but I'd be careful what you say. She has a way of twisting things.'

'Don't worry, I've got no intention of contacting her. But it's starting to freak me out, you know, this history with Mary and the house. Just when I think I know all there is to know, another thing comes up.'

Freddie, his skeleton mask slipping over his eyes, hurled himself at his mother's legs, howling.

The jet lag feeling washed over Ellie again.

'It feels like everyone else is in on a big secret,' she said, half to herself. 'And I'm the only one being kept in the dark.'

48. Then

Although the atmosphere in the flat had changed, Friday night at the Union was reassuringly the same. They pushed their way through the crowd of Freshers to where Tom and Danny sat at their usual table which was, as usual, covered with empty pint glasses.

'Well, hello, girls.' Danny spoke sloppily, like he had a mouthful of food.

'How much have you had?' Mia said, squeezing in next to him.

When he rolled his eyes, Ellie noticed the whites were tinged with pink. 'A few. Do you fancy another, mate?' he gestured at Tom's almost-full glass.

'Nah, I'm good, thanks,' Tom said, shuffling up the upholstered bench to let Ellie in. He put his arm around her and she leaned gratefully into him.

The music thudded in her temples. Everyone shouted to be heard. Danny in particular talked at full volume in the fake-jolly drunk way he did sometimes. Ellie hadn't seen him since before the summer and she'd been looking forward to catching up, the four of them together like always. But there was an edge to him tonight and the louder he grew, the quieter Mia became, retreating into the jacket she hadn't taken off and picking at the skin around her nails.

Vodka and lager mixed uneasily in Ellie's guts and damp patches spread under her arms.

'Can we go?' she said quietly to Tom.

But Danny interrupted. Loudly. 'You can't go yet, Ellie. We've got loads to catch up on, haven't we?'

Ellie saw Mia and Tom exchange an uneasy glance and her stomach spasmed. Danny's lips curled in a half-grin, half-sneer. The expression in his glittering eyes was unreadable.

'Did *you* have a good summer?' he asked.

Ellie put on her default smile and snuggled in closer to Tom. 'I worked in Debenhams for most of it, but yeah, it was good to spend time with my mum.'

'I went home and sweated my bollocks off in a margarine factory for very little money.' Danny sighed. He waved his pint glass in a vague semicircle. 'How about you, Mia and Tom?'

Both of them stared down at the table.

'Don't be shy,' Danny said, cheerfully. 'Tell us what you two got up to.'

'Don't be like that,' Mia said, quietly. 'Please.'

Tom tapped Ellie on the knee. 'Let's go.'

'Aw, don't go. You haven't told us what you got up to this summer.' Danny swilled lager round his glass. '*Mate.*'

'Danny,' Mia said as a warning.

Tom glanced at Mia and her shoulders gave a tiny *what shall we do?* twitch. A gesture of collusion that trickled fear down Ellie's spine. She flashbacked to walking into the kitchen after school to find Mum and Dad with their bad news faces on. Loss already hovering above them. Those quick, little glances. *Dad got his test results back today …*

Turning in a slow arc to look at each of them, she said, 'What's going on?'

Mia chewed her black-painted nails and refused to meet Ellie's gaze.

'Nothing,' she said. 'Danny's drunk, that's all.'

Danny slapped his hands on the table. 'Yes! Let's talk about getting drunk, shall we?'

Steel bands squeezed Ellie's chest, trapping her breath in her throat. She shook off Tom's arm.

'What are you on about, Danny?'

The bluster bled from him like he'd been punctured. 'I think you should ask Tom and Mia that question.'

'Tom?'

Tension hummed like electricity.

Tom hung his head. He didn't answer.

49. Now

'Wallpaper for the lounge,' Tom said, reversing into an empty space. 'Or paint?'

Within ten minutes of getting home from playgroup, they were in the car and heading for the retail park.

'Paint,' she replied. 'White with a hint of something.'

'What else?' he said.

'Shower curtain,' she said, manoeuvring the buggy up a kerb. 'Rug for the lounge. Light fittings. Bed for the spare room when Mum comes. Highchair and potty, thinking ahead. But I need to pop into Boots first.'

Tom stopped on the pavement as the automatic doors slid open.

'Listen, I need to get some screws and stuff for Dad. Why don't you give me the baby, I'll nip over to B&Q and we can meet back here? You've got your phone, right? You can ring me if you need me.'

'It's fine,' she said, jerking the pram out of his reach. 'I'll take Trinity.'

He threw her a puzzled look. 'OK, see you in ten minutes or so.'

Christmas had arrived early in Boots. She wove the buggy through the crowded aisles, stepping aside to let an elderly lady pass by the perfume and aftershave stands.

'Lovely wee thing,' the lady said, peering into the pram with a fond smile. 'Enjoy it while you can. One blink and they're away.'

'I will,' Ellie said, patting Trinity's leg. Soon she'd be toddling about on these tiny feet. One day she'd be a stroppy teen and then all too quickly, ready to forge her own path through the world wherever and however she wanted.

'Not too soon, eh?' Ellie whispered, tucking Mr Giraffe under the blanket.

She made her way to the baby aisle for pads and sterilising tablets. Picked up toothpaste en route to the checkout where several people already lined up at the counter. Ellie calmly checked her phone while in front, a tall man in a tweed cap expressed his irritation by staring pointedly at his watch and tutting loudly. A baby cried and the mum crouched down to pick up a dropped teddy. Rhythmic beeps sounded as the assistant scanned through nappies, baby wipes, sterilising tablets, Sudocrem.

Sudocrem!

The queue behind her snaked back to the sunglasses. If she went now, she'd lose her place. But if she left the pram for ten seconds … She could actually see the shelves of disposable nappies from here. The Sudocrem had to be just out of sight. Ten seconds. Twenty tops.

'Won't be a minute,' she murmured to no one and hurried towards the baby goods section, turning her head every other step to check on Trinity. Fine, no one had noticed she'd—

'Oh,' she said, halting abruptly. 'Sorry.'

She had almost walked straight into another shopper.

Old-fashioned updo. Same black dress. Same miserable expression. It was the woman from Moss Lane.

Ellie snatched a tub of cream and held it to her chest as she let out an uneasy laugh.

'We do keep bumping into each other, don't we?'

The woman's lips remained in a silent grim line.

'I think we may be neighbours. I live on Moss Lane?'

Without acknowledging she had heard, the woman continued up the aisle. Ellie shivered and her unease went up a gear. Several gears.

'Excuse me?' A haughty voice shouted across the shop. Heads

turned, including Ellie's. The tall man in the tweed cap stood at the checkout and pointed at the pram. 'Is this your child?'

'Oh God, yes.' Ellie scurried back and nudged the buggy up to the adjacent till, flustered by the weight of judgemental stares. 'Forgot this. Had to go and get it from, er …'

A man in a white tunic scanned her items. Above him, the round security mirror reflected the tops of heads. God, her roots needed doing. Tweed cap man blew his nose next to her.

And there, reflected in the rounded curve of the mirror, the woman in black stood next to the sunglasses. Ellie instantly dropped her gaze, catching eyes with the shouty man on the way. He narrowed his to literally look down his red-veined nose at her.

'Do you want a bag?' the assistant said.

She shook her head, taking out a crumpled bag for life.

'That'll be £19 exactly, please.'

On autopilot, she swiped her card. Sensing the woman's stare, she cast a furtive glance at the mirror. Yes, still there. Watching. Well, this time, she'd had enough. She'd find out who she was and what she wanted and how on earth she always seemed to know where Ellie was going to be. Self-consciously rubbing her neck, she turned.

No one stood by the sunglasses. The woman had disappeared.

She glanced at the mirror. The woman was still there.

How—?

Ellie grabbed the pram and ran.

She swerved the buggy around a stand of painkillers. Someone shouted behind her. The automatic doors slid open and she ran through.

Outside, the wind whirled scraps of paper and dry leaves around the car park. A plastic bag floated high above like a white cloud against the grey sky. She leaned against the pram handle as her legs suddenly refused to bear her weight.

Breathe. A few seconds, then she'd go to B&Q to wait for Tom.

This was getting out of hand. First at Nexus and now here.

How did the woman from Moss Lane keep finding her? It had to be different women conflated by Ellie's sleep-ravaged brain. After all, plenty of people wore glasses and black dresses. That made more sense. And those convex mirrors often created optical illusions, catching reflections at odd angles. Maybe—

A bony finger prodded her shoulder.

Terror rooted her to the spot. She didn't turn. Couldn't. Her chest was about to explode. *Please don't be her. Please don't be her. Please don't.*

'Excuse me,' the posh man in the tweed cap said impatiently, holding her bag for life at arm's length. 'You forgot your shopping.'

She snatched the bag with a muttered thank you and shoved the buggy towards B&Q.

'You're very welcome,' he called sarcastically behind her.

Drivers pulled in and out of spaces. A kid ran past with a balloon. People talked and laughed. Loud beats reverberated from a car stereo. Too many people. Too much noise.

Thank God. There was Tom striding out of B&Q. She didn't care that he had his mobile clamped to his ear and concern on his face. She didn't care when he frowned, flicking his gaze from Trinity to Ellie and back. She didn't even care when she heard him say quietly, 'Sorry Tanya, I'm going to have to call you later.'

All she cared about were the car keys in his hand.

'I need to go home,' she said, breathlessly. 'Now.'

50. Then

The Union's mix of music and loud conversation jangled in a discordant soundtrack.

Tom wouldn't meet her gaze. Danny, wet-lipped and red-eyed, scratched the back of his neck. And it was left to Mia to bite her lip and look down at the table.

'I'm sorry,' she said simply.

'What's going on?' Ellie said.

Mia's ragged black fingernails tore strips of printed paper from a beer mat.

'Why are you doing this?' Tom said suddenly to Danny. 'None of this has got anything to do with her.'

The expression of guilt that flickered across Danny's face quickly turned into a sneer.

'Well, *mate*, it's not fair to keep her in the dark. I mean, this affects her as much as anyone else. So go on, one of you tell her.'

No one spoke. Silence, weighted and awful, hung over their table while the rest of the bar buzzed with talk and laughter and happiness.

'Tell me,' Ellie said. 'Mia? Tom?'

'OK, first, it was my fault so don't blame Tom,' Mia said, her eyes finally meeting Ellie's. She laid her hands flat on the table. 'I had another row with Danny about seeing Josie while he was at home. You know, his ex. I got drunk and I was upset and … I kissed Tom. He stopped me. Then, as you can see' – she flapped her hands around Danny in a look-at-this-mess gesture – 'I made the mistake of believing I should confess and that's it. I swear it was my fault.'

She turned to Danny who had put his pint glass to his lips. 'Happy now?'

He shrugged and took a noisy swallow.

'Tom?' Ellie said quietly. 'Is it true?'

'Let's go,' he said, already pulling his coat on.

'For the record, nothing happened with Josie,' Danny said. Tom didn't reply.

Outside, the cool air fanned Ellie's burning cheeks. A bus trundled past and Tom grabbed her as though to run for it, but she pulled back.

'I want to walk,' she said, stepping out of the way of a bike.

Her brain couldn't take it in. Even though she had been dreading this, had imagined it, had almost willed it to existence, she just couldn't believe what Danny had said.

Tom and Mia?

Student life dominated the takeaway-lined streets around the Union. Groups walked or sat at bus shelters, smoking and singing and eating chips from polystyrene boxes. Cars beeped at drunks dawdling across the road.

But once they left the main drag, the night grew quieter. Only the occasional dog walker or late jogger crossed their path.

Tom was the first to break the silence.

'I'm sorry,' he said. 'We were going to tell you.'

We.

Tom and Mia. Mia and Tom. Talking. Conspiring.

She wrapped her arms around her chest to hold in the shudder building in her diaphragm. He stopped in front of her.

'Whatever you're picturing, I swear it wasn't as bad. Honestly. It was nothing.'

'Nothing to you, maybe,' she said tightly.

The glow of the streetlight caught the angles of Tom's face, twisting the features into something unfamiliar.

'I know it's no excuse, but we were both drunk and we were talking and Mia was really, really upset about Danny going for

227

a drink with Josie so I gave her a hug and she just … it just happened. But I promise as soon as I realised what was going on, I stopped it.'

'How long?'

'What do you mean?'

'How long before you realised what was going on? Ten seconds? Twenty? Thirty?'

'I didn't exactly set a timer,' he said. 'And I was drunk.'

'Ballpark figure.'

A gust of wind whispered through the trees. Tom shifted his weight from one foot to the other.

'A few minutes,' he admitted. 'But I swear, I never meant it to happen.'

Even though she'd played the *Tom cheats on me* scenario in her head hundreds of times, shock punched the breath from her lungs.

A few *minutes*?

'Tell me,' she said slowly. 'Exactly. Was it at Mia's house? In her *bedroom*?'

'No, nothing like that. Walking home from the pub, both hammered and she was upset. It's not like we're having an affair. It was nothing. One kiss.'

'She's my best friend and you're my boyfriend. Trust me, you can't call one kiss "nothing".'

A look of despair crossed Tom's face and his eyes shone in the streetlight. For a moment, he looked as though he might burst into tears.

Instead he raked his fingers through his too-long fringe.

'It just happened. What else can I say? I love you, Ellie.'

51. Now

Tom's electric toothbrush whirred distantly while the radiators groaned. Just the mundane sounds of a house and its occupants settling down for the night.

Not this occupant, though. Theories and speculation played like a compilation album of her greatest fears. No sooner had she grasped one unpalatable thought, than it morphed into a new terror.

He's set me up.

He's made me think I'm losing it.

He's going to have me sectioned again.

They're going to take the baby off me.

When you thought about it, it was the only explanation that made any sense. And she had to hand it to them, it was clever. Really clever.

Tom and Tanya – both detectives – treating her like a tricky case. Convince everyone your girlfriend is having a breakdown, get her out of the picture and play happy ever together. Problem solved. Case closed.

She leaned forward and hugged her knees.

Tom emerged in his boxer shorts from the bathroom. Slicking his damp hair back with his fingers, he said, 'Did you get any shampoo when you went to Boots?'

A floorboard creaked as he rifled through his T-shirt drawer, as though the house wanted a say in what was about to unfold.

'We're nearly out,' he continued, shutting the drawer. 'If not, I can pick some up on the way home tomorrow.'

Ellie's lips had gone numb, like she'd just had a filling. It was hard to form the question. 'Are you having an affair?'

'Am I what, love?' he said, pulling a T-shirt over his head.

'Having. An. Affair,' she repeated, enunciating each word clearly.

'Er, no.' He snorted. 'Who with?'

'Tanya.'

His head popped through the neck hole and he laughed. Actually threw his head back and *laughed*.

'It's not funny.' She banged her fist on the bedside table. Hot tears burned in the back of her throat, mangling her voice. 'I'm not stupid; I know what you're doing, both of you. Making that woman follow me. Messing with things in the house. Messing with my *head*. You've set me up so I think I'm going mad and I'll get sectioned again and then you can play happy families and pretend I don't exist.' Her voice wavered and rose. 'Pretend she's Trinity's mum and—'

She was crying too hard to finish. Angry, ugly sobs that shook her shoulders. Tears poured down her cheeks and dripped off her chin. She wiped her nose across the back of her hand, beyond caring.

Meanwhile, Tom stared, very much not laughing now. The mattress dipped as he sank down beside her and waited.

'First,' he said when the crying finally faded to gaspy, shuddering sobs, 'the last thing I would ever do is cheat on you or Trinity. And I mean that literally. You are my whole world and always will be. Second, absolutely no way does anyone think you're mad. Tired and stressed, yes. Mad, no.' He gently cupped her chin, flicking away the tears that gathered there. 'And finally, I am certainly not having an affair with anyone, including Tanya who is, by the way, very happily married.'

Ellie scoffed and jerked away. Adultery permeated every layer of the police force and she'd lost count of Tom's moral qualms over colleagues who had 'gone over the side'. As she held her hands up in a you-got-me-there gesture, she noticed they were shaking. Tom must have too because he clasped both in his.

'You spend more time with her than you do with me,' she said, amazed at the steadiness of her voice. 'And even when you're here, she's ringing you or you're sneaking off to talk to her.'

The reproach clearly stung. Tom's mouth contorted in an unhappy grimace.

'Tanya is happily married,' he continued, 'to a dentist called Kirsty. But even if she weren't, I still wouldn't be having an affair with her or anyone else because I love you.' He jumped off the bed. 'Here, let me show you something.'

He shook the jeans he'd been wearing earlier and with a soft thud, his phone landed on the floorboards.

With a couple of taps, the screen turned Facebook blue. A page belonging to the red-lipsticked Tanya Auguste appeared, the profile picture instantly recognisable as the woman Ellie had seen outside the station. The photo actually showed *two* loved-up women and the accompanying 'happily married to Kirsty Louise Lambert' status confirmed Tom's statement.

'See? And I know I'm working too much, but I just have to see this one job through to the end, you know? I wish I could, but I can't kiss Trinity goodnight and then forget the other kids, the ones I see onscreen at work, who aren't safe and loved and protected. But I promise, as soon as this operation is finished, I will apply for a transfer to another unit.' He sighed softly, his breath warm against her scalp. 'Is that what you got so stressed about at the shops today? Me and Tanya? Bloody hell.'

She slumped back onto the pillow, stunned, as he got under the covers beside her.

He wasn't having an affair!

Her suspicions shrivelled like scraps of burning paper. She felt dizzy with remorse and relief. This man who had never let her down, who had stayed with her through the worst moments of her life. Of course he wouldn't cheat.

'I love you and Trinity more than anything on the planet,' he

231

continued, re-tucking the duvet around her shoulders. 'You must know I would never do anything to hurt you.'

'I know,' she said in a subdued voice. 'I'm really sorry.'

She rolled onto her side and wriggled until her cheek was against his chest. He immediately put his arms around her, hugged her tight and his heart beat steadily against her ear.

Later, when he began to snore, Ellie carefully lifted his arm and extricated herself from his embrace. But he twisted, drawing her back into his arms.

'Are you awake?' he whispered into the darkness. She could just make out the gleam of his eyes.

'No,' she said. 'Go back to sleep.'

'When we were talking about Tanya before,' he continued groggily, 'what did you mean about a woman following you?'

The woman in black flickered and vanished.

'Nothing. Forget it,' she said.

She turned her back and pretended to fall asleep.

52. Now

It was still dark outside when Tom turned the bedroom light on.

'Big day today,' he said. 'I might not be contactable for a while, but you can always ring the station if there's an emergency.'

Ellie blinked and rubbed her eyes. 'What time is it?'

'Just gone five. Try and sleep a bit more before the baby wakes up.'

She lay back, listening to the sound of the shower. *Go back to sleep.* That was a joke. After a night navigating the foggy tunnels of her subconscious, sleep and wakefulness blurred until she couldn't tell where one ended and the other began.

By the time the sky had lightened to a uniform grey, Ellie had her hands clasped round her second cup of coffee and was observing the freshly scrubbed kitchen. She could hear the hum of the boiler, the occasional splash of water hitting the bottom of the sink and the noisy cawing of the birds circling over Mosswood.

One certainty shone through the brain fog: Tom wasn't cheating. How could she have doubted him?

Her imagination had gathered snippets of information and weaved them into an entirely false narrative. All these … *misunderstandings* weren't part of some elaborate set-up, they were the paranoid offspring of tiredness and imagination.

She rinsed the mug and set it, dripping, on the draining rack. *To work, to work.*

Where had the wallpaper scraper got to? If she closed her eyes, she could picture the flat blade glinting in the … lounge light? Kitchen light? She sifted through a pile of bits and bobs by the fruit bowl. Packets of screws, paint charts, bills, a new shower curtain still wrapped in plastic.

Her phone rang. Carol's voice came out a little too fast and a lot too cheery. 'Hi, love, sorry for calling so early, but I thought I'd catch you before you got too busy. You know, I woke up and I thought I'd give you a ring and see what you're up to today and what—'

'Have you spoken to Tom again?' Ellie interrupted.

She pictured her mum pinching her lower lip into a pout, the way she always did when she had something on her mind.

'Don't give him a hard time,' Carol said. 'He only rang me because he's worried and I'm glad he did. Anyway, I'm not just ringing about that. I've got some good news.'

'Your leg is on the mend?'

'Even better. I've booked my flight and I'm coming over at the end of next week.'

Her mum's note of triumph switched to distress as Ellie collapsed into noisy sobs.

'What's wrong, love?'

'Nothing. Hormones.' She tore off a piece of kitchen roll and blew her nose. 'I can't wait to see you and Trinity is desperate to meet her nanny.'

'Oh, love, you'll set me off.' Carol sniffed. 'What Tom has told me has worried me sick. I remember how hard things were when you were ill before, and I need to be there with you.'

Ellie ran her tongue over her bottom teeth and gave herself a few seconds before she answered evenly. 'I'm not ill, Mum. I was treated for PTSD and severe anxiety disorder ten years ago. Ten years down the line do you think every time you stub your toe you'll blame it on your broken leg?'

Carol didn't answer, but Ellie could hear her breathing.

'I think a lot of it is just being in the house on my own,' she said in a softer tone. 'I'm not used to the quiet. And I'm so tired. The normal new mum stuff.'

'I know, love,' Carol said with a sigh. 'In a few days, I'll be able to help and you can get all the sleep you want. And we can plan things to get you out of the house. There's always loads around Christmas. What about Tom?'

'We had a long talk yesterday and sorted a lot of things out. He's going to take some time off after this job.'

'He told me a bit about that,' Carol said. 'Not the details, but it sounded awful. Did he say when it'll be finished?'

'Tomorrow,' Ellie replied. 'There's a raid here and another somewhere abroad. He wouldn't tell me much either, but it's connected with children.'

'That must be tough for him.'

'Yeah,' Ellie said with a pang of guilt. She glanced at the baby sleeping peacefully in the Moses basket. 'It must.'

'Listen, I'm ordering some Christmas pressies online today to be sent to yours,' Carol said. 'And I thought I'd get us both one of those calendars done where you put your own photos in. So, do you want to have a look through your pics and send me your favourites of Trinity?'

'That's a nice idea,' Ellie said, already mentally flicking through her camera roll. 'Will do.'

After they'd said goodbye, she sat for a moment holding the phone in her lap. Her mum's words had struck a chord. While she'd been fixated on Tanya, Tom had been witnessing the worst of humanity then coming home with a smile to smooth the rough edges of Ellie's day. All while earning the money they needed and doing the shopping and the garden. Why should he come home to accusations and suspicion? Uncomplaining, unbegrudging Tom multitasked like a true hero, day after day. Ellie, on the other hand, could barely monotask without sliding down a rabbit hole of paranoia.

She lay on the sofa and snuggled into the fleece throw. She'd get on with stripping the wallpaper and tackling the bottomless laundry basket soon. But first, the photos. Her mum might not be able to see her granddaughter in real life just now, but thanks to the billion photo requests, she could watch her grow in real time, like time-lapse footage of a flower blooming. Or, Ellie thought as she scrolled through the pictures, one of those flicker books that brought still drawings to life. There were *hundreds*.

As she'd already curated the best ones for social media, that seemed a good way to narrow them down. Her news feed showed Danny and Josie and their adorable children playing frisbee with their giant shaggy dog. *Like.* Roger pushing Mum down the Paseo Maritimo in a wheelchair. *Like.* And with a stab of remorse, Jess, lipsticked and big-haired for a hen-do. *Love.* Another person she had to apologise to. Today. She would text her today.

I Love Uppermoss appeared in her news feed and, spurred on by Carol's attempts to kickstart her social life, she clicked the page. There were posts about lost dogs and found cats. Artisan markets. Houses for rent. Questions about catchment areas, electricians, the best way to get pollen off cashmere (Sellotape). Maybe when Mum arrived they could check out Baby Beats or Story Club at the library. Scroll. Scroll. Scroll.

Stop.

Her stomach drew into a tight ball.

There on the page was the photo from the *Stockfield Express*. Their house, sinister behind police tape, uniformed officer at the gate.

Did you see the house on Moss Lane sold?!! Someone had written underneath.

Common sense sent frantic messages – *Log out! Don't read it!* – that her hand and eyes refused to obey, and with horrified fascination she continued scrolling through the shocked emojis and comments.

Should have knocked it down.

You'd have to be desperate to sleep under that roof.

Can't blame them with the house prices round here.

The past is the past. What does it matter?

She picked at her nail polish, scattering little grey flakes in her lap. What had Asha said about Diane after Norah's article?

Trial by social media. Her fingers were poised to respond when a message pinged like a warning.

Where are my photos?!! it read.

Ellie sat back and breathed slowly down her nose. People had a right to their opinions. Let it go.

OK, so striped-onesie Trinity with an enigmatic smile? Mid-yawn. Swipe. Star-fishing hands. Swipe. Examining pudgy toes. Swipe. Gazing adoringly at Mr Giraffe. With so many gorgeous pictures to choose from, it was hard to make the selection.

A wash of exhaustion rinsed the caffeine from her bloodstream and pushed her down on the sofa. With a yawn, she wedged the cushion under her head, wriggled deeper into the blanket's soft embrace and let her eyelids close. Ten minutes while the baby napped, that's all she needed. Then she'd send the pictures. She put her phone on the coffee table. Tiny black dots swarmed behind her lids. She'd send Mum's photos in ten minutes.

Photos. They told the truth. Unlike eyes – shifty, deceptive things that fooled you into believing your boyfriend was being unfaithful. Or memories with their habit of editing events through a filter of emotion. Mirrors, too. Reflecting things that weren't really there. *People* who weren't there. No, photos were honest.

It was everything else you couldn't trust.

53. Now

The TV standby light shone in the corner. Outside, grey clouds darkened and, deep within the gloom, Trinity snuffled.

Ellie sprang upright, pulse racing. How long had she been asleep?

She checked in the Moses basket. Trinity stirred with a high-pitched grunt, then settled back again with her tiny, perfect fists curled either side of her head. Thank God. Totally fine. Ellie yawned and stretched her arms and legs in front of her, wiggling her toes back to life. Somehow she had slept through a missed call from Tom and a single heart emoji from Jess. And an unexpected message startled her to full alert:

Hi, wondering if you'd be free for a coffee? I could pop round to your house. Tell me when suits you best. Norah

Honestly, even for a journalist, the woman was shameless.

'Never,' Ellie said, pressing delete. 'Never suits me best.'

She switched the kettle on. Her phone dinged again.

Photos?! xx

Doing it now xx she tapped in quickly and, taking her tea, went back into the lounge.

Trinity had attained cuteness overload. Her perfect miniature fingers curled over the top of the blanket. Her lips curved in an almost smile that echoed Ellie's own. Sometimes she couldn't believe she had played any part in creating her. From the rosy whorls of her ears to the squidgy dimpled wrists and knees, every inch of this child was perfect.

'Not long till Nanny comes,' she whispered. 'Let's get one last picture.'

As she spoke, she pressed the camera app, then she clicked open the photo album she'd made for Mum for a final scroll-through.

What? Her finger hovered while her brain tried to make sense of what her eyes showed her.

She frantically swiped backwards. Trinity. Trinity. Trinity. There were twenty-five photos of her daughter. But the final photo wasn't a calendar-worthy cute shot of a baby. The final photo showed an indistinct figure standing in the garden looking out at Mosswood. The image clearly showed the pile of dead wood and tangled rose bushes. Even the lichen on the paving slabs stood out. But the figure itself was blurred and featureless. In theory, it could be a smudge. Or the shadow of a finger over the lens. From the angle, whoever took the photo – Ellie, because who else could it be? – must have leaned over the kitchen sink and held the phone to the window. The problem was she had no memory of taking that picture.

She dropped the phone as if it had scalded her.

Straight ahead, the mirror reflected the lounge's ordinariness: sofa, table, lamp. Nothing seemed out of place except her own blanched face. Gingerly holding the phone like the plastic case would burn her, she inched towards the hallway. A cold draught raised goose bumps down her spine. Had Tom come in silently to prank her? Was he hiding, waiting to jump out?

The silver E glinted innocently in the front door. There was no way a stranger could have got in. She paused on the kitchen threshold. Her fingers groped for the switch, afraid of what might be waiting.

Click.

Dishes on the rack. Overflowing laundry basket. Diane's cake tin rinsed to be returned. Back door firmly bolted top and bottom. There was no way *anyone* could have got in, not even Tom.

And the window?

No one stood by the rose beds.

Torn between confusion and fear, she opened the photos app

again. Maybe she'd missed some clue. But the picture had vanished from the camera roll. Or the deleted items folder. She tapped furiously. Recently uploaded? No. In the library and on the cloud, there was nothing but cute photos of Trinity.

Everything knotted together in one big confusing mess. If only she could delve inside her skull and unravel the tangled thoughts. The photo wasn't real. It certainly wasn't Tom playing tricks on her. And she wasn't even taking the same medication anymore.

She needed to grasp a single idea and follow the thread through to a logical conclusion.

There was *only* one logical conclusion.

'It's all in your head,' she told the kitchen walls.

As soon as the words were out, the kitchen shifted slightly. From the drying dishes to the crumpled clothes, everything looked the same on the surface. But the shadows cast by the furniture darkened. Cold air fluttered the bills on the table. And she knew without checking, there would be smears of mud on the floor and the door.

Less than a minute later, she was carrying both the baby and the cake tin towards Diane's porch.

Knock. Wait. Knock louder.

'Come on, come on,' she murmured, casting furtive glances through the green-black wall of conifers that divided the two gardens. From this angle there were no windows, no doors; number six was an expanse of blank, impassive brick.

It looked as though the house had something to hide.

54. Now

Diane, glasses nesting in her blonde hair, held a newspaper at the crossword page. Radio voices came up the hall and out onto the porch.

'Hello, Ellie. Is everything all right?'

Reminding herself to smile, Ellie held the cake tin out. 'Fine thanks. I'm returning this.'

Her neighbour folded the newspaper and placed it on the hall table. 'Bless you. You didn't have to do that.'

When there was no reply, she studied Ellie for a second then mimed a shudder. 'It's too cold to stand out there. Come in for a cuppa?'

Diane's kitchen was wonderfully normal. An Aga radiated heat and informal framed pictures on the wall depicted a happy family growing up. A pair of red wool gloves lay on top of a copy of *Gardener's World*. A British Wildlife calendar hung from a hook, reminders scribbled on almost every day. There was a teapot, an apron, wellies and the smell of something sweet baking. The heart of Diane's home beat strongly.

'Milk and sugar?'

'Just milk, please.'

Almost unbearably transported back to Anita and David's farm-house kitchen, Ellie felt her eyes sting. Diane clicked the radio off.

'Have a seat,' she said. 'Would you like me to hold the baby?'

Shaking her head, Ellie pulled Trinity closer, feeling the warm body safely sheltered by her own.

'Can't say I blame you,' Diane said, stroking Trinity under the chin. 'She's gorgeous.'

The kettle bubbled on the stovetop and Diane dropped teabags into a striped pot, talking about the weather, Christmas, babies. Her soft voice and unhurried movements soothed Ellie's frazzled nerves.

Diane set two cups on coasters.

'Asha said you've been busy with the house.'

'Still lots to do. Tom's dad has done most of it.'

The other woman dried her hands on a tea towel and took the lid off an Emma Bridgewater biscuit barrel.

'Yes, I met – Howard, is it? – a few days ago. Must be a godsend having someone handy around. Are your parents local too?'

Ellie took a chocolate digestive from the tin as she explained about her dad and Spain and Mum's broken leg.

'I'm sorry to hear that,' Diane said. 'Well, you're always welcome to pop round if you fancy a chat or need a hand.'

'Thanks.' Ellie swallowed the lump in her throat along with a bite of the biscuit. 'Sorry. I'm all over the place today.'

'No need to apologise, my love.' Diane pushed a box of tissues across the table. 'Would it help to talk?'

'Oh it's just Tom's been so busy at work.' She pressed a tissue to the corner of each eye in turn. 'And I'm tired and the tablets for my blood pressure were messing with my sleep and that's on top of everything with the house.'

Trinity moaned and Ellie jiggled her.

'Shall I pop her in Freddie's playpen to give your arms a rest?' Diane said, holding out her arms.

Ellie let the older woman take Trinity and settle her onto the cosy mat in the cosy playpen. It looked so cosy, in fact, she wanted to curl up in there herself and sleep for days in the warm tranquillity of Diane's kitchen.

'You've had an awful lot to cope with recently. It's perfectly natural to feel overwhelmed at times.'

'That's what the doctor said. But it's hard to explain without sounding, you know—' She mimed corkscrewing at the temple.

Diane laughed. 'I'll keep an open mind.'

Deep breath, Ellie.

'So, I met another of the neighbours when I came to view the house. She walked straight past me in the garden and now I keep seeing her. She's got dark hair. Wears glasses. Do you know who she is?'

Diane tilted her chin in affirmation. 'Dark hair and glasses sounds like Rita Cohen at number three. Have you spoken to her?'

'Not exactly. Every time I've met her, it's been a bit ...' She grimaced. 'Odd.'

'Ah.' Diane nodded. 'Please don't be offended. Poor Rita has dementia.'

Dementia?

'Jack, her husband, is having such a hard time,' Diane continued. 'I can't imagine he'll be able to cope for much longer. She's almost completely stopped talking and she keeps leaving the house at all hours of day and night.'

Diane carried on detailing Rita's gradual decline and recent wanderings while Ellie murmured politely, 'That's awful. How sad. Poor people.'

Meanwhile, she mentally reviewed the silent encounters with the woman in black. Excluding the nightmares, this curveball certainly moved things in the direction of 'Not crazy. Logical explanation.'

A neighbour with dementia who didn't speak and was prone to wander? *Well.*

It took significant willpower not to fling herself at Diane's knees, sobbing with gratitude.

'Is there anything else I should know?' Ellie said, when Diane finished. She picked at a thread hanging from her cuff. 'About Moss Lane, or Mary? It's my house and everyone seems to have a theory about what happened there, or they know something I don't.'

Diane lifted her glasses from the top of her head and pushed them into a case printed with roses.

'I'm not sure how much help I can be. I know it seems hard to believe, but I'd barely seen Mary for years. She never left the house. Wouldn't have visitors, except for the grocers in the village and the postman.'

'But you knew her when she was young?'

'Most of what I know came from the Cohens, actually. Rita was a teacher at Uppermoss High and from what she said, one day Mary was at school, the next she wasn't. No warning, she just stopped coming.'

'OK,' Ellie said, digesting the information. 'Someone told me Mary might have had a baby that was adopted.'

'Well, again, this is according to Rita, but apparently Mary had a boyfriend from another school for a short while and she was clearly pregnant when she stopped attending. She certainly would have had no choice but to give up her baby. Bill Brennan would never allow the stigma of an illegitimate child under his roof. I know you shouldn't speak ill of the dead, but the man was a despicable human being. Even taking his own life right behind the house was designed to cause maximum pain. You know he left a note so Mary would be the one to find him? Can you imagine the cruelty?'

She laid her palms on her flushed cheeks and exhaled loudly, a sound filled with misery and remorse.

'There hasn't been a day since Mary died that I haven't regretted not trying harder back then. When Bill Brennan said she'd gone to stay with relatives, we believed him. Nowadays, you'd question it. Thinking about that poor girl going through a pregnancy all alone only to have her child taken away. It doesn't bear thinking about.'

Ellie knew all about regret. Before she could stop herself, she had a flashback to Mia.

'It's not your fault.' She squeezed Diane's forearm and got a half-smile in return.

'Thank you. But I know I should have done more. It's no excuse that things were different then and I was busy with the children and my job at the clinic. I did try several times after her father died. I could feel her standing right behind the door, but she wouldn't open it. Of course, she was an adult by then so I had to respect the fact she wanted to be left alone.'

'Poor Mary,' Ellie said.

Apart from the wall clock ticking, the kitchen fell silent. The guilt in Diane's stricken features resonated with Ellie.

Could have done this. Should have done that.

'When I think of her dying in that awful way ...' Diane said, lost in contemplation. 'Yes, if I could turn the clock back, there are so many things I would do differently.'

55. Now

There were no delicious aromas of home baking in Ellie's own kitchen when she returned from Diane's with an open invitation to return whenever she wanted. Instead, dirty clothes and dirty worktops welcomed her home. Dirty floor too, which come to think of it, she'd already mopped. Or maybe that had been yesterday.

'Forget about perfect,' she muttered, slinging her jumper over the chair. After two cups of tea and the conversation with Diane, her anxiety had ebbed, but as ever, the housework remained.

She was in the nursery when Tom called to 'see what my two favourite girls are up to'.

In the background, a printer whirred and a keyboard click-clacked under urgent fingertips.

'I'm feeding Trinity,' she said, smiling down at their hungry daughter. 'How's the job going?'

'To plan so far, but we'll see.'

The tension in his voice was unmistakable and Ellie got the impression that he was less hopeful than he'd been. Even the usual background office noise – the laughs, the hubbub of conversation – seemed subdued.

'What have you been doing?' he continued.

'We went to Diane's for a coffee. And Mum rang to say she's booked a flight.'

She filled him in with some of the details.

'Sounds like you're having a good day,' Tom said.

He wasn't cheating on her. Mum would be here soon. Six Moss Lane belonged to them and the woman in black was a poor, confused neighbour.

'Yeah,' she said, a grin blooming. 'I am.'

Less than a minute later, the phone rang again. This time it was Mum on Facetime.

'Are you feeling any better now, love?' she said.

'*So* much better,' Ellie replied.

'I cannot wait to see my two beautiful girls,' Carol said with obvious longing. 'Can I have a peek at the baby now?'

Ellie lowered Trinity into the cot, her serene expression at odds with the clenched fists on either side of her head.

'Oh my goodness, she looks just like you did,' Carol whispered. 'Hello, gorgeous girl. Nanny can't wait to spoil you rotten. Now, tell your mummy to send me those photos.'

Trinity mumbled and stirred.

A fly strafed Ellie's ear. She flapped at it with her free hand. 'Bloody hell.'

'What's up?' Carol said.

'Massive bluebottle,' Ellie said in disgust. Another fat insect dived and she batted it away with the phone.

Her mum spoke distantly, 'What are you doing, Ellie? The screen's gone funny.'

Now there were two flies.

'I'll have to call you back in a minute.'

She tugged the chain on the blackout blind and wafted them towards the window with a copy of *The Tiger Who Came to Tea*. Their lazy barrel rolling over the cot continued.

She shoved the window. Cold air rushed in and the buzzing intensified. Turning, Ellie reeled in shock.

Flies.

Not one or two, but half a dozen or more above the cot. Red-eyed, plastic-winged. Worst of all was the grotesque spectacle of a bluebottle quivering on her daughter's wet bottom lip. Trinity's tongue lolled, an inviting red carpet. Batting at the obscene cloud as she went, Ellie snatched her up. Hesitated.

'Oh God,' she moaned softly, lifting one foot.

The stain had returned, spreading out from under the cot. Jet black against the pale grey carpet. She hopped back sharply, lost her balance and half-fell into the hallway, catching her hip agonisingly on the doorframe as she twisted awkwardly to protect the baby's precious skull.

Trinity conveyed her gratitude with an unrelenting *wah wah wah* that continued unbroken while Ellie turned the bath taps on, fumbled over the press studs and washed her thoroughly and carefully with antibacterial soap. When she finally hushed – cocooned in a warm towel – Ellie slid her back down the bathroom wall, sat on the floor and listened to the silence pulsing through the house. Slowly, holding the drowsy baby, she crept across the landing and put her ear to the door, straining to hear. But there was nothing. The buzzing had stopped.

OK. She pushed the door with one fingertip. Listened. Peered in.

Benign, friendly, welcoming. The room looked and smelled perfect. She switched the light on and cautiously dabbed the carpet with her toe. Showroom-perfect. No flies. No stain.

Almost as if they'd never been there at all.

Ellie shivered and closed the window.

Whatever had summoned the flies and the stain had gone for now. But her daughter's things would not be here when they came back.

56. Now

The Allen key slotted into the cot side first time. Stiff at first, she put her weight on it and it soon loosened. The base needed a screwdriver, not the flat-head sort, the other kind, which meant another trip to the toolbox and a check on Trinity mesmerised by the TV in their bedroom. Thank God for CBeebies.

Coaxing twenty tiny screws out of the base made her fingertips red and sore. After a few tries, she found a rhythm: insert, twist, twist harder. The last screw was stuck fast. She grunted and leaned her full weight on the screwdriver handle. But her palms were damp with sweat and it slipped into the web of skin between her thumb and index finger.

'God's sake!' She ran her hand under the cold tap and the water turned pink. She pressed a clean flannel against the cut, dabbed until the bleeding slowed. Not deep enough for stitches, but deep, nonetheless.

This time, the screw turned easily. She stacked the last slat and sat back on her heels, blowing a damp strand of hair from her eyes. The cot was a pile of dismantled parts.

Done.

She switched the light out and closed the door firmly behind her.

Dragging the nursing chair and the changing table into their bedroom had been easy, compared to reassembling the cot but finally, she had turned the last screw. She licked a smear of blood from her thumb and looked around the crowded room. There was barely any floor space left. Now came the hardest part of the whole operation: coming up with a convincing reason for emptying the nursery. What could she say that Tom would believe?

The Moses basket. That was it. She'd say lugging it up and down was a pain, so it made sense to keep it downstairs and move the cot in here.

The familiar sound of their car engine was the signal to gather the tools and glance at the nursery for a final time. Clean. Tidy. Bare.

Keys rattled downstairs and the front door creaked open.

'This is a nice surprise,' she said from the top of the stairs. 'I thought you were back late tonight.'

'I know.' Tom unwound his scarf and slipped his jacket off. 'Tanya said she'd stay late so I could get off early.'

'That's kind of her,' she said, descending slowly and carefully. The baby's fingers clutched at her top, the little nails surprisingly sharp.

'Yeah. Luckily, now we're not having an affair she has loads of spare time.'

He threw her an exaggerated wink as she reached the bottom step.

'Funny. How was your day?'

'Honestly? I couldn't take anymore. I have seen things today I never want to think about again.' He pulled his shoulders back and reached his arms out. 'But tomorrow. Tomorrow, we will have the bastards locked up. Fingers crossed. Anyway, how is my other beautiful girl?'

He cradled the baby tight, peppering her with tiny kisses and burying his nose in her neck, inhaling deeply as though the innocent baby-ness could cleanse him of the horrors of work.

'Great,' Ellie said. 'Do you want to do her bath?'

Half an hour later, she brought two plates piled high with spaghetti bolognese and garlic bread in from the kitchen while Tom lowered a freshly bathed and tranquil Trinity into the Moses basket.

She had her lines prepped. *Why did I move all the baby things out of the nursery? Oh, it's just easier to have all her stuff close by.*

OK, as excuses went it was pretty flimsy, but what else could she tell him? The truth? She could barely admit that to herself: she was afraid of the nursery. She watched him from the corner of her eye, waiting for her cue. *Moses basket downstairs. Easier.*

'God, this is good,' he said through a mouthful of spaghetti. 'I've hardly eaten all day.'

Well, that was strange. But if he wasn't going to bring the subject up then neither was she.

'How come?' she replied, picking up her fork.

'I lost my appetite. But you don't want to know why.'

'I do. Tell me.'

'OK, I'll give you the PG version.' He broke off a chunk of bread and mopped up the last of the sauce. 'First, I watched an hour of unimaginable webcam footage. Then, frame by frame, I cross-referenced all the tattoos, scars and body parts I saw with the ones we already have on the database. Then I signed off the paperwork for the raid and came home.'

'That sounds awful.' She squeezed his arm sympathetically, instantly regretting it as the cut on her hand sent out stinging barbs of pain.

'But if it goes our way tomorrow, it'll be worth it.' He scrolled through the TV menu. 'Stop me when you see something you fancy. Nothing heavy, though.'

'Anything but the chateau people, please.'

Canned laughter issued from the TV and Tom's answering chuckle vibrated through Ellie. When their plates were empty, she pulled the throw over both of them, its soft fleece as cosy as the warm lamplight illuminating the room. Sliding her hand up Tom's T-shirt, she laid her palm flat against the warmth of his belly. Here, in his arms, with their baby asleep and the house snug and secure, what would be the point in bringing up photos and flies? The shirt buttons pressed into her cheek as she buried her nose in his chest, breathing in the new-bread scent of him. So warm, so comfortable.

But she couldn't ignore her bladder any longer. She lifted his arm up.

'Back in a minute.'

The hall and stairs were in darkness, but a faint light glimmered on the landing. She faltered as her foot landed on the top step. The nursery door stood wide open and a slice of pastel light illuminated the carpet. The soft cadences of a lullaby drifted out. Hesitantly, she crept towards the light that pointed like a bright arrow into the dark room.

The nursery furniture stood where it always had. The cot under the window. The nursing chair to the side of it. The changing table against the chimney breast.

It didn't make sense.

She gripped the doorframe for support and the cut across her palm immediately stung. Questions ricocheted around her skull. The nursing chair, yes. Table, yes. But how could he have moved the cot? There hadn't been time for him to dismantle it and put it back together again.

Raucous TV laughter floated up the stairs and the noise shocked her limbs from their temporary paralysis. She rushed to the cot. Her fingertips met unyielding, hard wood then frantically traced the screws, tightly inserted in the holes, and when she dropped to her knees to peer at the slatted base, every piece was present and correct. Untouched. Unmoved.

At some point, she must have shouted out, because suddenly Tom stood in the doorway, holding the baby.

'What's up?' he said.

She jumped, slamming into the changing table.

'How did you do it so quick?'

'What do you mean?' he said, puzzled. 'Do what?'

'I moved everything this afternoon. It took ages to take the cot apart.'

Tom held his palm up in a placatory gesture.

'I'm really confused, Els. Are you saying you moved the cot?'

'And the chair and the table,' she added. 'Into our bedroom. But now they're back in the nursery. How do you explain that?'

The silence dragged on for a few seconds. Blood beat in her ears.

'I can't,' he said with a helpless shrug. 'Except … maybe you didn't move them?'

'Are you saying I'm *lying*?' High-pitched and borderline hysterical, she didn't recognise her own voice. Blood oozed, staining the cuff of her jumper and she thrust her hand out. 'The screwdriver slipped. And look at that.'

'That' was where the slats had bent the thick pile of the carpet, leaving striped indentations.

'Of course I don't think you're lying. But do you really believe I dismantled the cot, dragged it across to the nursery and reassembled it?'

Her jaw tight, she nodded once, quickly.

'But when? You'd have heard if I'd started shifting furniture.'

Tom continued talking, but the words were just noise.

A kaleidoscope of explanations dissolved and reassembled in her brain before she could make sense of them. How and what and who? He couldn't possibly have bathed Trinity, pulled the cot apart and put it back together, and moved the furniture in half an hour. A crack squad of removal men couldn't. Then suddenly, she was speaking out loud, her tongue tripping over the speed of her thoughts.

'First, I thought the side effects of the medication were making me imagine things, but then I got new tablets and it hasn't stopped. Or that being so tired and the stress of the move was making me confused and forgetful. Then I thought you must be gaslighting me to get me out of the way, but you're not cheating with Tanya, so why would you want me to go? And today Diane told me the woman in black is a neighbour with dementia, so I thought that explained everything. But now this. There's no way you could have moved the furniture back into the nursery without me hearing.'

'Slow down, love.' He laid Trinity in the cot and unwound paper from a loo roll.

Breathlessly, she asked, 'So what is going on?'

When she faltered, he pressed a wad against the bloodied gauze.

'I thought it must all be in my head, but it's not. It's *her*,' Ellie said, her voice tinny and strange. 'She never went away. I can feel her everywhere.'

Murmuring in affirmation, Tom leaned over the cot to stroke the baby's cheek. Trinity turned her head and smacked her lips in response.

'I understand,' he said quietly. 'I feel exactly the same.'

'Really?' She widened her eyes until the sockets ached.

'I can't stop thinking about what happened. How scared and confused she must have been. And I keep seeing her all the time.'

'You do?'

He nodded. 'The anniversary and Trinity's birthday has triggered so much for me too. Remember when it first happened and you saw her everywhere we went? Going past on a bus. Walking down the street. That time in the canteen right before you went to—' He paused and cleared his throat. 'Anyway, that's happening to me now. I keep catching myself reliving that night thinking what could I have done differently? And I know it's been hard for Dan too.'

There was a few seconds' silence. Ellie had been listening with mounting disbelief. This man she'd loved since she was eighteen years old was the one person on the planet who knew her inside out. How could he have read her so wrong?

'I'm not talking about *Mia*,' she said, aghast. 'I'm talking about Mary Brennan.'

The lines deepened across his forehead.

'Mary Brennan, the woman who used to live here?' he said. 'The one who died?'

Finally! She nodded eagerly. 'And I thought it was the PTSD back again, but this proves it. The cot proves it.'

'What proves what?' he said.

'Mary Brennan never left. She's still here. Everything that's happening to me is because of *her*.'

There. She'd said it. The vivid clarity was like diving into clean, cold water that washed away her confusion. She wasn't losing her mind and the cot was the proof.

Tom, however, was still struggling to understand.

Fleeting incomprehension and then disbelief swept over his face. He rested his forehead briefly on the nursery wall. In that moment, his phone rang. He exhaled sharply in irritation, checked the screen and answered tersely. 'Tanya? I'm just in the middle of something. Two minutes. I'll call you back.'

'Love,' he said, turning back to Ellie. 'Mary Brennan is dead and buried in the churchyard in Uppermoss. I get it's creepy that she died here, but like I said before, it's not the dead we need to worry about.'

His eyes darted briefly to Trinity and away again so quickly, Ellie almost didn't notice.

Almost.

Mothers can harm or even reject their babies.

Casually, she slid her fingers under her daughter's warm body, splaying them to support the fragile neck as she lifted. The wrinkled skin of prematurity that had given her a Shar Pei bagginess had plumped out, rounding those cheeks into rosy apples. And yet she was still so vulnerable. So easily harmed. So easily taken away.

Tom's phone shrilled again.

'Look, I'm going to have to take this,' he said, putting it to his ear. 'Just give me a minute.'

Ten seconds later, his shout of frustration reverberated through the house.

Buzzing her lips across the baby's silky ear, Ellie listened.

Tom had one hand braced on their bedroom wall, leaning his

weight into it. 'You have got to be joking,' he said. There was a long pause and when he spoke again, he didn't sound angry. He sounded defeated.

'I know you do ... yeah ... OK, early doors tomorrow. I'll try. Bye.'

The cords in his neck strained. He kicked the skirting board hard enough to rattle the photos on the chest of drawers.

'What's happened?' Ellie said.

'The main man was tipped off by someone at their end. We *had* him as well. Had the bastard.'

He punctuated the sentiment with a slap of the wall.

'Can I do anything to help?' Ellie said.

'No thanks, love.' He brought his tightly clenched knuckles to his mouth. 'I can't believe this has happened. Listen, I'm going to have to make some calls. I might as well sleep on the sofa. Can we talk about the cot thing tomorrow?'

Exhaustion and frustration gouged new tracks down the sides of his mouth. His entire body sagged, as though he'd aged ten years in ten minutes.

'Of course,' she said. 'Don't worry about that now.'

The spare duvet made soft whumping noises as Tom dragged it down the stairs.

She lay back and tried to sleep but her consciousness writhed. A tiny, traitorous part of it explored the idea of returning to Willow Lodge, or whatever the equivalent would be nowadays. A room efficiently cleaned by anonymous hands. Meals prepared, cooked and cleared away by the same. Nothing to do but read or watch TV. And an abundance of time with nothing to do but sleep. Even imagining it felt like sinking into a tempting mound of soft, comfortable pillows.

The web of skin between her thumb and finger throbbed as she fetched the Moses basket. It acted as a painful reminder that she *had* moved the cot. In her mind's eye she saw herself wrestling with the screwdriver, dragging the heavy wooden foot

256

and headboards into their bedroom, making a mental note of which was which.

But that was impossible.

And Tom couldn't have done it in the time.

And no one else was in the house.

57. Now

She woke to the sound of Tom moving around.

Bleary-eyed, she fumbled for the bedside light. The clock said 5.37, which was technically morning, but it was still pitch-dark. She flopped back on the pillow. If the whole purpose of sleep was to recharge your batteries, why did she wake up every morning even more drained than the day before?

'Morning, love,' Tom whispered. He had a towel wrapped round his waist and was drying his hair with another. 'Sorry, didn't mean to wake you.'

She rolled over and propped herself on her elbow. 'Have you heard any more about the job?'

He brushed a straggle of hair from her cheek. 'I did my best last night, but it's not enough. I'm going to have to go in. I just can't let these bastards go free. I *can't*. Dad's going to come and keep you company when the rush hour's died down. And I'll come home as soon as I've sorted this mess at work.'

Then I can sort this mess at home, she silently finished off for him.

A half-coughing cry interrupted from the Moses basket and Ellie gave up on any idea of going back to sleep.

After being winded and changed into a yellow dress and leggings, Trinity seemed content to be put on her tummy on the playmat while Ellie danced Mr Giraffe in front of her and tried to act normal. Dogs picked up on tension – she was sure of that. Did babies too? Even now, Trinity's infant brain could be rewiring itself, programming her mother's stress into her internal code.

'Look at Mr Giraffe!' she said brightly. 'He's having fun. We're all having fun. Not a care in the world.'

There was a ping from Ellie's phone.

Hi Ellie. Is 10 OK with you? Howard.

It was 8.20 now, so she had enough time to tidy up and get herself presentable. Her thumbs composed a quick reply: *Fine, here all day!*

She needed to focus on something other than her spinning thoughts. When Howard came, she would make a start on one of the myriad of DIY projects the house needed. Hang the new shower curtain. Strip some more wallpaper. Reattach the chunk of skirting Tom kicked off last night.

Jess had sent her a quick *how's it going* message and she fired off a quick reply. *All good thanks x.* And there was another from Norah:

Thought you might be interested in this. I'm writing another feature for the Stockfield Express. *Let's meet up for that coffee. Tomorrow? N*

'This' was a link to a Facebook page. Without thinking, Ellie clicked it.

Memories of Uppermoss High School

She clutched the phone, so tight the plastic case creaked. The screen displayed tiered rows of children with bad home haircuts, grinning awkwardly in front of a shiny navy-blue curtain. Standing, sitting on a bench or cross-legged on the floor, their brown flares, wing collars and hand-knitted jumpers were pure Seventies.

Only one of the pupils had been ringed in red.

Everything about the girl screamed *Don't look at me.* She shrank away from the camera and gazed at the floor, dipping her chin so the centre-parted dark hair hung on her hunched shoulders. Plain dark dress. Glasses. Ellie zoomed in. There was no mistaking it: the girl's hands were clasped protectively in front of a rounded stomach.

Uppermoss Secondary School 1979, the caption said.
Mary Brennan.

58. Now

'Ellie?'

Someone was saying her name.

A shadow fell across her, turning the insides of her eyelids from red to black. She scrabbled upright, scraping her back on wood. A woman plucked out AirPods. Her minty breath clouded the air. Nylon rustled as she bent down.

'Are you OK?'

Australian accent. For a blank, confused moment, she could only stare.

'It's me, Asha.'

Her feet stung. Dirt blackened the soles of her socks. Why wasn't she wearing shoes?

'What happened?'

Cold. Ellie cleared her throat, gazed around at the crowding trunks of trees. A low humming sounded, like a distant swarm of flies. Behind, the trunk of a tree burned like ice against her spine.

How did she get to Moss Pond? She tipped her head back. Saw bleached branches latticed against the grey sky. As she scrambled upright, she accidentally caught Asha, almost knocking her off balance.

'Hey, it's OK,' Asha said in the tone you'd use for a frightened animal. She brushed leafy debris from her jacket. 'Do you want me to walk home with you?'

Ellie nodded mutely.

'Your house is just' – Asha narrowed her eyes and gestured, waving one finger to the distance – 'over there.'

Bile burned up her chest and for a horrible moment, she

thought she would be sick. How did she get here? Shreds of memory swirled like the flakes in a snowglobe. The cot. Tom's work upset. Playing with Trinity. The text from Norah. Text from Howard. The photo of Mary Brennan.

'What time is it?' she said.

Asha clicked a button on her smartwatch. 'It's 9.20. Here, put this on.'

The waterproof fabric whispered as she zipped Ellie into her jacket, like a child.

'Have you banged your head?'

Had she? Ellie prodded her scalp gingerly. 'I don't think so.'

'Good. Can you walk?'

Bracing herself between Asha and the trunk of the tree, Ellie hobbled to standing. Her stiffened limbs suggested she'd been curled up in the same position for some time. Pins and needles shot up her calves and made her gasp, but there was no damage.

Tiny stones bit through her wet socks. Asha crooked out an elbow to link arms and Ellie leaned on her gratefully. Despite her slim frame, the other woman's arm was strong as steel. Still, they made slow progress with Asha holding low branches up for Ellie to stoop under.

'How did you get here?' Asha said gently. 'Can you remember?'

Ellie gave her head a little shake to help the swirling pieces fall into place. A photo. A girl.

'Is Tom at home?'

It took Ellie a few seconds to remember. 'No, he had to go to work early.'

Asha stopped so abruptly that Ellie stumbled on a tree root. She grabbed a branch and winced.

'Listen to me carefully,' Asha said urgently. She stood directly in front of Ellie, clasping her upper arms. 'If you're here and Tom's at work, who is looking after the baby?'

59. Now

Ellie felt the blood drain from her face. Even if she'd been wearing trainers, she couldn't have kept up with Asha. Stumbling behind, she watched the other woman side-step branches and tree roots, heard her swift feet beating across the forest floor.

By the time she entered the kitchen, her lungs raw and with blood hammering at her temples, Asha had lifted Trinity off the playmat and was cradling her.

'Hush, it's OK, honey,' she murmured.

Trinity's legs drummed furiously.

Stricken, Ellie reached out but Asha twisted the baby away.

'Why don't you wash your hands first?'

She stared. Front. Back. The dirt went up her wrists and smudged the cuffs of Asha's jacket. When she picked up the liquid soap, her fingers coated the bottle with dirt that blackened the white froth as she scrubbed.

'Where's the best place to change her?' Asha said.

'Nursery. Upstairs,' Ellie said faintly. She scrubbed at a stubborn patch with the dishcloth. 'I can do it.'

'No worries.' Asha jogged the baby and shushed her.

She led the way upstairs and Ellie obediently followed.

In the nursery, Trinity squalled on the changing mat, fists and feet punching the air in violent frog kicks while Asha stripped the dress and wet tights off.

Ellie couldn't speak. The baby had been spotless and now thick stripes of dried mud spoiled the yellow fabric.

'Easy, gorgeous girl,' Asha said, ripping open the tabs.

Jesus.

The stink of ammonia permeated the air. Visible chafed patches reddened the delicate folds and creases.

'Have you got any cream?'

She passed the tub over and glanced at the camera. Green light off. That was one small mercy, at least.

When Asha finished, she folded the nappy and dropped it in the bucket and wiped over the vinyl changing mat. 'Shall we put on some clean clothes?'

Ellie opened the drawer and picked out fresh tights and a clean pinafore.

With her nappy off, Trinity calmed down. Or maybe it was Asha's capable presence that soothed her. Either way, Asha dressed her with no fuss and when she'd fastened the final popper, she passed her to Ellie, saying, 'I think she might be hungry.'

Trinity immediately began to suck wetly on Ellie's T-shirt, triggering a fresh wave of mother guilt. How could she not remember when she'd last fed her? How could she not remember anything about the last hour?

'I'm really sorry to put you out,' Ellie said. Trinity lay on the feeding cushion. 'Thanks for helping.'

Asha stayed at the door. 'I'm popping over to Diane's to check she's OK to have Freddie for a bit longer. Then I'll come straight back.'

'That's nice of you, but we'll be fine now, thanks.'

'No trouble,' Asha insisted. 'I'll be back in ten, max.'

And she smiled like it was a done deal.

Ellie held it together until she was sure Asha had gone. Then she slumped in the chair, protecting the baby in a cocoon of her own body, and inhaled the blend of organic lavender and chamomile that made up Trinity's unique smell. Even during her stay at Willow Lodge, she had never lost a whole hour. Tears fell silently, dampening the feathery hair into stringy clumps.

Fate.

That's what her mum had said about finding 6 Moss Lane.

You made an infinite number of seemingly insignificant decisions every day, and – boom – the consequences floored you months, years down the line.

If the sun had been shining when she left work. If she hadn't stepped into the entrance of Raja Property Services. If the motorway had been open on the day of the auction. If she and Tom had stuck to their budget …

If, if, if.

Other fateful choices snaked further back through her life. If she hadn't applied for Henderson Hall. If Tom's work placement hadn't fallen through. If Mia had remembered her keys that night.

And now fate had led her to a house that ripped children and mothers apart.

Fate hadn't given her this house as a gift.

This house was her punishment.

60. Then

The clocks in Willow Lodge didn't work properly. Sometimes the hands moved so slowly, the world slowed to a halt. And other times, they spun round like wheels, faster and faster until a whole day could race by without anyone noticing. It made her dizzy. Or maybe it wasn't the clocks. Maybe it was the meds. In the four weeks since Mia died, she'd had a lot of those.

She watched a raindrop slide through the condensation on the window, cutting a clear path through the foggy view of the towering weeping willow tree and the staff car park.

Last night, she had woken to find herself screaming at the window and this morning had been forced to discuss her sleep-walking 'issues' in a group counselling session. Waste of time. Everyone wanted her to talk, but no one wanted to listen. If they genuinely wanted to help, they'd put her back on the sleeping tablets they'd given her a week ago, when she was admitted.

Those bitter white pills dissolving on her tongue triggered a sweet forgetfulness that started in her feet and spread upwards through her body before it numbed her face and finally, thank-fully, stilled her spiralling thoughts. But the doctor said they were habit-forming and apparently this was a 'Bad Thing' and 'To Be Avoided'.

Her finger squeaked on the windowpane. She'd drawn a love heart, and now she rubbed it out with her sleeve.

The nurse popped his head round the door. 'Your visitor's here. Shall I send him in?'

She nodded. Somewhere in the room, a fly rattled dementedly against the plastic casing of the overhead light. At some point there must have been a leak and a sepia patch bloomed across two of the ceiling tiles.

Next to the door was a noticeboard with two printed A4 sheets on it: *CCTV is in operation throughout this building.* And: *If you want to leave Willow Lodge, please just ask a nurse.* That was a joke. When she'd asked ultra-politely if they'd call her a cab, they'd said no.

A familiar outline showed through the toughened glass in the door and her traitorous heart leapt.

'Hi,' Tom said quietly.

How dare he look so good? His smile faltered as his eyes flicked down to the bandages on her wrists and, without a word, she pulled her sleeves down to cover them.

'How are you doing?' he said, pulling out a chair. 'Are you sleeping at all?'

Shrug.

'What's the food like?' he said.

She picked the ragged skin of her cuticles.

'I spoke to your mum. She said she'll be here about ten tomorrow and to ask if you needed anything, like clothes or shampoo or books or … stuff.'

She shook her head and bit the skin round her nail.

From the corridor came a sudden scream. Tom turned in alarm and half stood, hesitated, then sat down. Rapid footsteps ran past.

'Never a dull moment, eh?' he said with strained jollity.

There was a pause. Ellie pulled a tissue from her sleeve and began methodically tearing it into strips.

Tom cleared his throat and Ellie could sense the effort that was going into keeping his voice upbeat. 'I spoke to Danny last night about him coming back to Manchester. So we were talking and we thought you could stay in our flat for good. Or the three of us could find a bigger place. Or if you don't want that, we can help you find somewhere else.'

She dropped the pieces of torn-up tissue on the windowsill and pinched them into a heap with her fingers.

'Please talk to me.' He looked away and she realised he was trying to blink away tears.

Then, very slowly, she turned her back on Tom. She could hear his misery but it didn't touch her. Nothing touched her now. He was as insignificant as the bluebottle rattling against the glass, unaware that the windows didn't open at Willow Lodge.

'Don't throw away two years of work. Especially when you're on track for a First. Please, Ellie.'

She put her hand on the glass separating her from the rain-soaked outside world. Through the haze, the car park was like an Impressionist painting, smears of colour and vague shapes that made more sense the further away you got.

'And it's only been two months, but they're helping you here aren't they? And uni would help you catch up. I bet they'd let you back part-time, you know, if it was too much to handle all at once.'

Even though the air in Willow Lodge was always stifling, the windowpane felt cool against her palm. Cool and smooth. She rested her forehead against it.

'Please don't push me away,' he said and the strained voice didn't sound like his. 'I know you're mad at me for calling the ambulance, but I had to do something. You had a complete meltdown in the canteen. You weren't making any sense and you hadn't slept or eaten for days and you saw Mia everywhere and—'

'Leave me alone, Tom.'

From a distance, she tested her feelings and concluded that letting go felt good. Like unscrewing a valve to relieve the pressure. So she did it again and this time, she added a rhythmic bang of the window to each syllable.

'Get out, get out, get OUT.'

Two staff members barged through the door. One of them stood by Ellie while the other ushered Tom through the door. The last glimpse Ellie had of him was his beautiful, traitorous face.

He didn't look concerned anymore, he looked afraid.

61. Now

Howard.

She'd completely forgotten he was coming. And now the sputter of his ancient van on the drive had her leaping off the nursing chair, sending the baby into startled crying. Despite the sudden kick of adrenalin, getting to the front door was like wading through waist-deep mud.

'Ellie, are you in there, love?'

She opened the door. He stood in the porch wearing work boots, paint-spattered overalls, and a worried expression.

'Thought I might have missed you,' he said.

'We're here,' she said, failing to grapple Trinity to stillness.

'And is Grandad's little girl OK?'

Howard leaned in and let the baby grab his finger.

'Of course she is,' Ellie snapped. 'Why wouldn't she be?'

Bewilderment set around his lined eyes. He cleared his throat. 'No reason, love. Am I all right to come in?'

She ushered him quickly inside and, after scanning the driveway, locked the door.

Howard put his toolbox down on the kitchen floor. His puzzled expression was now tinged with alarm.

'Are you sure everything is all right, love? You look a bit …' he groped for the right term '… flustered.'

'I'm just tired.' The baby battered her fists on Ellie's shoulder. 'We're fine, thanks.'

'I'll get on with the garden then, if you don't mind.'

'Hold on,' she said and thrust Trinity at him before he could object. She took her phone out and flicked to Mary's class photo.

'The one circled in red,' she said. 'Is that the woman you saw in our garden? The one who didn't speak to you?'

Clutching the baby awkwardly, he pushed his glass down his nose and peered.

'She's a lot younger but it's her. Dark hair, big glasses?'

There was a silence. Howard frowned in concentration.

'Is it her?' Ellie insisted. 'I thought it must be Rita, but now I'm not sure.'

'I don't think I know a Rita,' he said, handing the baby back. He picked up his toolbox and walked to the back door. 'Sorry, love, I really can't tell. Will you be all right for ten minutes while I'm in the garden?'

'Sure, yes. Go ahead,' she murmured.

If only she could reach in to tilt the girl's chin to get a clear look. Ellie flicked her fingers to enlarge the photo, zooming in on Mary Brennan's downcast face.

She jumped at the bluebottle buzz of the doorbell. Peering into the hall, she saw two figures, their faces rippled in the dimpled glass of the porch.

Shit.

She'd forgotten about Asha. Her pulse launched into a sprint. The letterbox rattled, the brass lid flipped open.

'Ellie?' Diane spoke very kindly. 'Can we come in?'

Trinity squawked in sudden surprise as Ellie's fingers tightened.

'Is that Trinity there with you?' Diane said. 'Please can you open the door?'

Through the kitchen window, she could see Howard leaning on his spade, a plume of smoke curling into the air above him. If they went to try the back door, they would see him and that would be game over. She smoothed her hair down, straightened her top and turned the key.

Asha stood behind Diane, wiping Freddie's nose with a tissue.

'Sorry, it's not a good time,' Ellie said.

The two other women exchanged panicky glances.

269

'We came round to see how you are,' Diane said. 'Asha told me about what happened at Moss Pond. And with the baby. Is Tom coming home from work soon? Would you like us to call him?'

From the back garden came the sound of splintering wood.

'No. We're fine,' she replied. 'My father-in-law is here now. That's his van.'

'Ellie, please can you let us in for a chat?' Asha pleaded. 'Two minutes, that's all.'

'It's really not a good time. I'm about to … get in the shower,' she said brightly. 'Thanks for coming round, though. We are fine, honestly. And Tom's dad is here, like I said. He's looking after us now.'

She shut the door and flattened herself against the wall until they retreated up the driveway.

But what if they hadn't gone back next door? She clenched her fist and held it to her mouth. What if they went down the passageway to find Howard? They'd tell him she'd left the baby and then he would tell Tom and what would come next didn't bear thinking about. *Get to him first.* She boiled the kettle, poured milk in a mug and bashed the teabag with a spoon to hurry it along.

'Thought you might fancy a brew,' she called, looking over her shoulder. No sign of Asha or Diane. Good.

The path to the rose bed was well trodden now and the grass lay flat. It was still cold out here but watery rays of sunlight broke through the cloud.

Steam curled from the mug into the cold air. The anaemic tea inside was the colour of mushroom soup.

'Thanks,' Howard said, taking it. 'Look, love. You can tell me to mind my own business, but are you sure you're all right? You don't seem yourself.'

She cast a furtive glance at the passageway then peered at the hedge that marked the boundary with Diane's place. Under her feet, the black earth pulsed and wavered. She felt suddenly dizzy, as though she were standing on the deck of a ship.

'I'm fine,' she said faintly. 'Trinity's having a sleep. I'll just go and watch TV for a while.'

'Do you want me to call Tom?' He put his foot on the step of the spade.

'Honestly, no need. I'm fine. I'll just—' She jerked her thumb at the kitchen. As she did, a flutter of movement from next door attracted her attention. The blinds in the conservatory swayed, as though someone had been peering between the slats only a second ago. Good. They could see her talking with Howard. Bringing him a cup of tea. Doing normal things.

'I'll go back in,' she finished weakly.

Inside, she leaned against the back door briefly, and rolled her shoulders back to ease the discomfort of too tight straps and a bra stuffed with rocks. The washing machine rose to a noisy spin. Yellow flashed through the glass door as the mud washed from the dress Trinity had worn that morning. *You don't deserve her*, the mechanical whirring seemed to say. *You don't deserve her*.

It was inevitable that Tom would find out she had left the baby. How could Diane *not* tell him? Wasn't even a question of if, but when. Or – dread crackled through her like an electric current – what if Diane bypassed Tom completely? What if, even now, she was on the phone to social services?

Overdue a feed, Trinity squirmed in the bouncer. Each of her grumbles drove the guilt in a little deeper. Anything could have happened in the missing hour.

Upstairs, she plumped the pillows against the headboard. The nursing chair was more comfortable, but she couldn't do it. Not today. Trinity began to suck and Ellie took the TV remote off the bedside table. Nothing taxing. She needed the mental chewing gum of daytime TV. Something involving a fake living room and faker camaraderie. Something like this.

An older woman in a floral dress sat on a sofa bookended by two presenters wearing matching sympathetic expressions. At the bottom of the screen was a caption: *They made me give up my baby.*

The woman was in the middle of condensing a lifetime's heart-break into three minutes.

Silver-haired man was asking, 'And how did your parents react when you told them you were pregnant?'

'I was only a child myself,' she said in a Birmingham accent, smoothing her hands down her thighs. 'They were angry. Disappointed. There was no discussion. I wasn't allowed to keep the baby and that was that.'

Shiny bob nodded slowly. 'And were you allowed to hold her or care for her at all?'

Tears rolled down the guest's cheeks. She plucked a tissue from the box on the coffee table. 'I never even saw her. They took her away as soon as she was born.'

Without warning, the picture darkened, cutting away from the studio to a dimly lit staircase.

Ellie jerked upright, grabbing Trinity just in time before she rolled off the bed.

Their staircase again. Same swirly Seventies carpet, same textured wallpaper. A man's plump fingers curled around the banister. *Their* banister. Flick, flick, flick. Every channel showed the same clip. *Their* landing.

She jabbed the power button, but it wouldn't turn off. But when she tried to get up to switch it off at the wall, an intense pressure, like tight hospital sheets, pinned her to the bed. Helplessly, she watched the screen as the hand drew back the bolts. The nursery door opened on a few books on a thin plywood shelf. The chimney breast was covered in yellow floral wallpaper. A single bulb cast jaundiced light over the hump under the blanket while beneath the bed, the floor glistened.

The figure in the bed cried out.

Finally, the screen went black.

62. Then

It wasn't the alarm that woke her but the sound of Mia retching. Ellie looked at her clock: 5.15. So that's why she hadn't answered her texts last night. The toilet flushed twice. The kitchen tap ran and Mia's bedroom door opened and closed. Must have been quite a bender.

Ellie must have fallen asleep, because the next time she checked, it was after seven. This time, it was voices that woke her. Or, more precisely, one voice. Murmuring interspersed with long pauses told her Mia was on the phone.

'How can you even say that?'

No whispering there. Quite the opposite, in fact. Followed by a thud that sounded the way a phone would if you threw it across the room. The soft crying started almost immediately and Ellie chewed her lip. Knock on the wall? Go and see? Uncertain of the best course of action, she opted for inaction and lay in bed until the crying stopped and she could creep into the kitchen.

Late-night chips had set hard on the plate. Grease coagulated round a crusted smear of brown sauce. Bits floated in the scummy water in the sink and a fly buzzed. Ellie wrinkled her nose as she opened the window to shoo it out.

How late had Mia got back? She squirted green liquid over the dirty dishes and began to scrub. She hadn't heard her come in. Assumed she was staying over with Danny.

Wiping the dust from the telly and the coffee table, she decided against vacuuming. Let Mia sleep off the hangover. Instead, she opened the balcony doors and hung the damp tea towel on the line next to a sports bra Mia had forgotten to bring in.

Still no sign. Ellie couldn't let her miss the first seminar of the new term.

She rapped lightly on the closed bedroom door. 'Are you up?'

Nearly half ten on a Thursday and Mia hadn't got dressed. Last night's eyeliner clumped in the corners of her eyes and her hair needed a good brush. The M pendant Danny had given her last Christmas hung on a black cord around her neck, glinting against her black T-shirt.

'Sorry,' she said through a yawn. 'Long night.'

'You do look the worse for wear. Did you go anywhere good?'

'The flat then out for chips.'

'Do you want me to make you something?' Ellie said. 'Remember you've got to go in for twelve.'

Mia gave a tired smile. 'I'm not hungry, thanks.'

'How about a bit of toast? You can't go out on an empty stomach …'

'I don't think I'll make it in today,' she said with a grimace.

Behind her, the bed was unmade. Clothes littered the floor and spilled out of the half-open drawers. The curtains were closed and the air was stale.

'You can't miss your induction,' Ellie said, stepping forward. 'Why don't you have a shower and I'll tidy up?'

Mia blocked the doorway, fiddling with the black cord around her neck. 'Thanks but I just need to be on my own.'

'Well, at least let me make you a cup of tea.'

Mia rubbed her eye sockets. Flakes of old mascara sprinkled across her cheekbones. 'Jesus, Ellie,' she said. 'I want to be on my own. Can't you take a hint?'

Ellie swayed as she clung to the yellow pole on the tram, her emotions pinballing from anger to humiliation and back again. Her feet followed the well-worn path to her usual seat in the lecture hall. She took her coat off and placed her notebook and pen on the desk, ready for the induction session. But white noise came from the lecturer's mouth, a meaningless backdrop to the anger bubbling inside her like a boiling kettle.

How dare Mia speak to her like that?

It had been a week since the revelation at the Union. For the first two days, Ellie burned with anger and humiliation. Stupid cliché. Her best friend and her boyfriend going behind her back.

But gradually, she'd reasoned herself into something approaching forgiveness. On a practical level, the contract tied the pair of them together until next summer and nine months in a toxic flat-share did not appeal. Plus there was no faking Mia's hollow-eyed contrition. Any fool could see she was genuinely mortified. Then there was Tom. Ellie ached with misery at the idea of not seeing him again. Was it worth throwing everything away over one error of judgement? One mistake.

With a jolt, she realised the lecturer had taken her glasses off and was packing books into her bag. Rustling and chatter filled the hall. The girl next to her yawned extravagantly. What had the induction even been about? Ellie looked at the spiky doodles covering the page and flipped her notebook shut. That was Mia's fault. Making her lose focus.

Can't you take the hint? After all she had done. All she'd forgiven.

By the time she got off the tram and turned for home, black clouds were massed above her head. A storm was brewing outside and inside, her pinballing emotions had landed on fury.

63. Now

The sparkling mirror over the fireplace reflected a woman who had managed to shower and blow-dry her hair. Her top was only very slightly wrinkled and even her socks matched.

Ellie tested her happy face. Convincing enough. This is a woman in control, her reflection said. This is a woman who would never reject or harm her baby.

The key clicked in the lock and Tom said loudly, 'Something smells good.'

'In the kitchen,' she called.

A pan of chilli simmered on the hob. Trinity radiated cuteness while Ellie tried to radiate normality.

'I've missed you so much today.' Tom lifted the baby up and buried his nose in her neck. Then turned to plant a smacking kiss on Ellie's lips. 'And I've missed you today as well. How was Dad?'

'Great, really helpful. I did ask if he wanted to stay for dinner, but he had a darts match lined up.' She tapped the wooden spoon against the pan and scraped a cluster of mince against the side. 'How was your day?'

'Oh you know.' He kicked his trainers off. 'Damage limitation. Have I got time for a quick shower?'

'Five minutes.'

He kissed Ellie again. 'You look beautiful. House looks great. You've been busy.'

While Tom went to change, she cut the top off a rice pouch and stuck it in the microwave. Next, she warmed two plates in the oven. When the microwave pinged, she shook out the rice and spooned chilli from the pan. The chilli bubbled like lava; steam rose off the heaped meat and glistening sauce. Steam fogged the kitchen windows. Everything was under control.

Tom had changed into saggy joggers and a retro Manchester City top. He roughly scrubbed his hair then combed it back with his fingers and stuffed the wet towel in the machine.

'Bloody hell, I am starving. Mmm.' He gave a chef's kiss and smiled at Trinity in her bouncer. 'Daddy is a lucky guy.'

'Hurry up before it gets cold,' Ellie said passing him a cold beer and the bottle opener.

The baby gurgled contentedly in the bouncer.

'I could get used to this,' Tom said.

Ellie flashed her perfect 1950s housewife smile and sat down. 'Have you sorted the problem at work?' she said.

While Tom rambled on about Interpol and the CPS and the dark web, she pretended to listen intently, even managing to chip in occasionally, until both plates were empty and he began to clear away.

Despite the superficial easiness, something simmered under the surface and she saw them both suddenly as actors on a stage spouting dialogue written by someone else. But that was fine. The longer she could keep them both playing their parts, the longer she could put off the inevitable questions and explanations that would keep spiralling because the only explanation was Mary Brennan.

A door slammed outside and her body instantly tensed. Was it Diane? Asha?

'Major Tom to mother ship? Come in, mother ship.'

With a wan smile, she focused her eyes on his. 'Sorry, I was miles away. What did you say?'

As he spoke, he clattered the cutlery into the sink. 'Dad said you weren't yourself today and' – he switched the hot tap on – 'I know we're both knackered, but we really need to talk about what happened last night with the nursery and the cot.'

'Oh that.' She flapped her hand dismissively. 'I meant to tell you, I made a mistake.'

As he turned she fixed a silly-me smile in place.

'I know, ridiculous,' she continued, rolling her eyes. 'What happened was I was going to move the stuff, then I got distracted and forgot. But I really thought I had done it. Sorry. Blame it on the baby brain!'

From the look he gave her, Ellie knew the feeble lie hadn't fooled him for a second, but before he could respond, the doorbell interrupted.

Cortisol kicked through her system, rattling her heart in her ribcage.

'Don't answer it,' she blurted out. 'Please.'

He narrowed his eyes and watched her carefully.

The doorbell rang a second time.

'I'll be back in a minute.'

The wind rushed down the hall and into the kitchen. Something in the garden toppled over, landing with a noisy thud on the concrete.

'Hi, Diane,' she heard Tom say. 'Come in.'

64. Then

Mia perched on the edge of the sofa with her jacket folded over her rucksack. On the coffee table, several coffee mugs and an overflowing ashtray jostled for space with piles of paper. The air reeked of charcoal dust and stale smoke.

Ellie pointedly opened the balcony doors, letting the rising wind roar in to scatter Mia's sketches on the floor.

'Hi,' Mia said. 'How was your day?' She smiled, and the smile conveyed so much: apology, sadness, affection.

'I was a bitch before,' Mia went on, gathering up the fallen paintings and putting her phone on top. 'Sorry. I've got a lot on my mind and I don't feel too good.'

'Well, don't smoke then,' Ellie snapped. 'Seriously, you promised you wouldn't smoke in here. All my stuff's going to stink.'

Mia didn't answer. She wilted rather than sat on the sofa and pulled her knees up to her chin. Her skin was so drained that Ellie could see spidery veins on her eyelids and dark circles that had nothing to do with mascara. Angry-looking spots clustered along her jawline. Even her lips seemed bloodless. In that unflattering black dress and with hair tied in a messy updo, she was almost unrecognisable.

'By the way, Tom asked if you wanted anything bringing back from the restaurant,' Mia said.

Ellie turned slowly. 'When did you speak to Tom?'

Mia flapped vaguely at the biker jacket slung over the rucksack. 'He dropped my coat round on his way to work.'

'Why didn't Danny bring it?'

Her eyes glittered. 'He doesn't want to see me.'

Tom was here? Alone, with Mia?

Ellie undid her laces and, with shaking hands, set her shoes neatly against the skirting board. She dug her hands deep into the pockets of her jeans.

'Anyway, I'm going out for a bit. I need to talk to Danny.' She picked up her jacket and walked to the door. 'I just wanted to catch you to apologise about earlier.'

She slid her key in the lock. Hesitated, then dug her black-varnished thumbnail into the textured wallpaper. 'Sorry.' She drew in a sharp breath. 'It's just that—'

When she didn't continue, Ellie's heart thudded painfully. *Tom and Mia. Tom and Mia.*

'Just *what*?' she said sharply.

Turning, Mia hung her head until all Ellie could see was the scruffy topknot and the bumps of her spine through the shapeless black dress.

'I need to speak to Danny first.'

Dig, dig, dig went the thumbnail.

Something nasty caught in Ellie's throat and she pulled at the neck of her jumper. 'Is this about Tom?'

Shouldering her bag, Mia sighed. 'I've said I'm sorry so many times and I really, really am.'

But a surge of panic made Ellie grab Mia's arm. 'It is Tom, isn't it? That's why he was here.'

'I really can't deal with this today,' Mia said irritably shaking her off. 'Stop being paranoid. Not everything is about *you*.'

As soon as the flat door slammed shut, Ellie burst into tears. Horrible, racking tears that streamed relentlessly down her cheeks. She couldn't shake the misery all evening. And even though she put her happy face on when Tom arrived with a paper bag of goodies, he wasn't fooled.

'What's up?'

'Nothing. Why?'

He used the side of his fork to bisect a spring roll. 'Danny's been funny with me all day. Now I come to yours, and you're the same.'

Lightning flashed white through the balcony doors, followed by a deep growl of thunder. Ellie got up and closed the windows as the first fat drops of rain fell.

The rain poured for the rest of that evening. Wind rattled the balcony and scraped tendrils of ivy across the glass while they watched a movie involving a bank robbery. Or maybe a jewel heist. By the end of it, Ellie was none the wiser. But, thanks to the empty bottles lined like skittles on the kitchen worktop, she was significantly drunker.

Paranoid?

Tom was soon snoring, but Ellie queasily watched the angled corners of her attic bedroom tilt and swim. How could she be expected to trust either of them? She'd checked her phone about a hundred times and Mia hadn't called or texted to apologise. Consumed by anger, she lay listening to creaks and groans as the storm shook the old building to its foundations.

65. Now

To be fair, Diane had been sympathetic, apologetic even, using phrases like 'I'd hate you to think I am a nosy neighbour' and 'acting with the best of intentions'. And at least she'd spoken to them rather than telling tales to social services.

Not that it made much difference to Tom, who was currently leaning against the worktop staring at Ellie as though he barely recognised her.

'It wasn't as bad as she made out,' Ellie said, focusing on the leftover congealed chilli in the pan. Her head had begun to ache. 'I went for a walk, that's all.'

Anxiety lined Tom's features and saturated his voice. 'Asha found you asleep in the woods, Els. She said you were completely out of it. Didn't know where you were or how you got there. There is a line and leaving the baby on her own with the back door wide open crosses that line. I promise you I'm not blaming you, but we can't go on like this. Talk to me.'

The memory of finding Trinity, alone and screaming in the house made her flinch like a physical pain. No matter how outlandish the truth sounded, she couldn't let Tom think she'd abandoned their daughter deliberately.

'It's not what you think,' she began slowly. 'I'm going to tell you something and it's going to sound really, really weird but I need you to hear me out. No comments, no judgement till I've finished.'

He pulled out a chair and braced his hands against his knees. 'Go on.'

'Do you remember how we said no more secrets?' she said. 'You have to trust me. There's something wrong with this house.' She held up a warning finger as Tom opened his mouth. 'Hear me out.'

Nodding mutely, he tapped his thighs like he was typing a report on an invisible keyboard.

'A lot of things have happened since we moved in. Things I can't explain. And I know you're going to say it's all in my head and I'm tired or it's the medication or Mia or whatever, but I swear it's not.'

Slow down. Ellie heard herself gabbling, as though the lid had come off a shaken bottle releasing an unstoppable fountain of words.

'The keys. I know I had them that day at the park. I know it. And when the lightbulbs exploded, there was a woman singing upstairs. I've heard a baby crying that wasn't there. And I haven't sleepwalked for years, have I? Even when I did, I only walked, I didn't go through cupboards or end up sitting under a tree.' She paused to draw a panting breath, reluctant to disrupt the energetic rush. 'And I thought maybe it was me: I was a nutjob. But then the cot moved.'

'But you just told me you'd made a mistake, remember?' He rubbed his eyes. 'That you got confused.'

'I was lying!' she said, her tight throat forcing out a near squeak. 'I just wanted to get you off my back. There is no logical explanation for furniture moving by itself.'

Tom neutralised his expression. 'OK. But for argument's sake, if you can imagine keys moving, how do you know you didn't imagine the cot?'

She stifled a sigh. That was the trouble with Tom. His job had siphoned off his imagination, taking with it the ability to understand that between black and white, right and wrong, there were things that couldn't be investigated, solved and filed.

Her sleeve rode up as she thrust her arm at him. 'Because I cut my hand. Remember? That's proof that I didn't imagine it.'

Brown in the middle and burgundy around the edges, a scab had begun to form over where the screwdriver had slipped.

There was a pause while Tom interlocked his fingers on the table's scarred wooden surface. Watching the scepticism radiate from him sapped her energy. She could see his mind ticking, assimilating what she was saying, sifting through it, trying to convert the unpalatable truth into a logical explanation.

'OK, today. Why Moss Pond?' she continued. 'I'll tell you. Because it's where William Brennan hanged himself. Mary's father. And I don't know why any of this is happening to me. To us. But I do know it's all tied up with Mary Brennan. She's trying to tell me something.'

'No,' Tom said gently. 'All this about missing keys, a woman in the garden. Sleepwalking.' He stopped for a beat. 'Cutting yourself, Ellie. You must see it's about Mia.'

She shook her head violently. 'No.'

'Mary Brennan is dead,' he said.

The shout swelled up from the ground, reverberating through her body before it exploded from her.

'So is Mia!'

66. Then

'Are you sure you're OK?' Tom said.

She almost laughed.

Weeks had passed since Mia died and Ellie was still very far from OK. She rested her forearms on the tabletop, cold Formica chilling her skin. The tell-tale zigzag lines of an impending migraine flickered at the sides of her vision. If only she could drop her forehead on the table and sleep and sleep.

Steam rose from damp clothes, while outside the late October skies drizzled. Around them, the uni canteen heaved with students chatting, laughing, living. Between them, a cardboard packet contained a sandwich of limp rocket and plasticky sliced cheese. Tom nudged it towards her.

'At least eat something.'

Obediently, she peeled back the plastic film. A process began: salivary glands activated, chew, swallow the bolus of food. The bread tasted of nothing. The slimy lump sliding down her throat repulsed her and she gagged.

'You've got to eat something.'

Over the past few weeks, it seemed every time he spoke to her, his voice held that note of anguish. She should care. On some level she actually wanted to care.

But she didn't.

A glass shell shielded her from the rest of the world. It developed another layer, transparent and shatterproof every morning. It protected her during the police interviews. It had got her through Anita and David helping to sort the flat. It had got her through the horror of Mia's funeral yesterday.

'A celebration of a life lived to the full' – that's how Anita and David painted the service. Colourful clothes, please. No lilies. Roses were Mia's favourite flower. Donations to a local dog shelter she'd volunteered at would be welcome. The music was upbeat, the walls decorated with her artwork and the eulogy punctuated with hilarious anecdotes and video clips of Mia. Just twenty years to make so many friends. To do so many things. How was that possible?

The wake, held in a marquee in the garden, rocked with laughter rather than sobbing and it was, as everyone felt the need to observe, exactly what Mia would have wanted. Safe inside her glass bubble, Ellie didn't have to listen or care. Or to point out that what Mia would really have wanted was not to be dead.

And now, here she was back in Manchester with Tom. Sitting in the canteen with normal students and being expected to drop back into her old life as though nothing had happened. A girl on the table next to her turned, her eyes boring into Ellie. Suddenly, the whole canteen was looking at her, whispering, judging. *You know the dead girl? That's her flatmate. The one who was there.*

'I'm not hungry,' Ellie said and pushed the plate away.

Until Tom grabbed her hands in his warm grasp, she didn't realise how cold she was. Her whole body carved in ice.

'Me and your mum are worried about you,' Tom said. 'You won't talk to anyone. You haven't visited the counsellor. You don't eat. You're sleepwalking.' He hushed his voice, leaned in closer. 'Did you know you've started talking to thin air?'

His eyes shone with unshed tears.

'I'm out of my depth here,' he said thickly. 'I don't know what to do to help. And I'm scared.'

She turned to stare out of the window. And that's when she saw her.

The girl's long dark ponytail swished as she pushed the door open. She wore a black leather jacket over a jumper shot through with glittery threads. She had high cheekbones, a straight nose, and huge eyes ringed with liner.

Ellie shrank back in the plastic chair and let out a low moan. Tom shot her a look of confusion. 'What's wrong?'
The girl turned her head and flashed that familiar smile.
Ellie began to whimper.

67. Now

From a distance, she heard Tom saying her name.

Her blurred vision sharpened, revealing her own maternity-jean-clad thighs, the worn denim soft against her forehead.

'Keep your head down,' Tom pressed his palm gently between her shoulder blades. 'You fainted.'

'I'm OK,' she said. Or tried to say – her tongue lolled, too big for her mouth. The veins at her temples pulsed and her thoughts were muffled in a thick layer of bubble wrap. Giddy with rushing blood, she struggled to sit upright. 'I'm OK,' she said more clearly now. 'I just want to have a lie-down.'

With Tom's help, she climbed the stairs and sank gratefully onto the bed. Everything from Tom popping painkillers from a blister pack to her swallowing them down with a glass of water hammered in her ears. The headache clawed at the base of her skull and she closed her eyes.

'You know I would never do anything to hurt our daughter,' she said faintly when he returned with the baby.

'Of course I do,' he said with desperation in his voice. 'But none of this is right. I think your PTSD is back, Ellie. Everything fits – the sleepwalking, the paranoia, the delusions ... We need to get you some help before things get worse. Tomorrow. No arguments.'

With pain crawling across her scalp and burrowing into her eye sockets, an argument was the last thing she needed.

'OK,' she whispered and pulled the duvet over her head.

By the time the dawn finally seeped around the curtains, Ellie had been half-awake for hours. The headache lingered faintly like the thin grey fog outside. She had hoped to sink into oblivion for a while, but the birds of Mosswood had other ideas. Even burrowing under the pillow couldn't block out their raucous cawing. Crows, rooks, magpies – it sounded like every bird in the country had gathered directly above her bedroom. She could hear their claws scrabbling on the roof tiles.

Tom slept on, face down and with his arms wrapped around the pillow, his nostrils clicking with each in-breath. Even after all these years, his ability to sleep through anything still amazed her. She carefully wriggled free of the duvet and crept to the nursery. Peered at the carpet. Sniffed the air. Closed her eyes and tuned in to the atmosphere.

Nothing to be afraid of.

Still, she wedged the door wide before gathering Trinity up and laying the small, precious bundle on the changing table. Unfasten tabs, remove nappy. Lift. Wipe. Place fresh nappy. Fasten new tabs. Feed. Her body autopiloted through the baby's early morning routine, while her mind whirred with frantic activity.

'Morning, love. You're up early.'

She hadn't heard Tom get up, but here he was with the inside of his wrists propped against the top of the nursery door. He bowed forward, the movement releasing a waft of day-old aftershave.

'The birds were making such a racket,' she said.

She pulled a pair of soft jersey dungarees from the drawer and fleetingly held them to her nose. She remembered buying them the day after her twenty-week scan, the black-and-white printout neatly folded in her purse. She'd been so happy, so optimistic, so excited about becoming a mum.

'How's your head?'

'Better, thanks.'

He bounced on his toes, swaying against the doorframe. 'Are you still up for going to the doctor's?'

'Definitely,' she said.

Tapping fingertips joined the bouncing. Immediately, her senses sharpened. Why was he so nervous?

'I've got to go out for a short while,' he said. 'But Diane's going to come over and keep you company until I get back. OK?'

'I don't need a babysitter.' She clicked the press studs into place. 'When did you arrange that?'

'Last night when you'd gone to bed. This used to be her job, remember, when she was a health visitor. In fact, she's going to ring the clinic for us this morning and get you an emergency appointment with the same doctor you saw last time.'

She let herself be hugged from behind, felt his chin lightly resting on the top of her head and his body lightly press against her spine. At least until the enormity of his words sank in. She jerked her shoulders to dislodge him.

With one hand anchoring the baby to the changing mat, she turned, light-headed with anger at his stupidity.

'For God's sake, Tom. Diane knows I left the baby on her own yesterday. If she tells the clinic that, we're screwed! They'll have to report us for child neglect. They'll take her off us.'

'Hey,' he said, edging towards her. 'It's OK. No one is taking the baby. You know I would never let that happen. And she is just going to be here for a couple of hours while I hand everything over to Tanya. I've taken the rest of the week off and then your mum will be here. OK?'

Mum.

She pressed down on the panic, starving it of oxygen until it subsided. Keep going. Once Mum was here, everything would be fine.

With a squeeze of her shoulder, Tom headed for the shower.

She slumped into the nursing chair and lifted her T-shirt. Trinity wriggled into position.

A puzzle, that's what this was. She had been given a jumbled pile of pieces with Mary somewhere at the heart of it. Frustrating snatches of the full picture flashed in her mind, only to vanish before she could grasp them. She needed all the pieces before she could slot them together.

Now she just needed someone who could help her to find them.

68. Now

At exactly eight thirty, the front doorbell rang.

'Hi, Diane,' Tom said. 'Come in.'

Ellie kissed the top of Trinity's head and pressed her face into the soft warmth, inhaling the irresistible baby scent. In the unlikely event she was ever called upon to identify her daughter purely by smell, she'd know that part baby wash, part fabric softener, part unique Trinity-ness anywhere.

'Thanks. Now, Dr Monk is fully booked this morning, but she has managed to squeeze Ellie in at twelve noon. Does that sound OK?'

'That's great,' Tom said. He stood at the bottom of the stairs. 'Ellie, Diane's here. I'll be back in time for the doctor's.'

After Tom left, Diane did her best to put Ellie at ease. She didn't mention Moss Pond or the weirdness at the front door afterwards. She didn't interfere or try to take over or try to engage her in any discussion about her mental state. She asked if Ellie needed help with anything and when Ellie declined, Diane settled on the sofa with her crossword and a cup of tea. In short, she did everything possible to mitigate the truth of the matter: she was here because no one trusted Ellie with the baby. And after yesterday, she wasn't sure she trusted herself.

Her phone pinged a message alert. *OK. See you soon. Norah*

Voluntarily spending time with Norah held all the appeal of an episiotomy, but the idea had come while she fed Trinity. This woman had made it her business to find out everything about the history of 6 Moss Lane, so unappealing as it was, she could be the only person who could help Ellie figure out what the hell was happening.

She'd deleted Norah's previous texts, but after rummaging through her bag, found the screwed-up business card with her number stuck to a half-melted packet of Polos.

Hi, are you free this morning? We could take the kids to the playground? Ellie

Norah had pinged straight back. *Shall I come to your house? The kids can play in the garden? N*

Ellie scoffed at the blatant rubbernecking attempt. No chance. After a few more exchanges, Norah had finally agreed to the playground.

'Diane? I'm just popping into the village to take Trinity to the park,' she said, one arm already in the sleeve of her coat.

'Oh.' Clearly ill at ease, her neighbour put her crossword on the table. 'Erm, well why don't I come with you? We could go in my car.'

'Thanks, but I'm meeting a friend. Sort of,' Ellie said. Christ, this was awkward. 'It's Norah. I think you know her from playgroup.'

'Oh,' Diane said again. She took her glasses off and folded them. 'Well, I can at least give you a lift. I've got a few errands to run in the village.'

They were loading the buggy into the car when Diane stopped and waved. An elderly couple had emerged from the house across the road. Both had their heads thrust low and forward as they shuffled along.

'Morning, Rita. Morning, Jack,' Diane called.

The man raised a hand in greeting, but the woman gave no sign she had heard.

The boot slammed shut and Diane turned to Ellie. 'Did you say you'd already met Rita?'

Ellie stared at the woman hobbling out of sight. So this was Rita, the wandering neighbour with dementia.

Black hair streaked with grey peeped out from under Rita's hat. Not much of her face was visible thanks to the swathe of scarf and the turned-up coat collar. But she definitely wore glasses and her feet were clad in broad flat shoes.

Was she the woman in black? Maybe, maybe not. From this distance, it was impossible to tell.

'Are you all right?' Diane said, eyeing her with concern. 'You look like you've seen a ghost.'

Ellie gave a polite laugh and opened the passenger door.

As Diane drove the short distance to Uppermoss village, she kept up a running commentary about local landmarks and interesting facts about the village. Meanwhile, Ellie nodded, pretending to listen while she desperately tried to fit Rita into the puzzle. In many ways, the poor wandering neighbour piece made sense. It would explain the rudeness and the lack of respect for private property. Maybe someone had driven her to Boots to pick up a prescription. Or Nexus for a spot of Christmas shopping.

Ellie still hadn't made her mind up when they arrived at the church car park. They were putting Trinity in the buggy when a silver Range Rover pulled up. The driver wound the window down.

'Hi, Ellie. Won't be a second.' She raised her eyebrows. 'Hello, Diane.'

Diane nodded curtly in reply and turned back to Ellie. 'So, let me know when you're ready. I won't be far.'

Disregarding the 'Blue Badge Holders Only' sign, Norah had reversed expertly into the one remaining space. The door slammed and twin girls raced out. Norah lifted the baby out of the car, cradling him against the long camel coat that skimmed her slender frame. An Instagram-worthy snapshot of the perfect mother.

Until she opened her mouth, anyway.

'What a week I've had,' she said, barely glancing in Ellie's direction as she settled the infant into the Porsche of prams. 'This one's teething and those two little shits have run me ragged.

Never stop bickering, sticking their noses in everything so I don't get a moment's peace.'

The little shits clattered up the ladder and onto the fort, startling a pigeon. The gate opened with a creak as Ellie followed Norah to a bench. The cold metal slats chilled through her thighs and she pulled her coat down as far as it would go.

'I must admit I was hoping we could meet at the house,' Norah went on. 'I've never been there. I'd love to see inside.'

Before Ellie could reply, thudding feet hurtled towards the bench. The little girl's wavy chestnut hair was parted to the side and held with a clip and Ellie was instantly reminded of the twins in *The Shining*. An inappropriate giggle tickled her throat.

'Push me on the swings,' the little girl said, pulling at her mother's cuff.

Norah unpeeled the grubby fingers with a dismissive 'Mummy's busy, darling. Get your sister to do it.'

See the trials of my life, she stated with an eye-roll while twiddling the keys of her Range Rover. Ellie tipped her head back in acknowledgement then smoothed her own daughter's rosy cheek in a fervent promise she would always, always be pushed on the swings. Trinity, snug in her pram-suit, blew tiny spit bubbles and Ellie's heart swelled with love.

'Actually, you can probably see Mary Brennan's …' Norah half stood with one elbow braced on the top of the bench. Narrowing her eyes towards the churchyard, she pointed. 'Yes. Do you see the big stone cross to the left of the angel? Mary is buried directly in front. It's a sad little grave, really. Anyway, how are you getting on up there?'

'Good,' she said, choosing her words carefully. 'But I was hoping you might be able to help me to learn more about Mary.'

Norah deflated visibly. 'Oh. I thought you might have had something to tell *me*.' Sitting up straighter, she smoothed her hands down her thighs in thinly disguised irritation. 'What do you want to know?'

If Norah had been a different kind of person, perhaps Ellie would have been able to confide in her, and the temptation was there anyway, just to see Norah's mind well and truly blown. But instead she said carefully, 'Was there anyone Mary was close to who might know more about her? Maybe about the child she had adopted?'

Norah gave a derisory snort. 'She rotted in that house for two weeks and not one person noticed, not even Diane. Who, in my opinion, is the only person who *could* know the details of the adoption but claims not to. I think you can safely assume the answer is no. She wasn't close to anyone. No friends and her only known relative was her cousin.'

'Catherine Wilson?'

Norah nodded. 'Who was born and lived in Canada. And some more distant cousins scattered around the UK.'

'Do you think it would be possible to trace who adopted Mary's baby?'

Norah tilted her head to one side, considering. 'It's an interesting thought,' she said. 'Forcible adoption is a juicy human-interest angle. Selective mutism. Dying alone. Then there's William Brennan's suicide. Was it the guilt at giving away his only grandchild? Or fear of the skeletons in the closet at the council? That could work.'

'Juicy,' Ellie said, a shade too sarcastically.

Norah shot her a sharp glance, but twin one diverted her attention. Running up to the bench, stuffing her skirt between her legs she shouted, 'Mummy, Mummy. My wee is coming out.'

'Mine too,' the other added, hopping on the spot.

'I'll have to take them into the church. I'll be two minutes,' she said, waving a finger at Ellie. 'Don't go.'

With a loud tut, Norah threw her bag and coat over the pram. The baby began to howl as the pram wheels bounced across the rubberised surface of the playground.

Ellie watched her herding the twins towards the parish hall

and felt a flicker of sympathy. Maybe one child *was* nothing compared to three. She twisted back around to look at her perfect daughter and as she did, a sudden movement drew her gaze to the churchyard.

Across the lichen-covered headstones, stood a woman. A woman dressed in black with thick black glasses and her hair tied up.

A woman who, from here, did not look like poor, frail Rita Cohen.

69. Now

The vibration deep within her bag alerted her to a call. Dazed, she tapped the green button.

'Hello?'

Diane's tone was determinedly light, but panic hovered at the edges. 'Ellie, dear. Where are you?'

Good question. She scanned the surrounding hedgerows. In front and behind her, the road wound like a narrow concrete ribbon. Close by, a lone horse munched nettles in a field.

'On the road out of Uppermoss. Heading towards Moss Lane.'

'And are you OK?'

That was a harder question. Trinity's eyes were wide, alert to the world around her. As Ellie brushed a stray eyelash from her cheek, her daughter smiled and gurgled.

'We're fine.'

There was no mistaking Diane's tone this time. Pure relief. 'Thank goodness. I went to the playground and Norah said you'd disappeared. Hang on right where—'

She heard a background slam and the timbre of Diane's voice changed as the phone switched to hands-free.

'Can you hear me? Tom is going to meet you at the health centre and I'm on my way to you.'

Ellie took her phone from her ear and the screen lit up as notifications flashed, one after the other. Missed calls, missed texts, missed voicemails, the last from Tom, five minutes ago at 11.40.

The horse lifted its head and snorted, blowing frosty air from its nostrils. She steadied the pram with her hip and stuffed her hands in her armpits. Pins and needles tingled as she wiggled her frozen toes. She could say where she was, but if Diane had asked her *how* she came to be on the road out of Uppermoss, she couldn't have answered. One minute she had been at St Michael's, the next her phone was ringing and she was here.

How much time had she lost?

A flock of migrating birds formed a ragged V against the low, grey-white sky, honking chaotically as they flew in search of warmer climes. On this dreary winter's day, rags of low-lying mist swathed the fields, obscuring the muddy earth.

From the depths of her pram-suit, Trinity gave a little squawk. Ellie held her close, the warmth providing solid comfort.

'I love you so much,' she whispered, her lips against the velvet nap of the baby's earlobe. 'And it's true: I really don't deserve you.'

Diane's car rounded the corner, flashing the hazard lights as she pulled up at the kerb.

'There you are,' she said, concern and relief etched across her kind face. 'It's time to go.'

70. Now

The photo above Dr Monk's PC showed three children with huge ice-cream cones somewhere blue-skied and sandy. Perfect, like kids in an advert. Whatever they were selling, Ellie needed a lifetime's supply.

Dr Monk finished reading the screen, picked up her pen and smiled expectantly.

'How have you been getting on with the new medication?'

'OK, I think.'

'Diane said you've been having some issues. And last time you mentioned you were concerned about tiredness and not sleeping. How do you feel you're coping now?'

'I—' Ellie breathed in deeply. 'Sorry. It's hard to know where to start.'

'Take your time,' the doctor said with an encouraging smile.

'It's complicated. I've started sleepwalking. And I was convinced my boyfriend was gaslighting me and having an affair and he isn't. *Really* isn't. I'm just so tired, sometimes I can't tell what's real and what's in my head and time just blurs.'

She paused. What else? *I think my house is haunted.*

If she told the doctor about Mary Brennan, then they really would take Trinity off her.

I'm cracking up.

No, Dr Monk didn't need to know that.

Take it slow.

'They're waking nightmares, I suppose,' she finished off with a shrug.

'I see. And have you had any ideas about what's triggering them?'

'My boyfriend thinks it's connected to something that happened to me when I was younger,' she said slowly. 'My best friend died when I was twenty and I was … I was there when it happened. I saw her.' She swallowed hard. 'And afterwards, I was diagnosed with PTSD and severe anxiety disorder and ended up spending twenty-eight days in a mental health unit.'

From the way her finger moved on the mouse, Dr Monk was scrolling through Ellie's records. With half an eye on the screen, she said, 'And why does he think it's having an effect on you now?'

'Well, I've been fine since I came out of Willow Lodge – that's the unit. I was over the PTSD and my anxiety has been manageable but then I had my daughter and it's like it has all come back. Sleepwalking, panic attacks, confusion. I feel like I can't trust what I'm hearing or seeing.'

Dr Monk's fingernails click-clacked across the keyboard. 'Mmm-mm. It's like we said last time, you've had a difficult time. It's perfectly understandable.'

'But it's more than that,' Ellie said.

Something shifted inside a locked room deep inside her mind. And the truth about Mia, the truth no one else knew existed about that night, began to stir.

'My daughter was born on the tenth anniversary of my friend's death,' she said, staring down at her lap. 'Everyone thinks it's a coincidence, but she was early. She wasn't meant to be born on that day. And when we came out of hospital, we moved into a new house and nothing has been right since then.' She twisted her fingers together. 'And it's all because I don't deserve a baby. I don't deserve to be happy.'

Dr Monk sat back in her chair. 'What makes you say that?'

In another room, a phone rang. Muffled voices came through the thin partition wall. Ellie picked at the scab where the screwdriver had slipped. It had started to heal, but now fresh blood oozed from the ragged edges.

'Because I did something bad.'

There. It was out.

Over the last ten years, she'd imagined this moment countless times. Sometimes it took place in an interview room with an angle-poise lamp shining in her eyes. Sometimes a neutral space with Tom, maybe a restaurant or bar. Or Danny. She'd come close on the phone to her mum, especially after a few glasses of wine. Mainly though, she was in the farmhouse kitchen with David and Anita.

She had never envisaged a stifling room in Uppermoss Health Centre.

'And I've never told anyone this before,' she said, drawing in a deep, shuddering breath. 'No one knows. Not even my boyfriend.'

She stared down at her spread fingers.

'You said you did something bad,' Dr Monk prompted gently. 'What did you do?'

Deep inside Ellie's mind, a lock clicked and a long-sealed door began to open.

71. Then

Ellie shoved her hair out of her eyes and patted along the bedside table till she found her phone.

I can't find my keys. Can you let me in? xx

The nerve of the girl! Ellie clicked from vibrate to silent then let it slide through her fingers to the floor. At the thud, Tom stirred slightly and she wrapped her arms around him. Closed her eyes. A minute later, his own mobile buzzed deep within a pile of discarded clothes, light shining through the fabric of his jeans. Head throbbing from too much alcohol, she stretched her arm, pulling them towards her.

Missed Call from Mia G.

A second later, a text appeared. *Lost keys. Please let me in. M x*

Ellie switched Tom's phone to silent and lifted the corner of the duvet and carefully climbed in. A booming sounded above the storm, like an oil drum rolling on concrete.

'Wassat?' he murmured on a waft of beery breath.

'I don't know. It's still dead windy. Maybe the bins blew over. Go back to sleep.'

A minute later: Crack!

Something hit the window.

Crack, crack!

Tom rolled on his back, flung his hand over his eyes, and murmured unintelligible sleep phrases.

Ellie got up again to lift the curtain a fraction of an inch.

The courtyard was petrol-black, slick with water. Rain lashed Mia's pale upturned face and slicked her hair to her head. Soaked

303

by the downpour, the shapeless black dress clung to her legs. As Ellie watched, she scooped up a handful of gravel.

'Ellie?' she called hoarsely. 'Please can you come down and let me in?'

Shit, she'd been seen.

She put her hand on the catch. Two more stones hit the window. Hard.

Crack! Crack!

Wind and rain rushed in, threatening to fling the frame back. The net curtain billowed inwards.

'Stop it, you'll smash the glass,' she hissed, fighting through the thin fabric.

'Let me in then,' Mia said. 'I'm getting soaked out here. Chuck me your keys if you don't want to come down.'

Without another word, Ellie pulled the window closed. She picked her keys up off the bedside table and, checking Mia's selfish behaviour hadn't woken Tom, crept into the lounge and unlocked the balcony doors.

'At last,' Mia said in a low voice, hunching into her jacket. 'Chuck me the keys.'

Ellie put her hands on her hips. 'Have you lost your keys *again*?'

Mia tutted loudly. 'I dunno. Does it matter?'

'Well, yes. Because we'll have to tell the landlady and get the locks changed again. It's going to cost a fortune. She might even kick us out this time.'

Down below, Mia twisted her soaking hair over one shoulder and pushed wet strands back from her cheeks and forehead.

'Are you drunk? Stop being so bloody self-righteous. Just throw them down.'

Something in her tone snapped the last shred of Ellie's patience. White-hot fury erupted through her. She barely noticed the keys biting into the soft flesh of her palm.

'I don't know where mine are either,' she lied.

Rain streamed down Mia's cheeks. 'Can you come down and let me in, then?'

'I really can't deal with this today,' Ellie said, careful to enunciate each syllable clearly. 'Can't you go back to Danny's?'

Mia stared, open-mouthed, then set her jaw. 'Right then, if you're going to be like that.' She slung her rucksack on the step. 'I'll climb up.'

'Go for it,' Ellie replied coldly. 'I'm going back to bed.'

She didn't, though. Instead she retreated behind the curtain and watched Mia push her sleeves to her elbows.

Her dad would have said the Manchester night was blowing a hooley. It entered the flat like a noisy intruder, rifling through notebooks and piles of artwork. Loosened the tendrils of ivy scratching the window. A deep metallic groan came from the drainpipe as Mia put her foot on the first bracket.

When Mia hesitated, the first hooks of doubt tugged at Ellie's conscience, but her anger shut them down. *Look at her. Confident. Assured. Remember the farmhouse? She's done this a million times before. Serves her right.*

Mia had reached the first floor already, hand over hand, occasionally dislodging small bits of mortar. A gust of wind tore a long strand of ivy from the wall and fluttered it like a streamer. She looked up, blinking in the rain. Mascara and eyeliner tracked black rivulets down her cheeks, turning her eyes into two deep black holes.

The balcony groaned as she grabbed the railing. She grunted, trying to haul herself over, but the sides were too high. The whole thing swayed under her weight and more tiny fragments of stone fell to the ground.

'Help me then,' she said impatiently. 'I know you're there. I can see you behind the curtain.'

The keys burned in Ellie's fist. She dropped them to the floor and scuffled them out of the way. But not before Mia saw them.

Her eyes widened. 'You lying cow!'

Leaning over the balcony railing, she grasped Ellie's arm tightly. But as her fingers dug in, a ferocious blast rocked the balcony. Mia lost her footing and swayed back, pulling Ellie with her. Ellie felt herself lurch out of the flat onto the thin metal platform. Her hipbones hit the railings and the ground rushed towards her. Instinct took over. She flung her arms out to right herself, and the momentum shook Mia's hand free. For a dizzying second, her friend's mouth opened in a wordless plea. She scrabbled for the balcony but only caught the ivy. Ellie stepped forward; reached out, grasping.

But it was too late. Her fingertips brushed Mia's sleeve then clutched thin air.

There was a ripping sound as the ivy detached from the wall. Then a scream. Then a horrible, sickening crunch.

After that, things moved very quickly.

Movement came from other flats. Lights came on. Windows opened. A neighbour called out.

Tom came running out of the bedroom. 'What's happening?'

He didn't wait for an answer. The door slammed against the wall and she could hear his bare feet slapping against the stone stairs. The clicks of doors unlocking came up the stair well accompanied by murmuring voices. Then someone switched the exterior light on.

The huge swathe of ivy hung from the building's façade and draped over the porch. Falling masonry had dented the car parked directly under their balcony.

Faint with disbelief, Ellie watched a bare-chested Tom run out and stop dead. Staggering, he grabbed fistfuls of his own hair and in a voice impossible to forget, shouted, 'No!'

Mia lay perfectly still with her neck at the wrong angle. A halo of blood oozed around her head, a glistening darker patch on the wet tarmac.

The next thing Ellie knew she was standing outside. Blue flashing lights reflected on the dressing gowns and drained faces of the neighbours crowding behind police tape. Someone had put a blanket over the twisted body on the ground.

Tom ran over, trying to get her to go inside and she realised she was crying; they were both crying. Then Tom was bent double, vomiting ropes of saliva. Then Ellie was kneeling in a patch of weed-filled earth, throwing up. Her hands, her feet, her shins were streaked with mud. At one point, a paramedic shone a light in her eyes. Someone put a jacket around her and led her inside. She felt the mud drying between her toes. A policewoman asked her some questions and a kind neighbour passed her a mug of hot sweet tea.

And all of it – the people, the noise, the twisted hump lying motionless under the blanket – shrank to a nugget of unspeakable, granite-hard truth.

Mia was dead. And Ellie had killed her.

72. Now

'You didn't kill her,' Dr Monk said, sliding a box of tissues across the desk.

'I could have let her in,' Ellie said. 'I could have thrown her the keys. I heard the storm and I knew the building was falling to bits and I said *go for it.*'

She folded a tissue in half. 'She was holding on to me when she fell. It was my fault she died.'

Dr Monk was filled with compassion. 'No, it was a terrible accident. However mad you were with her, whatever you said in the heat of the moment, whatever happened, you are not to blame. Now ...' She started tapping on the keyboard. 'What I'd like to do, if you'll let me, is flag you as an urgent case to our mental health team. I'll do the referral while you're here and you should hear from a nurse within the next twenty-four hours. They can arrange an assessment and see what we can do about getting to the root of the problem.'

'My boyfriend thinks having Trinity has brought everything about Mia to the surface,' Ellie said. 'And he doesn't even know the truth about what I did. He thinks I went into the lounge because I heard her fall. So do the police, my mum, *her parents.*' Her voice cracked with emotion. 'I lied to everybody because I panicked. And now so much time has passed, what would they think of me?'

Dr Monk finished typing and leaned towards Ellie. 'It's not up to me to judge your actions or to tell you to confess or otherwise, but maybe if you spoke to your boyfriend, that might help?'

'No,' Ellie said vehemently. 'I lied to the police about what happened and now he *is* the police. If I brought it up now, he could lose his job.'

'Well, it is certainly true that a major life event can reopen these old wounds, allowing unresolved feelings to come flooding back. And there's nothing more life-changing than having a baby.' The other woman half-smiled. 'Apart from moving house, and you've done that too.'

Tears flowed freely down Ellie's face now and she scrubbed another tissue across her wet cheeks. 'That's the other thing. We bought the house on Moss Lane where Mary Brennan died. And I didn't know anything about it and people keep telling me these awful, sad stories.' She blew her nose. 'Have you heard about what happened?'

Dr Monk kept her professional composure, only raising her eyebrows slightly. 'Yes, I have. Mary was one of our patients at the practice. How has that made you feel?'

'I was freaked out at first. But now feel I belong there,' she said slowly. 'Because that house is a place that has known so much unhappiness and I don't deserve to be happy. Not after what I did to Mia.'

The doctor leaned forward. 'But surely your baby deserves to be happy?'

For a moment, the only sound was Ellie's congested breathing. Babies.

Everything always came back to babies.

73. Then

Sweat glued Ellie's thighs to the leather sofa. Duct tape covered a split in the seat cushion and she picked at the curled edges.

Danny's closed bedroom door vibrated with thumping bass. Tom bit his lip and glanced over. 'I'm worried he's going to do something stupid.'

Pick, pick, pick.

He slammed his hands on the kitchen worktop. 'Why didn't we hear the phone?'

Ellie tugged harder and the duct tape ripped free. Nasty yellow stuffing spilled out. She kept waiting for someone to say they knew what she did. That she was responsible for Mia's death.

But no one had.

Danny finally stumbled out of his room at teatime. Ellie, who had been dozing, sat up. Tom jumped off the sofa.

'Mate,' Tom said.

His crumpled clothes stank of smoke and sweat and his eyes were red and swollen. He looked like the dazed survivor of an apocalypse. 'My mum and dad rang. They'll be here in a bit. I'm going home.'

'Do you want a drink? Something to eat?' Tom said.

'Nah.' Danny wiped his nose with his sleeve. 'I just want a shower. I need to pack.'

'We can do that, can't we, Els?'

'Sure,' she said, poking stuffing back in the hole. The tape wouldn't stick back down.

Danny was a portrait of grief. He clenched his fists and let out a guttural roar. A fraction too late, Tom stepped forward, not quick enough to prevent Danny aiming a punch at the door.

'Mate. No.'

He easily shook him off. Wood splintered as he pummelled to the beat of the words: 'It's. My. Fault.'

Ellie jumped up, strode quickly to the kitchen. Images invaded her head. Mia, in her shapeless black dress, digging her nails into the wallpaper. Mia in the courtyard asking to be let in. Windmilling her arms, dislodging Mia's fingers.

Mia's face.

Mia on the ground, broken.

With robotic efficiency, Ellie fashioned an icepack from frozen peas and a tea towel.

'Can you move your fingers?' Tom was saying.

The knuckles swelled, discolouring by the second. Red and indigo. When Tom carefully wrapped them in the tea towel, Danny didn't flinch.

'You need to go to A & E,' Tom said. 'I'll ring a cab and we can tell your mum and dad to meet us there.'

'It's my fault,' Danny said, snot mingling with the tears that ran down his cheeks. 'She told me she didn't have her keys and I said *so what?*'

At the mention of keys, Ellie paced rapid circles in the kitchen. Her chest grew tight and she clawed her T-shirt. This was it, she was going to have to tell the truth.

She told me she was going to climb up and I said, 'Go for it.'

With one sentence, she could ease Danny's guilt. All she had to do was confess.

In the lounge, Danny drew a shuddering breath. 'I shouldn't have kicked her out. I was scared, that's all. I panicked and even though I knew there was a storm and she'd have to walk home, I told her to go. I told her I needed space to think.'

'Think about what?' Tom said.

Silence followed. Ellie wasn't sure if Danny had fallen asleep or passed out or what.

'Why were you scared?' Tom prompted.

There was a long silence.

When Danny finally spoke, the last piece of Ellie shattered.

'Mia told me she was eight weeks pregnant. We were going to have a baby.'

74. Now

'I killed my friends' baby. And that's why I don't deserve one of my own.'

She'd said it. She'd opened the door that held the past and no matter where the truth went, she'd never be able to lock it in again.

Dr Monk leaned forward and locked her gaze with Ellie's.

'You didn't kill anyone. What happened to your friend was not your fault. It was a terrible, awful accident and for your own sake as well as your daughter's, you have to stop heaping the blame on yourself.'

From the corridor came the sound of a baby crying. Ellie squeezed the damp tissue into a ball. Little white flecks stuck to her fingertips. From the night Mia and her unborn baby died, guilt had lived inside her like a secret bitter heart, beating a painful rhythm no one else could hear. *You don't deserve to be happy.*

'The fact you have carried this suffering shows you're a caring and compassionate human being,' the doctor continued, fingers rattling over the keyboard. 'And you absolutely deserve to be a mum and to be happy. Your daughter deserves to have you. I do think you need specialist help and that's why I'm making this urgent referral to the mental health team.

'You should hear from them in the next few hours. Definitely within twenty-four. Please ring the surgery if you need us before then. And in the meantime, go home and just enjoy your family.'

She wiggled the mouse then firmly tapped the return button with her fingernail. The sound had a mechanical quality to it. Like the click of a lock, the drawing of a bolt. A door opening.

75. Now

'I couldn't resist them,' Carol said holding a pair of daisy-printed bootees to the camera. 'What do you think?'

'That we're going to have to get a bigger house if you don't stop buying her stuff,' Ellie said.

Roger's midsection passed behind her mum. 'Another bloody pair of shoes? She's had a baby not a centipede, Carol.'

'Cheeky sod,' her mum said, pretending to swipe him. 'And anyway, it's my granddaughter's first Christmas. I'm contractually obliged to spoil her.'

'Can't wait to see you,' Ellie said.

'Me too, love. Not long now. You sound so much brighter,' her mum continued. 'The doctor helped then?'

Ellie let the unspoken *I told you so* slide.

'I've got an appointment with the mental health team tomorrow. But to be honest, just talking to the doctor really helped.'

'That's wonderful,' her mum said with palpable relief. 'Oh, I cannot wait to see my beautiful girls.'

'We can't wait to see you either,' Ellie said. 'I love you, Mum.'

She put the phone in her pocket and stared out of the bedroom window. A perfect winter sunset streaked the sky above Mosswood with peach and gold. The first stars would soon appear, glimmering in the indigo sky. From the bathroom came the sound of Trinity splashing and Tom singing.

Speaking the truth for the first time had been cathartic. Just hearing someone say *it wasn't your fault* lifted some of the weight. She prodded the guilt experimentally, like a sore tooth, and felt a twinge of pain. More habit-forming than any meds they handed out at Willow Lodge, the guilt would never leave her, but what she had to do for Trinity's sake – for all their sakes – was find a way to make her peace with it.

'Can you pass me a clean onesie?' Tom called from the bathroom. 'I forgot to bring one in.'

'Sure,' she replied, walking over to the nursery.

Jungle animals smiled down on her. The room was cosy and peaceful and warm. Everything she could ever want for her daughter.

She opened the top drawer, releasing the scent of lavender. Tom had been right all along – this was all about Mia, not Mary Brennan, a woman she had never even met. And that's what she would be talking about tomorrow at her appointment. How dreams and stories and tiredness and guilt had got jumbled up in her head. Mia's baby who never got chance to be born. Mary's baby forcibly adopted. And underpinning everything, fear that she didn't deserve a baby of her own.

Everything always came back to babies.

She picked out a sleepsuit patterned with stars and rainbows. Cute.

She smiled.

Everything was going to be fine.

76. Now

Hours later. She woke up cold. No, not just cold, frozen solid. Fingers and toes simultaneously burning and numb while breath streamed from her nostrils in vaporous clouds. For a second, her eyelids refused to open until she prised them apart. Her brain felt foggy. Doped. She couldn't understand how the bedroom window had come to be wrenched back on its hinges.

Tom slept on, face down with his arms wrapped around the pillow. She placed the back of her hand quickly on his neck. It burned. The heat of Tom's skin in marked contrast to the ice of her own. Was she dreaming?

Singing.

Faint, in the arctic chill, the first few notes rang with the clarity of ice. She strained her ears. The volume increased.

Mary, Mary, quite contrary,
How does your garden grow?

Ellie's teeth started to chatter.

Careful not to disturb Tom's deep slumber, she climbed over him.

Out of bed, the icy air stung her bare skin, raising goose bumps on her arms as she shut the window. Low clouds parted, revealing a smudged thumbprint moon above trees like cardboard cut-outs. So quiet. So still. None of the comforting bustle of the city streets, only acres of darkness.

Taking her dressing gown from the hook, she clawed her toes into her slippers.

'This isn't real,' she whispered. 'This is a dream.'

She tiptoed across the bedroom, stopping dead at the slight

creak on the threshold, but Tom didn't move a muscle. On the landing, light fell from the open nursery and lay in a sliver of gold across the green swirls of the carpet.

Ellie narrowed her eyes. There was mud on the landing carpet. Mud on the walls. Dirty streaks on the handle that absolutely were not there when she went to bed three hours earlier. As she dabbed the wall, crumbling the wet soil between her fingertips, the night-light stuttered on the same line: *Pretty maids all in a row. Pretty maids all in a row. Pretty maids all in a row.*

Saliva rushed to her mouth and she had to put out a hand to steady herself. Telling the truth was supposed to draw a line under this.

How could it still be happening?

She was sleepwalking; she had to be. Having a nightmare and walking in her sleep. *Go back to bed!* she ordered herself. But her feet moved on, out of her control.

An arctic breath chilled down her spine. It seemed impossible, but the cold intensified as she entered the nursery. Pastel lights flickered across the ceiling projected by the night-light. As she touched the handle, something oozed from under the cot. A glistening darker patch on the grey carpet.

For a second, the room shimmered and she saw, lit by a dim bulb, a yellow chimney breast, and a kneeling girl with her mouth open. Long black hair stringy with sweat. Ellie blinked and when she opened her eyes, Trinity's nursery reappeared.

Trinity.

At the same instant the name formed in her mind, she heard the distant cry of a baby. She hurried into their bedroom. The Moses basket was empty.

Shouting resulted in nothing more than a hoarse croaking so she grabbed Tom's shoulders, shaking him hard enough to hurt her hands. He let out a gentle snore and turned over.

Wake up! she screamed in her head. *The baby's gone.*

A frail cry came from the garden. Stumbling over Tom's

discarded clothes, she hurried to the window, had her hand on the sill when the cry stopped abruptly.

A tiny bundle lay on the concrete beneath the kitchen window. A lighter patch of blanket on the dark ground.

Everything came into sharp focus. She took the stairs two at a time, righting herself on the banister when she stumbled. A hundred knives stabbed her ankle, but she kept going, flying through the kitchen and out into the petrol-black night.

The shock of the cold stole her breath away. She gasped and the bitterness burned in her lungs. Behind her, the door slammed shut, forced by an invisible power so strong the whole house shook.

Ellie barely registered the deafening blast. Her hand crept to her mouth and she let out a silent moan. The world receded; the house, the garden, herself sucked into a black hole where nothing existed except horror.

On the concrete, the tiny, blanketed heap lay perfectly still.

Ellie had known fear before, but never like this. Her entire body vibrated with the thudding behind her ribs.

She took a tentative step. Reached out a trembling hand, hesitated and drew back. Couldn't. Had to.

Propelled by dread, she stroked the sad bundle with her fingertips. Tugged.

The fabric unfolded like a flower. Empty.

It was just a blanket.

She sank to her knees and held the soft wool to her face, her silent sobs a tidal wave of relief. But it was short-lived. Where was the baby?

As her eyes grew accustomed to the dark, dense black shifted and separated into individual, identifiable shapes. Trees, bushes. The pile of broken wood by the rose bed. Shadows cloaked the garden, silent and still, and from those shadows came the sudden perfect sound of her daughter crying and she saw a flash of white against the black soil of the rose bed.

'*Mummy's coming,*' she shouted. The sound rang out in the clear night air.

She sprinted across the lawn, and had almost reached the baby when she stumbled, falling square on one of the stepping stones. Her knee exploded with pain.

'*Trinity!*'

A square of light appeared as Tom switched the bedroom light on.

She scooped up their daughter, cosy in her stars and rainbows sleepsuit, and hugged her tightly. Despite the wintry chill, the baby's rosy skin radiated warmth.

'Sssh, shh,' she said, rocking Trinity close to her chest. 'Mummy's got you. You're safe now.'

The lights on Diane's conservatory flicked on, throwing a shaft of light across their garden that illuminated a hole, roughly rectangular in shape, in the earth to her left. Despite the icy chill, sweat trickled down her forehead, dampening her hair. She shoved it back with the base of her hand, feeling mud smear her skin. Was something glinting in the dark earth?

She heard Tom shout, 'What are you doing?' and Diane call, 'Ellie? Tom?'

The sound of the back door was like something snapping in Ellie's head, thrusting her back into the real world. Rapid feet approached and a wavering beam of torchlight found her squinting at the sudden glare.

'Ellie, what the hell are you doing?' Tom said.

She shuffled on her knees and lifted the baby off the grass. Rocking back on her heels, she wiped the sweat from her forehead.

'The torch,' Ellie gasped. 'Shine the torch in there.'

'Hello?' Diane called from the passageway at the side of the house. She hurried towards them, tying the sash on her dressing gown. 'Is everything all right?'

'Can you hold Trinity?' Ellie said, thrusting her into the other woman's arms before she had a chance to answer. The baby's sleepsuit was streaked with mud.

Ellie used her hands to dig out the earth around the edge of the hole.

'What is it?' Tom said, peering in. 'I can't see what's – oh God.'

The torch beam trembled on decaying cloth. A tiny bundle, the size of a new-born. A glint of something white.

'Ellie,' Tom said gently pulling her away. 'Stop.'

Six months later

Ellie looks at the almost-full suitcase on her bed. A lawnmower hums somewhere in the distance and above the mechanical sound, birds break into cheerful song. Even though it's only just gone eight, spring sunshine floods the garden. Right in the centre, where the rose bed used to be, cherry tree blossom flutters like pink confetti. It's only been there a few weeks, but given time and the right care, this sapling will grow into a beautiful, living memorial to Mary Brennan and her daughter.

It's been six months since the night they found the tiny skeleton. The police had arrived within minutes of Tom's phone call, followed by the forensic team who, with infinite care, excavated the burial site.

For weeks afterwards, the frozen garden had been an open wound tended by white-boiler-suited specialists, but nothing else was found. Soon, the fresh green turf Tom and Howard laid will look as though it has always been here.

There have been times over the last few months when she couldn't bear the thought of visiting 6 Moss Lane again, let alone living there.

First, when the forensic team arrived with their excavators and, hot on their heels, the plague of journalists and social media trolls. Then came the ghouls who flew their drones over day and night; rubberneckers gawking over the fence from Mosswood and endless well-meaning strangers, leaving flowers and teddy bears at the end of the drive. Mary and her daughter, ignored in life, went viral in death.

But the initial fascination eventually tailed off. Her mum, Roger and Howard cleared the flowers away and Diane and Asha washed the teddies to donate to St Michael's. The TV crews packed up and other sad stories now fill the pages of the papers.

And here they are. They moved back in a few days ago and already, the house feels like home.

Mary will never completely go away, Ellie understands that. One day, Trinity will come home from school, innocent ears ringing with playground gossip and Ellie will have to tell her what happened at 6 Moss Lane. She hopes Trinity will understand why they stayed. Not just about the financial commitment or the fact they would lose so much if they sold up (although this has obviously played a part). But because they owe it to Mary Brennan and her daughter to let go of the past and make this house a happy home.

Her phone buzzes on the bedside table. It's a message from Jess: *Hope it goes well. Give me a call when you get back and we'll do something fun x*

She replies with a love heart and thumbs-up, thankful for Jess's steady friendship.

Footsteps climb the stairs. Her mum peers around the door.

'Do you want me to make some sandwiches for the journey?'

Ellie rummages through the top drawer. 'No, it's OK. We'll have to stop at the services to change the baby anyway, so we can get something there.'

'Give me a shout if you need any help packing,' Carol says before lowering her voice to a whisper as she enters the nursery. 'I'll take Trinity's bag down. She's still fast asleep.'

'Thanks, Mum.'

Her mum has always taken the shocking news in her stride. When Tom and Ellie immediately moved back in with Howard, Carol booked into a nearby hotel – and she hadn't left. Roger joined her soon afterwards and now they are renting a flat in the village. Just for the time being.

Ellie can't help but think about those first few days now, as she folds pyjamas and puts them into the suitcase.

After the police excavated the rose bed and took the tiny bundle away, they contacted Catherine Wilson, the Canadian cousin, who provided the DNA sample that proved 'in all probability' that this was Mary's baby. The coroner's report had made for difficult reading: the bones were that of a new-born girl and the cause of death was 'probably asphyxiation'.

Almost equally hard to read was the speculation in the papers. Norah, however, had written surprisingly sensitive pieces for several national papers. After piecing the evidence together – the forensics, interviews with Mary's classmates and her father's colleagues – she'd concluded the most likely scenario was that instead of arranging a secret adoption, William Brennan had smothered his granddaughter and buried her in the garden, leaving his daughter too traumatised to speak. Unable to live with the guilt, he'd taken his own life at Moss Pond.

Catherine Wilson had helped to slot the final pieces of the puzzle together. She remembered her mother – Bill Brennan's estranged sister – burning a letter she'd received after her brother's death. A suicide note of sorts, in which he alluded to an act of anger and intolerable guilt.

When the police finally released the tiny skeleton, Catherine flew over from Canada to organise the simple funeral. The vicar of St Michael's delivered a moving service and the police kept reporters away. The small group of mourners comprised Ellie and Tom, Carol, Roger and Howard. Diane and Asha and Jack Cohen from number three as well as Tanya and the investigating officers from Tom's work.

Poor Rita died shortly before the funeral, and Ellie has not seen the woman in black since the day she met Norah in the playground. The day she told Dr Monk the truth about Mia's death. After her months of therapy, Ellie can see the connection clearly now.

'We need to get going soon,' Tom calls up the stairs. 'Twenty minutes at the latest.'

'Nearly ready,' she says.

In the end, Tom's big case at work ended in the arrest of almost a dozen people. Despite the success, and his good working relationship with Tanya, he has put in for a transfer to a different unit.

Trinity stirs in the nursery, whimpers, then settles back down. Ellie watches her eyeballs move behind her closed lids. What do babies dream about?

She thinks about three women and their three daughters: Mary, Mia and Ellie, their lives forever intertwined.

Tomorrow would have been Mia's birthday, and they are travelling to Surrey for a celebration at the farmhouse. Danny and Josie will be there with their kids, as well as family and a couple of old school friends. David and Anita invite Ellie every year, but this is the first time she has accepted. The last time she visited was for Mia's funeral.

She crams socks and pants into the gaps at the side of the case and zips it up. Some nights, when she is on the edge of sleep, she finds herself in the attic flat listening to Mia call her name. Other times, she is gouging mud from the rose bed under the silent gaze of Mary Brennan.

While she will always blame herself for Mia's death, the ongoing therapy Dr Monk helped to arrange has enabled her to manage the guilt. She doesn't sleepwalk anymore. It is slow work but she has begun to accept that she can't change the past. To learn how to live in the moment. To understand that the only person she needs forgiveness from is herself.

Downstairs, Tom is closing windows and asking Carol if she's seen the house keys. Trinity stirs and cries a little louder.

'Mummy's coming,' Ellie calls and picks the suitcase off the bed.

Trinity pouts, releasing the familiar notes of her hunger.

'Shhh,' Ellie settles her onto the feeding cushion and into

the routine that is so familiar now, it's hard to believe she ever struggled.

As Trinity sucks, a cloud passes over the sun, casting a dark shadow across the grey carpet.

'Ellie,' Tom shouts from the hall. 'Have you seen the house keys? I could've sworn I put them in the basket.'

'No,' she replies. 'I'm just feeding Trinity then I'll be down.'

A breeze blows in through the open nursery window, fluttering the curtains and rippling goose bumps up her arms. A fly buzzes close by and a flicker of unease stirs in her gut.

'Got them!' Tom rattles the keys in triumph. 'They were in my jacket.'

The sun comes out, flooding the room with light and warmth. She shuts the window.

She hears the car boot slam shut. They're giving Carol a lift back to the rented house where Roger is waiting, and a few minutes are spent making sure everyone has everything they need. Ellie passes Trinity to Carol who expertly straps her in the car seat and sits beside her.

'Can you lock up, Els?' Tom asks, tapping the postcode into the satnav.

The silver E glints as she locks the back door. She frowns. Tom, or maybe Carol, has tracked mud across the kitchen floor, but she doesn't have time to mop it. They need to leave now if they are to miss the worst of the traffic.

The downstairs windows are shut. The back door is locked. Good to go. Taking her handbag and coat from the end of the banister, she glances back at the empty hall.

She is about to step outside into the sun when she hears it. Or thinks she does. Maybe it's the breeze or her imagination.

Clutching the keys so tightly they dig into her palm, she strains her ears to listen.

Upstairs, very softly, a woman is singing *Mary Mary*.

Acknowledgements

Special thanks to my wonderful agent, Anne Clark, for believing in this book, and to Sarah Goodey for her brilliant editorial insights. Ditto Helena Newton. Thanks to all the team at HQ Digital.

Thanks also to everyone who helped me along the way: the guys at MMU who read early drafts and gave invaluable feedback, especially Emrys H., Lara W. and Lisa R. Ditto Ellie C. To Lesley B. for kindly sharing her midwifely wisdom and D. C. R. F. for policing knowledge and general cheerleading. Any mistakes are entirely mine. To Amanda P. for many years of always being there. Love and thanks to Christina and Edward K. Ross M. and my writing companions Smudge, Minnie and Lola. And always Tim and Christian for their endless patience, support and cups of tea.

Dear Reader,

Firstly, thank you so much for choosing to read *The Perfect House*. My own TBR skyscraper grows by the day, so I greatly appreciate making it to the top of yours! I hope you enjoyed reading about the inhabitants (past and present) of number six Moss Lane.

I've always been interested in the personal histories of houses – who the previous occupants were and what their lives were like. When I renovated my first house, I stripped the wallpaper to find drawings by children who had lived there years before, which was intriguing (and slightly creepy). That fascination sparked the idea of writing about a house with sinister secrets.

As well as bricks and mortar, babies play a huge role in the book, linking the lives of the three women in unexpected ways. Ellie's pregnancy complications have a psychological as well as physical impact on her, releasing memories she has kept under lock and key for years. How do you think Ellie's own past impacts on her feelings about the house? Does her sense of isolation and guilt shape how she tries to make sense of 6 Moss Lane's story? Or do you think there are supernatural forces at play? Maybe it's a combination of the two?

If you've enjoyed reading *The Perfect House* it would be amazing if you could post a review. Writing a book means spending long, long hours on your own and getting lovely feedback from readers makes it all worthwhile! I also spend too much time talking books, dogs and the environment on social media, so please come and find me on Twitter @rachinthefax, Facebook R. P. Bolton or Instagram @rachinthefax

Hope to see you again in my next book!
Love,
R.P. Bolton x

Dear Reader,

We hope you enjoyed reading this book. If you did, we'd be so appreciative if you left a review. It really helps us and the author to bring more books like this to you.

Here at HQ Digital we are dedicated to publishing fiction that will keep you turning the pages into the early hours. Don't want to miss a thing? To find out more about our books, promotions, discover exclusive content and enter competitions you can keep in touch in the following ways:

JOIN OUR COMMUNITY:

Sign up to our new email newsletter:
http://smarturl.it/SignUpHQ

Read our new blog www.hqstories.co.uk

🐦 https://twitter.com/HQStories

f www.facebook.com/HQStories

BUDDING WRITER?

We're also looking for authors to join the HQ Digital family!
Find out more here:

https://www.hqstories.co.uk/want-to-write-for-us/

Thanks for reading, from the HQ Digital team

H Q

If you enjoyed *The Perfect House*, then why not try another page-turning thriller from HQ Digital?

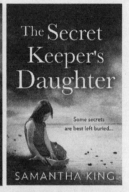

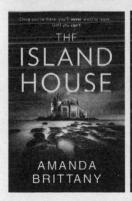